THE HAVE-NOTS

Katharina Hacker

THE HAVE-NOTS

*Translated from the German
by Helen Atkins*

Europa
editions

Europa Editions
116 East 16th Street
New York, N.Y. 10003
www.europaeditions.com
info@europaeditions.com

Copyright © 2006 by Suhrkamp Verlag, Frankfurt am Main
First Publication 2008 by Europa Editions

Translation by Helen Atkins
Original Title: *Die Habenichtse*
Translation copyright © 2007 by Europa Editions

Library of Congress Cataloging in Publication Data is available
ISBN 978-1-933372-41-9

Hacker, Katharina
The Have-Nots

Book design by Emanuele Ragnisco
www.mekkanografici.com

Prepress by Plan.ed – Rome

Printed in Italy
Arti Grafiche La Moderna – Rome

The translation of this work was supported by a grant from the
Goethe-Institut, which is funded by the Ministry of Foreign Affairs.

CONTENTS

THE HAVE-NOTS

1.

Everything will be different now, Dave announced as the removal van rumbled away, and, hoisting Sara onto his shoulders for the first time in a long while, he galloped down the street with her, all the way to the church, where a clergyman standing outside gave them a friendly wave. The trees were just starting to change their color, –just a bit, do you see, because it's only September, said Dave, stopping under a plane tree to let Sara pull off a leaf. –Isn't it big, she said in amazement, and after he had put her down, he gently held it up to her face. –Bigger than your face, he gravely declared. –Why are we here? she asked again, and he patiently explained. –This is where you live now, he concluded. She thought about it. –But yesterday it wasn't, she said uncertainly, –no, it wasn't, he agreed, not yesterday, we only moved here yesterday. –And we wouldn't be here, she said, if Auntie Martha was still alive. –No, if Auntie Martha was still alive we'd still be living in Clapham, Dave confirmed, but that's enough of that, he thought. –Up you come, he said, bending his knees. She swung a leg over his head and grabbed hold of his hair. –Not my hair! he yelled, and off they went, down the street and back again. –Can you remember this? he asked her: 47, Lady Margaret Road. She dutifully repeated it. –You need to know that in case you get lost, he impressed on her, adding solemnly: now that you'll be going to nursery school. –Now that I'll be going to nursery school, she echoed, as she rode at a gallop towards her new home.

The Victorian houses formed a single, unbroken terrace, differing only in the detail of their frontages; some, but not all, had a basement flat. Where there was no such "garden flat," the garden—a narrow strip enclosed by a brick wall—belonged to the ground-floor flat. From the street a small entrance led down to the cellar, which had once been used for storing coal and now housed decrepit items of furniture, old mattresses and broken television sets. There was also a child's bed, and Sara's father cursed as he lugged it upstairs. –But you should be glad it's there, her mother told him, disappointed, and then they argued about the throw on the sofa, which had a pattern of jungle creepers with a huge tiger in their midst. The sofa stood in the bay window, and anyone passing by could see the tiger's colors glowing amongst the greenery.

–There's Polly! cried Sara as she rode up to the front door on Dave's shoulders. The black-and-white cat leaped up onto the back of the sofa and stretched out with its paws touching the tiger's head. –There's Polly, Dave repeated, but he was listening to his father's angry voice, and when they rang the bell Mum opened the door and looked straight past them, her face rigid.

–You'll see, said Dave that evening, sitting on the edge of her bed and stroking her hair, –this is quite different from Clapham. –Because the houses are different? asked Sara. –Because the houses are different, and the people as well, he said. Dad'll find a job, and did you see how Mum was smiling? Sara was dubious but said nothing. –You'll go to school, said Dave, that's definite, and he stood up and got into his own bed. –Dave? she started to ask, but he was already asleep.

The next day was a Monday. She was woken by voices in the hall, and then the door slammed. Nobody came to get her up; then the door closed again and there was silence. She got out of bed and went over to the window, where a small bus had stopped. The driver folded down some steps and stood smoking while he waited for an old lady to emerge from the house opposite and clamber aboard the bus, and then he folded the steps up again, got in at the front and drove off. Dave was gone, and so were her parents, but Polly came and rubbed up against her legs. There were still some packing cases in the living room, her toys were in a packing case, too, and the day dragged on until afternoon, when Dave came home at last, wearing his new school uniform. He noticed the smell at once and found the spot where she had crouched down behind the sofa and messed her pants; it was only a little stain and he gave her a gentle prod: –What's in it for me if I don't tell? Then he helped her to rinse the things through; he looked sad. –We'll hang them out of the window, he said, Mum won't notice. He searched for her doll—it was in one of the packing cases in the living room—and while he emptied things out she hid behind the sofa and stroked Polly. –Come on, help me, Dave said later on: he was holding some plates and cutlery in his hands. You'll see, he said, Mum will bring some food when she comes home, and this evening we'll be sitting round the table, all four of us. –And Polly, said Sara. –And Polly, Dave agreed.

2.

Prominently mounted on a low brown shelf unit, the television sent shadows flickering across the parquet floor, shadows of the collapsing towers, of people letting go of the buildings and leaping to their deaths. On the dining table, glasses and plates had been set out for at least thirty guests, but most had not turned up. That afternoon Ginka had bought three bottles of gin and a case of Schweppes, –for those who need something stronger than wine, she said, pointing towards Jakob, whose first visit this was. He had arrived back from New York that morning; only the previous day he had been at the World Trade Center, and the others gathered around him as if he were a survivor, asking questions which he left unanswered, unable to concentrate. Isabelle went off into Ginka's study to phone Alexa, but her answering machine kicked in, and Isabelle wondered where Alexa and Clara were spending the evening. In front of the television Isabelle had almost burst into tears, but now, as she stood with the telephone in her hand, listening to Alexa's brief recorded message, she felt it was absurd to cry over total strangers while leaving countless other deaths unmourned. There was a small grey sofa in Ginka's study, the leather covering was worn, a cushion was out of place, and a pale stripe showed where someone had tried to clean off a mark. She sat down and after a moment's hesitation untied her shoelaces and put her feet up on the back of the sofa, intending to shut her eyes just for a few minutes, when there was a knock and Jakob came into the room.

Without further ado he sat down beside her, so that her feet were almost touching his neck. –You don't remember, he said, stating it as a fact. She looked without curiosity at the reddish-blond hair, the rather too soft features, the rounded cheeks that made his mouth look smaller but were redeemed by the strong nose and high forehead: he was good-looking, pleasant-looking at any rate. No, she didn't remember. On a small, slender-legged antique table stood a glass holding three faded roses; the stalks had already darkened, and a leaf floated, magnified, in the gleaming water. Ginka called out something, addressing it either to her or to this man who now gently took her hand, held it in his own, slightly moist one, and waited. Freiburg, she thought. Despite the miles traveled, the years, the countless decisions and small everyday actions, her memory spewed out its recollections: the tree trunks wet with rain, bare and dark in the twilight, the sparse undergrowth that looked ragged and windswept, though no gale could ever have penetrated so far into the forest, and the steep climb up to the Bromberg, where in summer the ground under the beeches was as grassy as in a clearing, because the trees were spaced far apart as though each one wished to dwell in undisturbed peace. In amazement she spoke his name. Jakob. She remembered that walk ten years ago, the forest, the twilight and the damp, the confusion that had made her reach for Jakob's hand, though she knew she would go back to her lover and their chaotic, humiliating life together. A shaft of light from the half-open door picked out the three roses.

Jakob breathed calmly and evenly; her face was still unlined, possibly the mole had become a little larger, while her throat seemed softer and he would have liked to kiss it. Her eyes returned his gaze confidently; she had been frightened in the wood, back then, and had let him take her back to his poorly heated student room. He could tell that she had not been waiting for him all this time.

Ginka appeared in the doorway, her high heels making her wince. When she found the two of them on the sofa together she burst out laughing and called out some remark to the others, but no one caught what she said.

At home once more, Isabelle made another vain attempt to contact Alexa. The television was on and the plane was heading, in a perfect straight line, for the second tower.

The following morning she was the first to arrive at the office. She switched on the computer and opened the windows: the cobblestones were fresh and lustrous after yesterday's rain, but the brick arches of the S-Bahn viaduct looked dull in comparison, as if dozing away the time until their final decay. On Isabelle's desk were some designs she had printed out the day before to show to Andras and Peter, but there had not been time. The proprietors' names, Pannier & Tarnow, stood out in vigorous, bright blue lettering beneath the firm's trading name, "*Hausordnung*—Berlin Property Management." She liked these small commissions, which the two men found irksome: company nameplate, prospectus, letterhead, business cards, and that was it. Not much, but it was all grist to the mill. Only the prospectus still remained to be done.

At twelve o'clock, after Peter had finally turned up, she took her lunch break. She walked to the Hackescher Markt, which was quieter than normal for this time of day, though the cafés and restaurants were open and tourists sat at the tables, visibly unsure whether to continue with their sightseeing program or not. The newspapers with the photographs were everywhere. In a close-fitting calf-length skirt but with trainers on her feet, Isabelle walked as far as Oranienburger Strasse, where there were more police than usual outside the synagogue, then retraced her steps and finally turned into Rosenthaler Strasse. The sky was overcast, the street and the shop windows milky, the people themselves like figures concealed behind a thin blanket, as if they needed to wait and see what might happen, or perhaps hide away—and what should one be thinking, what expression should one be wearing? Isabelle stopped in front of a shoe shop to study her reflection, which showed no emotion. She worked the elastic band free from her hair. Light brown, moderately thick hair. A face that avoided being ordinary only by being too perfect, a symmetrical pale oval. She bent her nose to the right and then to the left. Beside her a little girl, who seemed to have popped up from nowhere, imitated her actions and then grinned at her and ran off, in tiny, bright pink pumps. Isabelle glanced down at her own shoes and went into the shop. The sales assistant, looking up resentfully, pushed her open newspaper off the counter and let it drop to the floor, heedlessly causing the people frozen in midair in the photograph to plummet still further. Jakob had said he would be waiting for her at eight o'clock at the Angel of Death bar, and the problem, Isabelle thought, was not the shoes themselves but how to walk in them. She had the assistant bring her a pair with low half-moon heels and long pointed toes, in a varying mix of matte black and brown. They were secured over the instep by a strip of black elastic on each side. Clattering on the thin new wooden flooring, which already showed scratches, Isabelle paraded up and down in front of the mirror. –I've got a date this evening, she said, and . . . –This evening? the assistant queried, as if Isabelle had just announced a funeral. It was nonsensical to imagine a scenario—like something out of a B-movie—where it was not Jakob who showed up but her Freiburg lover, with the smell of hay on his clothes that seemed so incongruous. Like Jakob, he would recognize her at once, because she had hardly changed since she was twenty, still had the same smooth, innocent face.

She continued to pace up and down in front of the mirror, gazing down at her feet. The assistant looked on, crossing her legs in their long tight trousers, playing with her shoes, high-heeled pink confections with a golden insect in place of a buckle, making a face and saying nothing. She had forgotten to put some music on, but what kind of music did one play on a day like this? And the cars outside—it was as if they were going slower than usual. Through the shop window a child could be seen astride a bicycle, his mother holding on to the luggage rack. Jakob had left no doubt that they would see each other this evening in the Angel of Death, and after that too. Then we'll see how it goes. He hadn't needed to say that, and he hadn't been smiling anymore when Ginka, giggling, closed the door with exaggerated tact. Tap, tap, went the half-moon heels on the wooden floor. Some music would have been a help now, a rhythm, a sentimental song, and the assistant went over to the counter and reached down towards a hi-fi, gracefully bending from the hips, her legs straight, only her small bottom sticking out behind; her blouse slid up, exposing part of her back, almost white, very slender, and below it the slight round-ing where her buttocks began, smooth and firm. –They look great. Really, the assistant said indifferently.

That morning Isabelle had at last got through to Alexa. –For goodness' sake, why shouldn't we be all right? (and Clara could be heard laughing in the background) –what are you worrying about? As always, Isabelle had felt a pang at having to play second fiddle, at not coming first with Alexa, not ever, and after all why should she—just because they had shared an apartment for two years? But Jakob would be expecting her this evening. –I'll be waiting for you, he'd said, and then he had left. In her first year in Berlin Isabelle had thrown herself into an orgy of clothes-buying, determined to shake off the provincial aura of Heidelberg and Freiburg, but Hanna had laughed at her. Alexa had moved in with Clara, and since then Isabelle had hoarded her money, as if she were hoarding her past and her future so as to remain intact in the narrow gap between them; she never touched the money that her parents sent her, to use in whatever way you wish, as her father wrote every Christmas and birthday. Isabelle slipped the shoes off, stood there on the wooden floor in her black nylon stockings, and nodded to the assistant. 279 marks. Outside a tram moved off, squealing. Decisively Isabelle dropped her trainers into the paper bag that the assistant was holding open and then slipped the new shoes on again. The heels click-clacked on the pavement; the child with the bicycle, a little boy, looked up at her, beamed as he mounted the saddle and shakily pedaled away. He almost fell off when he turned to look back at her. Children liked her, as if she herself were only a child in disguise. An older version of a fourteen-year-old, Alexa had said, and she had bought some children's underwear made of terry toweling and photographed Isabelle in it. Up in the sky a helicopter was circling.

3

Jakob had woken early and was walking to the office. After yesterday's rain the streets were drying out, but it was a chilly and disagreeable day. In March he had turned thirty-three; a synopsis of each year gone by seemed to take up less and less space. From now on time would pass differently, more slowly; for what was past, the synopsis sufficed, just a few notes to give a general idea, he thought, an uncomplicated matter requiring only a brief commentary. The grave faces of the few people in the streets irritated him: nothing bad had happened to them, and there was no reason to suppose that anything would. Since his mother's death he himself had been spared any misfortune. She had died shortly before his twelfth birthday, and Aunt Fini had moved in with him and his father; she had cooked the midday meal, her expression betraying a secret satisfaction that her younger brother could not manage without her and that his marriage to a petty-bourgeois girl from Pomerania had been a failure. Due to her death. For several weeks Jakob had hardly spoken, certainly not to Aunt Fini, who, little by little, cleared out her sister-in-law Anngrit's study, aggrieved that she could not find fault with the Biedermeier secretaire, a gift from her brother to his wife. But she cleared the letters and photographs out of the drawers and arranged for other pieces of furniture to be taken away, two armchairs, a small table, the brightly colored Jacobsen chairs that Anngrit Holbach had bought in the seventies, some transparent inflatable plastic stools and some lamps. Not until four years later, when Aunt Fini had to move out to make way for Gertrud, her brother's new girlfriend, did it strike Jakob how different the house was now. He tried to remember his mother, the bright colors and simple shapes she had loved, and he yearned for the moment when he could move out, when he need no longer open the door into the dark stillness of the house. Gertrud's confidence in the future was also quickly exhausted. She would come home before his father in the evening, laden with shopping bags, call out Jakob's name and play her old cassettes in the kitchen: the Beatles, Fats Waller, Thelonious Monk. But it did not last long, nothing lasted long in that house, which they occupied like people in transit, being careful with furniture that was not theirs, just waiting for the day of departure. His father ended up alone there, for Gertrud had told Jakob that when he left she would leave, too. He did not imagine that she had stayed for his sake, but he was certainly in love with her. When they parted—she had hired a minibus and driven him and all his things to Freiburg—she kissed him on the mouth. The two of them had carried his mattress up to his new room, and for months he bitterly regretted not sleeping with her. Soon afterwards he had a fling with his housemate; he slept with her, but kept alive the memory of Gertrud, who did indeed leave his father, and waited for a letter that never came. It was only a full three years later, when he sat down next to Isabelle at a lecture on the history of law, that he fell in love again.

He had Hans. From kindergarten, Jakob would reply when anyone asked how he knew Hans. The truth was they had met in Freiburg on the day after Jakob's arrival, the day when he had bought himself some new shoes and gone to eat in the university canteen for the first time, wearing the expensive Bally shoes with which he wanted to mark a beginning, *his* beginning—the point from which he might or might not lay down memories of his own but would at least be free to shake off the ones that other people's petty recollection of the past tried to foist on him. They had each come to Freiburg alone, having no friends or schoolmates who were also studying law there, and they chanced to stand next to each other in the queue for the canteen, in the draft of warm air, facing the grimy, graffiti-covered concrete and breathing in the cooking smells that turned Jakob's stomach and merely surprised Hans. Step by step they shuffled forward, passing a bookstall, day after day they would stand here, and Jakob's eyes were fixed on the new brown leather of his shoes, on the seams that looked dependable and would last. Because he was not paying attention he bumped into Hans, who was standing in front of him, holding his student card in his hand as though expecting to be challenged at any moment. He came from a small village in the Black Forest where his parents had a farm.

The first four semesters passed quickly. They hiked along the Beggars' Way to Stauffen and on to Basle. They hitchhiked to Strasbourg. One year Hans took Jakob home with him for Christmas.

While Hans attended lectures on art history and never missed a major exhibition in Basle or Stuttgart, Jakob preferred to go to films or concerts; for a few weeks at a time he would take a keen interest in politics and read several newspapers a day, including foreign ones. On the day after the Wall came down he went to a travel agent's first thing in the morning, waited for the owner to arrive and booked two flights to Berlin. They were to fly from Stuttgart, and he hired a car and set off with Hans, but they were late reaching the airport and missed their flight. Later Jakob's curiosity waned; he was put off by the Modrow and de Maizière governments and by the comments made by his father, who suddenly took to phoning him almost daily. He felt as if the ground were being cut from under his feet: his country, the Federal Republic, was disappearing, so that he was emigrating willy-nilly, without moving from the spot. This mood, too, soon passed. Hans laughed at him. But then the unification treaty and the law to settle disputes over the ownership of property did become a long-term preoccupation. A conversation with his father on the subject put an end to the telephone calls; that Christmas Aunt Fini explained to him, not without a touch of malice, that this legislation brought back uncomfortable memories for his father. In the fifties Herr Holbach had been afraid he might lose his firm, which had been bought for a very respectable sum from Jakob's grandfather's Jewish business partner. You never knew what the future might hold, she said. Jakob resolved to find out more, but the word "Aryanization" initially made him shy away, and that autumn he met Isabelle. Their one walk together took them up the Bromberg; down in the valley, shrouded in mist and drizzle, lay Freiburg, which swallowed Isabelle up again after a single night. In 1992 Jakob took his First State Examination and knew that he had found the area of law that suited him: that of disputed property rights. He and Hans had agreed to move to Berlin together. In 1993 they both began their practical training in Berlin, Jakob with the firm of Golbert & Schreiber, which specialized in restitution cases, particularly concerning real estate in Berlin and Brandenburg. He did not, however, dismiss the thought of Isabelle from his mind. In his personal life he disliked thinking in terms of cause and effect: thus he refused to consider a possible link between his interest in restitution and the fact that his father had almost been involved in a case of that kind, and an essential component of his love for Isabelle was the chance nature of their meeting. But there was also a sense in which she had to be restored to him: he had waited a long time, and however you looked at it, this waiting in itself constituted a claim.

Jakob was certainly no materialist, he merely distrusted anything that seemed mysterious, and disliked hidden motives, or changes that produced no visible effect. He liked dealing with houses and plots of land. He had enjoyed traveling in Brandenburg: it brought to mind an era unknown to him, as if his memory were able to expand beyond the confines of his own experience. He felt, as he passed through the villages on his way to some land registry where he had to check the records of changes of ownership, that while one could not break the chains of causality, which he so disliked, there was a sense of one temporal axis intersecting with another. After the end of the war, when his mother had crossed Brandenburg on her way from Pomerania, it must have looked very much as he was seeing it now. Stone-surfaced roads that passed through sleepy, isolated villages where windows were kept firmly shut against possible intruders. Greed and fear on the faces of the people he spoke to. A touch of subservience, mingled sometimes with hope, sometimes with hatred. Rarely resignation. Often the faces seemed lost in reverie, the eyes layered over with the deposits of the history that, page by page, registry entry by registry entry, he was trying to reconstruct. It was like taking apart a jigsaw that presented a deceptive picture and rearranging the pieces in their proper order. *Those persons who were guided in their actions by the duly enacted laws of the former GDR and who acted properly according to those laws shall be deemed to be of good character and deserving of the protection of the law.* By now he knew that sentence from Fieberg and Reichenbach's introduction to the law of property by heart. He had deliberately bought himself an old Golf, not a new car. Even so, to most people he was still an emissary of the victorious powers, the Soviet Union no longer being one of them.

At the end of his training period he was offered a permanent position with Golbert & Schreiber. Herr Schreiber himself and Robert, who joined the firm at the same time as Jakob, worked on claims made under paragraph 1, subparagraph 6 of the law of property: *This law is to be applied to property law claims made by individuals and groups who in the period between 30 January 1933 and 8 May 1945 were persecuted on racial, political, religious or ideological grounds and who consequently lost their property through forced sale, expropriation, or otherwise.* He himself specialized in questions of priority in relation to investment. If a former owner could not be found, an investor was entitled to proceed with his plans regardless of the unresolved ownership issue. Pending the definitive resolution of such issues, life had to go on.

Hans had stayed on in the first apartment they had shared, in Wiener Strasse. Even long after Jakob had moved out, they still congregated there every few days, he and Jonas, Marianne and Patrick, along with all their fluctuating acquaintances, mostly painters like Jonas and Patrick or else specialists in German studies, journalists, never a lawyer. They sat at the long, wobbly table, which Patrick, with a chipboard panel and two extra legs, had extended to a length of eight feet, and it was tacitly understood that everyone should bring something to eat or at least a bottle of wine. Later on, after Hans had finished his practical training and passed the Second State Examination, and then had got his first job and was earning enough, he bought big new pots and pans and a second stove, had wine delivered, and insisted that those of his friends who were barely keeping their heads above water with grants and—all too rarely—the sale of a picture must not bring anything, except perhaps a drawing, a print or a photograph. In one of his two big rooms, which he had redecorated, he had a plan chest. The walls were painted white and left bare.

Unlike Hans, Jakob liked to keep moving house. Books and clothes into boxes, and out they went. He would give away his bed, table, and chairs and buy new ones, and so Hans too was always pretty well supplied with furnishings and household equipment. –You idiot, who do you think I bought this bed for? I certainly didn't plan to sleep in it myself for the next ten years. It was one of the games between them which had been working so well and for so long that at times Jakob could almost believe that there would be *no* rude awakening one day. Not in relation to Hans. Perhaps not at all. From kindergarten, Jakob would answer when they were asked how they knew each other, and by now it was almost the truth, they had known each other for as long as they could, or chose to, remember. As neither of them had a long-term girlfriend they were almost regarded as a couple. Why Hans remained single, not even Jakob knew. He himself never met a woman he could really fall for, and so he waited for Isabelle. He had, not entirely seriously, set himself a time limit of ten years. If he had not found Isabelle again by 2001 he would forget her.

When Golbert & Schreiber made him a partner in August 2001, he invited Hans for a celebratory meal at Diekmann's restaurant, and afterwards they went on to the Angel of Death. By pure chance it was Hans who pushed his way towards the bar to get them a couple of whiskies, while Jakob listened with half an ear to the voices around him. Isabelle. For the first time in ten years he heard her name. It hadn't been difficult to get chatting to Ginka. When she invited him to her party on September 11th, he brought forward an appointment with a New York investor to the ninth and asked his secretary, Julia, to rebook his flight.

He thought of that name, which had surprised him back then, and of her face, with its regular features and oddly absent air as though she were waiting for something, but without curiosity. She had been totally unlike the girls reading law, and had said she wanted to study painting or design. He remembered her face, her small breasts, and the fact that he had not felt awkward with her even for a moment. I've found Isabelle again, he told Hans with a grin before they left the Angel of Death.

And he really had found her again. It had been the wrong

day for a party, and all afternoon he had feared that the invitation was void, that the party would have been cancelled, but then he had taken a taxi to Schlüterstrasse, rung the bell and been admitted without further ado. And there she was: Isabelle.

During his lunch break, after a morning spent in the office unable to concentrate, he had wandered restlessly towards Potsdamer Platz and then back again to Mauerstrasse. He did not want to see the newspapers or pick up snatches of conversation. Only the day before yesterday he had been there. But he had left in time. He had been spared: Isabelle, he thought, had saved him.

4.

Mae was beside herself, clinging to him on the landing, sobbing. Completely hysterical. Jim could hear the television. They had all three been on the road, he and Albert and Ben, and he had been arguing with Ben, while Albert said nothing but insisted on playing the same CD over and over again, which revolted Jim as much as if Albert had taken a leak in the car. It wasn't the music itself but the way Albert listened to it, pretentiously waving his hands about and only taking hold of the wheel when absolutely necessary. Or when a police car appeared, which today was happening more often than it usually did on their route in from the south, especially around the Docklands area and the approach roads near Silvertown. Jim cursed, because this time Ben was clearly right to be nervous. What the hell were the police doing here? But Albert refused to put the radio on and only turned the music up louder. Basses, a backing group, an artificial, electronic-sounding woman's voice, *because it's been so long that I can't explain, and it's been so long, right now, so wrong*: he couldn't shake it off, that relentless, enervating voice, and now, just minutes later—Albert had dropped him off in Pentonville Road—Mae's hysterical sobbing. His hand struck her on the temple because she either ducked or stumbled. Grabbing her under the armpits, he dragged her into the living room just as, on the screen, the second of the towers collapsed in slow motion—or was it just trick photography? And then he made the connection between the images on television and Mae's hysteria, between the police cars and the images. But he still didn't understand what was going on. Mae was talking about people who had died, rocking to and fro as if she had a baby in her arms; later she kept on repeating what she had heard, that nothing would ever be the same again, the whole world, their lives, and that night, when she had at last fallen asleep, she started whimpering. A long-drawn-out, ceaseless whimpering until he prodded or shook her, a tiny mewling sound, never-ending, like a loop, as if the measurement of time had changed, as if following the slow collapse of the towers, everything had to happen in slow motion. For days Mae did nothing to keep the kitchen or the living room tidy. At some point the window was left open, the carpet got wet and it stank, Mae said it stank but did nothing. The smell persisted even after Jim had unceremoniously ripped out the carpet. This was no sort of life. What did any of that have to do with Mae, or with him? Long strips of adhesive on the floorboards. And the way she just sat around on the sofa, the yellow sofa—yellow once, nearly new once—that Albert had brought them, just as he'd brought the table and chairs. "Homes for my employees," Ben parroted. Ben, who was proud to be Albert's right-hand man and was always sucking up to him. The miserable toe-rag had taken a fancy to Mae, and he knew how to wind Jim up, arriving uninvited and criticizing the state of the place: there was an evil smell, and nothing in the fridge. They had a couple of quite big jobs coming up, in the suburbs and even further out: Albert had hit on the idea of burgling people who had moved out of London and felt safe now, felt safe especially in the afternoons, in the daytime, in the small suburbs and little towns where life was so peaceful that they didn't have burglar alarms fitted and even left their windows open, trusting each other. No more burglaries, he had announced a year ago, but that had changed now, and Jim saw the gardens, little houses with gardens in front or all round them. It was ten years since he'd

been out of London, and now here were all these houses, nicely kept, peaceful. He and Mae hadn't even got a bed, only a
mattress. Field Street, that was a laugh, nothing green for miles
around, just noise and building sites and dirt. What Mae did,
where she went once he was out of the house, Jim didn't know.
Down the street towards King's Cross, where Albert had
picked her up. So much noise here, it made Mae's coughing
seem quiet. And he thought of all the programs aimed at help-
ing dropouts. But who could believe in them? Anti-drugs, anti-
prostitution, anti-crime. He wanted to get away, with Mae. She
would lie stretched out on the sofa and say she wanted to stop,
she promised to stop. She would stand at the window when he
left and be lying on the sofa when he returned, her body would
go limp as soon as he put his arms around her, and when he
penetrated her she would cough and cough until he thought he
would go deaf. –Stop that, for God's sake! He must get enough
money together for them to leave here. No more burglaries,
just drugs, Albert had said. But then they did do more burglaries, and Jim joined in so as to get a few thousand pounds
together at last. But now there were more police crawling all
over the place, checking up on everybody. The late autumn was
cold and wet. The windows wouldn't close properly, or else
Mae forgot to close them. The heating either didn't work or
worked too well, it got unbearably hot in the flat and it stank;
Ben had been round and brought her something, some pills.
There she was at the window, standing erect in a close-fitting
blue woolen dress, dark blue, no shoes. Looking like a school-
girl. Her rather big but attractive thighs were clearly defined.
There was Mae, hanging onto the door, her eyes half closed.
There was Mae, catching sight of him, laughing, laughing and
falling onto the sofa. Yellow, it had been yellow once. Leaning
forward and retching, mucus dripping from her mouth; she
kept getting thinner.

She said she loathed the dust and that it was no better here than over there, in New York, that the dust killed so many people, and nobody talked about it, about the people who died. She wanted some tea. December came; in the New Year, Jim said, they'd leave the city, start a new life as soon as he had the money, move to the country. She wanted some tea, wanted him to bring some scones and cake. The building site around King's Cross was getting bigger and bigger, even the Midland Grand Hotel was being renovated. Albert said that in a few years this would be a good, affluent neighborhood, they'd be glad to be living on Field Street. Jim said that if Mae didn't see a doctor soon and give up the tablets she wouldn't need a place to live at all.

Mostly they sat in front of the television, and Mae would fall asleep. Though he couldn't put his finger on it, he felt sure there was a trap somewhere. Her face. He went out, pulling the door to behind him, and listened; went down the stairs, stood outside in the street and listened. An icy wind was whipping dust and scraps of paper along the road. Plastic bags. A cigarette packet. A boy peeped out of a doorway and waved. January passed. But the war's been over for ages, he told her; the towers, the dead people, the women in veils, but she lay curled up on the sofa, crying. Ben came round every few days. She denied it, but Jim was sure of it. And when he sat beside her in the dim glow of the television, telling her how they would have a garden, with a wall that he would put up with his own hands, and he knew what he was talking about because his father had been a bricklayer, and how the roses would bloom in the summer, those were the only times when she looked at him and smiled. They could have tea in the garden, under a cherry tree, a walnut tree: our life, he tried to tell her, she should think of that, of the garden and how they would drink tea under a cherry tree or a walnut tree, bringing the tray straight out from the kitchen into the garden, the cherry tree covered in blossom. It was still cold, but soon they'd be able to go for walks, they could catch the tube to Richmond or Kew and walk along the Thames. He'd take her to Kew Gardens, neither of them had ever been there but it was supposed to be lovely, everybody said so. Her face had grown thinner, she hardly ate anything, she smoked too much, he said, but he smoked too, and Ben kept coming and bringing her tablets. Amphetamines, Valium, as soon as Jim was out of the house. Jim took her by the shoulders and shook her. Life, he tried to tell her; he tried to reason with her, to make her stop letting Ben in, and in just a few more weeks or months they'd be able to get away, out of London, and make a new start somewhere in the country, perhaps even get married. That was life: making a new start. That was life: not dying. They could go to Richmond or Kew, they could go to the seaside. But Mae said that he was full of hatred, and then he forgot her birthday.

He suspected that Ben had told her about Alice. It was not this betrayal that made him angry, but something more profound that he couldn't express, just as he couldn't say why he saw Mae and thought that he was too far away from her, that she couldn't hear when he called her name. Worse still, she didn't like sleeping with him. Had never liked sleeping with him, he thought. Alice had been something else, she had given herself to him, she liked him, she taunted him, and then she'd stolen three hundred pounds from him. Drunk, completely gone to the dogs. There were so many things that you loved, or hated, without being able to explain why. Alice had been a slag, with a face like a small animal's, sharp-featured, cunning, and she'd certainly known how to cheat him. She'd got what she deserved. Her room in Arlington Road had made him feel sick, with the dirty crockery and needles, and the radio that she never turned off. Like an animal, he said to Albert, furious because Ben accused him of treating her badly.

–Who are you to look down on anybody? Albert, of all people, had said that. Mae had turned twenty-five and Jim had forgotten her birthday. –You're full of hatred, Mae said. He wanted to take her to the cinema. But there were police everywhere, checking up on people, she said, and she wouldn't go on the tube. –But why should anything happen to us, looking the way we do? Do I look like an Arab? Do you? he asked her. He was full of hatred, Mae repeated, and Ben turned up and stood there listening to it all. Two days later Jim couldn't pick a straightforward front-door lock and they had to give up and abandon the job. Albert put his hand on Jim's shoulder and laughed uproariously until Jim shook himself free and angrily ran off. Albert had never paid him his share: –I'm keeping it for you, it's all properly written down, he reassured him, just be patient for a bit longer. What did Albert take him for? He paid for their place in Field Street, that poky, stinking dump, your flat, he said, and actually expected him and Mae to be grateful. And yet it *had* been a sort of home, despite the ill-fitting windows, despite the stench, except that Mae lay curled up on the sofa, saying she could still see the dead people and the live ones jumping from the windows into the abyss, she could hear their screams, she could hear what the people trapped in the lifts and the corridors were saying. And the hatred, Mae said, the anger that would be vented on them too, him and her: how could we not have known that they hated us from the depths of their souls? He had nothing to say. The sirens went wailing along the road, from right to left and back again. –And the dead people that we've forgotten, said Mae, they're calling us. Jim flung the window open to let in some fresh air. It was February. The noise of the construction machinery came right into the room. Once they went for a walk, as far as the canal and then along it, heading for the park and the aviary, but it was too much for Mae. She sat down on a bench beside the canal, saying that she couldn't go any further, and he went on alone.

Later he thought that that was the first time she had disappeared, when she stayed sitting alone on the bench, in a little coat that she didn't button up although it was cold; he had turned round again and looked back, but her head was bowed. So he went on until he couldn't see her anymore, and she disappeared, although she was sitting still, not moving.

The next day he told Albert that in future he wanted fifty per cent, and he wanted it cash in hand. Albert laughed, but he himself had once told Jim that when you stop being afraid, people do what you want, and so it proved in this case. Albert agreed, though he asked Jim to be patient for a while, but he did agree and was willing to shake hands on it. They wanted to get out of the city and move to the country, but he didn't tell Albert that, and then he met Damian, who said he could stay in his flat if he liked, for a few months or longer, a proper two-roomed flat in Kentish Town, and it even had a small garden. But when Jim got home he smelled the gas and thought, what difference does it make *what* you choke on, but then he did break into a run and throw open the windows and switch the oven off. She was lying there like an animal on the kitchen floor, and he didn't tell her about Damian's offer but just stood there in the kitchen as the smell of gas grew fainter, downing one beer after another. In the back yard he could see a child playing with a washing line, catching wild horses, throwing the rope like a lasso, and in the yard next door a young lad was bending over a moped, making a clatter with screwdrivers and spare parts; lights were coming on in the windows.

Spring came. A year before they had gone out to West Finchley and had pancakes, his treat, and he had held the door open for her and bought her flowers—tulips—and for Easter a little soft toy rabbit. They had often spent half the night sitting in front of the television with their arms around each other, and on Sundays he got her to do a roast with potatoes and vegetables. He remembered it all as he stood looking out at the yard, he remembered standing at the window a few days ago just like this, thinking of last spring. –Listen, that girl . . . , Albert began, and then shrugged. –She's no good for you. Jim refused to listen, and anyway it was Ben who wouldn't leave Mae alone, turning her against Jim, bringing stuff for her, amphetamines, and Valium. It had been bound to come to this sooner or later. Jim saw that Mae was bleeding. She was lying on the floor in front of the sofa, bleeding and crying. She had said she could see the dead people, the dead and the dying, she never stopped talking about them, and he forgot what she had looked like last spring and even in the late summer, her oval, symmetrical face framed by fair hair, her eyes that were sometimes grey and sometimes green. There was a childlike quality about her, she'd been soft and smooth and not thin, but not fat either, everything had been just right. He had held her close, with both his arms around her, and she belonged to him; her neck, as he put his arms around it, had seemed to him as fragile as a kitten's. They would move to the country and have tea in the garden. He went into the kitchen to calm himself down, but then he heard her telephoning, calling Ben. –Come quickly, she begged, not meaning Jim, and she screamed when he appeared with a knife in his hand. Ben arrived ten minutes later, letting himself in: Mae must have given him a key. Now she was lying motionless, and Jim stood up and walked straight past him. Ben was pale. –You'd better make yourself scarce, he said, and reached for the phone.

He stood outside the house for a while and then slowly started walking; everything seemed to consist of outlines, nothing more than outlines. He could even recall his parents sitting at the table waiting for him, and the three of them waiting for his brother who'd be home any minute—this was before his brother got ill. He could remember that, even though something was missing, as if there was a gap in his thoughts where something had just happened, and so he stood there in

Pentonville Road until he heard an ambulance siren and moved on. You remembered happy times as something you had really experienced. But now there were only the outlines, and the fear when you didn't know what had happened. Jim felt for the key Damian had given him, and took the tube up to Kentish Town. He found the street, Lady Margaret Road, and it was quiet there; a cat bounded across the road, black and white, and hid under a car.

A few days later, Albert called him. He said nothing about Mae, and Jim didn't ask.

5

It was still Hanna's key that Isabelle used to open the main door to the building where the agency was. On the day before going into hospital for the last time, Hanna had given her the key, with that smile of hers that grew ever more radiant the paler her skin, the more hollow her cheeks became, until nothing was left but grey eyes and her full lips. Hanna had embraced Isabelle and poked her gently in the ribs with her skeletal hand. –Come on, we'll see each other at least once more. In fact it had been more than once, for Death seemed confused, distracted by the affectionate whispering at Hanna's bedside, by Isabelle's face, more childlike than ever, and by Peter's calmness, because now, at last, he subdued his rage and checked the rancorous, corrosive utterances that had added to the bitterness of the last few months. Isabelle brought the key with her on every visit to the hospital, hoping that Hanna would ask for it back. But then the inevitable moment arrived, Andras let her know, and they hurried to the Charité together. Hanna's lips were pressed tightly together and she made no sound; the doctors could not tell whether she was in pain. Sometimes she opened her eyes, but they seemed to take nothing in and to express nothing but the resolve to die. Peter came at night and slept on a camp bed that the nurses put up for him. In the daytime he kept away from both the hospital and the office, and so Andras and Isabelle found themselves alone together all day long and in the evenings too, because Isabelle was reluctant to go back to the empty apartment where Alexa never came now except to pack or unpack something. The night when it was all over, Isabelle slept at Andras's apartment; he put clean linen on the bed for her and slept on the worn red sofa that stood in his living room like some ridiculous stage prop. At five in the morning they were woken by a telephone call from Peter asking them to look after the agency and saying that he would be back in a month's time. Hanna had died on October 5, 1996; on that day, for the first time, Isabelle had unlocked the main entrance door and the door to the office using Hanna's key, and had found a short letter on her desk, a kind of will, making over Hanna's share in the agency to her. For Isabelle, who had never studied graphic design except for a few months in London, this was an accolade, and for a few minutes she collapsed, stunned, into Andras's arms. It was then, five years ago, that she had resolved to start being serious about her work and her life in Berlin, but something had always eluded her, albeit in an agreeable way, and, after all, even as Hanna's assistant she had worked late into the evening just as often as she did now.

When she opened the office door, holding the paper bag containing her old trainers, she almost fell over Andras, who was down on all fours with his tongue out, looking worried, as though he was going to have to lick up something that had been spilled. For a moment he seemed frozen in that position, then he leapt to his feet, while Peter, seated at his desk, gave a sudden bark of laughter—angry laughter.

–Andras, he said, was showing me how rescue dogs work, with all that rubble and the ash clogging their noses. Andras glanced at Isabelle's feet. –You've bought some new shoes.

–You make me sick, the pair of you, said Peter, almost knocking his chair over as he stood up. One acts like a lunatic and the other has nothing better to do than go shopping. After the door had closed behind him, Isabelle at last opened her mouth. –What's the matter with you two?

But Andras was gazing in silence at Isabelle's shoes. Taking the bag from her hand, he pulled out the trainers one at a time, placed them on his desk and gently ran a finger over the laces, the tongue, the toe. –Andras, don't do that! It was quiet, here too it was quiet. An S-Bahn train jerkily approached and came to a halt. Andras turned full circle two or three times, then sat down on the desktop. The train had started away again, had picked up speed and was gone before Isabelle's eyes had taken it in, but already the next train was there, stopping, jolting forward a few yards, stopping again. The faces that appeared at the windows seemed to be pressed not against window glass but against a lens that made them appear magnified and distorted.

–You're quite pale, murmured Andras. He hesitated and then went into the outer office, which also served as a kitchen, complete with jars of honey, crockery, tea bags, an espresso machine, a portable two-ring stove that was as heavy as a safe, and the gas bottle under the sink. He put the kettle on, laid a tray with a cup, a sugar bowl, and a milk jug, which he forgot to fill, waited for the water to boil and made the tea. Isabelle and Hanna had worked in the back office and the two men in the front one. After Hanna's death Andras had joined Isabelle in the back office, where he had strung wires along the wall to hang his designs on, and Isabelle's, too. Green lino in the back office, red in the front one, and the outer office was blue. Isabelle's desk stood at right angles to the wall, in between the two windows that had the main line and S-Bahn trains passing in front of them. Next to the computer, whose screen appeared to hover above a ball, were some small, brightly colored bowls containing erasers, sharpeners and little bottles of colored ink, while a number of glass jars held pens and pencils. Andras had encouraged her to start drawing freehand again and even to paint in watercolors, which she hadn't done since her school-days. She had grown used to his style of working and often spent hours drawing street scenes, interiors, or whole series of pictures before finally starting to tackle the project in hand. –It works, she had told Peter triumphantly, you can see that, it's not wasting time, quite the opposite. She loved the agency. *New Concept—New Life,* that was what it had been, for her at any rate, when she had arrived in Berlin. An ad for a roommate had led her to Alexa, and through Alexa she had found Hanna. She owed everything to Alexa, had clung to her until Alexa went to live with Clara, finally forcing Isabelle to look for an apartment of her own.

Setting down the tray, Andras went out again and returned with biscuits and a jar of honey, then sat down. –You do look pale, have some tea. This time yesterday Isabelle had been wondering whether she should help Ginka with her preparations, and had been looking ahead, not with unmixed pleasure, to the evening, the hurly-burly and the alcohol, the inescapable choreography of these gatherings in which Ginka took such a pride. Ginka openly admitted that in general she preferred guests who were single, and not even the attendance of ten couples on the verge of their golden wedding anniversaries would have deterred her from turning her party into a singles occasion. Within minutes of their arrival she drove a wedge between partners with a few mordant phrases, a compliment or a mocking, condescending remark, hitting, with unerring instinct, the precise spot that would set loving couples at odds with each other and make each partner wish for pleasanter and more exciting company, at least for this one evening. They might have resented this, had not the outcome vindicated Ginka's tactics—in less than half an hour, the pairs had separated and everyone was doing their utmost to be charming and entertaining so as to captivate someone on this whirling carousel, knowing that otherwise they would be thrown off it, cast out of these rooms filled with laughter and chatter into the darkness that seemed to surround them. When Ginka's guests were leaving, she found the right words to set them sliding down a slope, as it were, back into their marriages and liaisons, feeling, it is true, a slight prick of discontent but obediently consenting to trot back out into the night beside the partner they had arrived with. Those who were genuinely single she tried to pair off, and here too her instinct was unrivalled, though she privately admitted to Isabelle that it was illogical to play the matchmaker and then complain that there were fewer and fewer singles around. She included Isabelle in her match-making schemes, though she accompanied her offers with a threat to show her the door if she dared to turn into a bore like all the other women just past thirty who suddenly married, had children and possibly even gave up working.

Andras placed a hand on her knee. –Don't take it so much to heart. There probably aren't as many dead as they think right now. His voice, normally so pleasant and calm, sounded hollow; he ran his hand through his thick hair, above his slightly too broad face. She followed the direction of his eyes, which were fixed on her shoes. It was not the World Trade Center that was disturbing him but the new shoes, the tension emanating from Isabelle, waves that his sensory apparatus picked up without being able to interpret or process them. Isabelle reminded him of a captured animal that remains deceptively still while preparing its bid to escape, indifferent to everything but its own moment of decision. –Isabelle? She took the cup and warmed her hands on it. He dared not ask her about Ginka's party. After leaving the office yesterday, she had not gone home to change but had gone straight to Charlottenburg, in jeans, sneakers and a brown-and-yellow-hooped T-shirt. Andras could not fail to notice that most men found Isabelle as attractive as he did. But she had treated him from the start as an older brother, teasing him in a familiar, sometimes condescending way, tormenting him as one only does when one is utterly sure of somebody. For the hundredth time he asked himself why he didn't go home to Budapest—pack his few possessions and drive off without a backward glance, straight to Budapest where his brother-in-law László wanted the two of them to set up a graphic-design and advertising agency. For a while he had told himself that he did not trust László's enthusiasm, or that he could not face the thought of living with his parents, moving back into the house from which he had been dispatched at fourteen to his aunt and his uncle in Germany. But he knew that these were just excuses.

–This time yesterday, Isabelle said at last, and then relapsed into silence. Andras shook his head. Someone would pay for what had happened, would pay the price for the fact that here, whether in Germany or the USA, people felt that they had been robbed of the reality that was their right. The world will have that reality bombed into it, he thought, until people here feel secure again, secure with the old injustice that they find familiar and comfortable. –Someone will pay, he said at last, and you can be sure it won't be those who are responsible.

Isabelle looked at him with tears in her eyes. –Before they actually died, I mean, they must have been so frightened. She saw Jakob, suddenly saw him walking by her side across the university square in Freiburg, sitting beside her in the lecture theatre. He had escaped death. She would never have learned of his death, never have remembered him: he would have vanished in the indifference of her forgetting and of his death. Andras stood up to fetch her a tissue. He felt angry. He came back, gently wiped away her tears, and handed her the tissue. She looked really unhappy, unhappy and guilty, like the time when she had finally realized why Hanna shaved her head. But that had been five or six years ago, and she was more grown-up now. –Come round to my place this evening, I'll make us something to eat, goulash if you like. He stood up and crossed to the window. Three men and two women were walking along Dircksenstrasse, right in the middle of the road, arm in arm and laughing. Nothing as it was before, Andras thought bitterly, and then he felt so afraid that he wanted to run out into the street and keep going, to Monbijou Park, along the Spree, on and on until he had left the city behind him.

6.

Towards six o'clock the sky clouded over, and from the west, like a solid wall, dusk and storm together bore down upon the city, silently at first, the wind dropping as though to listen for something, until suddenly the rain came, a cloudburst above which nothing else could be heard. Andras stood at the window. The rain hung like a heavy tarpaulin over the roofs, lights glimmering feebly beneath it, the television tower struggled to free itself from the blackness, and the giant video screens on the far side of Alexanderplatz cast pallid shadows. Three years ago he had stood like this at the window and decided that it really was time to leave. Looking out, he had calculated that it would take only a small van to transport his books, some of the shelving, the heavy little chest of drawers, and the red sofa to Budapest. To one of those cellar spaces, he thought, that his parents had gradually colonized, slatted compartments whose doors hung crookedly on their hinges, held in place by padlocks; behind those doors were empty crates once used for coal, for potatoes, for firewood and kindling, and boxes full of screws, nails, string, all the things that had been kept for decades in the drawers and cupboards of the cramped apartment because they might come in handy some day. And he, too, here in Berlin, had saved every paper clip, every elastic band, every treasury tag, padded envelopes, empty tins, glass jars; every few months he gathered them all up and put them out in the refuse containers at night, unobserved as far as he knew, and for the few days that followed he kept away from the yard, and even avoided meeting the other tenants on the stairs, until the containers were emptied. These days he no longer breathed a sigh of relief after such clearances, because they were so short-lived. Within a week odd items started to accumulate again, a small cardboard box, a piece of string with no knots in it, useful things, undoubtedly, and it was better to abandon his resolutions and just have a good turn-out every six months.

Cars battled their way up Choriner Strasse, their headlights flickering; the trees, still in leaf, obscured the street lamps, which gave only the most meager light. The house fronts opposite were just as the Second World War and socialism had left them, while, a few buildings further along, garish colors marked the vanguard of delicatessens and cafés. –Just don't get like those early retirers, his brother-in-law László had warned him. Lifestyle, mobile phones, but underneath all the brand names they're a pathetic lot. In Germany you can punch somebody on the nose and they think it's cool. In Budapest they send three guys with knives after you if you play games with them.

Andras tapped on the windowpane as if he wanted to catch the attention of someone outside, or tell them to be quiet. Now the wind was tearing pieces out of the rain, like long grey strips of cloth. Andras listened out for someone approaching the door, but Isabelle would ring the bell. If she came. Seven o'clock.

A knocking sound came from the rear wall: for all these years Andras had wondered what could be knocking there, where one house met the next. Never loud, it was now almost drowned out by gusts of wind. Over by the wall stood his Uncle Janos's worn red sofa, which Aunt Sofi had offered to Andras as she might have grumpily held out to him yet another plastic bag full of old damask tablecloths and serving spoons. She had taken hold of the back of the sofa and made as if to push it a few inches towards the door, –if you want it, take it with you, right now, I won't wait; but then she had in fact used the transaction—a van had to be hired, a friend had to help with the carrying—as an excuse to delay her departure for Budapest and stay on in the already empty apartment, pouring out complaints day after day: when was Andras finally going to collect the sofa, what would Uncle Janos say, why did the light bulbs keep failing, wouldn't Andras like to keep the serving cutlery and the knife rests and the table cover after all, and although it was still warm, late-summer weather, she had sat on that same sofa wearing a fur stole, humming old nursery tunes. –You should come with me, come home. Even now he still found stray hairs from the fur (a Siberian silver fox, according to Aunt Sofi) on the sofa cover and on his pullovers, and Aunt Sofi was dead. –You're annoying him, she had told Andras when they said goodbye, pointing behind her as though his Uncle Janos were sitting there.

He had stayed here. Ever since Isabelle had begun to work for the agency it had been inconceivable that he should leave Berlin and no longer hear her voice, a clear, childlike voice without depth, sometimes unexpectedly hesitating or breaking off, a voice which sailed smoothly along like a little folded newspaper boat that would suddenly sink, or went hurtling away like a schoolbag on the back of a running child, its colors flashing as it bobbed up and down. What astonished him was her good nature and a sort of serenity, resting on an indestructible core of optimism, and every now and then an angry outburst or some sign of the petty, controlled meanness that almost everyone carries around with them like a dirty handkerchief. But he loved Isabelle. He could think of nothing but her, and, at last, after struggling and berating himself and calling himself to order, he finally, definitively accepted that he would find no proper place in life either way, whether in Budapest or in Berlin. And who was there to weigh him and find him wanting? He was a marginal figure, a stranger, a well-behaved, unobtrusive vagabond. Twenty-seven years ago his parents had taken him to the airport, sending him on a visit to his aunt and uncle in West Berlin without telling him that he would not be coming back. His mother's tears had ruined the departure for him—his first trip to the West, no reason to cry—and his fourteen-year-old's churlishness had concealed his own anxiety, which burst to the surface some months later after his first love, Anja, finished with him and he realized that he was never going back to Budapest. –When your parents have retired, Aunt Sofi consoled him, flapping a hand to silence Uncle Janos's snort, they'll come and visit us. But Uncle Janos's silence was more eloquent, and Andras understood. As soon as his German was good enough he wrote letters full of yearning to Anja in Wilmersdorf; he refused to write to his parents and younger sister. He refused to write anything in Hungarian at all until, five years later, his childhood friend László came to live in East Berlin. From there he wrote to Andras, and Andras replied, though without responding directly to his friend's eager questions. The years, the whole course of his youth and beyond, passed like one of the afternoons he spent on Wilmersdorfer Strasse or Potsdamer Strasse. Alone or with a group of other lads, spitting on the ground, smoking, waiting for girls, it was like an eternal suburb that you longed to escape from, just to get away, never mind where to; then later beer, a few petty thefts (Andras never made it beyond a Braun electric shaver) and books, and his friends laughed at him, he had to be home by ten o'clock, even at seventeen, and when he went with the others to Stuttgarter Platz, some of them on bicycles, others on foot or riding without a ticket to the Zoo station, he was nervous. The bit of shoplifting. A joint. Demonstrations. Girls. Andras had piano lessons but made no progress. Aunt Sofi never noticed that he hardly spoke, because she was always talking herself, and Uncle Janos maintained an even more obdurate silence than his nephew. –Don't get involved, Aunt Sofi would say in an agitated tone if Andras brought a newspaper home, that's no concern of ours. Not of yours, for sure—the thought seemed to launch itself into empty space—Uncle-ghost, Aunt-ghost, two tiresome yet touching old fossils, as out of place as a pony and trap on the Kurfürstendamm. And his aunt's crush on the astronaut Neil Armstrong. Oh, to have just one dance with him! Uncle Janos made no comment on that either, but set out for the hospital early and came home later and later. Andras only really noticed his existence when, in 1977, Janos Szirtes bought a television set and took an interest in the terrorist events of the so-called German autumn. –It's hard to know the right way to live, his uncle said to him, killing a few people doesn't do much good. He pointed to his nephew's flared trousers: why don't you send your sister a pair? One of his unforgivable omissions, Andras knew, but the list of these was so long that the only thing to do was to forget it again at once, like the question of what chronology counted now that nothing separated Berlin from Budapest anymore. The dividing lines of "before Berlin" and "after the Wall came down" were invalidated afresh by each visit home, leaving a sort of trickle that purported to be a continuum. Three years wasted, he could have been back in Budapest long ago. –When are you finally going to get married? his mother would ask, and recently his sister and even László had joined in, as though that was the most effective way to make him see that he had no business staying in Berlin now that his aunt and uncle were dead. Right up to the end, Aunt Sofi had gone on living in the dreary apartment block in Potsdamer Strasse, where the entrance hall stank of men's piss and the noise from the street came in through the windows, washing around the piano when Andras did a bit of practicing for once or Aunt Sofi played one of the two Mozart sonatas that she so loved. She played badly, inexplicably badly, and at one time Andras had suspected that her studies at the Budapest Conservatoire were no more than a family myth. He was wrong, as his father explained to him: before her escape in 1956 she had been expected to make a career as a pianist, which had been one of her reasons for going, but the escape had proved too traumatic, and through an illness that lasted for several weeks she had lost her musical memory and imagination. They had found a cheap apartment with all mod cons, kitchen and shower, not too far from the Steglitz hospital, and above all cheap, so that he, Andras, would be free to study whatever he wanted. That his uncle had been working for years at the Steglitz hospital not as a doctor but as a male nurse, right up to the early eighties, was another thing that Andras only learned from his parents. –You have so much to thank them for. They made such sacrifices for you. He *was* grateful, and if he in turn lied to them for years, concealing from them the fact that he had quickly abandoned his study of art in favor of graphic design, he was hardly to blame: there was a certain ironic inevitability about it. They paid his rent for a north-facing studio and a student room, on condition that he did not go and live in Kreuzberg, which Aunt Sofi regarded as a sink of iniquity, or engage in politics, another source of nightmare visions. Andras let friends use his studio in Crellestrasse and did his own drawing in his tiny room a few houses along—drawing and tearing up what he had drawn, as though he had to add his quota to the family's failures, as though this were the sacrifice he had to make in order to reach a decision at last. Not in order to get somewhere, but to remain somewhere, to circumvent the influence of the imagination and will to achieve that had played such a baneful role in his family. Andras had told no one but Isabelle of his paintings and drawings "before Berlin," and when, during one of his visits to Budapest, his mother had fetched the folders from the cellar, carefully wrapped in brown paper, he had taken some of them back with him to Berlin to show to Isabelle. Street scenes on a tiny scale, which on closer inspection were bizarre and disturbing: the human figures seemed to be made of the same porous material as the housefronts, as if the over-decorated late nineteenth-century architecture mocked the monotonous and mystifying conditions under which people lived. Why had he given all that up, Isabelle asked, but he did not know. He would have liked to put out the light; perhaps Isabelle herself assumed that he had lured her here in order to kiss her, in his fresh white shirt which, even outside the circle of light in which she sat studying his drawings and paintings, showed up brightly, revealing where he stood. As in an old-fashioned story she rummaged for something in her handbag, but without finding it, as she began to talk, to tell him about her own childhood, and this tale of a childhood, like all such tales, was like a rainy, desultory walk through the zoo, where, behind the same old name boards, the same old animals either remained in hiding or apathetically allowed themselves to be seen. Or like albums of photographs, complex products of light conditions and the chemical properties of the paper which, beneath a membrane of tissue paper, fades but by its very fading asserts itself and demands an inner eye that will do battle against oblivion. In this way Andras's memory became imprinted with that anecdote about how her sick mother's enormous grand piano had been lifted up, was gliding smooth-ly through the air towards the astonished five-year-old, and would have passed safely over the top of her head had not one of the men carrying it suddenly noticed the child and pan-icked, his warning cry almost bringing about the very disaster he feared. The piano started to tip sideways and would not stop, perhaps terror made the men's hands grow damp with sweat (though surely they wore gloves?), the instrument con-tinued its sideways lurch for another second and then crashed down onto the granite steps, making a piteous sound, less loud than one would have expected, but landing in such an unfortunate way that one leg snapped off and the frame split apart. Had the disaster happened or had it been avoided? Her nanny, Mimsel, had grabbed her and held her in her arms, even though blood was flowing copiously from a cut near her left eye—the scar was not visible to Andras, who had sat down again on the sofa next to her, his drawings and paintings like a ghostly presence in front of them; he should have run his finger over the scar to detect it by touch. He did not do so, yet another omission to add to the list. All of a sudden he understood that the events of every childhood, whether a happy or an unhappy one, formed a catalog of survival and of not belonging, a story of exile and of shame. Mimsel had taken Isabelle to hospital, but the real drama, she told Andras, was the illness of her mother, who took not to her bed but to a chaise longue to await her death; after a year of real or imaginary sickness, however, death performed an about-turn and vanished again into the mists of its temporal uncertainty, leaving Frau Metzel to the indefensible eternity of a life already laid aside. If her impending death had plunged Isabelle's father, a well-known Heidelberg lawyer, into despair, so too did its failure to come to pass, and in his dismay he organized a gigantic party which ushered in the second, depressing phase of Isabelle's childhood, a ceaseless round of social gatherings at which her allotted place was behind piles of plates and under huge trays of cocktails, taking the role of the ugly duckling. Certain that he was the first male recipient of this narrative, Andras did not underestimate the gift. But these set pieces and anecdotes were not enough to create a real story, and it all remained strangely lifeless, suggesting nothing to Andras and Isabelle but to go on sitting demurely side by side like brother and sister, thereby at least avoiding the awkwardness of an affair between colleagues, and it was only Andras who fervently hoped that things might after all turn out differently between them. But he could think of no way of breaching the cocoon that encased her.

–You should propose to her in the eastern European melancholic style, kissing her hand and presenting her with red roses, László had told him later—too late—and although Andras still found the idea in poor taste, he had felt bound to register it as another omission, because it would at least have been better than the notion he had hesitantly entertained of conquering her as a lover. Hesitantly, because he was not sure how convincing he would be as a surprise lover, but above all because it was not what he wanted. He loved her, that was the heartbreakingly simple fact.

After all this time, it made little difference now whether that evening represented a missed opportunity or simply underlined the harsh truth. Isabelle had so resolutely cast the two of them as brother and sister that he was the one she had felt able to tell, before anyone else, that she had met Jakob again. And this really did mean it was time to relinquish all hope. As her knight, faithful unto death, he had turned himself into a tragicomic figure. The role fitted him like a glove, it had become part of him.

Go back to Budapest. Stop clinging to a forlorn hope.

Forlornly the sound of passing cars drifted up to him; the church clock was already striking nine. She would not be coming now.

7

L ate that afternoon it emerged that his colleague Robert had still been in New York. Of the thirty-two lawyers at Golbert & Schreiber it was Robert with whom Jakob had most in common. They worked in adjoining offices, sharing the same secretary, Julia, and they knew that one of them—probably Robert—was going to be sent to London. The two of them, both tall, the same age, with pleasant good looks, were regarded as friends: they met from time to time at an exhibition, or occasionally drank a glass of wine together in the Angel of Death. As to the possibility of spending a year or two in London, they had never discussed it; they both wanted to go, and both knew that neither would try to swing Schreiber's decision his way at the expense of the other. Having studied in London for a year, Robert was the more likely choice.

London was Jakob's first thought when Julia, maintaining her composure with an effort that made her look ugly, and only her hands agitatedly flapping up and down, came into his room with an e-mail she had printed out. –He had been going to catch the early morning flight to Chicago. I didn't see his second e-mail yesterday. Jakob's face burned; over and over again, stupidly, shamefully, the same thought kept passing through his mind: So I'll be the one going to London. When he stood up, it felt as if he were not actively moving but gliding from one position to another without having to do anything. The telephone was in his hand, and he dialed

Robert's mobile number and listened three times to the message, *The person you are trying to reach is not available at the moment*. He had arranged to meet Isabelle this evening. And there Julia stood, her eyes filling with tears. Schreiber's office was on the top floor, and Jakob walked straight through the outer office, passing Frau Busche without a word. Schreiber was furious if anybody disturbed him unannounced, they all feared his rages, but this time nothing was going to stop Jakob, not today, not from now on. Schreiber looked at him, stunned, and for a second Jakob's certainty was mingled with such profound grief and doubt that his hands shook. He had found Isabelle, and he would go to London, but if the price was Robert's death, it was higher than he had expected. He told Schreiber the news in just two sentences; even they seemed superfluous, like an all too predictable line of argument. There was little chance that Robert had survived. He had wanted to fit in a further meeting with a client in the World Trade Center before leaving for Chicago. Schreiber went through to the outer office and said something very quietly to Frau Busche, and Jakob noticed how dark it was in the room. Only a few isolated rays of sunlight stole through the heavy curtains, and the desk lamp shone on the dark blue carpet, which absorbed most of the light. –Bentham will take it hard, Schreiber said when he returned. Bentham was Schreiber's London associate. Frau Busche is trying to arrange through a friend of mine for a search to be made of all the hospitals.

The barman had to ask three times before Jakob heard him and ordered a whisky. He rubbed his forehead and eyes with his hands, reached for the glass, and took a good swig. Isabelle might come in through the door at any moment, and he wouldn't tell her about Robert, nor about Frau Busche, who had wept and stood up to put her arms around him as if she had to make sure that at least *he* was still alive. Something made him think of his mother's death, but there was nothing there, no link, no actual memory. It was a matter of waiting— not even very long—until the horror, until this episode too belonged to the past. At home he had taken off his sweaty shirt and had had a shower so as to wash away what, against his will, had spread like a thin film over his body. After a brief hesitation he had changed the bed and turned on the washing machine. There had been a message from his father on the answering machine, just a hello, and the somewhat enigmatic remark, *Well, it looks as if everything is all right.* He was sure his father wasn't worried, he didn't even know that Jakob had been in New York. The clock showed a quarter past eight. Glasses were being pushed to and fro across the bar counter: the place had filled up. There was probably a film starting soon at the Babylon; nobody was choosing to sit down although plenty of seats were free. A woman, whose hair stood out like a brush in all directions, laughed shrilly; looking in his direction, she raised her glass to him.

And there was Isabelle.

She was standing beside him, her smooth hair shining; as she lifted her face to his, someone inconsiderately reached forward for a beer bottle, thrusting his arm right between them before slowly withdrawing it. Just for a moment the man's arm blocked out Isabelle's face, which vanished, was obliterated, and for the second time today Jakob felt a pang of gnawing doubt, of grief. He almost expected to find that Isabelle had really vanished again, after all these years, proving to him that his ideas and plans counted for nothing. But there she still was, unaffected by the interruption, almost as if she had been able to see him during that moment. Smiling at him, she took a sip from his glass, making words of greeting superfluous. He waited until she had put the glass down and kissed her, very gently, on the mouth. They did not stay there for long.

*

Ten days later, Schreiber asked Jakob to go to Hanover to attend Robert's funeral on the fourth of October, and offered him the position in London from the start of 2003.

At the station it struck Jakob as surprising that the funeral was only taking place now, three weeks after Robert's death. The time had passed quickly; Jakob had managed only five or six meetings with Isabelle, but last night she had stayed with him, in his bed, and had still been asleep when he got up and crept out to go to the station.

It was a rainy, unpleasant day. Jakob went to the train's on-board bistro and stood there, bending forward slightly to look out at the flat, grey landscape while he had a coffee and a cigarette. It would be cold at the cemetery, but presumably there was no such thing as a good day to be buried when you were thirty-three, and given that there was no body there would probably be no coffin either and no grave, just a stone and a sermon. All he had to do was to offer his condolences to the parents, the condolences of the whole firm, and lay the wreath, which had been ordered by phone, on the spot that was not a grave. And hold his breath, fervently trying to believe that what had bound Robert and him together and now separated them was chance, coincidence, not a trade-off, just the enigmatic, incomprehensible intersection of two lines, as incomprehensible as the point where parallel lines do finally meet. They were diverging again, Jakob reflected, moving apart in immeasurably tiny steps. They would not meet again. The landscape pressed down upon him like nausea. –But you don't owe him anything, do you? Hans had asked when Jakob said he was going to Robert's funeral. There were the first houses now, the platform and immediately beyond it more houses, set in small gardens. He wished he had taken up Hans's offer to come with him.

It was indeed wet and windy, and contrary to all reason

there was a coffin and a grave; the procession of mourners clustered around to toss a handful of earth onto the empty coffin, to feel with their own hands, at last, the calamity that had befallen them three weeks earlier. Robert's parents stood close to the pile of freshly excavated earth, not shaking anyone's hand. They did not look up as the line of mourners re-formed under the clergyman's guidance, but raised their heads just once, simultaneously, aghast, staring at Jakob, at his hair, dark from the rain: he sensed that he served them as a measure so that on every day to come they would know what they had lost.

—In a way, he had said to Hans on the one occasion when they had spoken about his mother's death, death is a change of ownership. What used to belong to the deceased passes into the possession of others, and property is the least of it. The next thing is the body: it belongs to those who arrange for makeup to be used or not, for the body to be laid out or not, for burial or cremation. And then they appropriate the dead person's thoughts, hopes, and experiences—even their memory soon belongs to the relatives, in the name of their love, in the name of *their* memory. I'd rather people just forgot me when I'm dead.

It was his second funeral. He didn't want to pick up the little trowel that lay in a wooden box full of earth, he didn't know where the wreath was and whether he was supposed to go and find it; he didn't know if he should stay where he was, as Robert's parents were still staring at him. How small they were, so much smaller than their son.

The rain had darkened the leaves on the trees. Among all the black umbrellas a red one stood out vividly; hunched beneath it was an elderly woman whose face Jakob could not make out, but who gestured to him with a small, dispirited wave of her hand: move on, you've been at the graveside for far too long. At last they reached the exit and he got into a taxi, at last the train moved out of the station into the flat, grey landscape. He stood in the bistro, bending forward, smoking, drinking a beer. Hans came to pick him up. When he phoned Isabelle that evening she answered at once.

8.

There were good days; they began without warning, first thing, with sounds from the bathroom and the kitchen, the same ones as every morning, yet different: hammering on the bathroom door, and each time she was afraid of needing to go to the toilet just then, and so she lay cowering under the blankets, counting her fingers one by one, the way she read the numbers on the clock radio in the living room, which had no meaning because nobody took any notice of them, but somehow it made the minutes pass anyway, and if she was lucky it wouldn't be too long; then loud knocking again, that was Dave, and her father shouting, furious. And when Sara came out into the hall her mother grabbed her by the hand and dragged her to the door, –just get on with it and have a pee while your Dad's shaving, don't make such a fuss. But the door was locked, or worse still it wasn't locked and could be opened just a crack, wide enough for her to pass through, to be pushed through, stumbling, into the steam, into the fury, the huge naked body that pushed her aside because otherwise she got in his way, and she had to hurry, hurry to reach for the toilet lid, because there was always one more obstacle, even on the good days when her father got out of bed sober. He would lift her up and drop her on the toilet, and she had to let it out, onto the toilet lid, without a word, and suddenly it wasn't a good day anymore, they locked her in, pushed a chair under the door handle, turned out the light. They were away all day long; there was a tiny gap under the door that she pushed some toilet paper through when she heard Polly, and Polly tried to catch hold of it with her claws, but Sara quickly pulled it back again as though hoping to entice Polly to squeeze through the tiny gap and come to her. She could see Polly's paws. Then Polly got bored, and Sara crouched on the floor beside the bath and counted her fingers until she fell asleep, until eventually Dave arrived home and tried to get her to come out, but she resisted, crying with fear, and he soon gave up, but before pushing the chair back against the door, under the door handle, he helped her to clean up the toilet lid and the floor. On good days their front door banged in the morning because her father went storming out, yanking the door wide open and suddenly letting go, so that it swung back with full force and crashed shut; he dragged her mother out with him at the last moment, and if Mum wasn't quick enough she didn't manage to grab her coat or the big bag that had the cleaning cloths and a feather duster in it.

Outside they filled the street with their voices, sometimes a car braked, car doors slammed and then it was quiet. She waited, to make quite sure. And waited a bit longer. If she went to the window too soon, it would all run backwards, the voices would get louder, first outside the main door and then on the stairs, until the bell rang, –bloody hell, what's the good of having kids if they can't even open the door and take things in? Dave! Sara!

That was her. Sara. Sara without an "h," as Dave, who could read and write, had explained to her, and "h" was a letter you didn't hear, that didn't mean anything, a thing that wasn't there and was missing from her name. Sara. Sometimes the whole name vanished. She herself was still there, but the name had vanished, like the "h." Dave was Dave, that was certain. Dave called her "little cat." –Because you hide behind the sofa like a little cat. Look, even Polly sits *on* the sofa. On top of it.

On good days her name was there again, when her mother

laid the table and put out a whole loaf of sliced bread, and
there was sausage on a plate, and her father looked round with
a satisfied grin: –it's what I keep saying, we're doing bloody
fucking well for ourselves. And Sara's eyes looked at Dave,
pleading with him to get up and fetch some beer from the
fridge. Dave, Dave? He stood up, his face expressionless, and
before he could bang the cans down on the table she was in
front of him, holding out both hands, palms up, for him to give
them to her, and he did, with a face empty of expression.

On good days her father left the door to the little terrace
and the garden unlocked, or left the key in the door. –It's a par-
adise, with all those toys, but don't you let those other brats
indoors. Until midafternoon the other children were at school,
so nothing could happen. They seemed to know when her parents were out, and after school they would haul themselves up
onto the brick wall and throw a pebble at the window, and if
there was no reaction, if neither her mother nor her father nor
Dave appeared and shouted at them, they jumped down into
the garden where the toys were, useless, broken plastic toys,
pieces of toy railway track, a car without wheels, a scooter that
was no good, a few buckets and molds for playing with sand.
They had made off with the balls long ago, colored balls that
belonged to a game Dave had been given. Sometimes they just
sat there, leaning on the wall and talking in low voices, or they
climbed the tree, peered into the house, and threw stones if
they saw Sara cowering near the French window. She felt
frightened if Polly was outside, and more and more often Dave
was leaving the house first thing in the morning, before their
parents got up.

On bad days her parents stayed at home all day. Her mother took the plastic cover off the sewing machine she kept in the
children's bedroom and sent Sara out of the room. She locked
herself in, and Dad kept calling her and kicking the door until
he got fed up and went to sleep on the sofa. Dave claimed he

was going to school and grinned as he put on the school uniform that was too short for him. –Take care, little cat, he would say in the morning as he bent over Sara's bed.

9

B
ut why do you two want to get married? Alexa asked. A bookseller was hurriedly packing up his boxes and carrying them into his shop. A clock struck seven.

–It seems so appropriate, Isabelle answered hesitantly. To their right was the Milagro, but she knew that Alexa wouldn't remember it, their first meeting there, after Isabelle had found her number among the ads for roommates and phoned her. Alexa was not sentimental, anything but. –Here, she said without any obvious connection. You drag somebody around town all day, and it's only when it's already getting dark that you suddenly know where you ought to photograph him.

–Who was it?

–A saxophonist. I listened to some of his music and didn't like it. Rather like Garbarek, dreadful. Tomorrow I'm going to Brandenburg with him, to the Elbe. It's probably hopeless trying to photograph him in the city.

She turned towards Isabelle, who was smiling as she walked along beside her. –But I think Jakob's very nice, she said. It sounded like a promise, casually spoken but still a promise, a little bit of the general atmosphere of benevolence that was just perceptible, in the warm drizzle, in Bergmannstrasse with its brightly lit shops and cafés, all so familiar, and with Alexa at her side. Since moving in with Clara, Alexa held herself very erect because she did yoga, daily headstands, daily stretching and flexing exercises, slowly, taking deep breaths in and out. Isabelle breathed in slowly and held her breath. –I can't hold myself as straight as you when I walk, she said.

Alexa made no reply, but tugged edgily at her camera bag. –Do we really want to go for a meal? she asked. –No, Isabelle agreed, if you like, I'll just keep you company on the way back.

–Let's walk a little more, said Alexa, it's just that I don't feel hungry, I never do on days like this. The guy from Universal drove me crazy. I thought I'd be able to take the photo in Monbijou Park or somewhere on the Kreuzberg. We drove around in a taxi, at some point Clara joined us, and the saxophonist wanted to play for her, can you imagine that? She hates jazz. She pulled me behind a tree and kissed me, the guy nearly flipped.

Clara, thought Isabelle, feeling a slight throbbing in her temples, in her eyelids, a reminder of her wretchedness when Alexa moved out, telling Isabelle that she could stay on in the apartment and take over the tenancy if she liked. No more photographs, and neatly folded in the drawer the toweling underwear that Alexa had bought for her. –Come on, just a few quick snaps, it'll look fantastic, honestly. Isabelle's childlike body, cut off above the mouth, the small breasts, the slightly rounded stomach, the strong legs of a young girl. Alexa had photographed her so often that, although she thought it obscene, she finally pulled down the red toweling panties to below her pubic area, which was covered only by soft, invisible down.

Two boys of about ten came towards them. –Got any cigarettes? The smaller of the two was toying with a golf ball. Alexa walked on, pulling Isabelle along with her.—No, Isabelle called back over her shoulder, no cigarettes. She only just managed to dodge the ball. –You little bastards! Alexa launched herself at them like a Fury, but she was hampered by the camera bag and they easily got away. –What's the matter with you, perhaps you'd like to offer them a light as well? she snapped at Isabelle, who could only respond with an embarrassed smile. –Nothing's the matter, she said, I think I'm fine. She looked for the golf ball and picked it up. Oh, look, there's a heart drawn on it.

She would have liked to show the photos to Jakob, but did not dare. She could not discuss them with Alexa, to whom they were simply photos like many others she had taken. Everything was clear and uncomplicated, and yet it felt as if there were wires stretched across one's path that one might stumble over, into another life, a life in which Isabelle slept with Alexa and not with Jakob. She wasn't in love with Alexa, not anymore. But she kept the photos in a box under her bed like a talisman.

–And what about Andras? Alexa fumbled with the fastening of her camera case.

–Posters for a Russian dance group, a new literary café, a coffee shop somewhere in Zehlendorf. Peter's got a contract from the StattAuto car-sharing scheme, and a law firm has ordered business cards and letterhead.

–But *you* won't give up working when you're married?

She had meant to tell Alexa over supper, while they sat eating at the Zagato, reading for the hundredth time the notice saying, "Take your feet off the radiators, right now!" in surroundings that were a part of her past, like Bergmannstrasse: *penne all'arrabiata*, *penne paradiso*, no need to order, father and son behind the counter, photographs of cycle races and motor races on the wall. Isabelle had meant to tell her in the way you announce a piece of news, even though to her it didn't seem like something new, but like one of those facts that wait for years to be discovered but then instantly become as obvious and familiar as the air you breathe. Just as one day she had known for certain that her studies were a farce, or that from now on she would only visit her parents at Christmas. Just as one day she had realized that her parents' house was a shoe box, a grey and long-since outmoded shoe box, absurdly unsuitable as a setting for drama and misery, and when she recalled how her mother had sat at the piano every day, practicing for hours on end, it seemed as if everything had been doomed to failure right from the start, the dream of becoming a pianist no less than the illness, the supposed tumor which was nothing but a sad little blob in that dreary box that was her parents' pride and joy. I like Jakob's face, Isabelle had meant to say, and that she liked *him*, but Alexa had been so obviously preoccupied with the saxophonist and with Clara that she had blurted out the news of her wedding straight away. Alexa had not been particularly interested.

–What are you brooding about? Alexa asked, prodding Isabelle gently in the ribs. Let's go to the Zagato. She stopped, put her arms around Isabelle, and kissed her lightly on the lips, and Isabelle smiled. She liked Jakob, she'd be happy with him, and Alexa thought he was nice. –What about your new shoes? Alexa enquired with a grin, pointing to Isabelle's old trainers.

–I've still got a cough, Jakob said anxiously a week later, you won't get a good night's sleep.

–It doesn't matter, said Isabelle, I'll sleep tomorrow afternoon, I can go home at lunchtime and have an hour's nap then.

–When we move in together we'll have to buy some furniture, said Jakob.

–If it comes to the worst we can make a quick trip to IKEA. After an hour there we'll be so desperate that we'll either decide to do without furniture or round up everything we need in five minutes.

–There are a few things from my grandparents, if it doesn't bother you to live with my grandparents' furniture.

–What I'd like is a big drawing table—a room with good light and a big drawing table. I don't care about the rest, said Isabelle.

–There's an apartment in Wartburgstrasse, four rooms on the fourth floor, with a balcony.

As they sat in Isabelle's kitchen, Jakob's gaze strayed across the wooden floorboards, stained a light color, to the door through which he could see into the living room, a beige carpet on the wooden floor, a small white sofa, a table, and three chairs. It was Schreiber who had told him about Wartburgstrasse and the apartment that Robert had been in the final stages of buying; the contract was with the lawyer, a friend of Schreiber's, and the price was good, Schreiber had told him with a malicious smile: –You've seen his parents, they don't need an apartment in Berlin.

–I would register it in your name, if you agree, said Jakob, then you've still got a place here if you come to London with me next year. I'd really like you to come.

–But why should you buy me an apartment?

–It'll be ours, Jakob replied, I mean, when we're married, it'll be *our* apartment, won't it? If we weren't getting married, I wouldn't need it anyway. You can work there, it has a south-facing room with a bay window. All that's missing is the drawing table.

And then we'll move to London, he thought. Isabelle had stood up, and she disappeared into the bathroom. –Vicks, she said as she returned, holding the small blue jar with the green lid.

–What do you mean, Vicks?

–You rub it onto your chest, so that you inhale the vapors as you sleep.

–I never remember what I've dreamt, do you? Isabelle asked next morning. Jakob shook his head. He reached for her hand, which lay compliantly on the table.

As he stood up, he noticed that Isabelle seemed not to mind relinquishing his hand. They could go back to bed and sleep together until their warm, satisfied bodies separated again. She would always be within reach now, Jakob thought.

–Perhaps we don't actually dream of anything, he said, but only see vague images, like memories that we can't remember, do you know what I mean?

Her face had an alertness, a look of attentive scrutiny that he had not seen before.

10

T he three men always stood on the same corner, at the junction with the little street of small houses that were painted in different colors. Two in anoraks, while the third wore a jacket over a roll-neck sweater. They stood slightly to one side as if to avoid being in anyone's way—polite, with that air of reserve that Jim always found so bloody annoying. He put his hands in his trouser pockets, looked at them, hummed a snatch of a tune, and walked on. Nothing to get annoyed about. The three were having a conversation and didn't even look up, they were talking in soft, polite tones in one of those damned languages of theirs, as though they had a right to talk and not be understood by anybody, right out in the street, as if it was their own living room. "Peace Cabs" was the name of the taxi firm one house further on. Maybe they worked for it. The place looked like a pub, a pub for blacks only, painted in red, with a big counter, a few chairs, and a television. Water and fruit juice, and tea of course, thought Jim, it might just as well be some lousy religious club, Congregation of Jesus, Cabs for Peace, or more likely Mohammed, The Black Muslim Community, but nobody was bothered because they were so peaceable, with their own polite customs, and had nothing to do with those fucking junkies, who were mostly white anyway, right? Lousy little thieves, just like him. While these guys were clean, they wore jackets and pressed their trousers. Jim walked slowly so as to be able to peer into the poky house next door, a dimly lit hutch of a place with sheets of chipboard forming partitions between whatever was inside, you couldn't tell what there was, and just a single chair with a child sitting on it. Stopping, Jim took a pack of cigarettes from his jeans and lit up, since nothing was going on there, nothing at all, a peaceful scene, lamb and wolf, or rather lambs, for now a woman came in, poking her head through a door that he hadn't noticed, smiling broadly with gleaming white teeth, and the child ran to her, into her arms.

He coughed, still that cough, and it was stupid to be walking about outdoors in a T-shirt, but he wanted to feel the wind on him, the cold, damp wind. Jim straightened his shoulders, much stronger now from the bit of training, weights, push-ups, the kind of thing he did during the day out of boredom, in the flat that was so much better than anything he'd had before. A pure stroke of luck meeting Damian, who looked somehow unbalanced, with a kind of mad enthusiasm—completely off his head, Jim had immediately thought, but he hadn't found out the cause of it. He seemed a bit afraid of Jim even though he didn't owe him anything, there were just a few grams of cocaine he hadn't paid for, and maybe that was it, maybe that was why he shoved the key into Jim's hand, just like that. Crazy, as if he had some vast plan or knew something that nobody else knew. Jim hadn't immediately recognized him: Damian used to be posh, with stylish leather jackets and a car his parents had bought him, a car and this flat that he offered to Jim, in fact positively pressed on him, he wouldn't be needing it for a while anyway, a few months or even longer, and the bills were still being charged to his parents who lived on the continent and didn't bother to check up on anything. So Damian had claimed, and it seemed to be true, because nobody had ever demanded a penny from Jim in all the months that he'd spent in Lady Margaret Road, day in, day out, since he hardly went anywhere now except when it was really unavoidable or he started to feel restless. He'd really hit the jackpot, and just at the right moment too, just when Mae had disappeared and he'd finally had enough of Albert and Ben. Probably there was something not quite right with the flat, and with Damian's wild talk about an absolute clarity so real that you could touch it, so much stronger than anything else that he didn't need drugs anymore, just courage and determination, if you understand what I mean. But Jim didn't understand, not a word. He had only listened because the bit about the brightness interested him, a dazzling white light, Damian said, in which things were hidden just as they would be in the most impenetrable darkness, impossible to see, and perhaps, Jim thought, Mae was there, waiting for him, making signs to him. There wasn't much more to be got out of Damian, apart from the key, of course, and that enthusiasm which actually made him hug Jim and try to press his own face against his. But this garden flat was just what the doctor ordered. A yard or two from the main entrance to the house, a few steep steps led down to the basement, so that Jim had his own front door that he didn't have to share with anyone else.

He crossed the road, a motorcycle screaming past him, and there he was at the canal, the nice familiar canal with the lock. A few yards further on was Sainsbury's, its entrance on the other side of the car park, concrete pillars in front of it so that you didn't see the shopping trolleys or the fat mothers, with their plastic bags and exhausted faces, emerging from their palace of plenty. All he had left was thirty pounds and some small change. A drunk was lying in front of the bus stop, hat in hand, his nose bleeding. Jim gave him a cautious kick, and would have liked to follow it up with another, proper one, but some other people were starting to take notice—though they didn't bend down, obviously, didn't bend down to turn the old guy on his side, to see if he might be choking on his blood or his vomit; he stank. As for Jim, they were looking at him suspiciously because of his dirty, stained T-shirt and his unshaven face—but a nice face somehow, Mae said, they all said that. Jim looked up. Sure, a nice-looking lad, ten, fifteen years ago, and he still was, too. He grinned at the woman with the long legs, good long legs in little flat-heeled boots and a skirt that reached to just below her bum, just right for a grope: he grinned at her and tried to smile, but she simply turned her back, not even showing disgust, just turned away, and that was him disposed of, out of the picture. He should have gone straight down to the water by the lock, after all, but recently he had preferred to follow the road all the way to Camden Town tube station, which on the weekend disgorged crowds of cackling teenagers along with the current of stale air. On the other side of the road the last customers were just being chucked out of The World's End, though actually it wasn't time yet, and the second bar, in the less comfortable, draughty part of the pub, was still serving, but Jim chose not to go in. He would carry on walking, around the outside of the tube station and back towards the canal, and then slowly wander across the bridge and be waylaid by the kids who dealt drugs there all day long, while others showed off their leather gear and shoes and tattoos, hey, we're cool, you're cool. Over to the left was the vegetable market, the stalls cleared hours ago and left clean and tidy; on the side near the street rubbish was piled up, and an old woman rummaging around in it pulled something out, he couldn't see what it was, but something sour and acrid rose up into his mouth and he spat it out. It was no good, he'd have to phone Albert. Sooner or later. Thirty pounds left. London was big, but not big enough as far as the drugs trade was concerned, there were too many guys who knew Jim and had nothing to do but shoot their mouths off all day long, and who'd be only too glad of a chance to get into Albert's good books. And then there was Mae. Without Albert he'd never find her again. People disappeared, sometimes they turned up again, sometimes they didn't. Two girls came towards him, giggling, the plumper one in a tight skirt, her thick legs bare. Jim spat again, but the bitter taste persisted and so did a lump in his throat, however much he tried to clear it. You can die of hatred, Mae had said, and she had disappeared.

11

Two weeks before their move, the new bed was due to be delivered, and Jakob asked Isabelle to be there in the apartment because he had a meeting, but then he put off his client, Herr Strauss, until late evening and asked Julia to reserve a table at the Borchardt. He put some finishing touches to the restitution agreement confirming Strauss's title to the building at 178, Prenzlauer Allee; in his mind's eye he could see its shabby façade. Now he just needed to draft one final application document, to be sent to the regional office for the settlement of unresolved property issues, and soon it would all be sorted out and yet another building would be enveloped in scaffolding and renovated. The contracts with the Netto supermarket chain, which had opened a branch on the ground floor two years earlier, had had to be checked over, and everything had gone smoothly. There was nothing more to discuss, and Strauss was pleased that the meeting was postponed to the evening, as it meant he would not have to spend it alone. Jakob wondered yet again why this seventy-six-year-old man, childless and well to do, had spared neither cost nor effort to regain the property that had once belonged to his mother. It was simply too late. But Strauss himself, even supposing he had thought about it at all, would speak of the need for a challenge, particularly for older people, and about the way Prenzlauer Berg had developed and the interest shown by a publishing house in acquiring the whole building, with its enormous inner courtyard, and after that he would say no more. Jakob had got used to the look on many of his clients' faces when their cases were concluded, their uneasy silence, their inability to move on, their air of desolation. On the surface they might give an impression of triumph, of pride even, as in something unquestionably achieved, as though it had been the client himself and not his lawyer who had fought for the property and won. Yet often Jakob's clients clung to him, telephoning him just to hear the soothing voice of the experienced physician who understood their pain.

He had not told Isabelle that he would be able to come to Wartburgstrasse after all; he wanted to surprise her. He hurried down the stairs at five o'clock, past Schreiber, who, without comment, made room for him to pass, and hailed a taxi. By twenty past five he was in Wartburgstrasse. He searched for his key, but had evidently left it behind, and no one opened the door when he rang the bell. The windows—clearly visible from the other side of the road—were closed.

The previous evening Isabelle had been lying across his bed when, with an impatient gesture to him to keep quiet, she had suddenly arched her body with a tensing of her muscles that amazed him, appearing to lift herself off the mattress by sheer will-power. Then she had opened the zip of her jeans, undone the button, and lowered them with a wriggle of her hips. He was standing between the living room and the bedroom, narrow shafts of light from the living room were falling right across the bed, while for her he was no more than a dark silhouette. In the half-light her thighs looked more muscular than they were. He grew hard. His penis hurt, he wanted to put his hand in his pocket to touch it, loneliness and astonishment constricted his throat. No more than two minutes had elapsed when she sat up and provocatively, with feigned seriousness, pronounced her verdict. –You're right, we need a new bed.

He had suggested she should go, as he had to be up at five, but that was no reason, and she had asked, her features clear and inscrutable, whether she couldn't stay anyway. She still had not put her jeans back on, he did not dare ask her to; her panties were lacy in front, and beneath them the skin gleamed pale and smooth. He found it disconcerting that she had no pubic hair.

Now, in Wartburgstrasse, he gazed blankly down at the closely laid square paving stones, one of them cracked at the right-hand edge, made of reddish crushed stone or gravel. It was starting to rain.

Instead of changing to the U7 line for Schöneberg, she got out at Mehringdamm so as to walk part of the way, and it was only when she was out in the street that she realized how late it already was, but the delivery men would wait, Isabelle thought, and continued westwards. The trees at the foot of the Kreuzberg were still bare, the bed of the waterfall dry. Ascending gently, the road curved around towards the Monumentenstrasse Bridge, which passed over a broad expanse of railway lines, sandy areas and preparations for construction work; she could see the city far away, and the television tower in the distance, toy-sized, with the ball on its pointed stem. It was hazy, dusk was gathering and deceiving the eyes, so that the roofs and towers of Potsdamer Platz appeared to her to be moving sideways to take up new, safe positions, while the cranes, diggers and concrete-mixers looked like observers from another planet. Now that everyone felt threatened, captive and at the mercy of unpredictable guards, calm observation seemed only to veil the impending horror. There. A car accelerated with a puff of thin smoke from its exhaust, took the slope and drove over the bridge, then vanished in the gathering dusk, its rear lights showing up one last time, as if in farewell.

Only as she was on the point of colliding with him did she notice the man stepping away from the parapet: like her, he had been looking out across the railway lines and the sand—grey sand that was excavated locally and bright yellow sand that was specially transported here—and at the huge ragged cloud moving across the evening sky, while a fine drizzle was starting to fall from the part of the sky that was still almost clear. The man did not seem startled, but fixed his eyes on her as she stammered something, an apology, a greeting—she felt as if she had encountered him before. His face was pale, and despite the cold all he had on under his dark blue, none too clean anorak was a threadbare, washed-out T-shirt: he had an air of neglect, but the sharpness of the look he gave her stopped her in her tracks. She put out a hand to fend him off, but he only laughed, caught the hand, which was too light and childlike, in midair and thrust it aside. She was afraid he was going to hit her, his eyes, of a light blue, looked at her unwaveringly, he seemed to take pleasure in her fear, but then, suddenly lowering his head, he retreated with a lithe movement, and vanished from her field of vision. She could still hear him, and expected a push, an attack from behind, but nothing followed, nothing but stillness, a silence that lasted until a car approached. When she turned round the man was no longer to be seen, and as the tension in her gradually subsided she felt frightened as though by a waking dream that interposed itself between her and familiar objects, between her and her life which refused to shape itself into a stable, coherent whole, persistently breaking up into disparate elements. The man seemed to have vanished from the face of the earth: she even peered over the side of the bridge as though he might be dangling beneath it. Not a trace, of course not, the car was long gone and she was running out of time; hurrying on towards the Langenscheidtbrücke, which spanned the S-Bahn like a railway bridge in a children's book, she eventually passed the church of St. Paul the Apostle, quite out of breath by now, and reached Wartburgstrasse at last. The terraces of late nineteenth-century houses were as perfectly unscathed as if there had never been a war, and their façades looked faintly ridiculous. The light from the street lamps blended with the fading daylight, and a blackbird was singing lustily, Isabelle could make out its plump black body in a little bare tree, and over on a ledge another one was perched, trilling, with its feathers puffed out, as if there were a contest to be won. From here she would be able to see the delivery van. Suddenly she shrank from the thought of going up to the apartment on her own; when she felt in her jacket pocket for the key, she felt a little hole in the lining. The street was empty, only a window was rattling somewhere, a car slid out of a parking space and vanished, and right at the other end, just before the corner, a man standing in the drizzle looked up. Andras, she thought, recalling how he had said goodbye to her at the office, –ah, you're already off, and had smiled at her, a sad, chivalrous smile. But it was Jakob, his reddish-blond hair glinting as he looked at her and recognized her.

Later, lying on the mattresses, they huddled, shivering, under the clothes that they had hurriedly discarded, until Jakob leapt up and, glancing at the clock, kissed her, dressed hastily and left, turning again at the door to take a last look at her. She seemed to him smooth and very young and small.

He found a taxi straight away and urged the driver on, he was going to be late for his appointment, the taxi jumped the amber lights, and now it was raining harder.

12

He saw Ben coming down the hill, wearing a green-and-blue-checked shirt and looking, Jim thought, like some fat kid flapping and swinging his arms about and shouting. A little scene with all the right ingredients: a summer's day, warmth, a gentle breeze in the treetops, and picnic baskets on the grass, the way it used to be. But this was Ben, not some child, he really had got fat and was running, had suddenly started running as if they were after him. Now he was just underneath a kite that was twisting about, preparing to dive to earth as if it were gathering itself for a leap, and the boy holding the string was running up the hill to where three mighty oak trees formed a semicircle, stretching out their sturdy branches. –What are you so steamed up about? Albert had said. Just because he chased after her a bit and brought her some pills. Just chased after her, no more than that, only brought her some pills, his girlfriend Mae, who was on the floor, bleeding, and –don't start making trouble here, Albert had warned. Ben called the ambulance, what else should he have done? And who beat her up, you or Ben? Jim had no answer to that, because she had been lying on the floor bleeding, in front of the sofa, the telephone still in her hand, and Jim could clearly remember having been in the kitchen, drinking a beer. And that was all.

Now Ben reached the path and looked nervously around; the kite had become entangled in the middle oak tree's branches. As if somebody was lying in wait for him, Jim thought, grinning, –you fat slob, he muttered to himself, *you'll* see. There was a light breeze, thick tree roots criss-crossing the paths, and hedges full of roses, Jim thought to himself, full of humming and twittering, like that garden far away from London, with a wall, with dogroses and blackbirds in it and dusty, summery paths beyond. He liked blackbirds, and Mae had liked them, they had talked about it all, about a house and a garden, because there *were* thoughts like that, and hills and dog roses, too. If he closed his eyes he could see the garden before him. But then Ben called the ambulance, and Mae vanished. –Gone to ground, dropped out of sight, Albert scoffed, you can see how much she thinks about you, no phone calls, no messages, and Ben didn't know which hospital she had been taken to, or so he said. Nearly five months since she'd disappeared, and Jim was waiting, turning his head this way and that, still searching, expecting her to come, expecting her voice, at any moment.

Here was Ben, sweating, eyeing Jim sullenly, and Jim felt the weariness, which still came over him, after five months, as though all this waiting was the last shred of her life. Mae was so tired, he thought, perhaps she's happy now. He pulled a face as Ben stammered something, still sweating, and he didn't listen to him, just held out his hand, recklessly, out there on the path, demanding. But then they did walk towards the Ladies' Pond, as far as the notice that told them to go no further. They stood in the deep shadow watching the bright bodies suddenly flash into view among the thick foliage and vanish again, and Ben handed Jim what Albert had sent him to deliver, in a plastic bag, a little package with some magazines and sweets on top of it, –keep it simple, the simpler the better, and a message for Jim, the address of his new office, Albert wrote, in Brixton, where he'd be expecting him. The money was in Jim's pocket, in an envelope, an absurdly small amount, twenty pounds; Ben shifted nervously from one foot to the other, and Jim grinned.

It was childish to try to cheat Albert: Albert would yell at Ben, and if Jim didn't get in touch there'd be trouble. He took the bag, held out the envelope towards Ben, but then ran off. Childish, not worth the bother, even if it was a laugh to hear Ben puffing and panting behind him, indignant, surprised, and now the fat bastard had to run after him, his face bright red. Jim looked round, waved and then ran on, light on his feet, full of hatred. Albert wouldn't make a big fuss because despite everything Jim was a reliable partner, one of the few he had left now that they were all dispersed, having been driven out of King's Cross by the diggers and lorries and engineers; Albert moaned about this as if King's Cross had been his old granny's parlor, as if he hadn't already got places in Clapham and Holloway and Brixton, as well as in Camden. Now he could no longer hear Ben's labored breathing, and he looked back: Ben was trying to blend in with the crowd, though his red face gave him away a mile off, while Jim could pass for a jogger as he left the Heath and ran lightly across the street, past the white low-rise residential blocks that were supposed to be better built than the concrete boxes of the sixties and seventies. A taxi was blocking the road, cars were honking, a man stuck his head out of the window and shouted an obscenity, and Jim laughed. The place in Lady Margaret Road was perfect; Ben mustn't get wind of it whatever happened. He would shake him off some-where among the derelict sites where they were now building fitness studios and a restaurant. Jim knew the workshops and studios: someone had set up a printing workshop, and a few weeks ago Jim had sold three wraps there that he had snatched from the hand of a startled guy at Camden Lock. There was a little street that curved around and came out almost opposite Kentish Town station, where the road went uphill and there was a small paved area which for no obvious reason was cov-ered over with a glass roof supported on green metal columns, as if somebody had been trying to build a miniature version of a covered market. But the only people sitting on the benches were tramps with cans of beer or cider in their hands, who good-humoredly toasted the passing pedestrians and the schoolgirls in their green or black blazers and pleated checked skirts, or hauled themselves laboriously over to the entrance to the tube, where they sold the *Big Issue* or begged for tickets. A revolting bunch, and there was a woman among them, in a long lightweight summer coat, who smiled at him and he grinned back at her. He trotted up Leighton Road, turned left into the side street, and then looked behind him again. He had shaken Ben off. The fat pig. It wasn't just because of Mae. He was sick of Ben and Albert and the others. He was sick of the police, who hung around the whole time as if they were stopping everything getting blown up, houses, people, body parts, torn-off legs, he was sick of nothing happening. He was sick of the teenagers who came on the trains from God knows where, searching for something, eager, depraved, the girls who begged for a drink or a hit and then vanished again or crouched in doorways, huddled up and filthy. He was afraid of finding Mae there, back where she'd been before Albert had picked her up. He would never move away from London without Mae. But he wanted some peace. Every so often something would flash in his brain and whole hours or days would go missing, but all the same there was a dazzling white light, he only had to find it, had to find Mae.

13

The raindrops had merged into long streaks, and these had swollen to form bulges, blisters that burst and separated into thin, fast-moving threads whose ends looked venomous, but this was deceptive, for most would be swallowed up by a broader, much slower stream, unable to get out of its path. Only a few escaped, and they bumped into the crossbar of the window frame, into the putty, which was grey, almost black, and porous. What happened after that Sara couldn't see, even if she pressed her cheek tight against the glass and squinted downwards. Meanwhile the greedy, broad streams, thick as her finger, coursed down side by side in a sort of race, while the raindrops still fell from the sky one after another, splashed onto the street, formed puddles and were sucked into the drains, gurgling, gone for ever. Big, fat drops landed on the windowpane and paused for a second as if in surprise; in some of them something was imprisoned, shining and magnified, a tiny insect with translucent wings, a flake of soot, a speck of sand or dust. Whatever it was shimmered, shimmered for a long moment before it was snatched away, twirling, confused, or slipped gradually from sight, perhaps held back one last time to show itself in its rigid transparency, a tiny thing, helplessly washed away, that would never return to its original place.

Now and again bigger objects were also blown against the glass, a leaf decomposing after a long autumn and winter, the skeleton damaged, the veins thin; a bit of paper, some scrap that was not yet soaked through by the rain and had offered no resistance to the wind. And there were smears and blobs, thick and slimy as snot, blackish like the stuff that came out of your nose after a long journey on the tube. They sat on the glass like beetles; Sara searched all over the window for them, and then stared through the glass at the rain-drenched street. She wished the radio alarm clock worked: it stood on the mantelpiece, its numbers not changing, and Dave had promised to bring a battery home with him, a battery or even another clock just for her. On rainy days it was hard to tell whether it was still morning or already afternoon, hard to have any sense of how time was passing. The man with the hand cart didn't usually come when it was raining; she thought he wouldn't be able to ring his bell, which he always swung right up into the air, the raindrops would silence the clapper, and without his bell nobody would know that he was there in the street, outside the house, waiting to see if someone would ask him in. She thought he was asked into houses because he brought good luck and it was a good sign if he took something away with him because there were too many things in the house and some of them weren't needed anymore. The people in the house next door had asked him in once, and after that his cart had been piled high, so that he was forced to walk very, very slowly down the road, leaning forward in order to pull the weight behind him. Usually, though, there was nothing in his cart, or only a few broken things. She was surprised to see him approaching now through the rain, and he waved, waved at nothing, perhaps he was waving to her because he had caught sight of her at the window, and she ducked down onto the carpet, and when she propped herself up on both hands her head bumped against the radiator. Cautiously she straightened up again; a car was driving by—the cars made more noise in the rain, the sound of their wheels on the wet road louder than that of the engine, swishing, hissing—and had to swerve to avoid the man with

the cart. She peered out. He was standing right in front of the
house, waving again with his free hand, which was holding
something, not the bell but something else. Sara used the windowsill to pull herself up and stood on tiptoe. He gestured to
her to come outside, let go of the other handle of his cart and
signaled to her, pointing to what he was holding high up in the
air with his other hand, and she recognized it. Her fingers
gripped the windowsill; the wood was cracked, and a splinter
jabbed into her skin. Now he was standing quite still, she
couldn't see his face clearly, the rain was still falling, and he left
his cart standing in the road and stepped quickly onto the
pavement, right up to the low cast-iron railings, and his face
was twisted into a grin, he waved again, his mouth was open,
and for a moment she was afraid he would come even closer.
His gaze met hers. She put a hand to her eye, which was
swollen and painful, she felt sick again, like yesterday evening,
and in front of her the stripes grew blurred, parallel, very neat
vertical stripes that she had never noticed before, like grooves
scratched into the glass to help the rain run down and wash
away the streaks, long straight lines whose meaning she didn't
know because she didn't go to school. But then the windowpane returned to normal, and raindrops hit the glass, divided
into thin threads, and soon joined up with others.

–Hey, Missy! He was calling to her. It was as if he had called
her by her name, and she thought that Dave had sent him from
where he was secretly living, from that place that he only spoke
of in a whisper with a finger to his lips and a smile in his eyes,
because one day he was going to take her there with him, and
until then it was a secret. But there was the man suddenly grinning nastily and ramming the doll that he had been holding
aloft onto one of the spikes of the wrought-iron railings, impal-
ing her between her dirty white legs that stuck out under the
green dress, stiffly spread apart, and everything was silent, the
clock and time and the rain.

Later on it stopped raining, the water ebbed away, bubbling, down the drain by the letterbox, and the color of the asphalt grew lighter, while the sky, even though the black clouds had passed over, grew darker as though it had a green inner lining. Dave had shown it to her, had brought a piece of cloth, for a cloak, he said, a cloak that he would wear when he took her away with him to a place where lots of princesses were playing and waiting for her, and they would never be apart again. The cloak would protect him. –If you take the cloth and kiss it, it'll bring good luck, like this, see, and much later Polly came to the garden door and meowed, keeping her yellow eyes fixed on Sara, who approached slowly, her legs quite stiff from standing so long at the window. Come on, little cat, Dave would say if he were here, open the door for her, go out in the street and call her—the door to the terrace was locked—and while she's on her way you can run to the railings, they're quite close, and get your doll, and then you can all three go indoors together. All three of you. Polly's been outside for two days, and you've been looking for Dolly for a week, haven't you?

She was torn underneath and some yellowish stuffing was spilling out, her green arms hung down as if they were dislocated, but the face was right, and the smell too, although she was wet and the wool smelled like Polly when she came in from the rain. You see, Dave whispered, things get lost, but the important things turn up again, you find them again in the end.

14

Instead of going away they stayed in Berlin and went on excursions whenever Jakob was free, and he bought a car, a Golf, which he was going to pass on to Hans when they went to London, but in the meantime he drove Isabelle to Lake Stechlin or the Müggelsee. One hot day when they were walking across the Pfaueninsel, thunderclouds gathered and they snuggled up close to one another as they waited for the rain and wind to subside. They visited the zoo, stood in front of the enclosures without reading the information boards, and watched the animals as they lay in the sun, motionless and perhaps contented. They went to Schöneberg town hall and registered to be married in August. The long hours of daylight meant that Jakob arrived home before it began to get dark, and they ate on the rather narrow balcony or in the dining room, which had no more than a table and a few chairs in it because they had neither time nor inclination to furnish it properly. Isabelle was a bad cook, which Jakob found surprising, and he suggested they might cook a meal together with Hans. Isabelle liked Hans, and they also invited Andras, and Alexa and Clara came too; it got late and the table filled up with bottles, then at midnight Hans started making pancakes; it was dawn before they went their separate ways. After that Hans was a regular guest, sometimes bringing other friends along, or they would meet up at their old haunts, the Makabar or the Angel of Death. Jakob would join them later, and he usually left before the rest. He had given Isabelle a white anorak and a lurid green, almost see-through T-shirt, which she wore with mini-shorts: it was hot. –I've never seen her so happy, Alexa told Jakob, and Isabelle laughed. Despite the threat of recession the agency was flourishing, Universal Music were calling every week, a new magazine wanted a layout, a children's book publisher was asking for some illustrations. They would be moving to London during the winter, and Isabelle said she would carry on working just as before. In the afternoons she sometimes stayed at home, sitting on the balcony in the heat and sending her drawings to the office or to clients by e-mail; Jakob had bought her the big drawing table. She went out into the street and to the shop round the corner that the schoolchildren used, and watched them as they came running out of the door, drew on the pavements with chalk, and were collected around four o'clock or went off by themselves with their schoolbags and bicycles. One little girl was always left behind because she couldn't run fast enough, and would hide in a doorway until the others had all gone.

They wanted a simple wedding at the registry office, with just their witnesses, Ginka and Hans, but even Alexa protested, and so there was to be a party after all, a picnic in the park, without parents, Isabelle said, and went to Heidelberg to tell them.

The house, the grey shoe box almost smothered in Japanese creeper, looked welcoming, and as the taxi came to a stop her mother emerged from the house, ran pale-faced to her daughter und gave her a violent hug. –But Mummy, I'm only getting married, Isabelle said, and her mother laughed; it sounded like fabric being torn. The grey flagstone floor gleamed, and the living room where the grand piano had stood seemed empty again, as it had when her mother had lain silently in her own room. In that living room the nanny, Mimsel, had tried to dry Isabelle's tears with sweets and little jokes, while, frightened and mute, Isabelle had cowered where the piano had been, and like an avenging angel Mimsel had stood cursing outside her mistress's door. –Have you got a beer? asked Isabelle, while her mother's eyes took in the short skirt, the crinkle blouse, and Isabelle's figure, which beside her own extreme thinness seemed ample and wayward. Frau Metzel sent her daughter upstairs to freshen up, and went to the phone to let her husband know she had arrived. –Your father, she said as Isabelle came back down the stairs, is going to bring champagne. On the glass table in front of the black sofa were two glasses of Campari and a jug of orange juice. No, of course you won't be inviting us to your wedding, Frau Metzel dutifully echoed, and Isabelle was thinking that tomorrow she'd be stopping off in Frankfurt to meet her future father-in-law, who wasn't invited to the wedding either, because there was only going to be a picnic, nothing more. And then her father came and hugged her as though he was proud of her, –my grown-up daughter, and during the meal he smiled as if he were sitting alone in a restaurant, while Isabelle's fingers fondled the glasses that she hadn't been allowed to touch as a child.

It all went off satisfactorily, she told Jakob, and later their parents would come and visit them, in Berlin or in London, and they could go to Frankfurt or to Heidelberg for Christmas: "the young couple," Alexa mockingly called them, but even she had found the wedding quite moving, for not far from the fountain there was a long, festively laid table, provided by Andras, with his aunt's white damask tablecloths, and Hans made a speech. They were friends, and Isabelle cautiously twisted her wedding ring this way and that, as cautiously as if her finger had suddenly become fragile; she smiled at Jakob, he had waited all those years, and when it got dark Ginka brought some table lanterns. Hans attempted a handstand on the rim of the fountain; he was drunk and fell into the water. Alexa and Clara ranged themselves on either side of Isabelle, Jakob took some photographs, and eventually they wrapped themselves in blankets because it was getting chilly and dawn was on the way: they would wait to see the sun come up. The summer was drawing to a close, the trees in Wartburgstrasse were losing their leaves; Ginka said that it had been the loveliest summer for a long time, and everybody agreed.

15

A bird that was perched on the windowsill took off, fluttered against the pane and flew away unharmed. Andras went into the bathroom, looked in the mirror, which was covered in little white spots from shaving foam or toothpaste, considered whether to have another shave, and studied his shirt with the pink, light blue and green stripes which appeared to change their relative positions as he lifted his arms. He was conscious of the reawakened vanity that led him to wear something different every day, to try out a different color combination, a leather or a denim jacket, different shoes, calf-length boots with a slit at the side. He often went to the western part of Berlin, to the children's book publisher in Kantstrasse or the Alto gallery in Schlossstrasse. Magda, the gallery owner, phoned him almost daily—she needed flyers, business cards, a catalog, there was a young Hungarian artist he should meet, she found a thousand reasons to phone him, promised contacts with other galleries and with the Martin-Gropius-Bau, and kept her word. She would love to have him as a partner, she said jokingly, but said it more than once. The gallery was financed from property that had belonged to her late husband, three blocks of rented apartments in Frankfurt which she managed herself. She was wiry, almost too thin, with a deep tan acquired from working on the roof, she told him, and showed him the roof garden, big earthenware pots with oleanders, the pergola with a wisteria growing over it, and beneath it a stone table and two chairs. She liked Isabelle and was perceptive enough to realize how much Isabelle meant to Andras, though she refrained from comment. On his way home he drove past the Wartburgstrasse apartment. He could not help liking Jakob. He was not even jealous when Jakob put his arms round Isabelle and kissed her: this was how it was destined to be, it was something he had had no part in from the outset. Perhaps his only option now was to go back to Budapest, move into the apartment next door to László and his sister and spend more and more afternoons having coffee with his parents, as though by merely sitting still he could reconcile the compass points between which he moved, from east to west and back again, which were hardly the ideal coordinates for mapping out a life.

When the telephone rang he knew whose voice he would hear and whose he would not, and he listened dispiritedly and gave assenting replies. In the kitchen he washed up the things that had been standing there for days, the few items he used, isolated objects that were like a broken fence separating him from the towering mountain of his aunt's and uncle's expectations and their ultimate resignation. From a bad dream, his uncle had said, you wake up the wrong way round, facing in the wrong direction, but from happy dreams you never wake up at all. There was the sound of footsteps on the stairs, of someone trudging heavily but purposefully upwards, past the door to his apartment and on to where there was nothing but the attic, secured only by a token padlock. Now he could hear the footsteps above his head, followed by silence. Perhaps a homeless person was moving in there, with a blanket and a few plastic bags, and would try to get a small fire going. Andras sighed, he'd have to go and investigate. Then there were footsteps again, this time a woman's, and when Magda knocked Andras opened the door and without further ado took her in his arms. –There's a smell of winter on your stairs, she murmured, nestling her thin face against his shoulder, laughing.

Who have you been dreaming of, that girl of yours? Like a length of light, almost transparent fabric she interposed herself between him and his sorrow; as he stroked her rough, freckled skin he thought he heard Isabelle, whispering, anxious, but the plaintive little sound, he realized in a moment, had been made by Magda, who pressed closer to him, her thighs parted, with a modest desire that touched him, and it took him a further moment to understand that it was his own need that she was reflecting back to him.

—My poor love, she said, so casually and absently that he stayed lying where he was while she got up, put on her blouse and buttoned it, bent down to him again and kissed him. Perhaps we suit each other best like this, you with your Isabelle and me with my sadness about Friedrich. I married him because he wanted me to and I didn't know any different at the time, and now I dream about him and he seems so handsome. With a laugh, she crossed the adjacent living room, ran a hand over the red sofa, and sat down on it for a moment. He saw the pale skin of her thin legs: she looked like an old woman, fragile, vulnerable, and it was easy to imagine his aunt sitting beside her, nodding her head and silently recounting, from her store of endlessly convoluted stories, one that told of the rooms and houses in Budapest, going back to times before the century that made ghosts and victims of people.

—Let's go to Budapest, said Magda. Believe me, there's no better basis for a marriage than when the partners accept that they don't love each other. Andras stood up, pulled on his underpants and trousers, and, with his naked torso that seemed to him too big and heavy, too clumsy, moved towards her. Conscious of her scrutiny, he longed to be alone, to set out on his own for a walk, have a drink in some pub and exchange a few words with somebody, go out into the night again, take a taxi along Wartburgstrasse and come back at dawn, possibly drunk, and then think of Magda's body, of her tenderness that still, like a gossamer-thin tissue, separated him from Isabelle. He was grateful. He was grateful that she got dressed and prepared to leave, blowing him a kiss from the door, expecting no further embrace, expecting nothing except what she read in his eyes, that they would become lovers. Perhaps they would see each other no more than once a week, for supper, and sleep together like an old married couple, each with their own sorrow, their own happiness, but at least there would be someone to embrace this no longer youthful body, not for the sake of the moment but because of the time that was ebbing away—perhaps the only possible act of compassion, Magda thought. Time was chopped up into such small portions that it was not worth paying it any attention.

Four days later Andras invited her for supper. She saw that he did not want to kiss her, but he took her hand and stroked it, the wrinkled knuckles, the pretty, unvarnished fingernails, the thin, clearly visible veins, stroked it, so that for a while she could be oblivious of what for now was entrusted to his care. Perhaps, he thought, we really are too old to worry about whether it's enough. And he told her about the man in the attic, whom he had gone up to see since her last visit, about the tiny, dark face, the eyes turned on him in alarm, and the outbursts of rage, the swearing and shouting with which this same man waged a hopeless battle against marauding specters that he dared not put a name to. He had introduced himself as Herr Schmidt. –Just fancy, said Andras, that really is his name, Herr Schmidt. He says he had eight brothers and sisters and is the only one still living, as though he'd been condemned to live forever. –And what will you do with him? Magda asked. –I've bought him an electric hotplate and given him a saucepan. She laughed. He's got two plates and some cutlery of his own, Andras went on, and now he's going to invite me for a meal. The property managers have stopped coming here anyway, they're only waiting for me to move out so that they can put the whole place up for sale.

In due course Magda and Herr Schmidt met, and after Herr Schmidt had had a chance to cast an eye over Isabelle too he knocked on Andras's door and, squirming in deeper embarrassment than he had ever shown before, informed him that it would only lead to unhappiness if he married the younger of the two women. Andras had no difficulty in reassuring him, but he was cut to the quick. It was already November; in January Jakob would move to London and find an apartment, and Isabelle would follow on soon afterwards.

Andras celebrated Christmas with Magda; Jakob and Isabelle had taken up Hans's invitation and gone to the Black Forest.

On New Year's Eve they got together in Wartburgstrasse. Magda was in Rome. Andras cooked a five-course meal with Ginka, Isabelle laid the table. Hans brought along a petition on behalf of the prisoners in Guantánamo Bay. The next war was already looming on the horizon. Jakob told them that a colleague was putting it about that Mossad really had had a hand in the attack on the Twin Towers, and they would see to it that he wasn't made a partner at Golbert & Schreiber at any rate. At midnight they raised their glasses to a peaceful year, knowing full well that they thought it unlikely. But they drank to peace and, tacitly, to their continuing to be spared. Andras yearned for Magda, but when he held Isabelle in his arms and gave her a New Year's kiss he knew that he would give up anything and anybody if only she wanted him to. He kissed her on the lips, while Jakob was out on the balcony setting up fireworks, and she nestled in his arms, her young, pretty face lifted to his, and returned his kiss.

16

While he was still at the airport Jakob phoned the number of his future colleague Alistair. It was Maude, the secretary, who answered: –Oh, my goodness, said her voice, you've already arrived, how wonderful! and she told him that Alistair would be waiting for him at two o'clock at the entrance to the British Museum. –He'll certainly recognize you, don't you worry. Alistair is a man of extraordinary capacities.

Small planes were landing and taking off. He had never been through London City Airport before. A bare handful of passengers were making their way to the exit, and as it was only one o'clock he decided to take a train.

Alistair did recognize him straight away. Hurrying down the steps of the museum, he took him by the arm, without enquiring about his journey, and pulled him along the streets, talking cheerfully and far too fast for Jakob to follow, until they came to a small deli. Greeting the owners, two women of about forty, like old friends, he sat Jakob down on a chair and returned a few minutes later with two well-filled plates. –Amira thinks you look exhausted, he reported, and started chewing. Right, he said, Bentham is sixty-six, and now that he's sold his big practice he doesn't want any business partnerships: the loose relationship with you in Berlin is the only one he's maintained. He gives us a share of the profits because he has no children or family—his elder brother died soon after they emigrated. He'll probably give everything away in any case.

That would be just like him. He isn't always in the office, but he can be phoned at any time. It's worth doing, his instinct is virtually infallible. He wants to tell you himself what you'll be working on; very likely he'll get you to look after the handful of old people and their descendants still mourning the loss of their ancient ruins in East Germany. You know, lakeside plots with dachas where there used to be a fine villa. And buildings too. Bentham refuses to handle inheritance disputes. Have you got all that?

Alistair straightened up, smiling at Jakob, and signaled to Amira, who came over with two espressos and gave a friendly shake of the head as she eyed Jakob's still half-full plate. —Not until he's eaten it all up, she said to Alistair, holding the little cup high in the air as if to stop a child jumping up after it. —Amira, Jakob, said Alistair, introducing them and giving Jakob a gentle nudge. Jakob got to his feet and shook her hand. —I'll bring you a fresh espresso when you've finished eating, and don't let Alistair talk you into the ground! A moment later a glass of white wine appeared in front of Jakob, and Alistair nodded approvingly. —She likes you, he said, and then kept quiet until Jakob had finished. —I'm looking forward to my time in London, said Jakob, and blushed at the inanity of this remark. And you'll show me the house?

Alistair grinned, running his hand through his thick shock of fair hair. He had green eyes and freckles, his tie hung crookedly under an elegant jacket, and his very long eyelashes and an attractively curving mouth contrasted with the boniness of his face. —In Primrose Hill there's a very decent flat, four rooms, nice area and so on. And then there's a Victorian terraced house in Kentish Town. Not really the right sort of address for somebody working for Bentham, but he doesn't mind. He mentioned that you wouldn't be coming on your own and that in Berlin people are used to having plenty of space.

—My wife, Jakob said hesitantly and, as he realized with

amazement, for the first time. My wife will be joining me, she'll continue to work for her design agency from here.

–Primrose Hill is posh. Are you and your wife posh? Alistair laughed at his own question. There's a woman who comes to Amira's deli every Friday and reads the coffee cups. Bentham swears by her. If you can't make up your mind, wait till the day after tomorrow.

Later Jakob was not sure whether it was this piece of information that had decided him against even looking at Primrose Hill. Reading the coffee cups seemed to him something so exotic, in a deli obviously frequented by lawyers and business people, that he took fright and felt very provincial, or like a mere child setting out to travel the world. His mind was so taken up with the idea of a future that could be foretold, and with the photograph of a sturdily built, raven-haired woman that Alistair pointed out to him, that he forgot to say goodbye to Amira or to pay attention to where Alistair was taking him. After a hectic taxi ride that took them through a maze of cranes and construction-site hoardings, they got out close to Kentish Town station. –Then you'll be able to see right away how near it is to the underground, Alistair explained, as he turned into a road that went gently uphill and took a further turning off it. Tall plane trees lined a street of smart-looking houses, somewhere there were children playing—Jakob could hear their shouts and the sound of a ball bouncing—and the front door that Alistair went up to was dark blue, glazed but with a protective wrought-iron grille, and a light-colored carpet could be seen inside. The internal layout was pleasing, with two large rooms and a small bathroom on the ground floor— Isabelle's rooms, thought Jakob at once—a kitchen and a combined living and dining room on the first floor, and two bedrooms and a bathroom on the second. From the ground floor a few steps led to a terrace and from there into the garden, an undistinguished-looking strip of ground with a few rhododendrons and hydrangeas and a rather rough patch of grass. –Some of the internal walls have been removed, Alistair said. In the other houses around here each floor is a separate flat, quite a fair-sized one by London standards.

When they emerged onto the street again, Alistair continued: –Of course you could have a look in Notting Hill, too, or in Hampstead, there certainly are better areas, but there's a good mix here, the position is good too, and you'd have to pay twice as much anywhere else. The house belongs to Bentham; he'll let you have it for five hundred pounds a week, it really is a snip at that price. Alistair took Jakob's arm again, –let's go on foot, he said, and was already setting off, but then he changed his mind and suggested they should catch a bus to the northeastern corner of Regent's Park, because from there it wasn't far to walk, and it was a nice attractive route which would take them past the edge of the zoo and down the length of the park, almost all the way to Devonshire Street. At lunchtime they could sit in the park, Alistair added, and Mr. Bentham liked to discuss things while taking a walk there, even when it was raining, so Jakob would be well advised to get himself a rainproof jacket, a good one with a hood, or better still a half-length coat, because Mr. Bentham set great store by a smart appearance, as he would very shortly see for himself. Only now did Jakob notice that Alistair was the same height as he was, and Robert came into his mind. Alistair was fair-haired, livelier, more natural in his manner, though there could be a mischievous sparkle in his eyes, and as they walked along he talked about concerts and the devious means by which his elderly aunt would smuggle herself in without paying, because she spent all her money on polo ponies and vets' fees. –I tried to invite her to go with me, at my expense, but she just said she'd rather have the equivalent amount in cash: naturally she'd still gladly come with me, but without a ticket. They left the park, where Jakob had seen the railings of the zoo some distance away; now he felt excited, and here they were, in Devonshire Street. Alistair simply knocked on the heavy door, and some unseen person activated the buzzer. This was the porter, Andrew, who came towards them holding a thick book, his finger marking the page at which they had interrupted him. His wrinkled neck supported a very small head: the ears were the only large and fleshy parts of this man, whose eyes were those of a nocturnal creature and who immediately informed them that he was in charge of the lift, strongly advising them to use it only, if at all, when he was on hand. Not that the stairs looked much more trustworthy, Jakob noticed as they climbed to the first floor, since they were uneven from wear and the stair-carpet was frayed; the doors were much in need of a new coat of paint, as were the walls, while the library, apart from the incongruously vivid colors of new books and periodicals, seemed like the slumbering, unused library of a noble house, abandoned to dust, time, and dry, unidentified tapping sounds. But the impression was deceptive, for the fine old wooden tables were freshly polished, towards the back of the room there were five new Macintosh computers, and two men of about Jakob and Alistair's age were ensconced in heavy leather armchairs, reading, ignoring the visitors. –This is Bentham's floor, Alistair explained when they had left the second floor behind and were climbing up to the third, where Alistair pointed to a door that was ajar. He didn't actually come in with him, though Jakob only noticed this a few moments later, when he wanted to turn to him for guidance because the man sitting in an easy chair by the window—a gentleman in an immaculate black three-piece suit, wearing, in lieu of a tie, a silk cravat elegantly wound round his throat and sporting a small white flower in the buttonhole of his lapel—did not stir but merely contemplated him, weighing him up. A violent, disturbing sensation gripped Jakob, and he was conscious of his heart pounding. At last the man's torso moved; he seemed to rise up spontaneously without the support of his legs, his body responding not so much to his will as to some mental formula that produced a perfect relationship between the various loads—the broad chest, the stomach contained by the waistcoat, and the rather short legs—so as to avoid any expenditure of effort. The neck and face were large and fleshy, as were the nose, chin, and cheeks; bushy eyebrows almost covered the eyes, while the rather narrow lips formed a soft, lax mouth. His voice was so deep and mumbling that Jakob did not immediately catch what he said, and afterwards he could never recall what Bentham's first words had been or whether he had spoken them in German or in English, however long and often he thought about it.

What Jakob told Isabelle and Hans, when he was back in Berlin, amounted to a list of the tasks that awaited him at work. About his future office he said nothing; he had been surprised to find that the spacious room full of old furniture, including a sofa and a heavy wooden chest, was the one he wanted. It was undoubtedly shabby and not very light, Bentham had said; moreover, on the first floor—Alistair and two other colleagues had rooms on the second—there was a modern office he could have. It must be behind the reading room, Jakob thought. Next to Mr. Krapohl's—the librarian's—sanctum, Bentham had confirmed, and Jakob blushed. Maude, Bentham's secretary, had appeared from a small kitchen with a tray, shaking her head indignantly when she learned of their intentions: what "this room up here" needed above all else was to be thoroughly cleared out and decorated. She had subjected Jakob to a rigorous scrutiny, a plump woman of about fifty, wearing a hairnet, with red cheeks as if she had just come in from outside, from a garden, the pruners still in her hand. But what she was actually holding was the tray, laden with a teapot and two small bowls of biscuits, a plate of sandwiches, and a silver milk jug and sugar bowl that were as highly polished as if she meant

them to demonstrate that proper care and cleanliness were the
only defense against rampant disorder. On the way to
Liverpool Street Station Alistair had told Jakob that there was
an ongoing controversy about whether to continue using the
old grey file boxes or finally replace them with brighter, more
colorful ones. Bentham himself bought up secondhand files of
the old, traditional type wherever he saw them for sale: it was
one of those eccentricities of his that you just had to get used
to. If Jakob wanted to see a concrete embodiment of
Bentham's quirks, Alistair had said, he need only visit
Bentham's favorite museum, the former home of Sir John
Soane, which housed a crude and utterly bizarre assortment of
objects, packed in there—you could hardly say "displayed"—
in an impossibly cramped and incongruous fashion. And Jakob
sensed that he would not mention any of this when he returned
to Berlin. The house in Lady Margaret Road provided plenty
to talk about, and he described it enthusiastically to Isabelle,
passing over in silence the fact that there had been an apartment in Primrose Hill that he had not even looked at. He let
Hans glance through the documents that he had brought back
with him in order to do some preparatory work, and so all
three of them were happy, even if Hans could not share his
friends' mood of pleasurable anticipation. He would miss
them.

It was Andras who finally asked about Bentham—Andras,
who had never made any comment on their preparations for
the move, and had merely nodded when Isabelle and Jakob
had invited him to visit them in London. They were standing
together on the balcony, while Ginka, Hans and Isabelle were
in the kitchen; for a January evening it was uncommonly mild,
and Andras was smoking, drawing edgily on a cigarette, his
fourth that evening. Magda was expecting him in two hours'
time. He hesitated to cancel, and he hesitated to invite her to

Wartburgstrasse. But he didn't want to leave: this was one of the last evenings they would spend here. He was playing for time. Jakob seemed quite alarmed when he asked about Bentham.

–Hard to describe, Jakob said at last, he's not very tall, a bit on the plump side, and with legs that are too short for the upper part of his body, which is very powerfully built. He dresses impeccably, he's possibly rather vain, in fact he definitely is, though he obviously doesn't care about the appearance of the offices, which are positively shabby. He's got a picture by Lucian Freud on his wall—do you know his work? A picture of some white flowers, I've no idea what kind they are. Alistair told me that Freud did a portrait of Bentham. A large face, the sort of face that has a certain heaviness, the nose, the eyelids, every part of it has its own quite specific weight, do you know what I mean? Jakob blushed. Bentham had been neither friendly nor unfriendly towards him, or rather he had been friendly, but not in any way effusive. –He's quite unlike Schreiber, I've never met anyone like him before.

–Is he a Jew?

Jakob stared at Andras, nonplussed. –No idea. How should I know? Alistair said he came to England as a child. Why do you ask? Andras shrugged. Inside, Isabelle was laying the table. She wasn't looking towards the balcony; Andras watched her as she leaned forward with the upper part of her body, as her arms reached out, as she straightened up. She was wearing a close-fitting green blouse and black jeans, and had thick socks on her feet. –Perhaps because nobody here has ever asked *me*, apart from Hanna. That's odd, too. Or not, who knows?

–Are you Jewish? Jakob leaned on the balcony rail and looked down at the street.

–Yes, always have been.

–But why should we have asked you?

—Because my uncle and aunt were able to emigrate, because I obtained German citizenship, because a lot of Jews emigrated from Hungary. On the other hand, sure, why should anybody have asked me?

For a moment Jakob had a mental image of Bentham getting up out of his chair, coming forward and standing between Maude and Alistair, and he saw once again the tiny gesture with which Maude stroked Bentham's sleeve, and Alistair's expression, in which animation and mockery were mingled with affection.

He thought of September 11th, a year and a half ago, of his helpless agitation that had had nothing to do with New York, and of Bush's speech, "nothing the way it was before." Nothing had changed. There were "sleepers" waiting to carry out acts of terrorism, there had been the war in Afghanistan, houses destroyed, human beings burned to death, bodies hastily buried, and in remote, inaccessible mountains there were still Taliban or al-Qaeda fighters, names and things that meant no more to people here than the intrigues and dramatic crises in a television soap, and that everybody talked about just as they talked about *Big Brother*. And now they were all talking about war in Iraq. How many had been killed in the last Iraq war? Thousands, and Jakob remembered the panic buying in Freiburg, people who in all seriousness started stockpiling tinned food and warm blankets and organized torchlight processions in protest against the war, while Israel was being bombarded with rockets. September 11th had come to represent merely the watershed between an imagined carefree "before" and the anxious, aggressive wailing and moaning that was now increasing by the day. Only for Robert's parents, Jakob reflected, had everything really changed; and for himself. He had found Isabelle, and was going to move to London.

17

Angrily climbing over empty vegetable crates and poly-
styrene containers that stank of fish, Jim nearly tripped
over a cat that was crouching behind a cardboard box,
a grey tabby; he stared at it for a second, then bent down and
tickled it under the chin. Cautiously he felt for its throat and
gently stroked its neck and chest, and the creature, which had
frozen at first, relaxed and stood still, its tail erect, without
purring. –Hey, why don't you purr? He started to pick it up,
but there was something damp sticking to its belly, dirt or
blood, and the cat gave a wail of pain. Jim swore. He straightened up; he could hear the noise from Brixton Road, buses,
shouting too, and a woman's voice approaching, furious, shrill.
The cat had lain down. Jim kept still, suppressing the impulse
to turn round and look back along the narrow passage to the
street, where the woman was presumably now standing, he
imagined he could hear someone breathing, while the street
noise was like an oily liquid sloshing in regular waves between
the buildings. Once again he tripped over the cat, but ignored
it this time and pressed on, stepping over more crates and bags
of refuse until he came to a brown-painted door, which he
pushed open. At the foot of the stairs lay newspapers, advertising leaflets, tin cans; with a grimace he waded through it all
and climbed up to the third floor, past doors behind which the
traders stored their goods, vegetables, clothing, toys. The
doors were secured with padlocks. Only one was open, and a
boy looked at him for a second and hastily vanished; there was

a smell of cooking. Up at the top Albert was waiting. He grinned, his broad body filling the doorway. His thinning grey hair was neatly combed back and he was wearing a T-shirt; his right arm hung limply down, while his left hand was braced against the lintel of the door. Only a glimmer of light came from inside. Jim strained to hear any sound: he had told Albert, when he phoned him, that he wanted to see only him, not Ben, nor any of the bodyguards that Albert kept around him, characters he picked up in the same way as he had Jim. Scum off the streets. Aimless and mostly talentless too, fit for nothing. They nicked car radios, handbags, mobile phones, cameras, and would lie around for days, out of their heads, on the mattresses Albert provided in the various pads he had which were dotted all over the city, over as far as South Ealing. Bolt holes, cities of refuge, as Albert grandiosely called them, seven of them, like in the Old Testament, and he named these sleazy lodgings Paris, Rome, Jerusalem. Jim had stayed in Jerusalem for a time. It was right in the middle of Soho, above a Chinese restaurant, on a mezzanine floor crammed with freezer cabinets and shelves full of rice noodles and other foodstuffs, tucked away behind the room for the waiters and chefs. There Jim had slept, sharing a tiny toilet with the others, a washbasin without a mirror, and the stink of piss. The thin, pale-looking men had never spoken to him, possibly because they knew no English, or because that was the way Albert wanted it. Jim stowed the things he pinched in boxes that had contained noodles, Albert had them collected, and in return there was hash and sometimes cocaine, promises, hot meals. The leftovers, plenty of them and actually not bad. Jim learned to eat soup for breakfast, or cold meat. Cocaine was better than bad marijuana and beer; Soho was better than the doorways and bus shelters of King's Cross. Even so, that was where he was drawn back to, and twice Albert had had to round him up and had given him a beating. He had taken him to a barber's and put new clothes on him so as to send him out onto the streets, with his pretty-boy looks. To break him in he handed him over to two of his friends, and afterwards pressed the money into Jim's hand, –you've earned it, with your sweet face and your sweet arse. He was given a different room, too, tried to run away even so, but Albert's mob were everywhere, and then he got a thrashing. –Don't pretend you're not used to it from home. Two weeks under lock and key and forced to go cold turkey—some weird idea of Albert's—then sent back on the street, then on the run again, this time for three months because he avoided King's Cross, and the City and Brixton, and Clapham too, all the places where Albert was, but he couldn't cope on his own, tried his luck in the East End and this time got pulled in by the police and stuck in a clinic, and then went crawling back to Albert. When he recalled it he could still taste the blood in his mouth, because he bit his own tongue when one of Albert's pals pulled his pants down and forced him to bend over. After that Albert's face, and back to the dump in Soho. He couldn't get himself off the drugs and carried on thieving until Albert started taking him along on his expeditions, and it was only when Mae turned up that things changed, because Albert had a use for him and gave them the place in Field Street.

Albert was still standing grinning in the doorway, and it was clear to Jim that he would never tell him what he knew about Mae without expecting something in return. Always assuming that he did know anything. He wouldn't let Jim go, wouldn't leave him in peace, not in London. Too late Jim realized that somebody had come up the stairs behind him.

Just a moderate beating, Albert declared, sending the other two outside. Jim kept his eyes shut. From the next room he could hear Ben's voice. He moved his legs, thinking to himself that he was lying there like a baby. Cautiously he stretched out first his right leg, then his left. He still seemed to be bleeding; he could feel it tickling his chin, his neck. His left arm was unbearably painful, dislocated, he thought and closed his eyes tighter; like an animal, he thought, and felt the tears coming. He managed to jerk his dislocated shoulder back into place; the pain shot into his brain, severed him from his own body. His legs were straight now, and as Albert approached he knew what was going to happen. Albert came from in front and kicked his left kneecap; Jim screamed. When he came to again it was very quiet. With an effort he sat up, lost his balance, recovered it and propped himself up on his right hand; opening his eyes, he saw Albert's frightened face. The room contained only a table and a few chairs. So this was the new office Albert had referred to in his note, with its freshly painted walls, while the other room probably served as a storeroom for car radios, mobile phones, alarm systems, all the things that Albert sold around Charing Cross, used and new, each item representing another few pounds towards Albert's dream of a restaurant in Kensington. –Whatever must you think of me? Albert murmured with a show of sadness, putting out a hand to help Jim to his feet. You tried to take me for a ride, as you very well know.

Everyone is entitled to his own modest dream. A restaurant in Kensington. A house and a garden with a cherry tree in it. What Ben's was, Jim didn't know; he saw his broad face peeking through the crack of the door and shuddered. Oh, what the hell! No house, no cherry tree. Mae had disappeared, and they would force him to go on working for them. It didn't matter anyway, without Mae. He felt a burning shame. –We really just want to help you. Albert twisted his face into a pitying grin, and showed him a photo of Mae with the same wording that appeared on the "missing persons" posters at tube stations. It wasn't the first time Jim had recognized a face on one of the posters. Barely more than kids, most of them, who got off the trains, just like him, at Liverpool Street or King's Cross or St. Pancras, greedy and naïve, but soon starving, willing to latch onto anybody who promised them a few pounds and the chance to prolong their dream, whatever it was, willing to scrabble in the dirt for what they saw as life, real life—coura-geous even, in their way, even if they didn't know what they were rebelling against or why. And then, like himself and Albert, they fell back on a small, unattainable dream, an image of peace and tranquility which their over-stimulated brains held up deceptively before them, a childish oasis where all hope resided, and they imagined that they had found the thing they longed for, their pride, their goal. When it was too late. Jim had beaten a few of them up, on Albert's orders or because they were harassing him, and doing this had never affected him strongly: if anything it had brought a degree of calmness. Desperation, just briefly, which to begin with was no more than a fine crack and then suddenly hurt, like a knife cutting a piece out of his own head, cutting out memory. He had imag-ined himself telling Mae about it some time when they were sleeping together, when he was lying in her arms before falling asleep. In that crack there was always a light, too, a dazzling brightness. Mae's photo at the tube stations. Missing. If you have any information please contact—and then a private mobile phone number, or how was Albert thinking of doing it? Jim stared at the picture. He didn't possess a photo of her. He moved his arm cautiously, and gave a groan. He had to con-centrate. She was quite close, not within hailing distance but near enough, so that he only needed to reach out his hand to her. If only he could remember. The longing was so intense that he could hardly bear it, as if something had been torn out of him. Albert grinned. He went into the next room, came back with a wrap, and cut three lines. –Do you remember, Jim, all the rubbish you talked about making a clean break? About how you wanted to draw a line under everything and go and live in the country? Jim said nothing, but watched Albert and Ben leaning over the table and snorting the powder into their noses, nodding encouragingly to him. Behind them he seemed to see the faint outline of Mae's neck, also bent forward. He hated it when she sniffed drugs or took pills, he hated the expression on her face and her inane giggling as she tried to press herself against him and put her hand into his trousers. They had taunted him about having beaten her up. Taunted him about Alice. He went over to them and stood in front of Ben. –Don't you think you should say thank you? Ben asked. Albert intervened: –Leave him, let him sit down now. He pushed a chair towards Jim, went off, and returned with three cans of beer. There must be somebody in the back room, some-body who had come up the stairs behind Jim, the breathing, he hadn't just imagined it, a blow to the head, on the stairs, while Albert grinned at him. Now he felt sick. Thirteen years ago he had run away from his parents for the first time, at the age of thirteen, and then three years later he'd made it to London, on July 3, he'd celebrated that day every year until he met Mae, and since then he'd celebrated the day he first saw her, in August, he didn't even tell her the exact date, and she couldn't remember. He felt like a dummy, hollow, unable to move. On the floor, which was bare cement, his blood was drying. Albert followed the direction of his eyes, raised his can, and poured out a thin pool of beer over it. They would clean it up or else let it dry there, it was all the same to him. –You must realize you can't simply bail out and pull jobs on your own account. Albert's voice was businesslike now. –In return we'll help you search for Mae without you having the police breathing down your neck.

–I didn't do anything to Mae, Jim replied weakly; the pain in his left arm was getting worse again. Albert made a mollify-ing gesture. –How stupid do you think we are? Remember, Ben actually saw her.

Jim stared helplessly at Albert.

–And you beat Alice up, have you forgotten that too? This was Ben, breathing hard, indignant.

–Alice stole three hundred quid off me! Jim flushed red. He had left her lying there: she'd had a room in Arlington Road, a basement room, Albert had seen to it that she didn't make any trouble and had forced him and Ben to clear the room out because he suspected that there were a few grams of cocaine hidden there. Five years ago, maybe six. And he couldn't remember. Only that she'd rushed at him when he tried to hit her, and nothing after that. He wanted to jump up and rush at Albert. But before he was out of his chair Ben was already upon him, the door opened and a dark-haired man of Arab appearance stood there, knife in hand, his narrow face impassive. Jim punched Ben in the face and sat down again. –So now you've got an Arab for reinforcements, have you? He stared at the man, the regular, attractive features, the light brown skin, the offended or amused flash in the dark eyes.

–Because of cretins like you, said Albert calmly. This is Hisham. He may be an Arab, but he speaks better English than you do.

–Tell him to get me a beer.

Ben stood there, pale as a corpse, with a split lip. –You nearly killed her, I'm a witness to that. If it hadn't been for me she'd have bled to death.

Jim shook his head dully. He could only summon up vague outlines, Mae on the sofa with the telephone in her hand, nothing more than a nosebleed or a cut, and then he'd gone back into the kitchen. Had he had a knife in his hand? He'd stayed in the kitchen until Ben came through the door. He tried to remember, shook his head, and stood up. There was the sound of rain outside, he thought of the cat down there, and looked at Albert. –Okay, so tell me what you want.

Albert glanced over at Ben with a look of satisfaction. –For a start, the money you owe me, he said, and then we'll give you a little something to take away with you, how about that?

He slept uneasily. Once he woke up because he felt his heart was beating too slowly. He got out of bed and fetched a woolen blanket from the built-in cupboard; it had a musty, slightly doggy smell. Human or dog hair, his fingers searched and found some short hairs. The smell was penetrating, but he was freezing cold. He couldn't get warm. Hisham had come down the stairs with him, silent but polite, had almost spoken as they parted, with something in his eyes that resembled pity. Perhaps he too had seen the cat lying dead not far from the threshold; it had lost some more blood, as though someone had torn its wound open again.

Jim didn't ask himself whether he was being followed. He had gone by underground as far as King's Cross, had crossed over Pentonville Road and walked to Field Street, paying no attention to the people hanging around in the street, but out of the corner of his eye he had noticed a young woman. Younger than Mae. The stuff that Albert had given him would be easy to sell in Camden. Near the canal he had seen a fox that had calmly trotted straight past him and vanished through a hole in the fence onto a patch of waste ground that bordered the canal. That had been in Camden Street. He had paused for a minute, considered hailing a taxi; the pain in his arm was almost unbearable.

Once he was home he searched for some painkillers, but found only an empty packet. The living room was strewn with empty beer cans, clothes, dirty underwear. He gathered up socks with his right hand, knocked a beer can over and used a T-shirt to mop up any of the liquid that hadn't immediately soaked into the carpet. He had to open the window and let in some fresh air. Buy yourself some flowers, he thought derisively.

The following afternoon, on his way back from the laun-derette with a bagful of clean washing, he stopped at the flower stall by Kentish Town station and bought a few carna-tions, and a lily that cost only a pound. He couldn't locate a vase. He held the lily in his hand, found a place for the carna-tions in a beer glass, and sniffed the white bloom but didn't care for the smell. It was already starting to wilt. He washed the dishes and stowed beer away in the fridge, as well as sliced bread, cheese, eggs, and a packet of ham.

He and Mae had spent that last afternoon in the room in Field Street. They had quarreled. It was a funny thing, memo-ry, it always seemed to be lurking somewhere just out of reach.

Outside his window he could see a little girl stooping to pick something up, her hair, dark and stringy from the rain, hanging down over her face. She took a few hesitant steps, then stopped as if she didn't know where to go. He watched her attentively. She was wearing only a thin green sweater that was too big for her, the sleeves covered her hands, and her face looked pale and pinched. She seemed to be looking out for somebody, craning her neck, even standing on tiptoe, but nobody came and eventually she disappeared from view. Jim felt angry, as though she had gone off with something that belonged to him.

By the evening, when he went out to sell some of the stuff, he was still in a bad mood. Not a good omen, he thought, and crossed himself superstitiously.

Around noon the next day, at the Kentish Town stations, he saw the "missing" notices with the picture of Mae.

18

J akob handed her a list, sent to him by his Aunt Fini, of furniture that had belonged to his grandparents and greataunts: Isabelle need only put a cross against the things she wanted to take to London. As she was unable to decipher the old-style German handwriting, Jakob made her a fair copy, though it turned out shorter than the original because he left out the annotations regarding previous owners, color, and the condition of the polish. The furniture, along with cutlery, china, and bed linen, would be loaded up in Frankfurt and dispatched to London, and Jakob would be there to receive it.
–You don't have to do a thing, he told her.

She drove him to the airport, and through the glass panels she could see him, with his newspaper, on the far side of the security checks; he turned around, but there were reflections in the glass and his eyes searched but could not find her.

The following day Maude was waiting at the door of the law firm to welcome him on Bentham's behalf. She shared a room with Alistair's secretary Annie, a plump little creature with a snub nose, who would also be handling Jakob's mail. Mr. Krapohl, who was afflicted with a constant snuffle and a slight squint, offered him his services, holding in his hand a piece of paper on which book orders were noted down in tiny writing, and at five o'clock Maude tapped on his door on the third floor to bring him tea and scones. Through the window he could hear the steady swish of the February rain.

–We're off to the pub, Alistair called out to him after the

day's work had ended, and waited in the hall, his left foot worrying at a thinning patch of carpet, his thoughts already elsewhere. Bentham wouldn't be back in the office until the end of the week, Jakob eventually gathered; apparently there was nothing unusual in this. Outside the pub two of his future colleagues were already waiting, Paul and Anthony, who pushed him through the door, drank to his health, and soon switched from beer to whisky, carelessly stuffing their ties into their jacket pockets; the pub's dirty red carpet exuded a slightly sour smell. At eleven they were standing in the drizzle out in the street, where a girl joined them and gave Paul a lingering kiss on the mouth. Jakob was drunk. Alistair and Anthony went off, whispering, Paul got his motorbike and sounded the horn. The moon was creeping out from behind the roofs, Jakob fancied that he could smell the sea, and there was the girl back again, kissing Paul and then skipping over to Jakob, who by this time was sitting on the curb watching cars going by without drivers. She was wearing a short fur coat and a miniskirt, her blond hair was falling into Jakob's face, all three of them were laughing and bending over him. –Hey, everything okay? Paul was back again with his motorbike. Jakob turned away with a groan. The girl flinched when he abruptly raised his hand, –no worries! Alistair shouted to him, hauling him to his feet and pushing him into a taxi.

On his third day Annie knocked and brought him a kettle and a teapot, and Maude, coming in behind her, said that he should just tell them if he needed anything—a desk lamp, another chair instead of that ridiculous old chest, a blanket. The heating did its best, around midday some steam came whistling out of a valve for half an hour, then it was quiet again. Through the floor Jakob could sometimes hear music coming from Alistair's room, Bach or John Zorn, Alistair told him. He was contacted by his first client, a Mr. Miller, who was dissatisfied with the solicitor who had been handling his claim for the restitution of a house in Treptow. When Jakob went for a walk in his lunch break he often got lost in the little streets between Devonshire Street and Wigmore Street. A second client, a fork-lift truck manufacturer from Hamm, was interested in buying a British railway company and asked Jakob to meet him at Liverpool Street Station. They sat in a poorly lit café on the lower level of the station, and Jakob leafed desperately through a stack of documents that Mr. Krapohl had printed out for him, including several articles on the history of the English railway system. The weather continued to be horrible; Jakob was usually the first to arrive at the office, he loved his room even while he shivered with cold, and the house in Lady Margaret Road was still empty and uninviting. He was expecting the furniture at the weekend.

The moving van turned up in the afternoon, blocking the whole street when the driver abruptly pulled across to the right-hand side of the road; a car coming the opposite way only just managed to brake in time. The car driver seemed to be in a state of shock. He was an elderly man, who got out of his car with difficulty, holding onto the door with both hands and staring at the lorry with the German license plate, where there was no sign of any movement in the cab. Jakob, meanwhile, was standing on the ground floor, rattling at the windows because he had forgotten how to release the sashes; finally he dashed out into the road in his socks and rushed up to the old man, whose thin white hair was lifting in the breeze, the parchment-like skin reddening on his cheeks, but as Jakob started to apologize he gave a dignified shake of the head, vanished into the interior of his Austin and switched on the ignition. Furious and ashamed, Jakob turned around. The van driver was maneuvering, fortunately the road was empty now, but then a little girl suddenly appeared and was on the point of running out in front of the vehicle, when Jakob grabbed her by the arm; she was a pale little thing in a red woolly hat, with big gray eyes, who shrank back nervously, gazed intently at him, trying to make out what he wanted of her, and then ducked as though afraid of being punished. The moving men clambered down from the cab, shouting out a jumble of comments and excuses, the girl broke away, and there were Alistair and Paul and Anthony, waving, coming to lend a hand and celebrate his move into the house. –Not bad, said Alistair, looking around approvingly. Jakob's grandmother's Biedermeier chest of drawers was already standing in the street, one drawer had come open and was overflowing with old photos that Aunt Fini had never cleared out. A cabinet almost tipped over sideways; it had already acquired a scratch. Alistair was in discussion with a policeman, who was leaning out of his car window. The girl had disappeared. –The furniture first! Jakob called out tensely as the others marched up to the front door, all six of them, with Alistair at their head, arm in arm with one of the movers, laughing.

They had distributed themselves over the various floors, offering advice; the light-colored carpet was showing the first signs of dampness, a patch was spreading where Anthony had put down his umbrella. Isabelle's workroom now contained the chest of drawers, a secretaire, and a round table that was to be her drawing table. The room next to it had a sofa, two small armchairs with black-and-white-striped covers, and another little table. The big dining table and set of six chairs went up to the first floor, along with a glass-fronted bookcase and a sideboard, while the double bed and the cabinet with the scratch-mark were carried up to the second. –Wow, said Paul, you'll be living in style, won't you? He was holding a square mirror with a narrow black frame, which he set down carefully in the hall.

At last, each piece of furniture was where it belonged, he had put away the china, the washing machine was connected, and, as if to see how it felt, he sat and ate in the dining room, with a glass in front of him, a bottle of wine and a small bowl of rice crackers. They crunched between his teeth, the only sound breaking the silence. At night he was sometimes so restless that he had to get up, go over to the window and take deep breaths of the damp February air. Cats wandered across the road; once a white fox trotted along the pavement before jumping onto a wall and disappearing. The evening before Isabelle's arrival Jakob saw the little girl with the red woolly hat walking by the side of a youth in Kentish Town Road, carrying a bag of chips. As he turned into Lady Margaret Road he almost collided with somebody whose light-colored anorak came out of nowhere with the suddenness of a flashbulb going off, making Jakob blink, and the man hissed something with such venom that he was momentarily alarmed. The plane trees were still bare, but the cherry trees and the tulips were already in bloom. –So your young wife is coming tomorrow, Maude had said; he found the expression overdone and a bit kitschy, and it struck him that he was almost as impatient for Bentham's coming as he was for Isabelle's.

–She's going off tomorrow to join her husband in London, the secretary, Sonja, had told a client over the phone that lunchtime. But it's the right decision, Isabelle thought to herself. When she came back to Berlin for a visit in a few weeks' time she would find everything just as she had left it, both the office and the apartment, so there was nothing to worry about, even though her mother had phoned again out of the blue to ask her whether it wasn't dangerous in London given that war with Iraq might break out any day, and Andras, an unwilling eavesdropper on the conversation, pulled a disgusted face as he heard Isabelle's soothing phrases. –Good Lord, it's not Baghdad you're going to. She packed her laptop, Peter had found out the dial-up number she would need in London; he was still making improvements to their Web site, –it's nothing much to look at yet, he muttered, and Isabelle promised to send a picture of her workroom as soon as she arrived. –It's full of Biedermeier furniture, Andras said, grinning. There were always some little snide remarks before somebody went away. –Our numbers are dwindling, said Peter. Sonja looked at him, her face twisted for a moment, and bent over her newspaper again. The article was headed "War Almost Unavoidable Now." Troops being deployed, tanks, arms procurement, intensified security precautions, Washington on orange alert. Isabelle, clearing out her desk drawers, came upon a photograph of Hanna, black and white, her face already gaunt, like a view of a village, she suddenly thought, the angles of the houses standing out with unnatural sharpness against a darker background. Then the photographs that Alexa had taken of her: after moving to Wartburgstrasse she had brought the box to the office. Isabelle leaned sideways to prevent Andras, who was watching her closely, from seeing the pictures. Cut off above the mouth, the red toweling underwear, the stomach protruding a little, and she had her thighs slightly apart: it aroused her to see how obscene the photos were. –What's that? asked Andras. Child pornography? She could not help laughing to see his face, malicious, troubled. When shall I pick you up tomorrow? he asked.

At home there was almost nothing more to do. Three big suitcases were standing in the hall, the fridge was empty, there were some crumbs on the white-tiled floor, but after she had gone the cleaning lady would clear everything up and post the key to the office, there was a padded envelope waiting, already stamped and addressed. The telephone rang, to Isabelle it almost seemed inappropriate to answer it, and it was Ginka, the telephone rang again and it was Alexa, and then Hans called to ask her again how often he should check her post. She drank half a bottle of red wine and wished that Jakob were coming to fetch her.

Then it was already morning: she was woken by Andras's ring at the door. He came up the stairs with some food he had bought for their breakfast, sullen and tense. Isabelle vanished into the bathroom. He started to make a pot of espresso, and took cups and plates from the kitchen cupboards. The fridge was empty apart from a jar of capers. Goodbyes were never more than casual here. He thought of his Budapest relatives and their kisses, the swelling clamor of any departure that could be interpreted as a parting, the countless people who would form a procession on the way to the airport or railway station, even on the way to the front door if he was only going out to supper with someone. –Where you are, in Germany, his mother said, even the dead just steal quietly away. Tears came to her eyes whenever she thought of Uncle Janos and Aunt Sofi, their deathbeds and their funerals, of which she didn't have any photographs, and there were no letters, no lists of people who had sent flowers, not a vestige of a wave of farewell left hanging in the air. He didn't want Isabelle to go. He wanted her to understand what it meant to part, to be parting from him, who might go back to Budapest after all. As she emerged from the bathroom their eyes met. Something was different. For the first instant he feared he had angered her; then an absurd hope leapt up within him, a timorous joy that made his heart stand still. But no.

She would not stay. And into her eyes there came a look of hostility, of tension.

After Isabelle had passed through the security checks, Andras went out into the cold February wind and stood around until a bus driver, an older man with a walrus moustache, asked if he needed help. Andras nodded, smiling, then politely declined the offer and boarded the next bus.

At the office he found a note from Sonja: Magda had phoned. He went to her place for supper and stayed. When, at six the next morning, he got up quietly so as not to wake her and went on his way through the darkness, he suddenly knew what he had seen in Isabelle's face, and he walked with his head bowed against the wind and rain, bowed because he could not bear the determination in her eyes, the implacable aimlessness. She was already in London.

19

The aircraft made a soft landing, the tarmac sped away beneath the wheels, and then, just when it all seemed to be over, the plane suddenly started to weave from side to side, and a sharp lurch to the right brought a startled gasp from the passengers, people who in their own minds had already collected their luggage from the carousels and hurried towards the exits to meet their friends and relatives, no longer passengers but travelers who had arrived, who were leaving the airport terminal behind them and forgetting, instantly forgetting their vague fears and the precarious security situation. Terrorists, somebody whispered and was echoed by a second and a third voice, one passenger let out a short, anguished scream; the stewardesses in their seat belts were swaying, rocking from side to side, making incomprehensible signs. The plane was still weaving, then swerved sharply to the right, –brace, brace! instructed an agitated voice over the intercom, but Isabelle craned to look out of the window, saw a fire tender, then another, could not decide whether the roar of the engines had grown louder. Another shout over the intercom, unintelligible this time, followed by a crackling sound; a stewardess leapt to her feet and seized the microphone, but although her mouth was clearly moving, only one row in front of Isabelle, she was inaudible, and Isabelle's fear had something sudden and intensely stimulating about it. She gesticulated, the stewardess gesticulated towards Isabelle, who was still sitting bolt upright but finally lowered her head obediently, with a sense of triumph that outweighed her fear. At last a voice came over the intercom, –this is your captain speaking; foam, thought Isabelle, they could prepare the runway with foam. Absolutely no cause for alarm, simply a problem with our landing gear, please keep your seat belts fastened, we shall shortly be arriving at our gate. But something was smoking, Isabelle saw. The other passengers seemed to breathe a sigh of relief; some sat up again and started talking and laughing. The plane was still taxiing, then it seemed to sag and collapsed towards the right, but so slowly that it only scraped along the tarmac for a few yards, the wing possibly damaged, describing an arc, leaving a scar behind. Isabelle held on tight to the armrest, Jakob, she thought, he was waiting, not knowing what was happening to her. At last the plane came to a standstill, propped on one wing, tilted so that the passengers, like jointed dolls bent out of shape, leaned to the right in their seat belts, folded over one another. They would be evacuated using the chute, the stewardess told them, a safety measure in case there was any risk of an explosion, though that was extremely unlikely, and then something cracked—the passengers' self-control as they staggered from their seats and pushed towards the emergency exit, where a man was now standing, making signs to them. Isabelle was one of the last to be solicitously placed on the orange chute, and she slid down, almost enjoying it, as though this was truly the moment of her arrival in London. Although she had spent some time at a college in south London, she hardly knew anything of the city beyond the student hostel where she had had to stay: narrow corridors infested with cockroaches, filthy wash basins and stinking toilets. A smell that made you catch your breath. She had described it graphically to Jakob, cigarette butts, stale fat, carpets moldy where the rain leaked in through ill-fitting windows. At night, seven of them squeezing into one of the tiny rooms, vodka until they were drunk, throwing up on the carpet, coming late to class, which did not bother the teachers so long as the fees were paid, so long as they drew, and submitted some sort of portfolio.

The passengers were all talking at once now, excited, relieved, elbowing their way onto the buses, some complaining about the delay, others ridiculing their impatience; a bottle of perfume broke inside the bus. The luggage was to be unloaded right away, but instead of waiting, suddenly overcome with longing, Isabelle hurried out into the arrivals hall. Jakob was there. Something had permeated through to those outside, some sort of agitation, and he clasped her violently to him and did not let go. Then they stood there, uncertain what to do next. –Your luggage, shall we have it sent on, what happened anyway, how will you get back into the baggage hall? Trolleys full of luggage, children, airport staff in a hurry, business people, all went purposefully past them, families more slowly and cumbrously than the rest, with dolls, children's backpacks and small bags that tumbled off the trolleys, mothers with babies in their arms, and then came a whole sports club in blue jerseys and white track suit bottoms. Taking Isabelle gently by the shoulders, he turned her towards him and kissed her. –Let's go home, she urged him. She felt his hands, his breath. But then he looked away to speak to a man in uniform, and Isabelle was allowed back to the carousels, which were carrying her suitcases around and around, and she felt quite flat as she re-emerged with the cases.

–Now we'll go home, Jakob promised her, as he pushed the trolley. –Home, and then to a pub, and in between we can go for a walk. He had the whole afternoon off: Maude had sent him packing, even though he protested because Bentham was expected back in the office that afternoon. –Your wife's first day here! Maude was adamant. The taxi driver stowed the cases carefully in the boot. Though the sky was clear, the sun was pale, the countryside still dull. The trees bare, with only a light veil of green, nothing to warm the heart. Isabelle's hand sought his. –And Andras, was he very sad? The transition was proving unexpectedly difficult, Jakob felt, and was relieved when they reached the suburbs, houses that gave them a reason to look out of the windows, then, in Golders Green, shops and Orthodox Jews with their black hats, and Jakob pointed out a little girl pushing a huge pram; and there, at last, further south, were the hills of Hampstead Heath.

Handing the keys over to Isabelle—the taxi had already driven off—he carried the cases to the door. The lock was troublesome. Isabelle poked around half-heartedly with the key, pulled it out a little and pushed it back in, pressing herself up against the doorframe, and then turned round to Jakob. She had missed him, she suddenly realized; he was standing there smiling, not even noticing how long she was having to fiddle with the door, running his hand through his tousled, reddish fair hair. She had missed him; what she felt was something barely perceptible and new to her, and some day, she thought, some day she would know what it meant. Then at last the key slid into exactly the right position, and she went inside, holding the door open for him. –Where's my room? Jakob was still in the doorway, smiling, looking at her expectantly.

But she didn't reach out her hand, didn't draw him to her, didn't look for the bed that had to be somewhere, their conjugal bed. Yes, Andras had been very sad; for a moment she felt it as plainly as if the sadness had been her own. Then a sharp pulling away. Gone.

She opened the door on the right, glanced into her workroom, smiled: flowers on the table, the whole effect, she thought, the way you would like a guest house to be, old-fashioned, cozy.

–Your domain, Jakob said, waiting for her reaction, detached. And upstairs, the living and dining room and the kitchen. Like a repeated telephone message. I'll take your cases up in a minute. He was relieved that outside—Isabelle was looking out of the window—the little girl had not appeared, hobgoblin-like, creepy.

–What kind of trees are those?

–Plane trees.

Still leafless, their trunks patchy, the branches lopped. A car drove by, looking as though its left and right sides were reversed.

–It's as if no one were driving them, she exclaimed. Are we going to go out?

–Across the park and right down to the Thames, if you like.

–Isn't that too far?

–Not really, but we can go part of the way by underground. We need to get a passport photo of you for a photo card, and a monthly ticket, so you can travel as much as you like.

Isabelle unpacked her computer, listening as she did so to a noise that came not from above but from the side: it seemed one could hear the neighbors, their voices, an object bumping into something, being moved across the floor, a piece of furniture, or was it only Jakob after all?

She ran upstairs. Plenty of wardrobes, ample space for more clothes. –Sit down on the bed, she said, till I've unpacked, and tell me how you're getting on.

There he sat. She busily arranged things in the wardrobes, sorting his shirts into piles of light and dark-colored ones, for everyday use and for more special occasions, shirts for which he might or might not have cuff links, and although one wardrobe door came off its track and almost fell on Isabelle and then on Jakob—he leapt up and guided it back onto its track—she worked cheerfully and efficiently, belts over there, a drawer for socks and underwear here. He was sitting on the bed again. A ray of light slid through the window, passing across her face. Her hair was tied back with a black elastic band. She bent down towards the suitcase, straightened up, stretched. By this time he had told her about the firm's offices, though not his own room, and about Maude, the first evening at the pub, the square not far from the office, the pigeons there, and the old woman who fed them each morning, taking stale bread out of plastic bags, crumbling it and shouting abuse at passersby. The first buds; the way Regent's Park was coming to life. Just a few more weeks, then they must go to Kew Gardens when the rhododendrons were in bloom; it was right next to the Thames. He watched Isabelle in her tight jeans and blue sweater, her bottom in constant motion as she bent over, straightened up, a step to the right, a step to the left, precise as a figurine on a musical box: he wanted to reach out and touch it or ask her to keep still for a moment. Finally she went off into the bathroom, set out her face cream and deodorant and toothpaste on the shelf between the wash basin and the mirror, stood her shampoo on the edge of the bath, and found places for her other bits and pieces. Then her face appeared again, just as it would appear countless more times from behind a door, familiar, growing familiar of its own accord, without her intending it. He felt a sudden, stabbing sensation of habit, of love. But also of uncertainty, he reflected, because habit covered only part of the ground: other parts it only washed over for a time before having to retreat again because something still remained unpredictable.

At least *things* should return to their proper places, he thought, houses to those they belong to, plots of land to their rightful owners. Upheavals could be overcome and injustices redressed, because human beings were not *just* human beings (all too transient and careless and vulnerable, helplessly naked even under the protective layer of functioning laws), but also legal subjects. Justice, he reflected, existed only where it could take on material form, in land-registry entries, contracts of sale, notarized certificates, a thin thread that could be taken up and followed. Now Isabelle was putting away her own clothes, her blouses next to his shirts, her sweaters; she hesitated, different piles, bright colors. She had come to London with him. When he thought now of his travels in Brandenburg in the early nineties, of his elation at finding a clue, an important entry that could alter the outcome of a claim, he could see that although he had been naïve, he had nevertheless got to the heart of the matter. There was no such thing as justice in the abstract, but there was something like a state of justice that he wanted to help restore. People were given back their rights because they were legal subjects, part of a fabric woven of laws and history. He held fast to the idea of bringing order to things, even if he could not provide healing. Possessions were intermingled because people's lives were intermingled. Any violent separation must be prevented, or failing that its effects must be reversed. For the last time Isabelle bent down to the third suitcase. Jakob lightly ran his thumb over his wedding ring. Then she snapped the case shut. Now he could stop thinking about the neighbors' little girl, whose pale face he found so disturbing: his route between home and the office was different now, no hobgoblin popping up, and his life was that of a married man. *Of good character and deserving of the protection of the law*, as it said in Fieberg and Reichenbach's introduction to the law of property, even if not acting *in good faith*. He smiled inwardly at this injustice towards himself: he would do his best. Any change produced a state of affairs that was still confused, not yet ordered. He was on the point of telling Isabelle about his room at the law firm, and about Bentham himself, when she straightened up, with a laugh of surprise. How childlike and soft her chin was. She came towards him.

–Just think: I've forgotten to pack any shoes. She held her hands up. Empty. Behind her forehead, clear to see and yet insubstantial, impalpable, her thoughts and desires. She came closer to him, put her arms around his head, felt his soft hair, so much thinner than her own, he seemed vulnerable. The sun, low in the sky and just reaching over the wall of a small garden, was now shining straight into the room; a siren came nearer and died away again. He embraced her hips, his fingers feeling along the seams of her jeans. Patch pockets. Studs. How soft the skin underneath was when he opened the zip, and finally pulled the jeans down a little; his fingers paused there uncertainly, and then even softer skin, concealed, deceptive, he thought, as if touching it were an illusion; the tenderness of his kisses, while his thoughts roamed aimlessly. He wished she were not so pretty. Andras would have kissed her no differently, he thought, but she belonged to him, she stood before him, silently, and then suddenly he fell back onto the bed, and pulled her down with him.

They walked down the street hand in hand, past the greengrocers' and newsagents' shops, the boards with the *Evening Standard* headlines, the newspaper stands, and it was already starting to get dark; inspectors recalled, results of the latest opinion polls. *Our intelligence officials estimate that Saddam Hussein had the materials to produce as much as 500 tons of sarin, mustard and VX nerve agent. In such quantities, these chemical agents could also kill untold thousands. He's not accounted for these materials*, Jakob read in a magazine, while Isabelle sat in the photo booth, turning the stool to raise and lower it, but surely that's old news, he thought, that's the speech Bush made in January. The most difficult decision of my life, was that Blair? And from Turkey the news that it would not after all allow sixty-two thousand soldiers to cross its territory en route to Iraq. And again and again the weather, the danger posed by the heat. Sandstorms. The bodies squeezed into their protective suits. The curtain moved aside, Isabelle put one foot out of the booth, cautiously feeling for the floor, one hand on the rotating stool, then she straightened up and came and stood beside him. She glanced at one of the headlines and flinched. Behind the counter the assistant raised his head and scrutinized them with black, hard eyes. *The materials to produce as much as 500 tons of sarin, mustard and VX nerve agent,* Jakob read as the photo, slightly wavy, came out of the chute, and hung suspended in the warm air, the sound of the fan barely audible above the noise from the street outside. *What does the whole of our history teach us, I mean British history in particular? That if when you're faced with a threat you decide to avoid confronting it in the short term, then all that happens is that in the longer term you have to confront it and confront it in an even more deadly form.* Then the photos were dry, Isabelle smiling four times over in happy anticipation, –you can give me one, said Jakob, for my wallet, and they crossed the road. Isabelle filled out the form while Jakob paid, pocketed the change, and in the meantime the escalator had stopped working, so that they had to walk down the hundred and seventy-five steps of the spiral staircase. But they had barely reached the platform when out of the narrow tunnel a train arrived, gathered them up; warmth and measured speed, and bored faces side by side, swaying with the movements of the train, a sudden jerk now and then restoring the balance of face, neck and torso. They managed to get seats next to each other, their hands touched, they were tired and—with the tiny distrust induced by too great proximity—deeply connected and yet filled with a desire to move apart. Imperceptibly Isabelle shifted her weight from right to left. Her face reddened by the stuffy heat, she edged away from Jakob, who was watching the illuminated sign with the letters moving across it, suddenly afraid that instead of the name of the next station he might see *Warning. Terrorist alert.* The train jerked and came to a halt between stations, started moving again, and Jakob, too, pulled himself together, his face became firmer, more manly, and then there was the name Charing Cross and they got out. It was already dark, the busy lights of the cars, shops, cafés distorted the contours of things, there were pockets of turbulence, and as they were touched, jostled, looked at, they were torn out of their own life and thrust into something both futuristic and medieval, a milling throng of travelers, traders, thieves, street vendors crying their wares, beggars and mad people. The businessmen, unresting, their faces giving nothing away. The roaring acceleration of monstrously large buses, the stumbling, hurried but then lingering steps of indecisive people on the way to nowhere. Again and again Jakob and Isabelle were forced apart; he felt he had nothing to offer her, and began to be uneasy. It started to drizzle, the raindrops splintered the lights, but Isabelle seemed not to notice; he wanted to go shopping for shoes with her, perhaps walk past the office to show her where he worked. She was swept past him, then waited, and rubbed up against him when people coming the other way pushed her into him, turning her head this way and that, her lips slightly parted, like a little cousin whom one has invited for the weekend for some reason already forgotten, to pacify relatives whom one doesn't care about anyway, or because it seemed a nice idea to show such a very young woman around the city, and then a little erotic confusion has sprung up to complicate that straightforward relationship. Isabelle turned off to the right, into a side street, called to him, ran a few steps ahead, lured him on, hid behind a car, with a kind of high spirits that was both provocative and alien to him, and then—only one block away from Devonshire Street—she headed for a restaurant and pushed the door wide open with both hands, as though putting something to the test, and he followed her. Bentham and Alistair were sitting at the table nearest the door. For an interminable moment Jakob saw them both turning inquisitive eyes on Isabelle; she stumbled, a waiter dashed towards her, followed by another, and between them they pushed Jakob into the background, as the door swung to behind him. He noticed when Alistair, having gazed his fill at Isabelle, at her skimpy mint-green skirt and her trainers (they hadn't bought any shoes, Jakob thought guiltily), suddenly caught sight of him and his blond head shot up in surprise and amusement, while Isabelle handed one of the waiters her rain-jacket and her short T-shirt came into view, white, washed-out-looking. Jakob found himself standing in front of Bentham like a schoolboy. He could feel himself blushing. –I hope your whole walk hasn't been so hurried, remarked Bentham as he rose carefully to his feet, holding his heavy body in a precarious equilibrium above the plates on the table and extending a not very large hand first to Isabelle and then to Jakob. His touch was warm and comforting, at last Jakob was able to smile and murmur something; the eyes looking attentively at him were faded, the brown irises ringed with pale violet. A menu was held under Jakob's nose and a bottle of wine placed on the table; Bentham made a slight gesture and mumbled something that Jakob did not catch, but the waiters understood it at once and filled the glasses.

–Regent's Park is to be recommended at any time of year, but of course it often rains, said Bentham, looking at Alistair and Isabelle, who were standing uncertainly side by side, and Bentham stood up and made a hint of a bow. Isabelle took a seat; she was like a little training dinghy gathering speed, delightful, girlish, an optimist with a fair wind, and then Alistair said something, made some proposal that Isabelle agreed to and Bentham agreed to, but Jakob had been looking at Bentham and had heard nothing.

Some sound or other would wake her in the mornings, when the other half of the bed had already cooled down and the quilt was hanging stiffly over the side. She never knew what it was, and later, after she had gone down to the ground floor, she would hear the neighbors making a noise, not every day, but often enough for her to expect it. When the wind blew, it made the windows rattle. It was already early March, there were more and more signs of spring, and further opinion polls were being published on the question of war in Iraq; she would buy the *Guardian* at the kiosk next to the tube station, there was a food store in Falkland Road, and it was not far to the Sainsbury's supermarket in Camden Town. Ginka phoned, so did Alexa, even her father, all asking whether, with the American and British invasion of Iraq imminent, things weren't getting too dangerous, and whether she used the underground: it was inevitable, her father said, that something would happen, sooner or later. Jakob tried not to get home too late from the office. Alistair was their first dinner guest, and Isabelle gave him chicken with peas in mint sauce: she hadn't known that there really was such a thing as mint sauce. They would be getting an invitation from Bentham, Jakob said, and he bought a dark blue suit and two Paul Smith shirts; though they had been to Regent Street, Isabelle was still running around in trainers, which had turned grey beyond recognition in a week. Fruit trees were in blossom; there were flowers in the park and in the little front gardens, and daffodils in faded window boxes on the sill outside their bedroom. –It's snowing here, said Andras over the phone. I'm looking out of the window, those are snowflakes. We're overrun with clients. Everything's going along just the same as before, isn't that wonderful?

Now Jakob saw Bentham every day. He did not arrive before eleven, sat in Maude's room, then in the library with Mr. Krapohl, and eventually climbed the stairs, slowly, with heavy steps (he never used the lift), and stopped at Jakob's door, mumbling something, polite but not inviting closeness, a dancing bear who kept his skills to himself. At five o'clock Maude would bring a tray with a glass of hot milk and honey, because Bentham could not stand tea, not in the afternoon: he was, he told Jakob, an old man with an old voice, hot milk and honey

did it good, and Maude forbade him to drink whisky before
six. His jacket fitted tightly around his bulging stomach; he
had very small feet. All day long the telephone rang, and
Maude announced the names of the callers like a master of cer-
emonies, but she could only be heard by anyone who just happened to be on the stairs, and then she would press various
buttons, crossly, edgily, and often the clients had to call back
several times. –They do phone again, Alistair grinned, as you
see. And indeed they did, undaunted, full of hope, wanting
Bentham and his firm to settle matters that in other hands
dragged on endlessly or remained unresolved. –We don't
appear in court, naturally, and normally we don't even con-
clude the agreements, we just draft them, Alistair explained.
Bentham hates endless negotiations, he makes suggestions and
the client gets another lawyer to implement them, or not, as the
case may be. Bentham doesn't really care which. Maybe that's
why it works so well. But we need to have somebody in
Germany to push things through on the spot, and in court, if
that's what it takes.

But even where the cases in Germany were concerned,
Bentham did not seem inclined to hurry. –Don't rush, he
advised Jakob, go for walks with your wife, Maude will tell you
if there's anything urgent. You see, Bentham said, I simply
don't know if I should really wish it on somebody like Miller
to go and live in Berlin. What does he think he'll do there, at
sixty-five—build up a business? Devote himself to chasing
rental income? It's nearly always the wealthy people who still
hanker after their property, at any rate it's only the wealthy who
come to us, and they won't accept a settlement or compensation. Lonely people, very often, and the cases drag on. But you
shouldn't feel the need to rush, the way I expect you do in
Berlin.

Even so, Jakob stayed in the office until evening, until
Alistair or Bentham came to his room and packed him off

home. If Isabelle was disappointed, she did not show it. These nights, Jakob sometimes could not sleep and wondered whether she was also lying there awake. A person's breathing could be deceptive. It was as if each was secretly observing the other with the aid of a mirror. In the next few days Alistair was planning to show her the Soane Collection, which could be viewed once a month by candlelight; Jakob would be meeting a client and might join them later. Alexa had arranged to visit them and then cancelled, but Isabelle seemed not to mind too much. She worked during the day, or walked around the city, and he liked it when she told him over supper where she had been: she already knew London better than he did. Just for a moment, before he did drop off to sleep after all, the thought flashed through his mind that one could make a conscious decision to be happy, and, already half asleep, he saw nothing to cast doubt on that idea.

In the morning he was woken by the noise of an aircraft, which sounded as if it was laboriously scraping a gash in the sky. The weather was fine.

20

He ran along the corridor, past coats, cardboard boxes, empty drinks crates; for a moment the noises grew fainter, the music and voices from the dance floor, and Jim grinned: just a few more minutes, then the cops would arrive and the yelling would start, howls of anguish as if they were massacring the innocents, and now some idiot had turned up the PA system so high that any cry of warning, however loud, would go unheard. The doorman, who knew Albert and knew that Jim worked for him, had tipped him off. Some slime ball, he'd said with a grin, was earning himself a few pounds by passing on times and places to the police, who were only too glad to get their hands on whatever they could: coke, hash, a bit of speed and ecstasy, and with luck the dealer, too. Probably the doorman himself was the informer, Jim thought. But he didn't care either way, and he'd sold all the stuff that Albert had provided him with. Now he could here more noise, street noise this time; there was an open window somewhere, behind one of these doors, the guy had said, three were shut, the fourth one was open. He recoiled in fright: some joker had propped up a skeleton in front of the table and strung fairy lights along its right arm. Little bulbs climbing up its arm like insects. So here was the window, with cardboard where there ought to be panes of glass, and Jim slipped out.

Outside, a not very high wall, rubbish, cars, a workshop by the look of it. He ran a few yards, half-heartedly. Wet pavement, puddles, water splashing up, the night densely black and heavy with rain, the cars struggling to make any headway. In the pocket of his denim jacket he could feel the money. He'd seen the poster with the photo of Mae, Albert had had it put up in Kentish Town station, –so that you don't forget us, he'd said when Jim phoned him, raging. I wanted to make sure you'd ring, he'd told him, you can't give up a long working relationship like ours just like that, can you? And Jim had fallen into line. He wouldn't leave London without first having found Mae. As long as he could stay in Lady Margaret Road. Until Damian came back, he thought. As long as nobody tracked him down there.

The boy, Dave, who lived with his parents at number 47, was the only person he sometimes talked to. There was something about him that he liked. Next door, at number 49, a fairly young couple had moved in, certainly not new customers for him, not the husband, anyway, but the wife had caught Jim's eye, even though he had so far seen her only from behind, in a pert little raincoat and trainers: about as tall as Mae, and his heart had given a lurch when he saw her. Very similar in build. They had moved in in grand style, with furniture and packing cases that had china and possibly books in them. Jim had never been interested in how other people did that kind of thing, moving house, moving in, getting sorted out, all the boxes, all the things from the boxes piled up around you, so that in the midst of them you were safe and snug, but now it suddenly hit him. They had moved in, the two of them together, as if in an embrace that fended off the rain and everything else as well. Jim had got used to Lady Margaret Road, to the little garden where the squirrels raced up the tree trunks when he opened the door, and in the evening there was the smell of supper being cooked by the people upstairs, who didn't say hello to him, probably because their experience with Damian had not been good.

Two days later, when he met Albert on the northern edge of

Soho, his thoughts tumbled out despite himself. –In a proper flat—not the sort of dump you always put us in—you can be quite a different sort of person, not the kind of idiot that comes running when somebody whistles. You think we're just waiting for somebody to whistle for us, don't you? You whistle, and Ben tries to, but you can't do that with me anymore. What I mean is, in a real flat you think of things that wouldn't other- wise occur to you, because when all's said and done you *are* a person, do you know what I mean? Not just some hunted rab- bit with terrified eyes, but a person who gets up in the morn- ing and washes or something and even thinks of going to church, the way he did as a kid, because he'd like to have God's blessing or have somebody praying for him. You sud- denly remember things, and all the shit is like a thick crust with something different underneath it that you'd just forgotten. You suddenly remember that when you were a kid you had a little dog, well, not really a dog of your own, but as good as, because he came running over to you every day and you'd saved something for him.

–When my restaurants are up and running, Albert said mendaciously, I'll give you a job and you can work for me as a chef.

–Yeah, right, Jim snarled, a chef turning out fried eggs.

–Why won't you let me have my little dream too? Albert whined, and Jim clenched his teeth: this damned sentimentali- ty, Albert's and his own, this whining. All the same, Albert would get what he wanted one day, but Jim wouldn't. Mae, he thought. But he didn't hate Albert. The fat, florid face sparked no feeling of hatred in him. –Don't forget . . . Albert began, –that you rescued me from the streets, Jim finished in disgust. Good old Albert, all heart. Then you sent me back onto the streets to stick my arse out for your friends.

Each time the pub door swung open there was the sound of the rain, and people came in with newspapers and had weighty discussions about what was going to happen, next week, and when the balloon would go up, and about the demonstration, and whether Blair was right or Blix, talking as if they were actually being asked their opinion before some poor sods had their brains blown out in the desert sands. It made no difference what people said, Jim thought. Once a person was dead, Jim thought, it was as if he had a false name and no address anymore. Albert's face was red and puffy. He was worrying again about the surveillance, because they had stopped Ben in the street and insisted on going to his place, luckily there hadn't been anyone there, but of course it was obvious that he didn't live there alone, in that hole in Brixton, only a stone's throw from Albert's office. –What about your Arab? asked Jim. Is he going to volunteer for the Iraq war and die fighting against his brothers? He emptied his glass; there was another pint already waiting for him on the bar because the barmaid fancied him, she was smiling sweetly, while Albert was pulling a face as if he'd bitten into something nasty, because Jim was blowing his cigarette smoke into his face and nose. –Just imagine how it'll be here, he said, you'll get on an underground train and not know if you're going to come out alive. Albert's obsession, since September 11th. –You can't wait for something to happen here too, can you? grinned Jim; he bumped backwards into a fat, cheery man who apologized profusely when Jim glowered at him as though he was about to pick a fight with him, and then withdrew with his girlfriend to the other end of the bar. Albert was still blathering on about what would happen. –You just try evacuating a whole city, or the trains below ground, especially if a tunnel has collapsed. Jim cut him off, he wanted to leave now and held out an envelope to him—the less unobtrusively it was done the safer it was, that was Albert's method, which had worked perfectly so far—and Albert took the money but said he didn't have anything with him for Jim, who was already holding out his hand and now stared at him, stunned at first, then angry. –Do see it from my point of view, there was that whining tone again, I have to think of the future. That was why he didn't have anything on him: Albert was having nothing more to do with drugs, was drinking his beer like a law-abiding citizen, collecting his money, leaving the legwork to other people, that was all, and Jim couldn't make a scene here, in the pub. Behind the horrific images he conjured up, Albert was preparing his own retreat, like a squirrel, safe and cozy, with ample provisions. Jim had gone pale. –If you think I'm going to your bloody office in Brixton again to fetch the gear myself, you've got another think coming. And the way Albert was soothing and placating him: these people, Jim thought to himself, who can contemplate all kinds of disasters because they're so sure that nothing will ever happen to *them*. –And I'm not meeting up with Ben either, Jim persisted. Finally they agreed that Hisham would phone Jim. –Have you seen the poster of Mae? Albert asked as they parted, patting Jim on the shoulder.

As he walked up Kentish Town Road, he looked through the windows of Pang's Garden and saw Dave, who was just ordering a bag of chips. When he went in, Dave beamed at him and embarked on some long rigmarole, as if Jim were somebody who could sort things out, five pounds that he'd nicked for his little sister, and all the shouting, and why he wasn't going home tonight, although he didn't yet know where he'd sleep because the boys who'd said he could go to their place had lain in wait and attacked him. Jim ordered a small portion of chips and a spring roll; they sat on the green bench by the window, the only customers who didn't go straight out again but stayed inside to eat, idly observing the four or five Chinese who were doing some cooking or cleaning behind the counter and watching television at the same time. Then a trap door opened in the low ceiling, and three women climbed unsteadily down an extending ladder. –The 'tween deck, Jim casually remarked to the boy, they breed like rabbits up there, and then they come down and spread everywhere. Dave looked at him, taken aback, and after a second said boldly: –But they're really nice here. They've often given me food for my sister. The old man, probably the owner, was sitting in front of the television, spooning up a bowl of soup, while his wife polished the pans and their two sons whispered together.

Dave sat there, very straight, thinking of the first time he had seen Jim, in here: two of the boys from his school had been waiting outside, prepared to hang around until morning, banging on the window every so often, and Jim had immediately grasped what was going on. There was a smell of hot fat, but that was okay, and Dave had come here every day to meet Jim again, buying a bag of chips when he had the money. Then he met Jim in the street, in Lady Margaret Road, just a few houses along, and Jim had told him not to dare come ringing at his door. He had nothing against Dave himself, but he didn't like the boys who were always on his tail. Petty thieving and drugs, and bunking off school of course, big mouths and small knives. –I'm not going to get into drugs, Dave said earnestly, and Jim nodded.

Back home again, Jim locked the door behind him and tidied up. Then he lay down on the sofa and turned on the television. The clouds of smoke from the gas boiler billowed up in front of the window. Dave had probably been too scared to go home. And where was Mae? Jim thought, as he pictured Dave skulking through the streets and the couple from number 49 sitting cozily on their sofa in front of an imitation coal fire, with their arms around each other.

They met in the Edgware Road: as Jim came out of the underground, Hisham emerged from a shop and went quickly over to him. –I'd like to buy you a meal, he said; Jim was looking suspiciously behind him. –I'll buy you a meal, Hisham repeated with a shrug. I do still have something to make up to you. He held out the plastic bag to Jim straight away, an offer that Jim refused with a grin. –No, you carry it, he said. Some men were sitting outside a café with their hookahs. Inside the restaurant a program from an Arabic television channel was being projected, giant-sized, onto a wall, a waiter was balancing a tray full of teacups on his hand, and a young woman in a headscarf was eating on her own by the window, chewing her pita bread, tears running down her face. The traffic was bumper to bumper and noisy. There was the smell of grilled meat; small shops had unfamiliar kinds of fruit laid out in front, pale, scaly as a lizard's skin, and brown, knobbly objects that Hisham tested with his fingers, muttering something in Arabic that seemed to infuriate the shopkeeper, who after a moment's delay reared up like a snake, thrusting his head forward, his tongue darting in and out, and Jim moved closer to Hisham, childishly, as though to be sure of taking part if a fight broke out, but nothing of the kind happened. It was Hisham's look that calmed the shopkeeper down, his meek, gentle gaze, and Jim burst out laughing. They walked on, heading southwards, until they reached a modest-looking restaurant, where a boy of Dave's age came running out, bowed slightly to Hisham and led them to a table inside, to which tea was brought at once, and the boy laid the table carefully, with cloth napkins, his thin arms and hands arranging everything deftly, and then came small plates, meatballs, falafel, pickled cabbage, humus, so Hisham told him. Jim sat down, feeling ill at ease: his neck itched, he wanted to turn and look in every direction, out of suspicion, out of curiosity, because the smells were unfamiliar, because Hisham gave little signs or said unintelligible things, and the boy dashed into the kitchen, not obsequiously, just eagerly, almost excitedly, almost as if Jim's every wish was to be fulfilled. That was it: as if his every wish was to be fulfilled, read from his lips. Little grey-green olives. It was a ges-

ture from the boy that induced him to take some, to slide his
tongue, tentative, exploring, over the smooth, slightly bitter
skin, and to tear off a piece of the pita bread and dip it into the
light-colored purée. To take a bite of the brownish-green meatballs, while suspiciously watching Hisham's face as he too ate,
pausing only to give an instruction. More tea. A bowl of warm
water for dipping your fingers into, to clean them. There was
the scent of rose oil. The room was in semi-darkness, the door
did not fit properly and a gust of wind forced its way through
the crack; there were still no other customers, just the boy running in and out, eager, happy, the same age as Dave. But in
Brixton, Hisham had struck Jim down from behind without
even knowing him. Now he was gently offering him the lukewarm water, and Jim dipped his hands into it. A bright, piercing pain made Jim suddenly start up, knocking over the bowl
and sending the water pouring all over the table, soaking the
napkins, collecting in puddles among the cutlery, washing
crumbs to the edge of the table. Hisham did not stir from his
seat. Jim felt his face contorting, his mouth. –Don't, said
Hisham. There was always noise, noise coming in through the
crack of the door, noise from cars, all those cars, all those people pushing and jostling their way through the streets, all the
fear, and the jostling crowds in the railway stations and air-
ports, the crowds that forced you to stay still and wait, restless
and miserable, and at any moment something might happen,
the voices might grow loud again, sleepers might wake and forgotten memories rise to the surface. He felt a cold gust of wind,
the door moved and Jim grinned because, just as if this were
some kitschy soap opera, there was a young woman standing
outside, hesitant, waiting, and he closed his eyes and told himself that perhaps Hisham had found Mae for him. But there
was only a cold draft, the bitterness, anger, that helpless, gut-
wrenching pain. Hisham was still sitting there calmly, just looking at him, while the boy and his little brother ran up with

cloths, grabbed the soaked napkins, laughed, fished olive stones and olives out of the water, brought fresh napkins, more plates, more pita bread; the bigger boy brought a large serving-dish, skewers with grilled meat and onions and tomatoes, while the smaller one tugged at Jim's sleeve. –My wife's brothers, said Hisham, there were eight children in the family. He called out something. Once again the cold wind forced its way in through the door, and a couple came in, tourists, Jim thought; their entrance was a humiliation for him, because he was still stand-ing awkwardly by the table, his hands awkwardly half-raised above his hips, hands that were fixed and rigid as if embedded in invisible ice or frozen air. After a quick look at the two men the couple sat down. The little boy came running over again and stood right in front of Jim, his head tilted back, lifting his face to his, and then, pulling Jim's right hand out of its icy prison, he held it between his own so much smaller hands, as if to warm it. Then he released it, like a ball that would go bouncing away or a bird that had been anxiously waiting to escape. Jim found himself facing him, smiling, embarrassed, but he sat down and started to eat, while Hisham dexterously slid the last pieces of meat off the skewers.

The traffic on the Edgware Road was flowing smoothly, and Jim walked to Marylebone Road, not wanting to take the tube or a bus—quite a distance on foot, and he rubbed each hand with the other and waggled his fingers to warm them: the after-noon was dull and rainy, as if autumn had returned and once again you felt you were approaching the end of something. Irritably, pedestrians crowded up to the traffic lights and hur-ried, tightly bunched, across the road. A corpulent man bumped into Jim, turned right round to him, remarkably light on his feet, and stopped when he saw his face. A taxi coming towards them hooted. –Everyone seems in such a hurry to get home, said the man. I hope you'll accept my apologies. Unless you wish to make an issue of it. The taxi hooted again, and the man inclined his head politely, waved to the driver, and walked on. Other people passed between them, heads, more heads, and above them umbrellas. The park gates were still open, Jim could feel the nylon bag in his anorak pocket, a police car slowed down and turned its blue lights on, but he was invisible as he plunged into the darkening park, where only a few last joggers were still following their orbits; spring, he thought, and Mae had said that the end was always polite, that at least they buried you. Even if it was a disgrace when there was nobody to follow the coffin, carrying flowers and expressing regret. She talked about death far too much. She'd have liked Hisham, Jim thought, his courteous ways, and would have laughed at Jim for being so suspicious, always suspicious. It was almost as if she was waiting for him at home. You could picture a thing like that; why not, it cost nothing.

From the start she had been a bit absent-minded and inattentive; he had shaken her when he wasn't sure if she was drunk or wasted or just not paying attention, hard to tell with her, her smooth face almost expressionless, like a face cut out of a film or a photo, as if she thought he didn't matter and neither did she, nor Albert. Nor anybody. When you're lost there's no need to look for anything anymore, she'd said, and he'd felt like shaking her. It was as though she'd drifted away, become blurred before his very eyes. She'd lost weight, she who had been as soft as a young girl, with a child's rounded knees and elbows, and so surprised that he didn't leave, not without you, he'd said, I'm not going without you. And sometimes she had put on a vest of his and nothing else, just as she wore her sweaters over her bare skin, no bra underneath, tight, soft sweaters, light blue or red. –I'll buy you whatever you want, he'd said, but she didn't want anything, not a skirt, not a dress. She hardly ever went out of doors with him, hand in hand, or let him put his arm around her shoulders. Before he could persuade her to go out with him, she would frantically hunt for a jacket or a coat, even if it was warm. Once she said that it wasn't out of fear or even caution; her mouth gaped wide as she laughed. He grabbed her by the shoulders because she wouldn't stop laughing, her harmonious features distorted, her arms stretched out sideways. But a slap calmed her down. He had to calm her down: she didn't believe him. And that's why there was all that shit. She didn't believe that he loved her, that things would turn out okay. And Ben was sniffing around her and bringing her pills. Ben embracing her, his hands on her waist. The humiliation of spying on them both, of being jealous. And then she was gone.

–Jim, Jim, Albert had said. Why should the police be interested? After a year? Surely you don't think she lodged a complaint against you, that Mae reported you? Grinning. It was probably Ben who had knocked up the poster. But the point was that Albert or Ben had a photo, and he didn't. Almost as if she was waiting for him at home, or at least he tried to imagine that she was. It cost nothing, but then it did hurt, and he lost himself in his thoughts, picturing things; maybe it had something to do with living here, with having a home of sorts and even a garden.

Without lingering among the crowds around Camden Lock, Jim went home, opened the door, and locked it behind him. A little later Dave walked past, deliberately averting his head, very slowly. The couple from number 49 strolled down the street, perhaps on their way to the tube. They were not holding hands.

21

She stretched out flat on the floor and held her breath until Polly came and tickled her. As long as she didn't breathe or laugh she could hear the dust, each individual speck of dust, each movement, however slight, could hear something settling gently on her face, on her stomach, on her open palms, even though you couldn't see it as well as against the sunlight, in the shafts of light that Dave showed her, where everything moved, danced, twirled, –there are ever so many, Dave said, more than anyone could ever count up to. Can you feel it? For that was the kind of thing that one could learn, that he could teach her. Each separate particle of dust, too small for the eye to see. Though that meant nothing, Dave explained, being too small didn't matter if something was whole, if it was complete, like her feet or hands, or like a baby, which was tiny but still worth as much as you or me, he said, that's obvious, isn't it? So she needn't worry if she didn't grow, and if she wasn't allowed to go to school—but Dave looked away when she said that. –Some day they'll get onto him, he said, meaning Dad, and then somebody from the school will come and fetch you. What difference does it make how big you are, he said, and that a single speck of dust was complete and beautiful even if she couldn't see it with her naked eye. –Just look how the dust dances about, said Dave, and told her that whenever she was alone she didn't just have Polly and her doll but all those specks of dust, each one a tiny little girl with beautiful long hair, all of them princesses playing together, and if they didn't take any notice of Sara it was because she was so big. Invisibly they floated down, danced on her bare arms, even tried to call out to her, and if she lay very still and held her breath she could hear them calling, playing with old-fashioned toys, hoops and yo-yos and real doll's houses. She lay still so as to feel their little bodies landing on her, light as dust, and held her breath or breathed gently so as not to blow them away. Perhaps they had parachutes, like dandelions in springtime, white, gliding parachutes. Dave said he would soon take her to the Heath again, but their parents didn't let him take her with him, and besides, his school was near the Heath, you had to pass the huge gate where the other boys were always on guard, and even if you went a roundabout way the schoolboys would be somewhere on a bench or on the hill where people flew their kites, or they would be where people sat on benches talking and kissing. Dave never said anything, but Sara knew that he was afraid whenever they met one of them. His face would go pale and haggard and his hand would be sweaty. Sometimes he would start talking under his breath, so softly that not even she could understand what he said, he talked to himself, even in his sleep he talked: he only went quiet when their parents were around. –We'll go away, he told Sara, just you and me, as soon as I'm old enough.

But Sara knew it would never happen. –Yes, it will, he said, I'm the prince and I'll come on a horse and fetch you. But he wouldn't take her with him, just as he didn't take her swimming anymore, –I can't, little cat, he said, not looking her in the eye. If I take you I'll be in trouble right away. He carefully pulled her T-shirt off and made a face. She kept still, although it hurt when he ran his finger over the bruises. With their parachutes, Sara thought, they could go anywhere. It was better not to go swimming than for Dave to quarrel with their father on her account, because of her not being allowed to go swimming. Dave shouted at Dad that he was a murderer. And then Dad called for Sara to come to him, with something in his voice that frightened her, –come here, girl, and she had felt Dave's eyes on her but had not returned his look. Dave's eyes on her back, on her face, with all his strength he was willing her to turn towards him, return his look, run to him. She had betrayed him, –and what good did it do you? he asked bitterly, for her father made her kneel down, and then he ordered her to pull his belt, which he had undone, out of the loops, because he was her father. Dave's look, like that of a parachutist falling to earth because his parachute had failed to open. And then Dave tore himself away, stormed out of the house and into the street, and Mum didn't try to stop him, while Sara knelt in front of Dad and the belt whistled through the air. Parachutists relied on their parachute to open in good time, Dave had explained, they trusted to the air and the fabric that the parachute was made of, they shut their eyes and felt themselves falling, but without fear, and then they had a cord and gave it a sharp tug to make the fabric unfurl, so that they started gently gliding, floating, with a smile on their face. She hadn't understood, but hadn't wanted to ask questions, because Dave was not smiling but looking at her earnestly, as though she must surely understand what he was telling her. –If the cord breaks, for instance, then they fall to their death. That was the sort of look Dave had now, and she knelt there, whimpering as she felt the hand with which Dad was trying to pull her pants down. Because she was more afraid of being naked than of being beaten, she deliberately fell over sideways. Dave had run out of the house. And Dad let go of her again, swearing, and turned the belt round so that he had the soft end in his hand and it would make no difference whether she had her pants on or not, and Mum stood in the doorway, motionless, ready to send her to bed when it was over. –Why must you make him so angry? Mum asked. Mum didn't undress her and she didn't have to wash even though there were spots on her pants, nothing to speak of,

Mum said dismissively. Tomorrow it would all be over and done with, except that she had to lie still because it hurt, and it was noisy, as though the bruises that hurt her were making a noise. –That's the reason, Dave said, and she was sad because his voice sounded angry, it's because of the bruises that I can't take you, don't you understand? She had to shut her eyes tight to picture those tiny beings, princesses or fairies, drifting down on her and floating this way and that without hurting her, even if you couldn't hear them or see their dancing and twirling, and then she was alone and had to wait until Polly came back and licked her with her tongue, until her parents came home and shouted for her as though she were invisible. The prince, Sara said, has set out on his horse; he'll soon be back from hunting, but a hunt lasts at least three days. But what if the prince never comes back? Unhappy, restless, the tiny creatures ran hither and thither and held whispered discussions, casting furtive glances at Sara, who had brought them the message. She could tell that they were afraid. She nestled against the sofa and considered what she could do to reassure the fairies, to explain that princes always went off and came back again. Because he's the prince, she thought, but the words, though they sounded confident, still seemed too weak. She said that Dave was the prince and they were all waiting for him, that they must post sentries ready to receive him, by day or night, the way she herself waited, scarcely breathing, scarcely daring to fall asleep, because he might come back in the night, just for a few hours. –Little cat, said Dave, why don't you put clean clothes on? She could see he was sad. You know I'll be back. He said: –You know I won't leave you on your own. She told Mum this, one afternoon when there were just the two of them and Mum called out for her, after Sara had been invisible for a few hours, lying face down on her bed, in her room, where she had run as soon as she heard the key turning in the lock. Mum had not looked to see where she was. But after a few hours she suddenly called out and gave her a hug, she even asked if she'd had anything to eat, and Sara told her about the princesses and fairies, too small to be seen with the naked eye, and her mother's breath smelt sour. About how they floated, light as dandelion seeds, and how Dave was the prince who sallied forth and returned. But he hadn't been home for four days, and Mum started crying, silently, just the tears running down her face, and then she stood up.

22

In the newspapers it said that people should stock up with blankets, batteries, candles and tinned foods. There it was in the *Guardian*: blankets, batteries, candles, tinned foods. She bought some batteries. Batteries were something that they didn't have in the house, unlike candles, blankets and tinned foods, although actually they had no equipment that ran on batteries, as she realized when she was back in Lady Margaret Road, unpacking the bags with the rest of her shopping (fresh milk, two avocados for a pound, still green and hard) and thinking where to keep the batteries. Five packets of four batteries, in two sizes. Perhaps Jakob had something that required batteries. She put the avocados on the windowsill in the sun. Two weeks had gone by since her arrival, and she had settled in, she liked walking down Lady Margaret Road to Kentish Town, and she liked taking the tube into town, they had been to the opera, and Alistair was very nice. Some days it was boring working at home, she missed Andras and Peter and Sonja, but this was still only the beginning: she might be able to get commissions here, too, clients, but above all the time had finally come to apply herself seriously to illustrative work, illustrating children's books, drawing. She used to draw, and now she would do so again. And while Berlin voted against war, London was sending its soldiers into battle regardless of the protests and demonstrations, was calling on its people to stock up with batteries, blankets, candles, food, and in a few days' time Britain would be a country at war, in the desert, but there was no telling what might happen here, too. The weapons inspectors had left Iraq. –But they're not finding anything, said Alistair. They haven't found anything. And Turkey isn't opening up its airspace. What will come of it all? She didn't tell him about the batteries. It might be a false alarm, but it *was* an alarm. She showed Jakob the paper, talked about blankets, candles, batteries, but Jakob laughed; it wasn't that she took it really seriously or was actually afraid, but surely it was no laughing matter. He didn't mean to be unkind. Even so, she was annoyed with him: what was he so busy with? His client, Miller? The villa in Treptow? He put money in the bowl on top of the chest of drawers, he never forgot to leave a fresh banknote there: that was her housekeeping money, the money she used when she didn't draw some out of her Berlin account. –What do you want for supper this evening? asked Isabelle loudly and clearly, but Jakob had gone upstairs. She was more on edge than in Berlin, as though her metabolism was upset. Three or four times a week she cooked a hot meal in the evening. Carried bags of shopping into the kitchen, set them down on the refrigerator, started to unpack and put things away; this time she returned to the dining table and the newspaper, which was hanging over the back of a chair. –Maybe we do need a television after all, she called up to Jakob. His mobile phone rang, she could hear it through the ceiling, and then footsteps, his voice. She went into the kitchen, cut through the thick plastic and took hold of the cold, smooth meat. In the oven, she thought, with garlic and wine and thyme. Either butter or olive oil. Since her arrival in London, since that first supper with Alistair and the peas in mint sauce, she had started to enjoy cooking. Jakob's voice was audible, but not intended for her. Evidently he was still on the phone. A little lemon juice. Pepper. The oven slowly warmed up. She would do the rice in the oven too. The kitchen window opened onto the garden, which they had not yet used, not even set foot in, as if it were extraterritorial. In the mornings the living and dining room was dazzlingly bright: all the rooms facing the street became dazzlingly bright as soon as the sun came out, because there was nothing to get in its way, no obstruction from the bare branches of the plane trees. The carpets were almost white. –Should we get into the habit of taking our shoes off? she called up the stairs, but Jakob didn't hear her. Blankets. Candles. Because one might get cold. Because one might be frightened in the dark. The sound of his voice made it clear that she would get no aid and comfort from him. Candles, blankets. In Baghdad, of course, they expected to face sandstorms, heat. –But we have to think of what will happen to all those people, Alexa had said, as though, being in London, Isabelle were defending the invasion. Neither of them could remember how many had died in the previous Gulf War. Isabelle recalled the television image of a man who had fallen to his knees, sobbing, covering his face with his hands, because he was afraid he was about to be shot. There was no cruelty that one could not picture to oneself. Would I be able to picture it? Isabelle wondered. But she had no wish to. And Jakob was coming down the stairs, one slow step at a time. She wanted to fling her arms round his neck and feel safe in his embrace, safe enough to stroke his face, the stubble, the reddish eyebrows, the slightly too fleshy cheeks that had grown a little thinner in London. Had he grown thinner? They had been married for only seven months. She stood at the foot of the stairs, looking up, for the time it took him to come down. Then he was beside her, hesitant, thoughtful, still going over the telephone conversation in his head, displeased. –That was my father, he said at length, asking whether you wouldn't rather go back, back to Berlin, if it should turn out to be safer there. How stupid, Jakob added. Blankets and batteries, what a lot of nonsense, do you remember how it was during the first Iraq War? In Freiburg in 1990, when people stocked up with tins of food, probably throwing away what they'd bought after Chernobyl? All that anxiety for no reason at all. Didn't I want to send you to Berlin, my father asked, can you imagine it? You're not worried, are you?

She moved away from him and took a step towards the kitchen. Rub the chicken with lemon, then add the herbs. They smelt like hay, their aromas indistinct, too much alike. She wanted to bury her head in his shoulder. But Jakob was preoccupied with something that had nothing to do with either her or the war. When she came down to her workroom each morning she would hear the neighbors shouting at the tops of their voices, stamping, banging, what on earth were they up to on the other side of the wall, and then sometimes it was so quiet you could hear a pin drop, as if the house was deserted. The milk float would come along the street, not always at the same time, and an old man with a handcart would turn up, ringing his bell and collecting bulky items that people wanted to dispose of, possibly selling things too, and Isabelle considered what she might be able to give him next year, or the year after, when enough time had gone by. Yes, Jakob had got thinner, his face was thinner. She looked at him from the kitchen, he was standing in the dining-room doorway, apparently thinking, holding something in his hand, a ticket, a note. –It would be stupid to worry. Or would you like to go back to Berlin?

She must have pulled too hard at the chicken, there was a crack and the wing broke, twisting out of its socket, and she jumped as if it had been an electric shock, the noise, his question, which he repeated; outside, the sound of a siren faded into the distance. Did she want to go back to Berlin? She wasn't sure. There was something waiting for her here. The police car had turned around, the siren was coming nearer again. –Have you noticed, said Isabelle, how often they do that, the police cars, I mean? First they go one way and then a few minutes later they come back the opposite way. He opened a bottle of wine. Actually they drank something every evening, cider, or wine, ever since Freiburg, then in Berlin and now here too. And they would go on sitting facing each other, the two of them, eating chicken, drinking red wine, which they could buy anywhere, just as they could make a home anywhere, in Berlin, in London. –Everything is so quick nowadays, her father had said when she told him about the move. I mean, even if the two of you get married, even if you move to a different country, it's not such a big thing. She had felt slightly sorry for him, because really he would have liked to visit them in Berlin.

She didn't know what Jakob was thinking about when he seemed lost in his own thoughts, possibly the railway company that a client wanted to buy: perhaps that was a matter of great importance, more so than Miller and his villa in Treptow.

They sat at the table, eating. –There's going to be a big demonstration, said Isabelle, and Jakob, his mind obviously elsewhere, asked if she was thinking of going on it. Isabelle still hadn't bought any shoes. And then they went out again and walked down Lady Margaret Road. A chilly wind was getting up; the plane trees looked like old animals with nothing left to look forward to. In a garden flat Jakob noticed a bare light bulb dangling from the ceiling; he wanted to tell Isabelle, who was walking along beside him, her arm in his, wanted to point the light bulb out to her, and later, when they were already in bed, it occurred to him that she would have noticed something different, a jacket over the back of a chair, perhaps, a glass on the table in the living room, for it had seemed to be the living room.

–So Miller wants to meet you at Amira's? Bentham enquired dryly. He probably wants his coffee cup read. He'll ask Sahar whether his future holds the promise of a villa in Treptow, a new life, a new start in Berlin. You can be sure he won't divulge to you what Sahar has seen, and Amira will smile and ask if you'd like another piece of cake or a coffee. Have you seen it done yet? Those coffee cups, the fine cracks in the glaze, the lines round the rim of the mocha cup?

–But why do you laugh at him? asked Jakob. He's never been to see her, he only asked me to meet him in Amira's deli. He's entitled, surely?

–Do you mean to have his coffee cup read? Or do you mean to the villa in Treptow?

–Both, said Jakob, confused.

Bentham nodded. –Of course he's entitled, he said in a soothing tone.

Maude entered, carrying a tray with a glass of hot milk on it, and Alistair poked his head inquisitively round the door and called across to Jakob, with a laugh, that no one else could dissect a legal case as Bentham could, so completely that nothing was left, neither justice nor injustice. And Bentham, waving the remark aside, stood up and went over to the window, which was completely hidden behind heavy curtains, as in the days of the blackout, Jakob thought, though at that time Bentham had been no more than a child.

–Entitled? Miller entitled? Of course he's entitled. The property belongs to him, not to the German state or the Treuhand organization or some purchaser or other. You say Miller's going to go to Berlin? I'll go myself one of these days, Schreiber has been pressing me to go for years. But Miller hasn't actually *lost* anything. When he first started thinking about what did or didn't belong to him, he didn't even know about the property in Berlin.

–His parents told him about it, Jakob objected, unclear what point Bentham was making, as he mumbled, buried in his armchair again, groping for a rug.

–Yes, of course, his parents, since he was lucky and they survived, even if his grandparents were gassed. You misunderstand me. I'm not saying that he shouldn't try to obtain the value, the equivalent value of the house, in other words monetary compensation. Of course he should. What puzzles me is that he wants the house itself. The place, as if it were a place that was still intact, a part of his past. As if old age and sadness hadn't encroached on it. Sadness, and the horror of knowing that no place has remained untouched by the truth, by cold reality. As though there were a past that could still be put back together, after all these decades.

–But then why do you take on cases like that at all? asked Jakob.

Bentham got to his feet, looking for something in his desk, in the drawers underneath, looking for something or thinking.

–The past, families, inheritances, continuities. And we lawyers are always working retrospectively as historians of a past that is notionally just, an objective legality. Even though Miller got divorced at the age of sixty, and is going to consult a fortune-teller.

Jakob was sitting in the chair with the perfectly curved arm-rests, walnut, light-colored linen fabric, horsehair. Maude looked in at the door again, and shook her head.

–Given that there is no angel of history, there must at least be something else we can depend on, don't you think? Well, I think so too. But why can't it be the law, why can't it be simply the monetary value of something? Why insist on regaining what is lost, why insist that something be made whole again? It never is made whole again.

There it was, the thing he had been looking for, a cardboard folder held closed by a red rubber band, faded, perished, which broke in two and fell to the floor when Bentham tried to remove it, and he bent down but did not pick it up. Maude put her head in for a third time, this time gesticulating, with a telephone in her hand, making signs to Jakob, and Bentham acquiesced: we've finished, he nodded and returned to his desk, grumpy, mumbling, as if he had been prevented from getting on. But apparently amused. What about, thought Jakob, what was it?

Two hours later, there was Alistair in the doorway, come to collect him, having already spoken to Isabelle. Actually they had made plans for the early part of the evening, Jakob and Isabelle, they had agreed to go and buy some shoes at long last, and a woolen blanket, which couldn't do any harm, although today the weather was lovely—a high pressure system—and tomorrow would be sunny too, it was spring, very nearly spring. But Jakob had forgotten about their arrangement. From the library came the sound of a vacuum cleaner: Mrs. Gilman was there between eight and nine o'clock, and sometimes she sat down with Mr. Krapohl in the library, because she was in no hurry and hated the long journey back to Finchley, she said, and Alistair maintained that she was hoping to go for a meal with Mr. Krapohl, he had seen the two of them in the British Museum once, sitting together at a table, or had it been the Wallace Collection? –A nice couple, grinned Alistair as they passed the library, and actually Krapohl was "one of your lot," born in Germany, always had a cold but was extremely obliging, and had incidentally had a long chat earlier on with Isabelle, who had come two hours ago to pick Jakob up; she had been told that he was busy and had insisted that he mustn't be disturbed. Krapohl had assured her, Alistair told Jakob gleefully and with a touch of feline malice, that there was no need to worry about the war, whether it took place or not, though he, Alistair, felt bound to add that it would at best delay the terrorist attacks that were certain to come eventually. But for this evening, he said, he had proposed that they should all three meet at the National Film Theatre, which had a nice cafeteria, and he patted Jakob on the shoulder. Jakob stared at him in confusion.

Isabelle had left Mr. Krapohl and Alistair at six o'clock, and had walked along Devonshire Street, with its terraces of tall houses, and then turned south. She had had a coffee in Baker

Street before heading for the Thames and walking over Hungerford Bridge—the footbridge was not quite finished, but was already usable—to the South Bank, past the National Theatre and the National Film Theatre; booksellers were packing away their books and tables, and she walked downstream, past the sandbanks where criminals had once been left in chains to be engulfed by the tide. The South Bank had been flattened during the war, but who could imagine it now, the bombs, the Blitz, docks and houses ablaze? Here was Tate Modern, gigantic, blackish-brown, almost windowless, but some women in cocktail dresses were coming out of the main door, pink, light green; a man in a suit headed purposefully towards Isabelle, swerving only at the last moment to avoid her. Dusk was dissolving into darkness. On the opposite bank, London was switching on its lights. St. Paul's Cathedral glided by. Like portholes, windows sent their light bobbing across the water. Two boys cycled around, making their little bikes leap off the ground and perform tricks in mid-air. Dogs strained vainly at their leads, held back by their owners, and there were two toddlers also on leads, with white harnesses around their little chests. Jakob and Alistair would be expecting her at eight or half past in the NFT's cafeteria. And there she was back at Tate Modern; now an old man was standing in front of it, muttering and combing his hair, holding his head on one side, then fixing his eyes on the entrance door, which opened one last time before being locked by a stocky, dark-skinned man with a big bunch of keys. Time to go. Isabelle straightened her green corduroy skirt, which had twisted around ninety degrees, and looked down at her trainers, lifting up her right foot, then her left: the white material was a dirty grey, she would put it off no longer but would buy some shoes tomorrow, and a blanket as well.

–There you are: delightedly Alistair's green eyes explored her face, while she turned to Jakob and kissed him, but not on the mouth because he made an awkward movement so as to maintain his balance on his high stool, and his right hand reached out for her shoulder. Her kiss caught him on the temple. –We ought to go to the concert by John Adams, John Zorn, and John Woolrich, Alistair announced. –Where is it? asked Jakob indifferently. Alistair studied the program, –it's already started, he said and the two men looked at Isabelle. –I'm quite happy here, she said, but she was vaguely disappointed. It was as though nothing was ever going to happen, she thought, and Jakob loosened the knot in his tie and stood up to get her a cider.

Later, when they were waiting for a Northern Line train at Charing Cross, she saw some mice running about on the tracks, slithering out from behind the curved poster hoardings, black mice which would be grey, she told Jakob, if someone were to wash them, and she uneasily watched out for the train. But no harm would come to the mice, no harm ever had come to them, thought Jakob impatiently. He was in a bad mood when he got out at Kentish Town, he had tried to kiss her, and because the escalator had broken down again they had to climb up all the one hundred and seventy-five stairs. At the top, fixed to the window that looked out onto the street, were two posters, one about a missing person and the other an appeal for witnesses to a mugging that had proved fatal. –But that was yesterday! Isabelle exclaimed, while Jakob studied the girl on the other poster, a young woman, younger than Isabelle, and yet—the sight of it affected him strangely—the features in the photograph resembled Isabelle's, no doubt about it. Missing, last seen a year ago, he read, Mae Warren, twenty-six years old, height five foot six inches, fair hair, no distinguishing marks. He turned his head to look at Isabelle, at the mole on her cheek, but she was already ahead of him, standing in the doorway ready to go outside, and then she did go out into the street and walk on a few steps, so he could no longer see her.

*

What are missing here are the little non-essential things, Isabelle thought as she dusted. Alongside the compact stereo player about twenty CDs were lined up, on the chest of drawers were a vase of flowers and the bowl where Jakob put the housekeeping money. Two candlesticks stood on the mantelpiece above the fireplace, which the fitted carpet invaded like a ground-cover plant, its light color contrasting with the black wrought-iron surround above it. A faint odor of adhesive lingered in the room: the carpet had been laid not long before they moved in. On her table sat the laptop. Everything in its place. The children's book publisher had asked her to design a business card, which she had almost finished. She sat down at the table and checked the proportions again. Sketched a second design, a child in a short coat, running. She thought of Andras's drawings from Budapest: the little figures ran along the streets, and at the crossroads they fell into a pit or exploded. A gale was blowing the roof off a house, the people inside were standing at the windows, waving their arms about, and the fire brigade seemed frozen at the corner of the street, the firemen looking away. Isabelle gave a cry as in the house next door something was hurled against the wall. A chair? A television? Hysterical laughter, a voice getting louder and louder, like a siren. Isabelle had never heard the woman before. She stared in horror at the wall, which did not crack, did not open up, and on the other side everything went quiet again. And stayed quiet, while Isabelle sat there on tenterhooks, waiting. Red ink, black ink. The paper, thick sheets. She pushed the computer aside, unscrewed the lids of the little inkpots, and listened. Perhaps there was a thin voice making a humming sound, but perhaps it was some other sound, from outside, far away, an aircraft, a small aircraft on its approach to somewhere. No fire engine came around the corner, nothing happened. A door slammed. Isabelle switched on the radio. Desert

Storm, you couldn't see a yard in front of you, and so all traces
were obliterated, "embedded journalism" was the buzzword,
but you still didn't get to know what was going on; the opinion
polls remained stable, Tony Blair was going to be a loyal ally
whatever Germany and France might say. She sprang to her
feet and went quickly to the window, leaning forward to see
who was leaving the house next door: a woman, a man, a boy.
Isabelle breathed heavily, the glass misted over at once, while
outside three shadowy figures moved, the boy held fast by his
jacket or by the scruff of his neck, while the woman, thin,
standing slightly apart from them, looked up the street and
waved, although no one was coming. But she seemed to be
waiting for something. Isabelle wiped the windowpane but
could not make out the woman's face. The man, on the other
hand, was turned towards her, his face visible, contorted, as he
shouted at the boy. The boy, who was wearing a school blazer,
only came up to the man's ear. He was pointing towards the
house. One could see he was trying to argue, and was looking
out for something behind the windows. As Isabelle turned off
the radio and listened, the woman suddenly yelled, –Dave,
stop that right now!, and Isabelle went over to the wall,
nobody was watching her, nobody could see what she was
doing. In the recess next to the fireplace she pressed her ear to
the wall, startled by something that seemed like a noise made
by the wall itself, scarcely a noise, more like a substance with a
sound of its own, and she timidly moved her head away, but
then pressed her face to the cold surface once more, and this
time it seemed to be a voice, or just the expression of something, imploring, addressed to no one.

Back at the window, she saw that an old green Ford was
waiting with its engine running, and the woman got in without
lifting her head again, only raising her hands as if to fend something off or protest her innocence, while her husband (if he
was her husband) gave the boy a shove that propelled him a

few yards along the street and then also got into the car, which drove past the boy at walking speed before finally accelerating. She watched them go, the car, and the boy. The road, evenly bathed in sunlight, looked as though it went on forever; to the left, some distance away, she could make out part of the church. Next door remained quiet; she stood between the window and the wall, in front of the table on which her computer screen turned black before showing a confused mass of stars and the moon.

Tomorrow was St. Patrick's Day. Alistair had told her that Jakob ought to take her out to dinner, but neither of them knew why, or what the day signified. Perhaps the first bombs might fall tomorrow. Perhaps there would be the first fatalities. The weather was flawless.

23

J im saw that her trainers were dirty; her coat, which she had left unbuttoned because the sun was shining, slapped against her thighs, sturdy, not especially long thighs, he imagined that he could hear the gentle flapping sound of the material. She was walking ahead of him. Slightly too heavy but attractive legs, moving with a steady up and down, up and down rhythm, in trainers, in a knee-length coat, with bare calves, and the sun was shining as if it really were spring. He had been here for almost a year now. There were streets like this which defied the passage of time. The houses stood there, were renovated, were rented, people moved in and moved out, and yet everything stayed the same, quiet, peaceful. He remembered how he had opened the door with Damian's key, and the place had seemed just right for him and Mae. But he had left Mae behind with Ben, and an ambulance siren had been screaming in his ears as he ran off, taking Ben's advice, just get out of here. Mae would have liked this street and the little garden, even if it was only a narrow strip of ground with some grass. The young woman in front of him stopped and reached out a hand as though to touch one of the plane trees, whose trunks looked like spotted animal skins. Then she moved on again and turned off to the right. Her back straightened as if she were holding her breath. Jim hummed a few notes. For a moment he thought he might speak to her, he suddenly felt light and filled with hope, as if a curse had been lifted from him. His father cursed and swore, he had cursed Jim, and they cursed you in church, old people were always doing it, and you were cursed by your own misdeeds, Jim thought, humming, the wrong you did that was never punished, the things you didn't remember. You never did remember, he thought, stopping to light a cigarette. They had reached Leighton Road and were approaching Kentish Town station, and the woman took the yellow season-ticket holder out of her jacket pocket, fed the ticket into the slot, and passed through the barrier. A fat woman carrying bags of shopping pushed past Jim; the escalator, he saw, was out of order, you had to use the spiral staircase on the left. The fat woman complained vociferously, pulling at the sleeve of the blue-uniformed attendant who had come out of his glass cabin, there was a smell of chewing gum and cheap soap, and Jim slipped through the open barrier without a ticket; a current of stale air rose from the shaft, he could see the shallow stairs winding around the central column into the depths, and the worn handrail, the tiled walls. Down he went. The draft rising from the bowels of the earth made a soft whistling sound, otherwise all was quiet. And there was the young woman hurrying down the stairs, nimbly, noiselessly in her trainers. Jim pressed his lips together, his head was spinning, he felt he need only reach out his hand to touch her. He ran down the spiral stairs into the weak yellowish-green light, suddenly sweating because it was cramped and oppressive, –one of these days they'll blow up a tunnel, Albert had insisted, you'll see what it's like when a tunnel collapses and everybody starts screaming in the dark. An old man was feeling his way cautiously along, holding onto the handrail; Jim overtook him, going faster and faster, and here he was at the bottom, sure that she'd be heading for the centre, southbound, but even if he chose the right platform she might have got on a train and left. He stumbled, almost colliding with the wall, one last turn, six steps down to the platform. He was there, felt the draft getting stronger, saw the taillights, and the

digital indicator board was clattering. He didn't even know her
face. The air was full of dust and a smell of stuffy warmth, of
suffocation: he screwed up his mouth in disgust. The fat
woman was approaching, and the old man, and the indicator
board was showing the next train, Bank branch.

One day, in spite of Jim's prohibition, Dave was at the door,
wearing a filthy anorak that was too big for him and with a
bruise under his eye. He had been prepared for the contemptuous look with which Jim opened the door to him, and stood
there guiltily, but then Jim motioned him to come in and
fetched two beers from the fridge, banged one down angrily
onto the coffee table in front of the sofa and gestured to him
to sit down. Dave sat there, hunched up. He reminded Jim of
Hisham: he had something gentle about him, like the people
who demonstrated against the war, against evil, hundreds of
thousands of them, peaceable but determined, and Dave was
looking at him as if he believed in goodness. He sat there and
told Jim about an ambush they had lured him into, a few of the
boys from his school who wanted to volunteer for the army,
and he'd said something about it not being the Iraqis' fault, not
the people's fault, told Jim something about a fight he'd got
into because he was against the war, and Jim grinned and let
him talk, brought him a second beer, waited a bit, and when he
got sleepy gave him a blanket. Dave looked at him gratefully.
But Jim suddenly jerked the blanket away again, held it up in
the air as if he were playing with a dog, and Dave's face crumpled with fear, any minute now he would start crying, and he
was fidgeting nervously to and fro, trembling, because his
refuge was no good, his lying was no good. No refuge was any
good for long, Jim thought, it came apart at the edges like a
cardboard box. He saw the boy sitting there as if he were in a
cage and felt faintly disgusted. –Come off it, you got a thrashing from your dad. Didn't you? He took a step towards Dave,

felt an urge to kick him, and did, on his hip, which was bony. –Your dad, are you going to deny it? Dave squirmed, he had gone red, and Jim laughed, waving the blanket up and down and catching the light bulb with it, so that there was a shattering of glass and the splinters fell onto the sofa and the table; he hauled Dave up by his arm. –Ambush my foot, it was your dad. He looked at the boy standing there, caught out, ashamed, still blushing. –And you come to me with a pack of lies, you little bastard! Haven't got the guts to go home, is that it? The beer bottle tipped over. Jim waited, but Dave didn't move, didn't defend himself. Jim grabbed him by the hair and pulled him to the floor. Nothing, not so much as a whimper. Jim left him lying there, went over to the door leading to the garden, and opened it. On the brick wall a blackbird perched, singing. The pale yellow tips of slender twigs hung over the wall, evening was slowly falling, the day slowly drawing to its close; from the street or from other gardens came the sound of voices, and from somewhere the roar of a motor, music, a vacuum cleaner. Jim's face was reflected in the glazed door, looking bright, bright, and handsome. He stared at it. Handsome, bright— that's what Mae had said. The way he'd looked years ago, when he had been a nice-looking boy, just as Dave was now, and the teachers had told him it was a shame to waste his chances, and that he must come to school, he must stick it out, one teacher said to him when he turned up for P.E. with the bruises and welts his father had given him. Dave shouldn't have come. His own fault, and he knew it. He had put his trust in something, in Jim, in his good nature or whatever. Jim turned around. –Get up, he said. He went into the kitchen, got himself a beer, rummaged in a drawer and found himself a wrap, so pure and white and fine, screw it all, he thought, and expected to see Mae at any moment, hi Mae, there you are, lying on the sofa, under a blanket, looking at him, and the kids wanted to go to Iraq, the way he'd wanted to join the Foreign Legion because his father had beaten him, yanking his belt out of the loops, and later, too, when he was having his arse split open for Albert. But Dave had lied. He'd taken a beating, because somebody was always taking a beating, so why not Dave? He breathed out cautiously, cut a line, breathed in deeply. Dave had stood up, and was simply standing there with his arms hanging down at his sides, defiant, proud. –They do want to join the army, he said, the older ones. And it was because of my sister. Dad won't let her go to school. He says the authorities won't find us because we've moved to my aunt's flat, and that she's retarded because she doesn't grow, she's a disgrace to us. –Well, go and report him, said Jim, uninterested. Tell your teachers at school, they'll be round in no time, you can bet your life on it. –But he beats her, said Dave. Jim straightened up, clearer-headed now, shaking himself as if he could shake off what was going through his mind, the boy and Mae, the young woman with her bare legs, the trainers, nimble, full of expectation, the way she skipped down the stairs with her coat fluttering, and he knew exactly what she looked like, her hips and her breasts, even though he hadn't seen her face yet, and sometimes he thought that Mae was dead. That she was having a laugh at him. The voices, the dead people. It had just been an illusion, like an animal adapting its color to its surroundings. –Wipe the beer up, he told Dave. –I could go and get something to eat: Dave looked at him hopefully. –Shall I clear up here and go and get something to eat? –With my money? Jim mocked. Dave went red again. –No, he said, that's not what I meant.

Two hours later Dave was asleep on the sofa, clutching the blanket with both hands, his face calm and flushed. He didn't wake up when Jim turned on the television, turned it off again, and went out, locking the door behind him. When he returned it was almost morning; Dave really had cleared up during the night while he'd been out, and at seven o'clock he left.

The man from number 49—Dave had said they were Germans—walked past, reddish fair hair, well-groomed and well-built, the type who would buy something and then put his wallet away so carelessly that there was no fun in pinching it; well-built, well-groomed, and yet you could see he was worried. Perhaps about the war, which had started overnight, with bombs dropped on Baghdad, no ground troops, then one day later—it was the first day of spring—ground troops after all, and Jim left the television on, even though it made him angry because none of this had anything to do with him. Mae had hated it when he turned the television on in the morning, it was one of those things that she had principles about, eating together, sitting together at the table to eat and not using bad language, as if they had children, children with a promising future, and she didn't like it when he laughed at all that and lit a cigarette and smoked during the meal. He lay in front of the television, smoking. A radiator was dripping, and then the image on the screen was suddenly pulsing with light. Triumphant flashes of hits, if they were hits. Paint was peeling off the front door. There were no images of a shattered city, or white flags. They claimed Saddam was dead, then he was alive after all. They claimed there were hardly any dead, maybe four or five. Mae had said there were hardly any sparrows left, hardly any sparrows, wherever could they have gone? In the garden little yellowish birds hopped around; in the evening a blackbird sang from the top of the wall. The grass was growing, and next to the wall there were daffodils: he pictured Mae bending down, cutting the grass, planting flowers. The birds were very tame. Mae turned around to him, laughing. What had become of the things they'd had in Field Street, he didn't know. The television. Folding chairs that they'd bought. Even a sunshade, because they'd planned to go to Brighton.

An emergency drill had been held at a Circle Line station, chosen because it was closed anyway—had it been Chancery

Lane? But the lights had failed, setting off a panic, the medical equipment had been trampled underfoot and a doctor injured, and the lights hadn't come back on. Hisham phoned Jim, gave him an address in Holloway, they'd buy all the gear, he said, they were Serbs, Albanians, cigarette smugglers hoping to get into the drugs business before they got shot by a rival gang. Dave walked past, obediently keeping his head turned away.

Jim walked the twenty minutes to Holloway, and was met at the street corner that was the agreed rendezvous; they stepped into a doorway where three men were waiting, polite, dressed in cheap, thin anoraks, with hard, greedy eyes, and out in the street women were going by wearing too much makeup. No English people about, Jim thought. Headlines announced that a young woman had been killed, probably with a brick, and nobody had noticed anything even though it had happened in a park in broad daylight. He went into a pub not far from Archway, stood at the bar, humming, his paltry, miserable humming, and took a first mouthful. The barmaid was sizing him up out of the corner of her eye, while from the rear part of the pub the tinkling of a gaming machine could be heard. But Jim didn't look up and went on humming; at the age of twenty-eight he still couldn't whistle. A real boy whistles, his father had said with contempt. The barmaid leaned on the bar, smiling at him. –Are you thinking about your girl? Jim glanced at her briefly without replying. At the back of the pub the gaming machine tinkled again. The man who had handed over the money to him was probably forty or so, heavily built, with bad skin and shifty eyes. Jim turned his glass first one way and then the other. At thirteen he'd decided to run away from home. That was fifteen years ago now. He had believed in London: that had given him the strength finally to run away at sixteen. But it had been a shock to arrive and find himself standing outside the station, after all his imaginings of a life that was free and wild. With Mae he would have moved to the country. He needed to break away from Albert and find Mae and have enough money. From the kitchen came the smell of cooking; some stairs that were closed off with a cord led up to the first floor. And still there was the enervating tinkle of the gaming machine. Jim turned around, strode into the back room, made for the boy standing at the machine, who stared at him in fright, and shoved him so hard that he fell over. –Give it a rest, you little scumbag! The barmaid called, –Get lost, Gigi! and came over, smiling at Jim. Without a word the boy picked himself up and made off. Jim sensed the woman's eyes resting on him expectantly. Not his type, he saw when he turned round; an amply endowed brunette with a face that was heavily made up but looked trustworthy. So this was Holloway, like a bad smell, he thought, but she had showered, her hair smelled freshly washed, much thicker hair than Mae's: he took hold of it, which she allowed him to do, then she leaned her head on his shoulder in a friendly way that seemed perfectly natural, and smiled at him. It was pleasant, like a tangible object, a palpable sense of well-being; her hand felt for his and held it for a moment before releasing it as she cuddled up closer to him and steered him into a little cubbyhole, gently edging him in between buckets and a vacuum cleaner, a confined space with stale, dusty air and no room to lie down, but she was skilful and tender, so that he forgot everything and was surprised when he felt her lips, a gentle, affectionate kiss. –Dreamer, she said. The daylight out in the street was bright, and after two hundred yards he noticed the noise again, the suspicion in the eyes that rested on him, a woman with a small boy by her side giving him a wide berth. The air had a scent of summer about it, it had been raining, droplets glistened on the branches of a small tree, and a child came running towards him, only avoiding him at the last moment, so that as he passed Jim felt the draft and almost the warmth of the compact little body. He stumbled: there, right in the middle of the pavement, lay a plastic bag covering something, he pushed it aside with his foot, caught a glimpse of fur, a rat, and amid the roaring, hunking, wearisome traffic he stood immobile, helpless, while a cold wind sprang up and rain soaked through his anorak.

He couldn't remember the last time he'd been ill, really ill, not just drunk or suffering the effects of some pills or other, but with a fever, sweating feverishly like a child. Every touch hurt, as though his skin were transparent, permeable, leaving his nerves exposed, yet at the same time it was like a hard shell that he was trapped inside. With an effort he got up and made some tea, the kitchen cupboard was a complete mess, things of Damian's that he hadn't touched in a year, a jar of jam that had gone moldy, tinned food, dirty crockery; he smoked, coughed, his temperature went higher still, and he ended up lying on the sofa, unable to get to his feet when Dave called out and rang the bell, listening helplessly as Dave called his name, as Dave climbed back up the steps and went away. He fell asleep, woke up, too weak to get up and eat something, to cook some rice— there had been some rice in the cupboard, but he couldn't get up, he couldn't, and everything he could see seemed ripped into shreds, the living room, the kitchen in Field Street, proper saucepans on the stove, and Mae laughing at him, talking nonsense about the dead and laughing at him while he was sweating and in pain. Above the radiator black shadows were moving about, the young woman walked past the window, looking for him, and if he concentrated he could force her to turn around and show him her face. When he came to, it was broad daylight, the middle of the day. His mobile phone rang, stopped, rang again until he finally answered it without checking the number on the display. It was Hisham's voice. –I wondered what had become of you. The voice held no trace of mockery. –Haven't heard from you since Holloway, are you at home? –None of your bloody business, said Jim, pulling himself upright. –Okay, okay, but you sound ill, are you ill? Hisham asked gently. –You cocky bastard, said Jim and ended the call.

When evening came he went out because he was hungry. He walked down to Pang's Garden. The old man was sitting at a small green table spooning up his soup, slurping and swallowing, his elbow almost touching the screen of the television, which was switched on, while in the kitchen two young women were scouring pots and pans. Three men were working behind the counter, chatting and taking no notice of Jim. Two black men came in, looked over towards him, and whispered together. He gave a laugh, ordered another spring roll. It tasted bitter.

When he finally left, he saw the young woman walking away on the other side of the road; she looked across at him, but it was too dark to make out her face. He hummed something, almost the opening of a song, she was still looking in his direction, but then she went on her way, and Jim couldn't whistle.

24

All the excitement eventually died down. The demonstrators vanished from the streets and the war from the headlines. The chemical weapons had disappeared from the desert, having doubtless been nonexistent all along. Distant now, the combat continued. Rumors had Saddam captured, dead, then on the run again. Because one delivery had been unsatisfactory and the next one incomplete, the delivery van from *Hayes & Finch, Candle Manufacturers and Church Furnishers* made three appearances in Lady Margaret Road. Isabelle thought she could smell beeswax when the van door opened and a man carried some brown cardboard boxes, with a thick, extremely tall white candle on top, into the house diagonally opposite. So that was where the priest lived. The BBC voices pronounced the names "Basra" and "Nasiriya" with effortless fluency, there was talk of "pockets of resistance"; then the vocabulary changed again.

The telephone rang but Isabelle did not pick it up, and after the answering machine had played her message she heard Alistair's lively tones. –Your husband is ensconced in Bentham's room, until late, apparently, but maybe we could still go out somewhere? For the first time Isabelle wasn't sure whether she felt like making plans, it seemed that her every wish was being fulfilled, and yet there was something missing. Alexa had come for four days, had slept in Isabelle's workroom, and the two of them had visited the museums and drunk tea together: Isabelle particularly liked the Watteaus in the

Wallace Collection, the enigmatic gaiety of the *fêtes galantes* and the musicians, and the way the figures sat there expectantly, waiting for they knew not what. On the last morning she went with Alexa to Golders Green to put her on the bus to the airport, then returned home, stripped the bed and set the washing machine going. The days fitted like gloves. Jakob had stopped asking her whether she was bored or lonely. She showed him her sketches for the children's book, though the story hadn't turned out right, or at any rate wasn't the right story, she explained, for the little girl and the scenes that she was drawing; she liked it when he stood attentively behind her chair and praised her drawings. He asked her to take her clothes off; the curtains were not closed, he placed himself in front of her, in his suit, and then led her by the hand up to the bedroom. She liked sleeping with him, without being overly excited about it. When they ate at home, which was not often, he told her things from the office that she had already heard from Alistair, and Jakob was by no means as good an observer. Once they quarreled because Jakob broke the big plate from Aunt Fini, a white plate with a rose-patterned rim, a big, shallow plate that one might perhaps be able to glue together again, but broken it was, and Isabelle pronounced it a disaster. Jakob was surprised at the word, he thought she couldn't mean that seriously, a disaster, but she was genuinely angry at his carelessness. One morning when she was sitting in a café she had been approached by the man she had seen a few times in Lady Margaret Road, Jim, a good-looking man, younger than she was, with a narrow face and an attractive though slightly hard mouth. He had sat down at her table without asking, and had asked her name. –I just wanted to know what your name is, in case we meet again, he said, and was gone again immediately.

She e-mailed Peter with her designs for the prospectus of a private music school for children. –Are you pregnant? he e-mailed back, you do almost nothing but children's stuff these days. As for Andras, she'd heard nothing from him for some days.

She was inking in a red skirt for the little girl with the long hair when the noise started up again next door, something slammed into the wall, she heard a loud, agitated voice and then, a few moments later, as she colored in the green stockings, complete silence. Smoke was fluttering from the roof of the house opposite, and perhaps it was a faint, thin crying that she heard now. Carefully she laid the pen aside and noiselessly straightened up. She hesitated to stand up, as if by doing so she might interrupt something that had to take its course. It was quiet again. In her own house a door rattled: that was the wind, there was a draft even when all the windows were closed.

Three days later she met Jim as she was on her way to Hampstead Heath. He was standing in front of the old fire station that had been turned into a discotheque, giving short shrift to a boy who seemed to be trying to beg from him. Without asking where she was going, he fell in beside her, even taking her arm, and bought a bottle of Coke at a kiosk. He was wearing a white shirt and jeans. On the Heath he led her to the copse near the Ladies' Pond, took her jacket and spread it out on a bench, and plied her with questions in a way that was almost rude. He let her drink from the bottle and drank from it himself. They sat close together, his face too near to hers, he had long eyelashes and knew that he was good-looking. A bit too much like a cigarette advertisement, she thought. Then, leaping up and taking her by the hand, he pulled her after him into a thicket close to the pond, where he parted the twigs with their tender new foliage to show her three women of about fifty who were tentatively advancing, naked and giggling, into the water, which was still cold, their thick arms wrapped around their sagging breasts, their ungainly bottoms sticking out behind. He grinned as he watched Isabelle: she was riveted by the scene. She could feel his eyes on her. For a moment she feared that he would order her to take her clothes off. She was both aroused and afraid. Involuntarily she took a step backwards, stumbling when he burst out laughing. He turned and walked away, humming, his hands in his trouser pockets. Passing the bench without picking up her jacket or the Coke bottle, he went back to the path. There he waited, and as she followed, with the jacket over her arm and the bottle in her hand, she was conscious of her humiliation. He stood in the half-shadow, his face registering nothing, as if she were no more than a patch of brightness. There was a coldness in his eyes; she stumbled, the ground was uneven, full of thick roots and hollows. She knew she would not be able to persuade him to stay, and, sure enough, he left without a backward glance. When she emerged from the copse into the open, she saw him some distance below, at the edge of the Heath, walking through a crowd of schoolchildren who drew back and made way for him. Only one of them spoke to him, and Jim took the lanky boy, who was nervously kneading a pullover in his hands, along with him. She felt a pang. She took the half-full Coke bottle over to a bin. But his smell, Jim's smell, remained with her and she could not shake it off.

Back at the house she sat at her computer for a while, scanning some of her drawings. In them, a brother and sister went to Berlin's Winterfeldt market and bought some striped sweets for the girl, who had run away from home and now lived on a barge on the Spree with the captain, who in the end would marry her mother. But for now the girl was standing all alone in the twilight on the deck of the barge, under a washing line with kitchen towels fluttering on it, waiting to see if her new friends would appear on the bridge. Jakob phoned to say that he would be home late. Peter phoned to ask what had become of the estimate for a book prospectus. Alexa didn't phone. Andras sent a short, businesslike e-mail – he didn't know where the estimate

was, either. A magpie flew up outside the window. Next door
the man was shouting, no doubt yelling at his wife and son.

As dusk began to fall she decided not to wait for Jakob but
to go into town, on her own. She walked down Tottenham
Court Road and went on further, turning off left towards St.
Martin's Lane. Against a dull orange sky, chimneys huddled
together in threes and fours on the roofs; a class of schoolchildren came pouring out of a pizzeria, the girls waving their
bare arms about and giggling, and Isabelle followed them for a
while and saw how one girl hung back to kiss a much older
boy, who thrust a demanding knee between her thighs. Not
wanting to go home yet, Isabelle walked some way along
Oxford Street and in a boutique found some red leather boots,
bright cherry-red, which she bought. Yet that evening and
those that followed left her feeling dissatisfied. The boots
stood in the hall, cherry-red, while Isabelle slipped back into
her trainers; it was disappointing, and in addition she and
Jakob seemed to be on the verge of a quarrel, which they only
avoided, Isabelle thought to herself, because no subject arose.
They were both thankful when Anthony suggested they should
all go to see *King Lear* together the following evening, performed by a company that was in temporary premises but
offered one of the most thrilling productions, and the eager-
ness in his voice lifted her spirits, he was getting things moving, London, life in general, everything that was exciting, and
so when Isabelle saw him outside the theatre, waving the tickets, she rushed up to him with inordinate enthusiasm. She was
taken aback by the sight of the auditorium: the seats, very
tightly packed together, left about half of the space free, particularly a broad strip in front of the stage. Jakob arrived late,
sat down beside her, and gave her a hurried kiss, his upper arm
brushing against her shoulder. I can only understand about
half of this, he whispered to her after some time, feeling for her
hand, while she sat up very straight, hoping to read in the

actors' faces all that she was missing in their words and understand why the catastrophe was unavoidable. The murderous deeds were done, the pain rose to a shrill, unbearable pitch. –The Fool was the best, Alistair whispered to Jakob, and here were Lear's words, howling, pleading, –*And my poor fool is hang'd! No, no, no life! Why should a dog, a horse, a rat have life, and thou no breath at all? Thou'lt come no more*, and a few lines later the walls of the set began to collapse, silently at first, as if it were just a projection, then suddenly falling with a thunderous roar, crashing down into the space where the front rows of seats might have been, shattering, sending clouds of dust swirling upwards and leaving behind a scene of devastation. This was followed by an apprehensive silence and then once more, faintly, the voice of the dead Lear, *Thou'lt come no more, never, never, never, never, never.*

It was still echoing in her ears as she jumped up to hurry out before the others, but she was intercepted at the exit by the Fool, a short, grim-faced man, and as she pushed her way out into the street he followed her, muttering, muttering, standing close behind her, for she could not run away, she wanted to go on ahead but did not dare. It sounded like a curse. The others came out in a cheerful mood, walking side by side, three tall men, but only Alistair noticed the Fool at once and took a good look at him: –another admirer! he said teasingly to Isabelle. They went to an Arab snack bar, and by the time they were ready to set off for home the last tube train had gone, the grilles were just being lowered in front of the entrances and a few stragglers and nocturnal revelers were left standing about under the overhanging canopy at the front of the station. The bus stop for the night bus had been moved, whether to Pentonville Road or in the Camden direction, nobody knew, and Alistair suggested they should head towards Camden Town. The street was as empty as if the whole area were closed off, they started to walk up York Way, which was poorly lit, and again Isabelle heard Lear's voice, heard the Fool muttering. Walking in front of the others, she saw five men suddenly emerge from one of the scaffolding-clad buildings opposite and cross the road, and there was the bus stop, temporarily located on the narrow pavement which was wide enough for only one person. Here the five men gathered, staring towards her, light faces above black anoraks. Two of them were leaning against the wall and did not move out of the way, and so Isabelle stepped out into the empty road and walked on without a sideways glance. Jakob was bringing up the rear, and as he passed they grabbed him by his coat and swung him round, without speaking: the only sound came from Jakob, a stifled cry that made Isabelle turn instantly and look back. Three of the men pulled out knives, though not threateningly; they seized Anthony and Alistair, while the other two held Jakob, and they formed a tight semicircle around Isabelle. The wall was behind her, and she wondered irrelevantly what wall this was, stretching the whole length of the street without an entrance. One of the men approached to within inches of her, she could smell his breath and sweat, could feel the heat of his body. He stood there calmly as if emboldened by the pale, astonished horror of her companions, even Alistair had nothing to say for himself, and it flashed through Isabelle's mind that all this was comical, an attack that held less terror for her than the play, than the cry of *Never!* –Fancy doing it with us, darling? Which of these losers is yours? And she looked into his eyes, searching for something, thinking of the last few days, of the aimlessness, searching to see if there was something to be found in this man, while Jakob slumped to the ground. Then she started to laugh, looking at the man and stretching out her hands towards him: like a child, Alistair said later, amazed, shaking his head, and he didn't believe her when she said she had already seen the police car turning into York Way, though it *was* almost dark, the nearest street lamp some way off, the houses opposite covered in scaffolding, the windows crudely boarded up, dark, in short, so that the police car's headlights were clearly visible. She had seen it. Like a child she stretched out her hands and reached for his ears, held the warm earlobes between her fingers and pulled his face closer as if she were going to kiss him. She alone noticed that the police car had approached to within eight or ten yards and that the driver had wound down his window and was leaning out. Isabelle laughed again, then thrust the man away with all her might and ran through the gap towards the police, waving, gesticulating, suddenly frightened and desperate. Caught in a blaze of light, the five men released their captives and fled, running across the road and diving into a side street just beyond a building site, taking advantage of the head start they gained when the police officers stopped to ask Isabelle if she was hurt. Then the patrol car set off in pursuit, and along with the silence the dim light descended again on Isabelle and the other three, who looked dazed and were rubbing their wrists. Isabelle took half a step back as Jakob came towards her looking nervous and guilty, and she watched indifferently as Anthony raced off after the police and Alistair got out his mobile phone and waited to be connected. They were alone. Anthony came back. The wall was massive, reddish, it was the railway station, and behind it one could see the flashing lights on the gas holder and on a crane that reared up out of the roof of St. Pancras. Now Isabelle noticed that there were still signs on the dark, rundown buildings opposite, formerly cafés, small hotels, gaming establishments, that had been shabby for decades or more; any windows that were not boarded up were smashed, and the pavement was unevenly surfaced. Alistair had managed to order a taxi, and he and Jakob argued about whether they should wait for the police or not. –Are you crazy, they practically assault your wife and you're not even going to report them? The taxi arrived and they got in, the men downcast, ashamed, Isabelle thinking intently, as if she needed to discover what it was that had revealed itself for an instant, something that cut across the placid succession of things. They drove northwards, Anthony had given the cabbie the address of a club: he insisted that it was his fault for taking them to the play, and so this was his treat, he ordered whiskies without asking them and led Isabelle onto the dance floor. They danced, Anthony and Isabelle, Alistair and Isabelle; Jakob alone did not make the effort, but sat, more or less upright, on his bar stool, straightening himself with a jerk whenever he started to sag. She danced, Isabelle danced. She tried to recall the man's face, his eyes only inches from her face, she compared it with Jim's face, she was drunk and in high spirits, and when Alistair asked her if she had been afraid, she said no. –It's already become unreal, said Isabelle, although only two hours had elapsed, and by next morning nothing about it would be quite authentic anymore, because even one day later a thing like that turned into an anecdote, something she could tell Andras, Isabelle thought; but the two of them talked so rarely.

Next day she did phone the office; it was Sonja who answered, and so she told her all about it. Sonja wanted to know what Jakob had done, about which there was little to be said. That morning he had waited, still dejected, until she woke up. He hated violence so much, he had repeated over and over again, getting on her nerves; now she felt sorry for him. She wondered if he didn't notice the neighbors, never heard the noise because it was on the ground floor, in her room, or whether he ignored it because he hated violence, because he would not acknowledge the presence in his world of what he loathed. Wasn't there a tiny crack opening up there, a shift that provoked unease and curiosity, and disappointment? It was quiet, she wandered here and there in the house that was so untouched, she didn't feel like working, and so she went out, walked to the tube station and took a train to King's Cross, into the din of people and construction machinery and traffic. Everywhere there were newspaper stands, travelers, beggars, businessmen hurrying out of the station, families with suitcases and anxious faces. With a beaming smile, a tall woman with short blond curls ran up to a shorter man with a big head, and they threw their arms round each other; the man reminded Isabelle of Andras. York Way was quiet by day, too, and there was nobody waiting at the bus stop. In the sunshine the buildings looked even more dilapidated than by night. Something flashed, light reflecting off glass. A single stunted tree stirred in a draft; a paper bag lay on the asphalt. She absorbed everything she could see, a man in a hard hat on a crane some way off, the reddish wall. Sirens emitted two or three wailing notes, and then fell silent. At the spot where the men had appeared from behind the tarpaulins the previous night Isabelle stopped and stood still. Even things that happened directly to you faded and melted away. All there was here was a rundown neighborhood that was being demolished and rebuilt, nothing more. She buried herself in the little streets and alleys, refusing to accept that nothing was happening, that nothing *had* happened. It was warm, almost like summer; she was conscious of her thighs beneath her skirt, the dust on her feet.

As she rounded the corner Jim recognized her at once, and was confused and angry: she had no business here, on his old turf, which he had kept away from for so long, in these streets that Mae had walked along, that he had crossed with her. There she was, stroking her hands down her skirt. He felt in his trouser pocket for cigarettes, for his lighter, and began to smoke. But she wasn't spying on him, he thought, even if she was standing on the corner of Field Street as though she was waiting for somebody. The house where he and Mae had lived was unoccupied, and even the greengrocer wasn't there anymore, nobody he could ask, just scaffolding, a tarpaulin that covered the front of the building and flapped against the steel poles in the warm breeze. An occasional muffled thud from the excavations, like the beat of a drum, made itself heard above the noise of the traffic. Jim flicked his cigarette into a drain and fished the next one out of the packet. And she was coming nearer, with an indecisive, silly expression on her face she was coming nearer, walking, here, where he was searching for Mae; then she stumbled, twisting her head sharply to one side, looked up and recoiled when she recognized Jim. There's no place on earth with so many idiots and peeping Toms and murderers, Albert had declared, to calm Mae's fears of a terrorist attack. The dead, he said, would never be where you expected to find them. Isabelle approached him like a sleepwalker, and he grinned and took her by the arm, then encircled her waist, squeezing it so tight that she moaned, and made as if to kiss her. She looked into his eyes, at his mouth.

He looked furious; she wanted to explain, but after all he must have been waiting for her, must have been lying in wait for her, and she asked him something he didn't understand, whether he had been here last night, and was obviously disappointed when he let go of her, took a step back and started laughing. There he was, in a tight-fitting T-shirt beneath which she could see his powerful torso, the definition of his muscles, and again he merely turned on his heel, calling out something to her over his shoulder, –see you, a promise, a threat, before walking rapidly away. Field Street, she read on the street sign, confused, deflated. There was a mistake somewhere. If only one could go backwards, run back, rewind what had happened up to now, to erase or confirm it. But here there was just an empty street, something bright and barren, and so she set off, slowly at first, then faster, to Euston Road and beyond, westwards, and now she was running towards Warren Street, where she was held up by a cluster of people, newspaper vendors, sellers of belts, working people, tourists; somebody dropped a small bunch of flowers and the blooms were trodden under-foot. For a moment four schoolboys surrounded her, faces grinning above crooked, crumpled collars, and a man heaving a double bass along in front of him rammed it into Isabelle; pain and hurt feelings brought tears to her eyes, and as she threaded her way awkwardly out of the milling crowd she saw a flower-seller taking the last bunches out of her buckets, and a younger woman appeared behind her, grabbed the buckets and with a swinging motion emptied the water out onto the roadway. She seemed oddly familiar to Isabelle, but thin, almost gaunt, and as she straightened up and turned sideways Isabelle saw her face, disfigured by a scar that ran from temple to chin, fiery red, ugly. As if the wound itself were not enough, it had healed badly, and the face was marked, branded by the viciousness that ruined human faces. But perhaps it was an accident, Isabelle thought. Shocked at the sight, she had been unaware of being watched by the older woman, who advanced on her with an angry, contemptuous expression and shooed her away with a sweep of her hand, without a word, as one chases off a gawping child.

Blushing with shame, she hurried on, past small shops, a café with a green bench outside it, the Royal National Institute for the Blind, and here was the last street junction separating her from Jakob, here was the massive door with the wrought-iron bars.

25

J akob carried the carefully balanced pile of folders, notes, and copies to Bentham's room. He eased the door open with his shoulder, and there was Bentham seated behind his desk, straightening up with measured curiosity, holding a small figure in his hands. –Look at this, no, put the papers down somewhere first, he gestured around the room, –you need to touch him, here you are. He held out the figure to Jakob, who was standing there at a loss, balancing the pile of papers, uncertain what to do. –Behind you, there's some room on the chest, and as Jakob turned around the top sheet slid off and floated in a graceful curve to the floor. The wooden figure, a Buddha, was warm and smooth, but did not nestle comfortably in his hand, –that's right, said Bentham, he doesn't mould himself to your hand, you have to explore the posture with your fingers bit by bit, it has an austerity which takes time to yield up its secrets. He took the figure back from Jakob. –He was given to me by a lady I know in Israel, the only thing she inherited from her father: he had been the director of the Far Eastern Art Museum in Cologne, and had a large private collection which he donated to the museum. Fortunately his second wife was Aryan, which is how he survived, that's to say, he died in 1943 of a broken heart. His daughter was already in Israel. I handled her claim for restitution—and lost.

Bentham put the Buddha down on his desk again, looked at Jakob, and waved his hand as though there were someone else in the room. Then, rising to his feet, he went across to the chest of drawers and bent over the papers. –Count Helldorf, he said, ah, I see.

–He was the Chief of Police, and apparently he enabled a few wealthy families to leave the country, in return for enormous bribes, Jakob reported. An intermediary signed the contract for the Treptow villa on his behalf, that's why I've only just come across his name. –Leader of the S.A. in Berlin-Brandenburg from 1931 onwards, wasn't he? Bentham said. What a disagreeable individual. Executed, I believe?

Jakob nodded. –In August, 1944, in Plötzensee prison: he was arrested after the July 20th bomb plot. That's what makes the whole thing so complicated, he's regarded as a resistance fighter and therefore legally unexceptionable, and there's also the matter of the intermediary. There's a contract of sale which names an appropriate price, but letters from Miller's father make it clear that the amount actually paid was not even a tenth of that sum. After the war the intermediary's heirs got the house. Their name is Krüger. The man has probably studied law and thought he could handle the case himself. He claims that the relevant documents were destroyed in the war, and argues that his grandfather bought the villa in good faith. In other words, he knows nothing.

–It seems Helldorf really did help a few people, Bentham said.

And Miller, Jakob went on, had gone to Berlin on his own initiative, to Berlin and the area around Lake Stechlin, where the family was supposed to have had a country house. He had been met with hostility in both places, and in Treptow, moreover, he had been shocked by the rundown condition of the house, which had been subdivided into apartments, while the ground floor and basement had been given over to a shop selling computer and role-playing games. He had sent Jakob a copy of a letter, inconsiderately written in German and insolent in tone, from Krüger, who thought that he could resolve the matter on his own, by intimidation. Now Krüger was probably considering hiring a lawyer after all—Bult, the one who had come to the fore in the case about the Seehof plots of land and acted as press spokesman for the demonstrators, or, rather, counter-demonstrators.

–The Seehof plots, asked Bentham, wasn't it in connection with them that the comparison was drawn with Israel: that what Israel was doing to the Palestinians, the returning Jews were doing to the Germans now living there?

Again Jakob nodded. –In Treptow Krüger started by arguing on the basis of the investment already put into the property, which is laughable, of course, in view of the state of neglect the house has fallen into. I imagine Bult will bring him back into line.

–But, you know, Bentham said with a shrug, in the final analysis the old Roman principle still holds: a claim can be based on a period of unchallenged occupancy—in this case, the duration of a thousand-year Reich.

–I shall probably have to go over there, said Jakob. Bentham looked at him. –The idea doesn't exactly enthuse you? You'd rather stay here with us? Then don't be in a hurry to bring things to a head. Prepare yourself thoroughly. That's better, anyway, and instructive, too.

He bent down, looking for something in a drawer, and appeared to forget Jakob. Maude's knock at the door made him glance up again, but it was Jakob she wanted. –Your wife's downstairs, she said, beaming, as if this announcement gave her particular pleasure. –I told her you'd be down straight away. This was sternly directed at Bentham, who nodded his acquiescence, looking again at Jakob. –By all means, he said, go for a little walk. That always does one good.

Isabelle was standing in the hall, her hand clutching the banister; her agitation made Jakob feel uncomfortable, and he steered her outside, holding her firmly round the waist. Only when they were out in the street did he kiss her, noticing her soft, appealing skin and the beauty spot that seemed to have a life of its own, like a little animal, affectionate, but ready at any moment to disappear into its burrow. –Isabelle, said Jakob. She looked up at him with an embarrassed smile. –I didn't mean to disturb you, but it's been such a strange morning.

–You're not disturbing me.

–I mean, suddenly turning up at your office like this, she answered. It's because of yesterday, that's all. I've been worried about you.

–About me? Why about me?

–Jakob? she said, can we go home?

He heard how her voice sounded, quite ordinary, clear. Can we go home? He felt his body reacting faster than his brain. She wanted to go home, she wanted to go to bed with him, and he knew she was right: how easy it would be to do what she was suggesting, which would dispel the sense of danger and defeat that he had only managed to forget for a while because he was due to go and see Bentham. So easy, he thought, to sleep together, even without desire or passion, tenderly, because they were man and wife, because of their love, and they could laugh together about the humiliation that he wanted to forget. –It was nothing, just a few idiots, he said vaguely. She nodded hesitantly. –Look, let's go out for a meal this evening. There are still a couple of things I need to do. Or are you nervous on your own?

At the end of the street she turned and waved. Jakob went upstairs, but the door to Bentham's room was closed, not even slightly ajar but actually closed, and Jakob felt a stab, as if this were some kind of punishment. The railway-company purchase was complex and stimulating work. Jakob met the client, who was convinced that he, as a German, could build up a gigantic business, as he put it, simply because his trains would run on time and not break down or come off the rails as soon as there were "leaves on the line" or half an inch of snow. He was a big man with a rather expressionless face, who made Alistair and Anthony laugh when he arrived, breathing heavily, amiable and yet slightly menacing. Jakob devoted most of his days to reading, and ordered a whole list of historical works from Mr. Krapohl, who suggested additional titles, –but what about Bajohr, you must read Bajohr, too, and Friedländer, only the first volume has appeared so far but it's one of the best books on the subject, and Krapohl cleared a shelf for Jakob so that he could gather everything together, the books and also some material from the Internet relating to the Wertheim land in Leipziger Strasse and the property acquired and developed in recent years by Otto Beisheim, and Jakob read letters written by the owners of the land in Seehof and the transcripts from the Court of Administration in Berlin. –I've never made such an intensive study of Germany, Jakob told Hans over the phone, –I wonder whether I'd have been able to read all these books in Berlin. –Why not? Hans said touchily, and Jakob read him a passage from Friedländer's book about the Third Reich and the Jews, describing how in June, 1938, some children attacked a jeweler's shop and plundered it, and a little boy spat in the face of the Jewish proprietor.

During the early part of the afternoon Jakob would start looking out of the window every so often to examine the sky, the speed of the passing clouds, and the blue between them, to see whether the sun promised a fine evening—the early evening that Bentham preferred for his walks—for although Bentham himself was indifferent to the weather, it was only in fine weather that he would ask Jakob to accompany him on a short stroll through Regent's Park, as far as the zoo and back. There was no telling whether he was doing Jakob a favor or actually seeking his company. On these walks Jakob kept half a pace behind Bentham, who advanced resolutely, only occasionally turning his head to the right or left so that Jakob saw his profile, the steeply arching eyebrows, the nose, the full mouth, surprising for a man of his age, and noticed how the various features seemed rather ill-assorted and clumsy and yet created an effect of graceful mobility. Although Bentham must have been aware of Jakob's extensive scrutiny, he gave no sign of it, commenting instead on flowers, passersby, trees, or dogs that ran up when they saw him and then stopped at a respectful distance, wagging their tails. Jakob smiled, smiled at everything that Bentham pointed out to him, ducks, couples lying on the grass kissing, the wolves in their enclosure and their long-legged, restless pacing: just like a child, Jakob thought, meaning himself, and felt embarrassed. He loved the park, but whenever he went out on his own, because it was drizzling or because Bentham had not come into the office, or because it was the weekend, he hoped above all else to bump into him, and kept a constant lookout for a suit, generally light-colored these days, with the shoulders somewhat constricted inside it, which emphasized the narrow hips and the nonetheless heavy build: Bentham cut an elegant figure, advancing with dance steps, or rather dancing-bear steps, more speedily than one would suppose, immersed in thought and yet taking note of whatever was agreeable or amusing.

Now and again Alistair would pass a comment when he came up to Jakob's room on the third floor, or when they went out for a meal together. Although he would inquire about Miller or about Jakob's reading, it was clear that he really came to test out some idea that had occurred to him casting a remark into the conversation as one casts a line, certain that Jakob would bite. He was not inhibited by Bentham's presence on the same floor, and with his usual insouciance made no effort to lower his voice. To Jakob he seemed guileless yet subtly malicious, as though intent on savoring to the full his own love for Bentham. A bird, he said—speaking of Bentham—whose feathers were falling out, whose wings were losing their power, in spite of his unwavering vanity, which was hard to overlook, and indeed sometimes sharpness of mind, even of the legal mind, was inseparable from vanity, Alistair remarked as he was leaving the room. Bentham, he said, really enjoyed creating confusion, especially in a young man, he added on another occasion: in fact Bentham considered confusion to be highly desirable in general, not just in young men, for if one had too great a degree of certainty, how could one reflect on the relationship between jurisprudence and history, on how subversive, in effect, legal decisions were, and what an ingenious form of continuity something like reparations represented. The whole field of reparation claims, Alistair once said, was a strange one; had Jakob any idea how one's view of an issue like this was influenced by one's age? Calculations of losses and their settlement, that was how Jakob ought to view it. Like a lover's beauty and his death, and the way you rail against it all over again, but are wise enough not to do battle where there is no prospect of success. What this referred to, Jakob did not immediately grasp, only suspecting that it had something to do with Maude's unfailing solicitude towards Bentham, which gave the impression of having been practiced over many years.

Jakob never took the lift, which creaked and groaned on its cables, but always climbed up and down the stairs, his hand firmly gripping the banister thick with varnish. In the half-light that penetrated the windows or seeped out of the lamps, the worn carpet glowed, but one could feel underfoot how threadbare it was. These had been Bentham's offices for nearly forty years, Jakob gathered from Alistair's explanations, with their sometimes enigmatic undertones, and of course a lawyer who was still young, and an immigrant at that, could not normally have aspired to such a good address. It had been a gift. Maude, chancing to join them, provided a far more straightforward account: in 1967, she said, correcting Alistair, Mr. Bentham, then a handsome young man of thirty-two, had been offered the use of the premises by a patron—here Alistair sniggered—but he had soon been able to buy them outright, since his firm quickly became one of the most highly regarded in London. It was an exceptional achievement for someone who had arrived there all alone, with no possessions, nothing but a cardboard sign around his neck, and had been put up for adoption; eventually his parents had followed him and thereby escaped being murdered, but they had never really established themselves, especially as their other son had died soon after their arrival. –Fate treated him cruelly! she added, full of anxious concern for Bentham the child, even in retrospect. But fate, Jakob thought, was precisely the wrong word. He, too, hearing such stories, had originally thought in terms of fate, of a harsh destiny, of inexorability. He had seen German unification as an opportunity, even at this late date, to apply the rule of law to some tiny fraction of the old injustice. But he now began, for the first time, to view the Nazi era as something man-made, as politics, as a product of human action, of the human will.

That it was not Bentham's childhood that prompted Maude's fussing attentions when he left, sometimes a little shaky on his feet, at the end of the day—parting from him with a gesture that seemed to call on all good, kindly spirits to watch over him—was something Jakob suddenly understood when, one evening, he caught sight of Bentham not far from the Coliseum. Delight made his heart skip a beat, but the next moment it almost stopped, for Bentham was waiting for someone, evidently in vain, alone in his elegance and perfect composure. Passersby stared at him in wonderment as they brushed past him, and Jakob was glad to be too far away to catch any of the disparaging remarks to which Bentham, in his white suit, black bow tie, and light-colored, impeccable shoes, was surely exposed. He was confident of escaping his notice, since it was obvious that Bentham would see no one but the person he was waiting for, and Jakob continued on his way to a rendezvous with Isabelle, seeking solace with her, conscious that his feelings had been hurt. There was someone who was supremely important in Bentham's life.

When Alistair turned up in his room the following day, Jakob felt like a little mouse lured out into the open by the cat-like, playful slyness of Alistair's suggestions, by his sleek body, his never-empty hands that seemed to mock him with their careless animation. –Bentham is sure to leave early today, and I've arranged with Isabelle for us all to go and see *Sunset Boulevard* at the National Film Theatre. –But why should Bentham be going home early today? Jakob queried, annoyed at having to show his ignorance. –Today would have been his lover's birthday, Alistair responded, now come on, I'll pick you up here in an hour, Isabelle will be waiting for us at the N.F.T., and we can go on my Vespa, or would you rather walk? Jakob agreed to the plan but insisted on walking, and Alistair gave him a wave and disappeared. On the roof guttering some pigeons were sitting side by side with their feathers fluffed up, Jakob heard them cooing and went over to the window. A predecessor or a visitor had flicked some cigarette ends into the copper guttering. –If you smoke, lean well out of the window, Maude had told him right at the start, and now he smoked a cigarette, something he had not done in a long while, peering down at the street, listening to the voices, the cars, the sirens. Inside the building it was already quiet, it seemed as if Bentham really had left, as neither his gentle coughing nor his telephone was to be heard. Later, as Jakob was crossing Hungerford Bridge on the pedestrian walkway, alongside the rhythmically pounding trains, which seemed to be losing speed and power after their journey from the Continent, a youngish man came purposefully towards him, cutting through the crowd in an eye-catching get-up, with a glittering, close-fitting little jacket, and above it a handsome head of thick curls. He stopped in front of Jakob, smiled and even held out his hand and, when Jakob silently shook his head, touched his shoulder for the briefest of moments before walking on. Left with a confusing, insistent sense of regret, Jakob recounted the incident to Isabelle and Alistair, describing the attractive young man who had apparently made a pass at him, or how else should he interpret his behavior? Jakob asked—at a moment when Isabelle had gone to the bar—and Alistair, laughing, acted as though such a thing came as no surprise to him. –But why shouldn't another man fancy you? Jakob watched Isabelle, who was returning with three glasses and a bottle of wine and smiling at Alistair. He might have felt jealous, Jakob thought, but he didn't. When he asked if she wanted to go to Berlin with him, she said no.

After they had discussed the action Jakob would be taking in Berlin, Bentham rose to his feet, motioning to Jakob to remain seated. –Take your time, anyway. Incidentally, I shall also be away for a few days next week.

On this occasion, with his light-colored suit, he was wearing a white bow tie with black spots.

–I'm meeting Miller again tomorrow, he's found some more of his grandfather's letters.

–There's always something being unearthed, mumbled Bentham, even I shall start doing it one day. Who knows? I met Miller yesterday, and he was enthusing about the house as if it were his guarantee of eternal life. We have a past, so naturally we have the right to a future.

–But surely he really does have that right, Jakob protested. It was theft, a carelessly disguised theft, because von Helldorf had nothing to fear.

–Yes, a theft, certainly. But does one want the stolen property back? At one time I was sure of it, in the days—he pointed to the Buddha on his desk—when I was representing Mrs. Pinkus. It was the notion that something radical could be done, something to restore the truth, nothing less than the truth. As though Germany could give us Jews proof that there was such a thing as truth and justice after all, for us, for the whole world. When one no longer has that belief—and how absurd it seems now—one suspects that there was some element there, after all, of enacting the role of the Chosen People, first the suffering and then the restoration of justice, though of course I do not mean that unkindly. Things can be right and yet misguided. The impulse, I mean, was right. After all, our families were murdered, and many who were not murdered still perished. Then I had that court case, and the judge was one who had been directly involved in sanctioning the original Aryanizations. It was a farce.

–But we surely can't give up on that account.

–I would be more inclined to say that we've barely started.

Jakob lowered his eyes in confusion. Bentham was pacing to and fro. –You've had your grandparents' furniture brought over here, haven't you? I also own some old furniture: I bought it, as if that were a way to provide myself with a past, for of course there was nothing for me to inherit. Now I would probably change it all, but I'm too indolent, and I'm sentimental too. Those pieces of furniture have been with me for over thirty years. They've acquired a right of residence, so to speak. You could say that they've won their place in my memory by unchallenged occupancy. But now that I'm getting really old I wonder what all that signifies. A past, little cases, boxes, letters, photos, all the things you want because they help you to carry on believing that, despite everything, you can elude old age and death. Miller is like me in having no children or other relatives. And yet we are not prepared to give up our truth, we defend our conception of legality and our life against all affronts, old and new. After all, Miller and I are able to do that, while so many others perished. And of course Germany has an obligation. –Surely restitution is the least that Germany can do? Jakob asked. Bentham turned away, pushed papers and books on

Jakob's desk from the right side to the left, picked up one sheet and looked at it, curious to see what was on it. –Yes, that is the least Germany can do, he agreed. And it is nice, he said, looking squarely at Jakob, to have you here. And you get on so well with Alistair. When all's said and done, it is heartening when you manage to turn back even one tiny wheel, don't you think?

Jakob took a flight from London City Airport. Gazing down at the water, he thought of the film he had seen with Alistair and Isabelle, *The Hours*, and tried to picture Meryl Streep's face, but the water blocked it out, in a kind of imageless destruction, and he told himself that he would certainly read a book by Virginia Woolf sometime. Read *Jacob's Room*, Alistair had suggested. Most of the passengers waiting at the gate were tourists, cheerful travelers chatting, boasting, telling each other about things that they had evidently experienced together. A tall, lean man embraced a short, almost spherical woman who closed her eyes, speechless with happiness, and Jakob could hear her humming: totally and utterly happy, he thought.

From Tegel Jakob went straight to Mauerstrasse, where Schreiber was expecting him but was not free to see him. The other party's lawyer cancelled the appointment when Jakob was already in Treptow, and so he prowled around outside the villa, his presence announced by the barking of two dogs in the front garden, until a man shouted something at him in a venomous and menacing tone and led the two dogs by their collars to the garden gate, as if about to set them on him.

He walked in the direction of the park and on towards to the Soviet Memorial; there was a kindergarten nearby, and through the bushes, which were still light green, he caught glimpses of bright colors and heard the voices, clear and confident as if they were merrily calling out: here I am! The birds chirped and twittered, and Jakob marveled as he watched the large numbers of sparrows scraping out hollows and having dust baths: it was very dry, almost summery. On reaching the Spree, he saw the bay and considered hiring a boat for an hour, saw the little islands, the Liebesinsel and Kratzbruch, while to his right was the abandoned amusement park with its decaying dinosaurs, oversized swans and the naked arms of some roundabouts. A tramp sitting on a bench grinned insolently at him and waved, with a suggestive leer, at a young woman who was approaching with a tear-stained face, pushing a pram. Now the path, which had narrowed, ran directly alongside the river, with just a thin strip of woodland to the right, and on the opposite bank a factory with lorries, inaudible to Jakob, carrying their loads away. A small landing stage jutted out into the water, but there was no sign of a ferry, just a barge going past. It bore the name "Wroclaw," and there was no one to be seen on board, only a washing line with colorful print aprons fluttering on it, and a bicycle propped against the rail. The landing stage gave off the smell of warm wood and summer, fluffy clouds floated by, and, saddened as if by a loss, Jakob thought of Bentham. He remembered Fontane's *Stechlin* novel, the boat ride, the excursion to the Eierhäuschen, an incipient love. Restitution *was* a farce, since it was ultimately not about places but about lost years of life and of memory, about the memories that were denied to people or stolen from them. He wished he could dive into the water, head first and eyes closed, slip into a different skin and rise to the surface again, fresher, more lucid and with a vitality that he had never possessed. Surprised, he asked himself whether he had ever suffered a loss—he had lost his mother, but even so he did not mourn his childhood. The home he had grown up in meant little to him, the memory of his mother meant a great deal, and the two things together perhaps provided an outline that he only needed to fill in. *Part* of an outline, he mentally corrected himself, for Isabelle and Bentham were part of it too.

As he neared the underground station again he took out his

mobile and called Andras's number. Andras sounded a little surprised, but pleased, and they arranged to meet that evening.

Andras was half an hour late, a half-hour which passed so slowly that Jakob felt the whole of his afternoon walk would have fitted into it. He was startled when Andras came through the door of the Café Lenzig, because he looked as if he had grown taller, stronger, and he seemed to know intuitively what Jakob wanted to discuss with him.

–Isn't Bentham right? said Andras. You really did believe that you were restoring a kind of justice. But for that you need the Jews, whereas it's often quite clear that people here would rather see the Jewish Claims Conference in Hades. And the ghosts of the past, or their descendants, who are pretty much like ghosts anyway, conveniently provide the state with proof that in the Federal Republic everything has been handled admirably and is all straightened out, and only the G.D.R., with its loud protestations of innocence, behaved criminally. Politicians play off past law against the rights of the past, and claim to be acting in the name of truth.

–How do you mean? asked Jakob.

–The point is to justify the behavior of the Federal Republic. There may be a lot of people who don't actually want Jews living here, but that's the price that has to be paid for the state to be able to claim that it's founded on the rule of law. After all, the other consequences of the Nazi era are left well alone, or are even being served up now in a different way, with the suffering of the Germans, the bombing of German cities, marching steadily into the foreground. Don't get me wrong, of course I'm all for the restitution of the stolen property, and if it's in the form of the property itself, rather than compensation, that's fine by me. But, even so, I can understand why people find it bizarre. The descendants of those who were driven into exile or murdered are seeking to recover their ancestors' past, which was wiped out. And is there such a thing as German-Jewish coexistence? I'm not at all sure there is.

–But *you* live here, isn't that German-Jewish coexistence? And restitution doesn't mean that the beneficiaries have to live here.

–No, they don't have to live here—but in that case what your work aims to achieve is basically compensation, isn't it? Income from rents and that sort of thing. Ludicrously inadequate compensation for the destruction of what a person thought of as his life. And as for me, I live here as a Hungarian, or as a German, if you like. Who actually knows that I'm Jewish? Peter doesn't, Isabelle doesn't. Nobody asks, and I don't rub their noses in it. Why should I? I'm not certain myself what it means to me. Am I Jewish? Yes, of course. But first and foremost I'm a Hungarian in exile. One exotic identity eclipses the other. And the fact that Israel exists makes me feel more comfortable about living here.

–Have you ever been to Israel?

–Several times, I've got a few relatives living near Tel Aviv, though not as many as in Budapest. Andras leaned back. They don't need to tell their stories, it's enough to spend a day with them. It's a bit like a continuous procession, to shops, to other relatives, on errands, everything is a constant evocation of what only the older people still remember. For us, all of that is gradually fading—my sister and brother-in-law live no differently from you and Isabelle, I should imagine. But whenever I'm there my parents feel compelled to bring up, yet again, the subject of what they had to deprive me of by sending me away. They think it was my childhood, but actually I did spend my childhood with them. I've been away for so long that the stories of those who left and of those who stayed have all become focused on me. Their longings, their ambition, their failed loves and adulteries and lies.

Jakob glanced out of the window as if from there he could look up at his apartment, which he had found unchanged.

–I wonder if it was wise to go to London, he said. I feel as if something is slipping away from me there, but I don't know what.

–Is that why you wanted to see me? Andras asked kindly, almost tenderly.

–This afternoon I was thinking that there's a sort of outline around one's own life, and that that's all one needs—but I don't know what that really means. Things seem to be changing.

–Things?

Jakob was silent. Then Andras said: –Why shouldn't one live in two places? Why make these so-called decisions? Perhaps at some stage we can come to terms with our own outlines and understand that that's sufficient, more than sufficient.

The next day Jakob had to be at the Court of Administration. Hans picked him up there and they went for a meal, but both were cautious, disappointed, and Jakob tried in vain to think of something he could say to Hans. Come and visit us, he wanted to say, but didn't. Hans drove him to Tegel. At the moment of parting they held each other in a long embrace, and when he saw Hans smile, bravely and sadly and tenderly, he cautiously stroked his arm.

As the aircraft approached Heathrow, it circled in a wide sweep above the city. Jakob was able to make out Regent's Park and Great Portland Street, and tried unsuccessfully, restrained by his seat belt and admonished by a severe look from the stewardess, to strain upwards in his seat and perhaps catch a glimpse of Devonshire Street.

For the next few days Bentham did not come into the office, and no one told Jakob where he was.

26

It was Magda who left *him*: for the time being, she said, perhaps only for a while, so as to avoid a more unpleasant parting of the ways, which would certainly come if they left it too long and no longer knew what they expected or hoped for. So we're foundering on expectations, thought Andras, and was surprised to find that his slight initial bitterness quickly disappeared. He wandered around the city even more often than usual, noticing nothing, walking in circles, covering the same streets and squares over and over again. Occasionally he found himself in the outer suburbs, in Weissensee, or in Marzahn, where the concrete-slab buildings petered out towards the northeast, giving way to fields. At no point was he really unhappy: he simply went wherever his feet took him, and his mind was at ease. Everything was on hold, even his yearning for Isabelle. He had been irritated by the last newsy e-mail that she had sent him, two months ago, in which, agitated about the war and with a labored attempt at humor, she had told him how people were being urged to stock up on candles and batteries. But his annoyance was subsiding now, although her reaction, and the mixture of naïveté and unconvincing irony with which she described a store of provisions under the bed, seemed to him embarrassingly stupid. Because when it came down to it, thought Andras, she was unscathed. She had a remarkable talent for remaining unscathed even where something directly affected her, such as Alexa's decision to move out, Hanna's death, or her marriage: not so much a cat with nine lives as a puppy which never comes to any harm because it's so cute that nothing can possibly hurt it. He felt no longing for Isabelle, nor for Magda, and yet they filled the space in which he lived, the walks and the night hours when he stood at the open window, in the zone of urban darkness that lay between the lower end of Choriner Strasse and the bright lights of Alexanderplatz. He had taken up smoking again, finding it difficult at first, coughing, disliking the taste, but Herr Schmidt had offered him a cigarette one evening when they met on the stairs, and Andras had fallen in love with the glowing red dot, the ember of passing time. He stood at the window, with the smell of dust behind him, the apartment showing signs of neglect now that he never had visitors. The red sofa he had sat on with Isabelle, the bed in which he and Magda had slept. Their bodies, different as they were, merged into one, Magda's dry leanness, Isabelle's softness, the fulfilled, the unfulfilled. He was not sure there was any great difference. Often he would wake up too late to get to the agency on time, and then Peter would phone him, furious, demanding. Dutifully making haste, Andras would arrive at the office in Dircksenstrasse looking deeply abashed, and settle straight down to work. While he was getting everything done on time after all he would listen to the sounds that rose from the street, the footsteps and women's voices; now and then he would go right up to the window, see girls strolling past and ask himself how much this still concerned him, whether he still felt involved when he admired a dress, a swaying of hips, a pair of slender arms or ankles, all the things that attracted him and yet had become more remote. It was not that he had renounced them. At times he felt piqued, and made a point of noticing whether a woman's eyes glanced fleetingly at him, whether a woman he found attractive returned his look, whether he could distract her as she sat at a table with another man, or whether, if he briefly touched someone by accident in a cinema queue or some other crowded situation, the contact was welcome. When he got to know thirty-year-old Claire he was delighted by her hopefulness, her eager, shy way of touching him, but then he vanished, never to see her again. Not without misgivings, he examined whether that decision had been necessary. What he remembered of Claire was her gentle eyes, brown, just like a doe's, with something in them that seemed weightless, light to the point of self-abnegation, intangible. That appealed to him, because everything he was, everything that mattered to him, was gently drifting to the surface, floating on the air like leaves or like the fleecy poplar seeds that wafted so carelessly away. One of his walks took him to the western part of the city, to the woodland cemetery; it was a brilliantly sunny day at the end of May, and a crowd of mourners in their black clothes were covered in the downy fluff as they streamed from the graveside back towards the exit. He had not been to visit Hanna's grave since her funeral; now he saw how well-kept it was, and realized that Peter probably went each week without fail to weed or plant and to smooth the soil. The sandstone with Hanna's name already looked blurred, and bright green moss covered the weathered side of the stone; there was something comforting about that. On a second visit, towards evening, Andras saw some wild boar running away, disappearing under a hedge, and there were said to be foxes and other animals in the gardens in Heerstrasse and right into the city as far as Charlottenburg. He described it all in an e-mail to Isabelle: the scent of the acacias and lime trees, the play of the shadows of leaves cast by the street lamps, the railings, some very splendid, some comically crooked, that divided the houses and gardens from the street, the eerily broad road towards Spandau, and lastly the approach to the Olympic Stadium. *Do you remember*, he wrote, *what Bush said, that nothing is the way it was? Heerstrasse doesn't seem to have changed since the thirties, nor does the woodland cemetery. All unchanged. And yet how much everything must have changed, Hanna is dead, you're married and living in London, and I may take myself off to Budapest after all. Or I may just spend a few months there. I'll keep the apartment on in any case, and of course Herr Schmidt is still there too, he's made himself at home up in the attic, and although the property managers are looking for a buyer they haven't found one yet, so the two of us are staying on there, quite content with this temporary state of affairs.*

He assumed that Peter had told her about the agency's impending move. In Dircksenstrasse the lease was due for renewal, and the rent would be going up. Peter had proposed leaving the Mitte district rather than negotiating about the rent, –moving, he said, with a vehemence that startled Andras, and then they fell silent, both of them thinking of Hanna. Andras had undertaken to look into the possibility of moving to Potsdamer Strasse, and in a workshop in the rear part of a building he had found two printers who were interested in working regularly with their agency. Nothing has changed, he thought as he walked down Potsdamer Strasse after his meeting with them; it felt just as if he was walking home twenty or twenty-five years ago, and Aunt Sofi was sitting at the piano, playing with such a light and faultless touch that Uncle Janos and Andras sat silent and motionless on the sofa, and Uncle Janos was weeping. This is all that there is, Uncle Janos told Andras, you don't understand that, you're waiting, just as I waited. He laughed: I hope at least *you* will realize it before it's too late. Andras shook his head to chase the phantoms away. Stallholders were packing fruit, the first watermelons, back into their boxes and wheeling them away on tall, metal racks, making a great clatter but continuing to shout, still calling out what they had been calling out all day long: tomatoes, melons, cheap aubergines! Two pounds of apples for thirty-nine cents! They did not bend down to pick up what was lying around on the ground, and an old woman waited patiently a little way off, ready to gather it up; Andras tried to give her five euros, but she shook her head without looking at him. Two boys came running out of the ice-cream parlor opposite, pursued by the owner who was yelling angrily and, to add insult to injury, being mimicked by the young men sitting at the tables outside. A police patrol car approached, sounded its horn, and drove on. The people in the street were moving more slowly now, a steady flow, growing indistinct in the slowly gathering dusk. A few men sitting in silence outside a tearoom eyed Andras keenly, and he walked on, straight past the house where he had lived with Aunt Sofi and Uncle Janos; he only looked round when it was already too late, and did not stop. He had expected *some* message from Isabelle, a reply to his e-mail, a brief hello at least, a sign of continuing absence scratched into the insubstantial surface of time. He burst out laughing, at himself and his fanciful sentiments. He missed Hanna, really missed her: she would have helped him sort out his feelings about Isabelle—Isabelle whom he no longer missed but still cared for in a way he did not fully understand. That was why he had lost Magda. He still cared, even now, for the indecisive, confused girl that Isabelle had been when he first met her. Indecisive, he thought, that's what my life is, and hers, too. We know all about cause and effect, and yet it doesn't seem to apply to us, not really. So how are we to say whether anything has changed or not?

And the future played no part in this; it changed into the present, that was all. The plan to move to Potsdamer Strasse and give up the old office was as easy to carry out as his decision to give up painting. Isabelle would either rejoin them or not. He had not been surprised by his uncle's lie (that he worked as a doctor, when in fact he was only a nurse), nor by his aunt's failure at her beloved music. Budapest, whichever way he looked at it, was a faded memory, a ghost of a memory, though alive in its own way; and his parents had done what they had to do, for they believed they were saving one child, at least, by sending him to where they themselves would once have been murdered. All of it so foolish, and yet serious. There had been enough decisions made in his life, and the past, like an unwelcome guest grown to an inordinate size, expanded and stretched itself out like an old cat, sprawling gigantically on the table or the bed, its claws broken, but still a mass of fur and flesh that would have driven one away if only one had known where to go. –My dear, do move out of here, Magda had said, no matter whether to Budapest or to somewhere else in Berlin, in this hole you'll just go to rack and ruin. It would have been easy to move in with her, he was sure she was only waiting for him to ask: two rooms and a bathroom for him, separate from her own quarters, she wouldn't interfere, he knew, and would give him his own key to the back door. –Yet another opportunity for you to turn down? had been László's comment. And then Magda had gone. László tried again to lure him to Budapest; he came to Berlin, eleven pounds slimmer since he'd started going to the gym. –Directly overlooking the river, a fantastic view, power walking on the spot, he declared, grinning, and Andras really should get some new shirts. –And give that leather jacket to your tramp, you look a fright. But it was impossible to make any plans with Andras. –What are you still waiting for, what *does* interest you? László finally asked, exasperated. Nothing much, thought Andras, just the first warm evenings, the acacias, and Isabelle not answering. He was not interested in the past, that gigantic eastern-European-and-Jewish feline, growing unbidden, taking up ever more space. He could only avoid it by creeping surreptitiously past it.

Then he found a message from Isabelle, short and casual, with a drawing attached, showing a girl in a red coat, running. She was running away at speed, as if in a panic, and he read, *The child next door is the model for this, although I've never seen her in the street. She's probably not allowed out of the house, and is very pale.*

There was no mention of the new office; she merely sent Peter an authorization to act as her proxy. Hans was dealing with the contract, and Andras told László that he would come to Budapest for three weeks. –Yes, off you go, said Peter angrily, so long as *one* of us stays here to do all the work. Though you *could* find us a few new clients in Budapest. If nobody's drumming up any business here, we'd better start importing some from Budapest or London. What do you people think you're playing at? In case you've forgotten, the three of us all depend on the agency for our livelihood!

That night they worked until two in the morning, and when they were together again the following day and were leaning side by side at the window, Peter said: –That *was* what we wanted, wasn't it? A design agency? Sonja came to the door holding two telephones and making frantic gestures because a third one was ringing, but the two men ignored her and went on leaning out of the window in the sunshine, feeling comfortable with each other. –Even if Isabelle came it wouldn't be any easier, said Peter, but I expect you miss her.

–I don't miss her at all, that's just it. You know, not long ago, I went to the cemetery, to Hanna's grave. And Magda really has stopped contacting me. But I don't feel depressed. We carry on, and actually things are going very well, we're just older and possibly tire more easily, that's all. I've always assumed that at a certain point you work out what really matters to you, and then you come to a decision. But maybe that's not true at all. When I first met Jakob, that's when I started to worry. As though he was blindly searching for something, and Isabelle might go running off somewhere like the girl in the red coat.

–Nothing really matters to me anymore since Hanna died, said Peter slowly. I thought it was because of that, because of her death. The work goes on, the apartment has hardly changed, Sonja's moving in with me—I've been meaning to tell you that for some time. He laughed and ran his hand through his short grey hair. –Perhaps you'll get your Isabelle after all, though I'm not at all sure I should wish that on you. Magda is a different proposition.

Sonja came into the room with a note, and Peter went up to her and kissed her on the lips. –I've told him. Come on, Andras, give us your blessing!

A few nights later he suddenly started from his sleep, switched on the lamp with trembling hands and looked at the clock. Almost four, too late to phone Magda. But his dream had not been of her but of Isabelle; she had been standing in a bare room under neon lighting, naked and older than she was in reality, an aging woman in a childlike body, wearing a vacant, helpless expression. Andras got up and went into the bathroom: for the first time it bothered him that the mirror had so many tarnished spots. Wrapping a towel around his waist, he went to the window, lit a cigarette, coughed. The image would not go away, and he searched in it for Isabelle's face, the face that he loved, but what he saw remained strange and distressing, as if this was how her face was ultimately destined to be, so frightened and cold. But she hadn't been alone in the room, he remembered, and he recalled the grey carpet, stained and threadbare; even in his dream she had had to put her clothes back on and go, leaving the other person, whoever it was, behind. At six o'clock Andras took a shower, dressed and went out. He met the newspaper deliveryman, who spat on the ground in front of him. The morning smelled dusty and the light of dawn showed nothing to bring cheer: a newsagent unloading bundles of papers from a lorry, the traffic building up at last, two policemen casting an indifferent eye on him, a train passing by. How he clung to the belief that Isabelle was still the person he loved, intact, transparent, with no particular wishes, nothing to displease or repel one, nothing leading onwards, out of the present and into the turmoil of hope or desire or ambition. Old-fashioned, he thought, in her way, but perhaps she was sometimes unkind.

László had persuaded him to spend at least three weeks in Budapest, –for the sake of your sister and your parents. They were due to fly tomorrow.

At the office he found an e-mail from Isabelle. *Today for the very first time I saw our neighbors' child out in the street, following in her father's wake. It was like a scene from a Ken Loach film. She has straggly hair and is very pale. Her father left her standing there in the street and rushed off in a furious rage. I couldn't understand what it was he shouted at her. He was shouting, and I was standing at the open window, the way you often do yourself. To me that's London, as well as Jakob, of course, and all the things we do with Alistair. I suddenly felt quite homesick for Dircksenstrasse—but we are definitely moving from there, so Peter tells me. Hans has faxed me the contract. Peter also tells me you're going to Budapest. Have a good trip, Isabelle.*

In the evening he found Herr Schmidt waiting for him at the door to his apartment, standing erect and looking very embarrassed. –Listen, your lady-friend was here, he told Andras in a low tone, as if it were a secret. With the red hair, you know who I mean. Then, with a slight bow, he disappeared up the stairs before Andras had a chance to reply.

Magda had not left a message. Slowly he packed a suitcase with shirts and underwear and trousers, and before going to bed set the alarm. László was picking him up at eight.

27

The pianist had had to cancel, and someone else had stepped in. They were told this as they went in by an elderly man of neglected appearance, one of the old people living in a nearby council block who were glad of a cheap concert and a cup of tea. –But the tea's awful, Jakob whispered to Isabelle, as he balanced the plastic cup carefully in the palm of his hand. Placing themselves at one side of the foyer, they let their eyes roam over the shabby walls, the worn floor, the people milling this way and that—mostly regulars, it seemed, smiling and nodding amidst their crutches and wheel-chairs, while in among them a woman wearing a bright red dress and holding a purple fan made a vibrant splash of color. Jakob and Isabelle were received with much goodwill by the other concertgoers; they were the youngest there and stood close together like two children who have sneaked into a gath-ering of grown-ups, amused by the scene, expectant. People smiled at them or greeted them with a nod, appreciating their presence here in the Conway Hall—one man nodded more vigorously, delighted that here were two young people who were interested in music. They made a handsome couple among the flaccid, ill-dressed bodies, the mottled arms, the thinning hair, the fat or spindly legs, –like something from a Fellini film, Jakob whispered, pointing to a pair of massively swollen, bluish feet in sandals. Before setting out for the Conway Hall that afternoon they had slept together, and as they left the house Isabelle took Jakob's arm. It was a Sunday afternoon, and they went by underground as far as Warren Street and then walked through the quiet streets to Red Lion Square. –How quiet it is on a Sunday, Isabelle said to Jakob, everyone's having a siesta, the whole city is so peaceful. Jakob nodded, but they were just passing one of the CCTV cameras: this was the new Europe, subject to surveillance, prepared and counting the days, Jakob thought, and he put his arm round Isabelle. Were they safe? Yes, they were safe on this Sunday afternoon, making their way to Red Lion Square, though since it was tucked away they went wrong, continuing past Red Lion Street and wandering disorientated in the empty streets, with no one to ask. But they had plenty of time to spare. The threat was just another charade, like Bush on his warship, like the end of the war, he wanted to tell Isabelle; we shall remember it as something unreal and tasteless, but at some point it will become real and we *shall* be at risk. They walked along hand in hand. Bentham had told him about the Conway Hall, where there had been chamber concerts every Sunday for thirty years or more; it had been opened in 1929 and named after a pious American, Moncure Conway, who had donated money, who had wanted to make the world a better place, which was why there were these concerts costing only three pounds, with a cup of tea included—though that wasn't quite true, Jakob thought as they drank the tea out of plastic cups, because it was thirty pence extra. The place was very dusty. People greeted one another, some were taking their seats, and now there were, after all, some elegant woman in long dresses to be seen, and some men in light-colored suits, and Jakob anxiously looked out for Bentham. Although he had not said he would come, Jakob kept an eye on the door, for there was still some time to go before the music began. Then the doors were closed and the light settled dully on the rows of seating, the gallery and the wooden rostrum; the walls were cracked and yellowed, and the worn floorboards creaked beneath Jakob's shoes whenever he moved his feet. How shabby it all was: eccentric, ludicrous. The old man on his right accidentally prodded him in the ribs without noticing that he had done so. Slack, aged flesh, thought Jakob, and he fixed his eyes on the stage, where a woman in a yellow shawl and tight white trousers was standing, making some announcement, which prompted a shuffling of chairs: there was to be a further delay before the concert could begin, and three men started doing something with the grand piano. Isabelle kissed Jakob on the cheek as she stood up to go out again and have some more tea; how she takes everything in her stride, Jakob thought, and he too got up and went outside, into the mild, early summer air. The little square had been dug up for road works and was half closed off with barriers; a latecomer came hurrying over the wooden planks that had been laid across the torn-up asphalt and the water and drainage pipes. There she is, thought Jakob, sensing Isabelle's approach before he saw her, and as he turned to look at her he felt guilty. Two or three hours ago they had been lying in bed. He had stroked her stomach and hips, that soft, warm skin, conscious that there was nothing more agreeable to him, and now here he was, disgruntled, ungrateful, because his secret and quite unjustified hope of seeing Bentham was not being realized. A bell rang shrilly. He kissed Isabelle before they went back in; the woman in the yellow shawl was standing in front of the podium, beckoning, the grand piano had vanished and been replaced by a harpsichord at which an ill-shaven man was waiting, impatient to start. –It's not piano music! he called out to the audience, raising his long, brown-spotted hands. When he began, Jakob was taken aback, but apparently all was as it should be. Unused to the sound of the harpsichord, he made an effort to listen, looking down at his feet and then back again at the man who was playing, each note distinct, like a cold, sharp raindrop. There was something remorseless, vengeful, in the way he played, and the audience sat immobile, cowed: not a sound came from them, not a rustle, or the clearing of a throat. Jakob could not feel Isabelle's body but only saw her bare right arm, smooth, with no goose pimples. She sat motionless; she had forgotten him.

It was a rainy day in June. The Heath seemed empty, apart from two children down at the lower pond playing with a little wooden boat, and a woman jogging past, her face flushed and strained. As his eyes followed her, Jakob thought of the murderer who had killed four women with a brick or some other blunt object. One of them must have seen him, because she had been telephoning her mother in Norway at the moment of the attack, and according to the newspaper her mother had heard her quick cry of fear and the imploring, *Please don't!* before the connection was broken off. In Battersea Park there was to be a reconstruction of the second murder today, and the police were urging any possible witnesses to attend, anyone who had been there that afternoon two weeks ago, walking or jogging or exercising their dog. The dead woman had been found in a clump of bushes at around three o'clock.

It started drizzling again. Jakob walked up a hill towards a group of old trees. Isabelle had not wanted to come with him. Sunday was a day that neither of them really knew what to do with. They had been to the Portobello Road Market, the East End, Greenwich, the Durham Collection, and, last Sunday, the Conway Hall. One weekend soon they would go to Kew Gardens, before the last of the rhododendrons finished flowering.

He was reading up on transport, the rail network, the coordination between the various railway companies. Through Miller he had met a man who had regained possession of a house in the eastern part of Berlin five years ago and now lived there. –I wouldn't live anywhere else nowadays, he had told Jakob, it's the liveliest, most open-minded place in Europe!

Come and see me when you're back home again! For a moment Jakob had felt a touch of homesickness. But he liked London: Berlin seemed deserted by comparison. He was glad that Isabelle was not afraid, even after the attack on them near King's Cross. He himself had been more nervous since then. But you got used to it all, the homeless men and women that you had to step over as they lay stretched out across the pavement, the notices appealing for witnesses to muggings, the drug dealers around Camden Lock who followed you, making their whispered offers. He thought he had recognized one of their neighbors there, a young man who lived a few houses along from them; on one occasion he had followed them down Leighton Road, and Jakob had had the impression that Isabelle knew him, but he hadn't asked her: he had no right to ask. In Berlin they had not spent more of their time together than they did here, but there had been no secrets between them. Jakob stumbled; to the right of the path there was a thick, dark-looking clump of bushes, and he felt a momentary fear. By now he had reached the eastern edge of the Heath; on his right, fences overgrown with creepers screened off some small, detached villas. This must be the way to one of the bathing ponds, and sure enough, after a few yards, he came upon a notice that read *Kenwood Ladies' Pond*. Today, on a rainy, chilly Sunday, there was no one here, or at any rate no sound of anyone. He went a few paces along the path, treading softly and listening intently, until he reached a small, open gate. *No men permitted beyond this point.* After a brief hesitation he went through all the same; to his right he could now see an expanse of grass for sunbathing, and ten yards further on, through slender tree trunks, the water itself. A duck was quacking. It came waddling out of the bushes and into the open, heading towards the pond, which he now saw in its entirety, lead-colored, shimmering as a breath of wind rippled its surface; a haze blurred the boundary between water and air.

Jakob had reached the fence, a recently repaired fence, which was intended to halt his progress, its new planks still waiting to be stained; leaning over it, he felt the wood in his groin and pressed against it for a moment before climbing over. The grass beneath his feet was damp and yielding. From a wooden pontoon by the far bank a white ladder led down into the water. Now that the duck had fallen silent Jakob could hear the soft sound of the rain on the water, and looked around for shelter; under the dense canopy of a chestnut tree he found a rickety little bench, five yards from the bank. He had hardly sat down when the duck began to quack again, apparently in alarm; he could not see it among the reeds but it was clearly seeking safety further out in the water, and then there was a cracking of twigs and the sound of feet trampling a path through the undergrowth on the far side of the pond, followed by suppressed laughter—not a woman's laughter—and Jakob cautiously withdrew behind a scented bush, whose white blossom brushed his face. A young man came into view, naked but for his underpants, playfully showing off his strong, attractive body to someone who was still hidden by the leaves and branches; an arm appeared, very white against the other's tanned skin, and then a thickset body on legs that were too short, a heavy, hairy torso, apelike, ungainly, the face concealed by the dense mass of twigs, while the young man presented himself proudly, arms outstretched, laughing aloud as he swayed his hips from side to side and, inserting two fingers under the waistband of his underpants, let the elastic snap back against his tensed abdominal muscles. Suddenly he stopped. But it was the duck, not Jakob, that he had caught sight of, and he took a few steps into the water to shoo the bird away, forgetting his watching companion, only to turn to him again all the more winningly and wade back to the bank, peeling off his pants very slowly, keeping his gaze fixed comically and tenderly on his older friend—or client. He placed himself before him, calmly, submissively, and if he had been mocking the older man before, he now yielded, offered himself as a gift, reached for his penis and turned around. Jakob had a sense of being excluded, and although he felt affection, even love, for the young man, and for Isabelle, Alistair, Bentham, he was conscious of his hands among the wet twigs of the jasmine, useless and cold. The young man let himself drop into the water and rose to the surface again wet-haired and snorting, arms flailing as he lost his balance and neither the pond's bottom nor its ruffled surface helped him to steady himself. Then he stumbled back to the bank, where the older man was now waiting, in a shirt, in underpants, holding ready a large blue towel which he wrapped around the young man to warm him, rubbing him with vigorous, assured movements. Jakob could not make out their faces. He passed his fingers over his eyes as if that might localize the sharp pain that assailed him, but found that it was impossible, that he was only intensifying the pain that spread in direct response to every move that they made. Absorbed in the sensation of each other's touch, they did not hear Jakob as he started to stumble away. He turned to look back once more. By the older man's movement as he raised the towel, by the way he momentarily rested his right hand on the younger one's shoulders, Jakob at last recognized Bentham, in profile, half naked, his face obscured, and now Jakob saw, with abnormal clarity, the rather small hand, too small for the strong white arms, as it tenderly crept up over the shoulder and caressed the proffered neck. Jakob made no effort to be quiet as he hurried back across the grass to the main path, for they would not notice him, he thought, no voice called after him, and after only a few yards he began to doubt—a doubt which grew with every step he took towards the sports ground and the school— that it really had been Bentham; tears welled up in his eyes, making him stumble again, he had to take care not to get run over when he reached the road, and then he made a deliberate detour because he could not go home like this. Distraught. Excited. He tried to think of a way of describing the incident that he himself would find amusing and that he could repeat to Isabelle, turning something that had profoundly shaken him into an anecdote. Two naked men on the Heath, and himself as a peeping Tom in the bushes, bushes reserved for women. He would not tell her that it was Bentham. He was not sure that it had been. Nakedness alters people so much, he thought, to the point of making them unrecognizable. It was as though every-one had two bodies, and not even that expressed it adequate-ly, for his nakedness in Isabelle's eyes was something other than the nudity of the two men. But the gesture, the movement with which the hand had descended on to the young man's shoul-der, was Bentham's, and Jakob realized that it was one he had seen but never felt, that this was an intimacy reserved for Alistair. He felt unsteady on his feet, doubtful of finding his way home—home, where Isabelle would be expecting him. All at once he knew for certain that he would tell her nothing: per-haps it was a secret, regardless of whether or not it had been Bentham, and perhaps it made no difference whether or not a secret, a thing that must not be told, bore any relationship to the truth, to reality. Two men, naked, abandoning themselves to pleasure. Or was he being naïve, and had the trip to the pond been a terrible humiliation for the older man? Get your clothes off, out here in the cold June air, at the Ladies' Pond where you have no business to be and will be ignominiously chased away if anyone catches you. But only Jakob had seen them, and he had been too faint-hearted, too ashamed or too deeply stirred to call out. He need only have called out his name, Bentham's name—but of course that would have been impossible. He knew that he would never ask him about it, not tomorrow, nor the day after. Perhaps what he had witnessed had been joyful, a love scene. High spirits. A game. Or perhaps he had witnessed the humiliation of an ageing man. An old body, Jakob thought again, as if that might either repel him or calm his feelings. An old man's underpants. But then he realized that what preyed on his mind was not that the old man was so old, for he had long been aware of that, but that the young one had been so young. He had thought of himself as a gift, and now he pictured his own body, which would only look ridiculous if *he* posed in the water. He was surplus to requirements: Bentham had no need of *his* embrace.

How should he behave when he saw Isabelle, he wondered as he at last turned into Lady Margaret Road. But he need not have worried, for she was out. On her desk lay an ink drawing. The girl was climbing a tree, while an old man stood below, looking up. Isabelle was changing too, he sensed; it was as though each of them was venturing into unknown territory, and he feared what it might lead to. He sat down in her room to wait for her.

Bentham absented himself from the office all week, and this time Jakob was glad. When everyone else had gone home on the Thursday evening, leaving him alone on the top floor—he could hear Mrs. Gilman using the vacuum cleaner down in the library—he entered the empty room and, without switching on the light, stopped just inside the door. He stood there until Mrs. Gilman came up the stairs. At half past eight he finally left the office and decided to go home on foot. Regent's Park was still open; it was a pleasantly warm evening, and there were couples lying in the grass while others strolled along hand in hand or with their arms around each other. Jakob felt calm and contented, as though he had managed to solve a difficult problem. The generously proportioned park stretched out before him, affording a view right up to Primrose Hill; it was a piece of countryside right in the city, welcoming and benevolent, designed to ease the strains of urban living. Like the other men of his age wearing suits, their ties undone or stuffed into a pocket, he had left work and was on his way home. His body was dependable, he took conscious breaths, could feel the muscles working in his legs: he had a sense of well-being. His shoes were new and hand-made. Perhaps the summer evening was deceiving him, but what of it? He thought of Bentham, of Isabelle and Alistair and of Hans, too, with a tenderness that was new to him. There was no need to diminish distances, or even to bridge them.

Soon he reached the northwestern exit; he was sad to have to leave the park, but there was the attendant, waiting to lock the gate. At the traffic lights he caught sight of Maude, and cheerfully called her name. She turned around, startled, and then came quickly towards him. He could smell her scent, an old-fashioned scent that reminded him of his aunt; she was wearing a bright blue dress underneath a white summer coat. –I'm meeting my friend at the cinema, she explained as he looked at her inquiringly. –Though I don't even know what film we're going to. –Well, I'm sure she'll have made a good choice, Jakob said pleasantly, grabbing Maude's arm as she stepped into the road without noticing an oncoming car. –It's silly of me, she said, but I always worry about Mr. Bentham when he doesn't come into the office. She hesitated. You like him, don't you? He's been doing that for years, ever since his partner was killed. Taking a room in a hotel for a few days. Probably meeting . . . well, you know.

–I didn't know his friend was killed, Jakob said, embarrassed.

–In a motorcycle accident, fifteen years ago. They were in a crash, Mr. Bentham was almost unhurt but Graham died instantly. And now, in his old age, he can't bear the loneliness.

–Perhaps he's dealing with it in the right way, don't you think? I'm sure he knows what he's doing.

With an indignant look, Maude demanded: –The right way? With young men one knows nothing about?

–Was Graham his age?

–Twenty years younger. I shouldn't really talk about it. But I do worry about him, and you don't know *what* may be happening until he's safely back, and of course you can't ask questions.

–And he doesn't tell Alistair where he goes, either? Jakob immediately regretted his question when he saw how hurt Maude was.

–Why should he tell Alistair, when he doesn't tell me?

By now they had almost reached the cinema. A woman of Maude's age came towards them, waving. There was a dense crowd of people in front of the entrance, and a beggar was pushing his way through them. The traffic at the junction was stuck fast. Jakob bade a hasty farewell to Maude and her friend and walked up Kentish Town Road. A woman stepped into his path. She had three small children with her, one of them wearing an eye-patch, and she held out a piece of paper and seized his arm imploringly. Impatiently he shook her off, and she moved humbly aside, murmuring quietly to no one in particular. –Iraq, we're from Iraq, Jakob heard her say, and he walked on quickly, keeping a tight grip on his briefcase. A few yards further on he had to stop because the pavement was blocked by a mass of people, some of them shouting and yelling. Above the din a man's voice could be heard, preaching, so it seemed, but the laughter and heckling were too loud for Jakob to be able to make out what he was saying. But then the noise died down and everybody listened. Jakob's eyes moved to the young woman standing next to him, and he studied the rounded, dark-complexioned face. Above her nose her eyebrows touched, two delicate lines that met and joined. He was leaning back, hoping to continue observing her unnoticed, when she turned her head and looked at him with almond-shaped eyes, the almost black irises surrounded by immaculate whiteness. After a moment something in her look relaxed, the mistrust vanished, and Jakob was annoyed to find himself blushing, but he could not tear himself away. It was just a tiny change, he thought, from mistrust to warmth, perceptible in the eyes, in the line of the eyebrows, a nuance more like a code than a language, and once again he felt excluded. Any second now she would turn away. His ears picked up fragments of what the preacher—a powerfully built man with thick, unkempt hair and a fearless expression—was shouting. The woman turned away. What was the last thing he had read in her look? Disappointed curiosity. Pity.

–Is it Jesus you're waiting for? Mohammed? The Home Office? The preacher had turned half around and now stood facing Jakob. –You will not escape the despair of the slaughtered, the vengeance which is war and fear. You will eat dust, not the dust of the serpent, but the black dust of the underground tunnels. You will drag yourselves along over the tracks, over the ballast, praying that you may once more see the light of day. Your sweat will be stained black, and mortal fear will contort your face into the mask it already is. No matter how many floodlights are turned on you, the light is no help, you crouch there in your darkness, and at night you are seized with foreboding, is that not so? The fear mounts within you, as though you were criminals bound in chains on the sandbanks of the Thames as the tide comes in. What more are you waiting for before you try to save yourselves? What act of cruelty has not yet burned itself into your eyes? What cry of terror have you not yet heard?

He paused, lifting his face heavenwards, and then returned his gaze to his listeners, who were starting to grow restive—what had they been laughing about, earlier? Jakob wondered—and some people moved away, while others joined the throng, so that Jakob was propelled forwards. He braced his legs against the ground to avoid jostling the woman whose slender neck he saw before him, so close that he could distinguish individual tiny hairs in the fine down, lighter in color than her hair, and the vertebra that stood out like a button, delicate, fragile. He thrust his hands into his trouser pockets, fighting down the desire to stroke that neck, to turn the head gently towards him.

–Still you wait, patiently, blindly, and in the end you remember nothing. The street, do you see it? Do you see the beggars? Do you see the dead? Do you remember nothing? Do you know nothing? You do well to forget Jesus, it was not for you that he died: ask the dead for whom it was that he died on the cross. Ask yourselves, rather, for whom *you live*, for whom you breathe, for whom the summer is coming, for whom everything is flowering and the tension is mounting to a level that is unbearable. Do you see the beauty even here, how long the twilight lingers, how hesitantly the darkness creeps up to enfold you, while the sirens scream, while someone writhes in his own filth, while a few yards further on, a few hours later, someone dies, shot or stabbed, because you close your eyes and choose to see nothing, and your robbery has paid his passage to the realm of the dead. We are thieves, living here in the way we do. Each of our days borne on the backs of those who, bowed down by adversity, seek shelter, seek a reprieve. It remains to be seen, you say, whether disaster will strike us. But it *will* strike, it will strike us, and our heartlessness. We have no right to survive. We are naked. For the moment we are still alive, that is all.

–What does he mean? whispered Jakob, leaning forward slightly so that his breath should reach the smooth skin in front of him. She straightened up infinitesimally, turning her head a little to indicate that she had heard him, but without moving her shoulders. –He's nearly finished, was all that she said.

–Perhaps the victim lifted onto the stretcher by the medical attendants is still alive. Perhaps someone is still alive with a face cut to pieces by shards of glass. Perhaps another lives whose arm or leg has been ripped off. Perhaps there is one whimpering, hoping for death, in one of the prisons that we pay for. And what do *we* have, what certainty can we hold on to? Only that nothing has happened to us yet. Should we be grateful for that? you ask, and I say no. Not grateful, but humble. Stand up and be humble and refuse to accept the unbearable things that you see. Is the war over? It is over, you cry, but you know you are lying. You know that those destined to die already bear the mark on their foreheads. You know of the men and women who sob all night through and are filled with fear. They see their children die. They see their loved ones die. They see the dust that will not settle because *we* stir it up.

–My God, said Jakob. The orator straightened up, as if he had heard Jakob. –You will understand soon enough, he called to Jakob, you will understand, and today, this very day and some day in the future you will be happy. –But what is he actually saying? asked Jakob again, as the crowd broke up, untroubled, unmoved despite having listened so patiently. It was almost dark now. Jakob could feel eyes resting upon him with curiosity, and at last the woman in front of him turned around and smiled. –My name is Miriam, she said. As though at a signal, all other eyes drifted away from him, and their owners disappeared in the direction of the tube station or dispersed to left and right, and the preacher picked up a bag and a bedroll and disappeared too. –You're cold: Miriam took Jakob's hand as if it were a child's. –I'll make you some tea, she said, as though this were perfectly natural, come, it's not far from here, and she walked quickly along beside him, holding his hand. How kind she is, Jakob thought in a daze, how full of hope and confidence. He was trembling as they entered a room that had only a table and a sofa and some photographs above a low bookcase; the effect was inviting and yet sad. –May I take your shoes off for you? she asked when he was sitting on the sofa. Taking off her own sweater and slipping out of her jeans, she knelt half naked before him, smiling, untied his shoelaces, drew the shoes from his feet and took his right foot in both her hands. –He's called Jonah, the preacher, I mean. We've known each other for years. He was my teacher once, and then I met him in the street; he was wild at that time, desperate. When he started preaching—though it's hardly a sermon!—I thought he'd gone mad. He pointed to a man among the crowd and told me to take him home with me. He believes that we're constantly meeting people whom we *could* love, and even if life doesn't permit it, that's for purely accidental reasons, he said, which must not blind us to those we can show affection to. And I did as he asked, I don't know why. It has nothing to do with sex. Laughing softly, Miriam slid his right foot on to the floor and lifted the left one into her lap. –In a minute I'll make you a cup of tea.

He sat on the sofa, feeling wakeful and drowsy at the same time, looking at the bookcase, the photos, the unclouded life that they depicted: he saw Miriam hugging a child to her breast, smiling radiantly at the photographer and playfully tickling the child. He had lighter coloring than hers, green eyes, and he too looked happy, exuberant—far too happy, Jakob thought somberly, as though something in the room's atmosphere made it impossible that that happiness should have lasted. –Who's that? he asked Miriam as she came in with a teapot and two mugs, –in the photo? and he watched as she set down the pot and the two mugs on a stool. She had put on a short skirt. –My son Tim, she said. –Our son, Jonah's and mine. We were married, but after a few months he disappeared and I almost went out of my mind with worry. He wrote just one letter, which was illegible because he had spilt water over the ink, leaving only that ghost of his writing as a sign that he was still alive, and I left my place in Clapham and moved here. Tim was born. My parents supported me and I was even able to go back to studying. She tugged at her skirt with impatient, slender hands. –You aren't listening, she said, but Jakob did not hear. She sat down in front of the sofa. His hands were trembling again, and his feet too; she placed his feet in her lap and stroked them. But Isabelle would never do that, he thought, she shied away from such things, and in their caresses there was always something nonchalant, furtive, almost a fear of embarrassing each other or themselves, of uncovering what ought to remain hidden. He closed his eyes and felt Miriam removing his socks, touching each toe tentatively at first, then stroking it. He wanted to straighten up, but something forced him back against the sofa, something that constricted his heart and brought tears to his eyes. The photo, he thought, the strong childish body squirming to escape from Miriam's arms, wriggling with impatience, ready to run off, and he ran and ran, wild and brimming with happiness, across the road that was wet from rain, the asphalt dazzling in the evening light. Tim turned and waved, but the driver did not see that, for he did not see Tim, he saw nothing but the glaring light, and felt the impact. Then he braked. Jakob shuddered, something cracked, his body reared up and he opened his eyes, staring at Miriam in disbelief, and stretched out his arms towards her, confused by his longing and his grief. Why? he thought again and again. How can she bear it? Is that how it was? he wondered. He took her in his arms; the trembling was different now, less noticeable, like a thin gauze around his love and his anxiety. Memories became mingled with the smell of Miriam, with the smell of the June rain on Hampstead Heath; he saw the two men, the younger one showing off, mocking, but there was as much tenderness in that as in the gesture with which the older one carefully rubbed him dry. As he held Miriam close, he hoped that the older man really had been Bentham. He rocked her and knew that he must leave very soon, because she wished it. Dazed, submissive, he obeyed her signal, and when he left the house he paid no attention to where he had been but walked blindly on until he recognized a street and came to the canal, with its black, malodorous water that flowed sluggishly towards the park, towards the aviary whose denizens had long since fallen asleep on the branches, hidden among the leaves. Jakob let the darkness enfold him like a blanket, though his heart was beating violently and he clutched his briefcase with a clammy hand, distraught—the word flashed through his mind—and yet he walked perfectly sensibly past Camden Lock and turned right, noticed the man coming towards him and the car passing on his left, and heard the pounding of the bass speakers through its closed windows, behind which a woman sat, smoking. She braked, observed him in the rear-view mirror. Accelerated, left him behind. Just a movement of the foot, a split second in which the decision was taken whether or not to open the window and speak to someone—a mysterious linkage of eye and muscle. Thus was he weighed and found wanting. His perceptions were abnormally clear, he was conscious of his own feet in his shoes, in his socks, the familiar friction, and he stopped and stood still to recall Miriam's hands, her fingers that she had inserted between his toes, the thumb-tip with which she had stroked his nails while murmuring something he did not understand. It was a tiny segment of time that now forced itself between them, ready to expand, and his watch, which he shook free of the sleeve of his jacket, suddenly seemed to him like a musical clock with tiny figures turning in a circle, Miriam and himself, Isabelle and Bentham, following their circular course, and in their midst Death with his scythe. –No, we shall not meet again, Miriam had said, unless Jonah wishes it. She had waved goodbye to him, serenely, lovingly even, as if she knew what awaited him and wanted to give him courage.

Property, Bentham had said, is a form of loss: we merely pretend that it offers us stability and permanence. It is actually a mirror of transience, which we gaze into as fixedly as into our bathroom mirrors—and ultimately all that we see in either is that we grow older and die, though of course there are moments of beauty, are there not? Jakob's watch was showing half past ten; he ran his finger over it, over the glass beneath which the hands moved visibly or imperceptibly, each in its own rhythm, and he listened outside a house to the voices that carried through the open windows. He thought of the Watteau paintings that he had seen with Isabelle: Death, though unseen, was nonetheless present in those graceful movements, which halted time for a single, immeasurable moment that bore transience and loss within it. And now he was in Lady Margaret Road. The white fox ran out from under a parked car, leapt on to a wall, ran precariously along the top of it and vanished into one of the gardens in Countess Road. Isabelle was standing at the ground-floor window, just an outline, keeping perfectly still: perhaps she was waiting for him, perhaps she had been watching the fox. He waved to her; he was very happy. But she turned away, retreating into the room without having seen him, and silhouetted against the light she looked tense and thin.

28

D ave had told her that some people didn't live in the city but in the country, where everybody had a great big garden with apple trees, and they had animals, not just a cat like Polly but dogs and sheep too, sometimes even a pony that you could ride if you wanted to or hitch up to a little trap to drive through the countryside, past streams and over fields, until you got hungry and came back home. Everybody sat down at a long table and ate until they were tired. The children went off to school together every morning, running through the garden to the gate and waiting there for the others, and they would wait for Sara, too, and then all walk to school together, with their school bags and sandwiches and something to drink, because at dinner time they all ate their meal together, with soup and pudding too, and then they played until the bell rang. In next to no time you learned to read and write, Dave told her, and then he brought her a notebook, gave her a felt-tipped pen that had fallen out of Dad's pocket and drew some letters. A snake, he said, S for snake, S for Sara, and the pen was green and the snake was green, there were marks on her fingers that she hid, her hands in her pockets, and the pen under her mat-tress—her father's pen, green, and he searched and searched for it. Then Dave disappeared for several days, and nobody said anything: it was as if he had never existed. Mum didn't cry, and Dad lay on the sofa, spent half the day sleeping on the sofa, and all night too. Mum fed her in the kitchen, giving her bread and cheese, which Dave didn't like. He didn't come.

With her finger she drew the S on the tabletop and on the window, after Mum and Dad had left the house, because they were working: they had got jobs in a supermarket, Mum said. Sara breathed on the window and drew an S that quickly vanished again, and outside it was warm, the trees were growing, green leaves, thin branches pointing straight up into the air, or into the sky, which stayed light for a long time now, so long that the other children came into the garden more and more often, climbing over the wall. But they didn't knock on the door or throw balls, because they were hiding, or searching for someone, and they soon moved on, climbing over into the next garden. Dave didn't come. Next morning her mother woke her and sent her down to the shop in Falkland Road, just round to the right and a few yards along, where vegetables were laid out in boxes with nobody keeping an eye on them, and a man standing inside the dark shop looked at her with a sigh and said she didn't have enough money for all the things on her list. She drew an S on the back of it, because the man asked her her name and whether she went to school. It was a mistake to tell him—Dave would have pointed that out to her—but Dave wasn't here, and her father came, grabbed her by the arm and pulled her out into the street, and she crouched down by the rubbish bins because he'd said they would come and put her in prison. Through the window she could see Polly inside, appearing first on one windowsill, then on the other and finally lying down on the back of the sofa and going to sleep. From the house next door the man came out, and later the lady. The man didn't see her; the lady smiled at her, but when she came back she wasn't alone, another man was with her, and she said goodbye to him and pretended not to see Sara. That evening a car stopped outside the house and her father got out and picked her up. Her mother laid the table, there were two other men there, who stroked her hair, and then she was sent to bed without anyone asking if she was hungry. She lay down in

Dave's bed, and although he wasn't there she told him that she didn't feel a bit hungry anymore, and that she too wanted to go to where the big garden was, with all the apple trees. Dave always listened; the pillow smelled of him, but in the morning it felt damp and she was ashamed because she was afraid she had wet the bed.

She stood at the door to the garden, listening for any sounds, but there was only Polly's meowing as she wound herself around Sara's legs and rubbed herself against the door, wanting to be let out. The other children would throw small stones at Sara and laugh at her because she wore clothes that were too short, or old things of Dave's that were far too long, and because she didn't go to school yet, and because her father cut her hair because he wouldn't spend money on haircuts, not for a child. She never said, even to Dave, that she would always stay like this, that she was afraid she would always be a child, the way she was now, because she never got any bigger and wet her pants or the bed. She was retarded, Dad said, and although she didn't quite know what that meant, she knew that it couldn't be put right. It wasn't like an illness that might go away again if she stayed in bed and did as Mum told her. And anyway, Mum didn't tell her what to do, and there were some illnesses that didn't go away again and were so bad that nobody talked about them. Or else it wasn't an illness but something she'd said or done, and the children knew about it and that was why they laughed, and they threw stones at the window and pointed their fingers at her because she didn't learn anything and wasn't growing.

She pressed her ear to the windowpane. Polly was meowing. If she had the courage to open the door and go outside, she'd almost be like one of those people who didn't live in the city but out in the country, where they had sheep and a dog and even a pony. At least she had Polly, and she could run across the grass to the tree by the brick wall and imagine that it was an apple tree full of apples, and that Dave would come and take her by the hand and they would just keep going, into the woods, or to a pond with a rowboat, and he would row her across the pond. He'd promised to take her to the Heath, but he hadn't been home for days now. She touched the key that was in the door. Then she took hold of it and made as if to turn it in the lock. It wouldn't move. Now she tried with both hands, using all her strength. Her hands grew hot and sore and slipped off the key, and now she desperately wanted to turn it, to open the door and run out into the garden, down from the veranda that was full of junk and over the grass to the brick wall where a big patch of sunlight shone through the tree.

Then the key moved with a jerk, and there was a sudden rush of air, but there were also nice smells and it was warm, warmer than in the house. Polly squeezed out through the crack, ran down the two steps and then stopped and looked back at Sara. On the terrace was a table, a small table lying on its side. They could sit and eat outside now that they had a garden, it had seemed like a promise, all four of them sitting together out there—after Mum's Auntie Martha had died—and Dad had hoisted Sara up on to his shoulders to take her out into the garden, and told her they were here to stay. There had been so many promises, as soon as they'd moved Sara would go to nursery, Dad had said, and then for some reason everything had stayed the same as before. Because she wasn't growing, perhaps through some fault of her own. Dave never came home now. Beside the table was a chair standing on three legs, and here she also came upon her old teddy bear, Tod: he had vanished one day, and then Dave had told her that Tod had gone on a journey, a long train journey, Dave had said, to console her, but here he was, half under the table and half under the chair, all swollen up, and his tummy had actually burst open; she looked away. She took one pace forward—still holding the door, with her arm stretched right out behind her—and then another and another, and now she was standing on the first of the steps, and now the second, while Polly had already reached the far end of the grass and was sniffing at something, a plant growing by the wall, where the sunshine was. The grass was damp, she could feel it through her socks. You weren't supposed to go out just in socks, with no shoes on, and she took care to lift her legs high to make up for it. There was a plastic bucket lying there, and even a little green spade. She thought she might take her socks off so that they wouldn't get wet and messy. Beside the bucket something gleamed: it was a big piece of broken glass, the bottom of a bottle, and next to it stood a tiny horse, brown with a white fleck on its forehead and a black saddle on its back. Cautiously she reached out her hand for it. It really was a horse. She grasped it firmly, closing her fist round it, and then spread her fingers and watched it as if it was a beetle that might scuttle away. The horse was still there, and with all four legs too. She stood him up, and he galloped the length of her palm. If she put him down he could gallop and gallop, over hills and plains, in the warm, sweet-smelling breeze, past a giant flower as big as a tree, and on through the tall grass, crossing an endless prairie, on and on. The piece of broken glass was a lake for the horse to drink from. Holding the reins, Sara waited until he had drunk his fill; then she mounted him and off they went, faster and faster, until they reached the scorching sun, where a huge monster lay in wait, a terrible creature with claws and a frightful tail that lashed out at them, trying to kill them. But they dodged it, and with a quick, neat movement they took cover behind a hill and watched the gigantic beast from there. It was a dragon. It lay there motionless so as to trick them, its hissing breath the only sign that it was not asleep. Its flanks rose and fell as it lay there, fearless, you had to find the sword that could vanquish it, inflicting the fatal wound on its dragon body, you had to be fearless and bold, –and even if death comes we won't be afraid, Sara whispered. She stroked the horse's quivering back, speaking words of encouragement to him; then she even sang a song, softly, and the monster fell truly asleep and slept on the grass, stretched out, trusting. –We are bound for hell, Sara whispered. We are doomed, and you are doomed with us. With her finger she stroked the horse's quivering back, whispering soothing words. –But we won't surrender. The prize was freedom, the prize was a golden treasure, and every wish would come true. Jewels, and the enchanted tree at whose foot the monster lay, the tree that you touched, the tree you bowed down to so that all your wishes came true. And at the foot of the tree lay the monster. If only it were dead! –We must slay it, she whispered to her steed, who raised his head and, tossing his mane, whinnied his agreement, –we must slay it with a single blow. For though it was asleep now, if it woke, then all was lost. –With a single blow, Sara repeated, looking about her, searching, for every battle needs the right weapon, Dave said, and Dad said it too. And there it was, a club, lying ready for her, a thick branch, not too long, and picking it up she grasped it with both hands and swung it up into the air, high above her head, and Polly's whiskers twitched, she made a little contented sound and opened her eyes. –It's the monster, the horse whispered, shuddering, you must slay it to break the spell! Do you see its eyes? If its gaze once falls upon you, you will never grow and always be a child. It opened its eyes, both eyes, dark green and sleepy—if you ever hope to go to school like the others—and there was a small sound as if Polly were trying to say something, sleepily, but the horse begged and pleaded, and so she raised her arms, reaching high into the air to strike the blow against the enemy. As it lifted its head, ready to attack, Sara stretched up still higher, took a single step forward, and struck.

Polly's scream rent the silence. Fur bristling, she raced up the tree, hissing and spitting, on to the lowest branch and, unable to get a grip because her injured hind leg slipped off, crawled laboriously towards the wall. Now she had to jump, just the tiny distance separating the branch from the wall, and she pushed herself off with another screech of pain and leapt across. On the wall she seemed to feel safer. She licked her hind leg and paw, her eyes never leaving Sara, who still stood there, upstretched, rigid. Tears streamed down her face, but she felt only horror, something that was cold and piercing, as she saw Polly crouching there, hissing when Sara lowered her arms, her arms as cold as if someone had tipped white paint over them, white, gleaming paint that took her breath away and marked her, like the time when, for a joke, her father had plunged her arm into a bucket of paint right up to the shoulder, to make her easier to find, so that it'll be easier for us to see you; and there she stood. She bent down to pick up the brown horse, held it in her hand and hurled it over the wall, but it was too late. Polly flinched and crawled a few feet further along, getting as far away from Sara as possible. Only now did Sara notice that one of the windows next door was open and the lady was watching her. She was making no sign, just watching in silence; endless minutes passed before she leaned further out to get a better view, and then she called out, –what's the matter? Do you need help? Sara cowered in the grass, her arms wrapped around her shoulders. The sun was now hidden by clouds. The grass smelled damp and cold. She shook her head again and again, but did not move from the spot. There was Polly. She wanted to speak to her, she wanted to say she was sorry, to lure Polly to her and comfort her, but no sound came out of her mouth, and now Polly was softly wailing, a continuous, relentless sound. Sara heard it, and then she lowered her head and was sick, once and then again: yellow, bitter slime that made a yellow patch on the grass and gave off a bitter smell. Her stomach hurt, and she pressed her hands to her belly. Not daring to sob, she swallowed her tears and shifted herself slightly away from the stench, not raising her head. The moment of shame was about to come. Dave, if he came, would know at once what had happened. He would go away without looking at her. He wouldn't come back. Polly was somewhere around. There was silence. Perhaps she was dying. Perhaps she, Sara, would die too. It had grown cold. Then came the first drops, big and icy. She didn't move. Soon she was drenched, and cowered there, all feeling gone. A brief, passing shower, and a rattle as the window next door was closed. Shortly afterwards someone opened the barred French window which led out into the neighbors' garden.

29

They had had no use for the garden, since it consisted only of a long, narrow strip of lawn; they had left this unmown, and it was now a meadow. A hawthorn tree grew close to the wall, which was higher than Isabelle had thought. Stretching up, she could just reach the coping, but there was nothing for her fingers to cling on to. After a moment's indecision she tried to pull herself up, but slipped down again. She went back inside to get a chair; its legs sank into the ground, but it was an improvement nonetheless. At the third attempt she found a foothold and parts of the wall she could grip with her hands. She pulled herself up, and just as she was thinking she had done it, she suddenly slipped down again, hitting first her chin and then her elbow on the wall, and the chair tipped sideways, pitching her into the wet grass. The pain made itself felt only when she put her foot back into the gap; though this was not large enough, some loose mortar trickled from it, and she gouged out even more with the toe of her shoe until at last she was able to push herself off and swing her left leg over the top of the wall. She had a graze on her elbow, and a stabbing pain that passed between her ribs and right into her lung nearly took her breath away; it seized hold of her and, in a way that was almost a relief, drew together the scattered sensations of the last few months, the vague alarms and hopes and disappointments that had got caught up in a wide-meshed net. Too wide: the agency, her marriage, her drawings, London, Alistair and Jim, the noises from the house next door. She felt as though she needed to go back to the beginning, and the drawings were her only guide. Perched on hands and knees on top of the wall, she looked back towards the house that she lived in, and remembered what Andras had written in his last e-mail. *The girl in the red coat reminds me of that film "Don't Look Now." There's something mean about her, as though childhood were nothing but a hiding place that you lurk in, lying in wait for people.* The pain was subsiding, becoming diffused, however much she tried to hold on to it. There the girl lay, doubled up on the ground. She was wearing some kind of tracksuit bottoms and a grubby T-shirt that was too small for her. Isabelle's eyes rested without sympathy on the bare strip of childish flesh. The garden was strewn with rubbish and old toys, the terrace cluttered with beer bottles and kitchen equipment—she could make out a frying pan and a household bucket. Detritus, bags crammed with waste, and the child was shamming dead, like an animal, the stick lying beside her in the grass. It was still drizzling; she felt chilly. –For goodness' sake, get up! Had she said that out loud? At all events the girl had turned her head sideways and was watching her, registering every movement, every detail of Isabelle's face, with intense concentration. In a single leap Isabelle jumped down from the wall, furious because she had no idea how she would get back up there and into her own garden again. How idiotic, she thought with distaste, as she hesitated but then at last bent down to the girl, took her by the shoulders and pulled her up straight. –For goodness' sake get up! The T-shirt was damp, and she took off her cardigan, which was torn at the elbow, and wrapped it around the child. Now what? The girl's eyes never left her. Isabelle was still holding her by the shoulders, trying to evade that insistent stare; it was a contest that neither of them won. It was a battle. –What's your name? Isabelle asked without kindness, and while she was waiting for an answer the cat came towards them from the tree, still mistrustful and pausing before each step with its paw in the air, and sat down in front of them both. –Polly, said Sara. Then, her eyes still fixed on Isabelle, she said, –Sara, clinging to that as if otherwise she would be lost. The garden, where despite everything the grass was flourishing and there was even a rambling rose patiently spreading along a wall, was effectively a prison. From this side the wall was higher, the soil had apparently subsided more or never been banked up, and Isabelle had only herself to blame for getting into this ridiculous situation: now she would either have to collect some junk together so as to haul herself back up on to the wall, or else pass through a strange apartment, occupied by violent neighbors whom she didn't know, to reach the street where she would be left standing outside her own house without a key. The cat sat there, watching and waiting. It didn't move, the child was shivering, Isabelle's hand was going stiff and she could feel her expression hardening, but there was nothing for it, and turning towards the child she met her gaze. She felt as though the distance between them had been wiped out, as though her own mouth was filled with the bitter, sour taste of vomit and her own mind with fear and guilt. The cat uttered a plaintive sound, a little blood trickled from its nose, and it sneezed. What am I doing here? thought Isabelle. Once again she took Sara roughly by the shoulder and turned to look back at her own house. Jakob wasn't there. Jim, she thought, but she didn't know where he lived, whether at number forty-three or further down the street. Tell the child to shout for Jim, she thought. She took a step back in order to scrutinize the face more closely, the snub nose, the high forehead and straggly ash-blond hair. The thin-lipped mouth opened, but nothing came out; then, after Isabelle had shaken her, Sara knelt down in the damp grass, knelt there awkwardly and emitted a kind of cry, quite unintelligible, and then another. How ridiculous to suppose that that thin voice could carry over the garden walls. It had scarcely anything childlike, or indeed human, about it: you might as well expect the cat to start talking, and Isabelle bent down to Polly and picked her up. The animal snuggled into her arms, warm and trusting. Each caressing movement of Isabelle's communicated itself, as if by some inversion of logic, to Sara, who was still on her knees, trembling, trembling each time Isabelle's hand ran through Polly's fur, as though she were receiving electric shocks. –But I'm trying to help you, said Isabelle crossly. Sara started to cry, and Isabelle watched her in astonishment: silent, convulsive sobs. Isabelle gently put Polly down and looked around. On the terrace a table had been tipped on its side, its legs projecting horizontally into the void. The neglected garden served only as a dumping-ground for things that were broken or no longer needed. A blackbird landed on the wall, shook out its feathers, and warbled a song. From somewhere or other came the smell of something rotting. Waiting for her, only feet away, were her workroom, her computer, her nice clean house. The child was crying, while the cat rubbed up against Isabelle's legs, purring. –What have you done to her? Isabelle asked. She's hurt.

But the wound seemed to be only superficial; the blood was already drying. –Come on, it's not as bad as all that, Isabelle said impatiently. She surveyed the terrace and garden again. This could be anywhere, she thought, Bosnia, Baghdad, it was always the obverse of her own life. As if the measure of suffering were fixed, only its distribution variable. Timidly Sara straightened up from her squatting position and reached out her hand towards Polly to stroke her, but the cat leapt aside with a single bound. –You hit her, said Isabelle coldly, what do you expect? The girl raised her head and looked at Isabelle, and now her eyes were grey, challenging. –It's my cat, she said defiantly. She got up and stood close to Isabelle, guilt-ridden, ready to defend herself, torn between the two, thought Isabelle, feeling challenged and repelled. Purposefully she turned towards the wall, and the blackbird flew off; Sara and the cat did not move from her side. It would be easy to help the child up on to the wall, and here she was already, close beside her, her breath slightly sour-smelling, with both her arms stretched upwards. But it was the cat that Isabelle lifted up and put on the wall, before starting to look for some hold for herself, a crack or a ledge for her feet, and since the wall on this side was less well built or had never been repaired, she found what she was looking for; although her hands repeatedly slid off the wet bricks, she eventually managed to brace herself against the trunk of the tree. The material of her blouse tore. Sitting on top of the wall, she looked down at the girl, who was making no attempt to follow her. In speechless horror she was staring at Isabelle, and now there was no trace of anything childlike in her face, only hopelessness and suffering; Isabelle couldn't help laughing. A few words would suffice to pacify Sara; she could reach out her hand and pull her up too, to where the cat sat purring. What a farce, thought Isabelle, how stupid of me to get involved. Her mind made up, she jumped down into her own garden and, picking up the cat with both hands, set it down in the grass, which looked fresher here and had a pleasant smell. The door to her living room and workroom was open; her life, viewed from the outside, looked well-ordered and inviting, apparently untouched, like a birthday present that you haven't felt like unwrapping yet, but that is lying there ready. The cat was rubbing its head on Isabelle's calf, meowing. One could, it occurred to her, lift it back on to the wall and push it off on to the other side. Everything was ambivalent. Had she helped the girl, as had been her intention? Later she would listen, through the thin walls, to the noises from next door and know what was going on there almost as well as if she herself were taking part in it. She felt certain that Sara would not be able to get back into the house by herself, the door had been closed, and it was sure to be self-locking. Two or three hours to go, Isabelle thought, before Sara's parents came home. Before Jakob came back from the office. She picked up the cat, a lump of a creature, which flopped like a dead weight in her arms, uncertain what to expect next after having just soared through the air into a strange garden. Yes, put it back again, on the other side— whatever had she been thinking of, Isabelle asked herself. The animal seemed effortlessly to read her thoughts, even if the tensing of its body was imperceptible, a tiny shift in the position of its legs and head in preparation for being dropped. Then the warm body went limp again, as if Polly had come to the conclusion that she needn't fear such treatment after all, and she made herself comfortable, mewing softly, the very picture of a cat, Isabelle thought, seeing them both reflected in the French window as she climbed the two steps.

With her foot she pushed open the French window, which was ajar, and put Polly down in the living room. But it was clear that the animal felt ill at ease, only sitting down because the door was immediately shut again, and perhaps dazed by the different scents and movements; had it been able to talk it would probably have expressed a wish to be back beside the girl who was no doubt crying or being sick, rattling at the locked door, afraid of being punished or of the onset of darkness. Isabelle was glad when the telephone rang, and glad to hear Peter's matter-of-fact voice telling her about a new inquiry. A publisher of audio books wanted a cover, something original and not too expensive, –the usual story, Peter said, adding that he was busy with the move and Andras with his trip to Budapest. So this one's for you, he said, I need you to help me until Andras gets back. László's trying to persuade him to stay there, but he won't succeed. Peter's tired voice was neither friendly nor unfriendly, and he didn't ask her how she was. Polly mewed and followed Isabelle up the stairs to the kitchen, sniffed at the bowl of milk that she put down on the floor for her and watched while she cut up a piece of cold meat in a second dish. Isabelle enjoyed feeding the cat, and when she thought of Sara, who was probably sitting crying in the garden right now, but who at least had a cat, she considered her a comparatively lucky little girl. Having eaten her fill, Polly went on a tour of inspection and, like some secret policeman, mounted the stairs to examine the two remaining rooms, the bedroom and Jakob's study, not that he ever used it. The law firm was like an obsession that brooked no questions. But she too preferred not to have to explain how she spent her days; their mutual silence was like a down payment, Isabelle thought—on what, still remained to be seen. Leaving the cat upstairs, she went down to the ground floor and opened one of the front windows. It was already dusk, heavier clouds now obscured the sky, and there was a rather cold, gusty wind. In the street a fat man with a huge turban was passing, and two children in school uniform were walking along as sedately as a pair of elderly ladies. Any moment now, Jakob might come up the road, see her and wave to her. Polly jumped up on to the windowsill, startling her, and Isabelle took her firmly in both hands and held her out of the window. The cat writhed and struggled to get free. Isabelle let go of her. The animal seemed surprised; her legs buckled momentarily, perhaps she was too old for jumping, but then she got up again, squeezed between the bars of the little gate and disappeared under a parked car.

There were three bottles of red wine in the kitchen, one of them still half-full. Jakob had brought home some sushi. Alistair had arrived half an hour later; they had not eaten much, and Isabelle drank more than the others. Alistair lifted her into the air and whirled her around. –What a nice convenient size your wife is! And she had felt sick, but the feeling had passed. Jakob drank to her health, she emptied her glass and Alistair immediately refilled it. Both men had risen to their feet and now moved close to her, upright, expectant. Jakob turned his head towards Alistair and she sensed the looks exchanged above her head, felt the hands touching her back, Jakob's hand sliding over her hair, her forehead, in front of her eyes, play-fully holding them shut, while another hand found its way to her bottom, stroked the cheeks, ran a finger along the crack to the extent that her trousers allowed, and she waited for the hand to slide upwards again, to find the waistband and venture inside and forwards, she heard herself sigh as fingers started working on the buttons, the zip fastener, her mouth opened, this must be Alistair turning her on her own axis, she wasn't dizzy, she felt wide awake, someone gently pushed a thumb into her mouth, now she had to shut her eyes herself, she felt a breath on her ear and then someone was blowing gently into it, that must be Jakob, one look from her would stop all three of them, but it was still too soon, a few minutes more and she could open her eyes. She held her breath, a tongue, it must be Jakob's tongue, caressed her ear, and if that was Jakob, then it was Alistair who was kneeling in front of her, clasping her around the legs and putting his head between her thighs, and she heard something, sensed a movement close to her, perhaps Jakob's hand stroking Alistair's hair, his neck, and very soon now she would see the two men naked, it was time they took their clothes off, she thought impatiently—Jakob, who was embracing Alistair, who was holding her in his arms. But no hand touched her breasts, and the tongue withdrew from her ear; there was only a hand fondling the nape of her neck, but it tickled and wasn't pleasurable anymore: one of them was spoiling everything, breaking the mood. Still reluctant to believe it, closing her eyes tightly and stretching her body as if to offer it afresh, she felt desire ebbing away, and automatical-ly held on to her panties which a hand was tugging at, not ten-derly but roughly, it must be Alistair: as she touched his hand, his anger hit her like a blow; fingernails dug into her arm and he forced her hand inside her panties and lower until her fingers touched her still wet vulva, and she forgot the rough grasp and his anger as she tenderly felt for the soft skin, something that seemed thin and infinitely old, that was not herself but an old woman, a body that no longer sparked desire but only pity. Her hand was pulled away, Jakob, she thought, putting an end to it all. He let her be shamed; she sensed Alistair's displeasure and was powerless against it. Jakob picked her up in his arms and carried her—she really was incapable of walking by herself—up the stairs and into the bedroom, where he laid her on the bed and covered her over, without undressing her. Her hand was still resting on her sex; she had not opened her eyes. She heard footsteps, quiet voices: they were both still there, perhaps kissing, and Isabelle lay there and felt the humiliation becoming part of her body.

Later she was sick. A little self-control and you can always make it to the bathroom, her mother used to tell her reproachfully, and she did make it. Jakob would not get to know about it, not because he was so fast asleep but because he had bedded down in Isabelle's workroom downstairs. He came back up in the morning, however, knelt down by the bed and caressed her as she lay apparently asleep, for she pretended to be asleep, so that he could believe that nothing had happened. And that was the noose that she placed around her own neck. She should have reached out a hand to him and drawn him to her, she should have slept with him, to make it up between them. After he had gone she lay still, listening to the rain; one could feel, through the closed windows, that it had turned chilly. Around eleven o'clock the sun came out, and Isabelle took the two empty bottles and the half-full one to the bins, but it was no warmer. She only registered the fact that a car had stopped outside the house next door when the passenger door slammed, the thickset man stomped up to the front door, eyeing her without a word, and a blond woman got out of the back of the car, shouting something in a voice that sounded hoarse. She was wearing green tracksuit bottoms and a pink sweatshirt; no doubt she had been pretty once, and she was probably scarcely older than Isabelle. The man stepped outside again and furiously pulled the key out of the lock. –Why can't that bloody kid even open the door?

–You and your fat arse, the woman answered; then the door was slammed shut.

The street, still damp, gleamed as though freshly washed; Isabelle had not showered, and was wearing yesterday's clothes. Alistair had left at some point, and presumably, like Jakob, he had been at the office for some time now, occupied with some other matter that was not new, but then nothing was new, and wasn't that a good thing, wasn't that what they had wanted? She felt a sudden longing for Berlin. The previous day's humiliation remained with her, and however much she tried not to think about it, she couldn't help wondering whether Sara's parents had only come home just now, and not yesterday evening.

The streets were no darker than those in Berlin, but hardly any of the windows had a light showing, and the street-name signs in Sanskrit unsettled her. Any of the houses might conceal refugees, or enslaved women workers. Men eyed her, while adolescent boys came up to try and entice her into one of the innumerable Indian or Bengali restaurants. This was not her first excursion into the East End, but it was the first time she had ventured there on her own. She had strolled around two uninteresting clothes shops (loose-fitting embroidered smocks, hooded jackets, boots in lurid colors), bought a small wooden mortar and pestle in an Indian supermarket, stared from the outside at bookshops and at shop windows full of cassettes and CDs, and wondered what there was about the buildings, some renovated, some decaying and almost village-like, to make this part of the city so famous. It was desolate, with a rather hostile atmosphere. A giant of a man followed persistently on her heels; finally she sought refuge in one of the two bagel shops on Brick Lane and stood by the mirrored wall opposite the counter to eat a bagel and drink two mugs of very hot, strong tea, while her huge pursuer watched her so soulfully through the window that she was quite tempted to invite him in and offer him a cup too. The woman in charge, darting about between sausages, an enormous roast and the cash till, was sizing her up out of the corner of her eye. –He'll go away again, don't you worry. Everything goes eventually. Isabelle nodded, uncertain whether she had understood her correctly. –He's not yours, is he, not your boyfriend, I mean? She carved off a slice of meat and cut it into pieces. –That's the way to do it, cut them up into little bits, not have everything in one. Husband, lover, boyfriend, best mate. It's better for everybody that way, and you look as if the chickens have taken your last crumb. Hesitantly Isabelle moved closer to the counter. –We've only been here a few months.

–Yes, I can tell that from the way you talk. From Germany, right?

–From Berlin.

–Listen, I've got a daughter your age, pretty, like you, and a good girl. *She*'s a bit of a delicate flower, too, keeps herself to herself, never wants to get involved. Except for the war—she *did* spend half a day on the march against the war, because basically there's a sort of principle involved, isn't there? Look at you, Mum, she says, your first husband beat you, the second one left you, and you've done nothing but slave away here all these years. Just look at yourself, Mum. Fair enough, I tell her. But I loved those fellows, both of them, even if they weren't much good. I went running after one of them, bawling my eyes out, so what? And I've got you, I tell her. You want to avoid the misery I've had? Okay. But then what *have* you had at the end of it all?

–But surely she can still have children, if she's my age.

–Well, she won't, and even if she does it won't make any difference. I'm only saying this because you remind me of her. You're not happy either. And there's something brewing. All the same to me, really. Only I think it'll be something bad.

Isabelle looked out at the street, which was empty. –Well, I don't want to poke my nose in, said the woman. Lover boy's taken himself off, anyhow. With a nod of finality, as though that was enough tea, enough warmth for a chilly day in June, and more than enough talking, she disappeared into the back of the shop where enormous baking trays stacked high with bagels were waiting to go into the oven.

Isabelle left the little mortar and pestle behind, but she had already gone five hundred yards when she remembered and she didn't want to turn back. Flush Street, Plumbers Row, she made a series of wide loops, coming upon another gallery here, a small printing house there, and two young women in crotch-length miniskirts walked straight towards her, not giving way and forcing her off the pavement; then, finding that she had completely lost her bearings in the little side streets, she headed for a telephone box and dialed the office number. Jakob had gone out for a walk with Bentham, Maude told her, but Alistair was on hand, and he described a restaurant in Plumbers Row where all three of them could meet in an hour's time. –Just go back to the Whitechapel Gallery and get them to tell you the way. Or shall I pick you up there?

But it was Jakob she saw first, and she ran towards him as if he were her savior, as if he were, after all, the knight who would magnanimously protect her. He took her in his arms and then led her by the shortest route to Bengal's Secret, where Alistair was already waiting in the queue. –It's always like this here, he called out to them, but it's worth it, you'll see. And indeed, when they had been shown to a table, it was soon laden with all the good things Alistair had ordered, meat and vegetables and rice, and they were kept constantly supplied with fresh jugs of water. –London saps your strength, Alistair declared earnestly, you two don't eat nearly enough. –And then we'll go for a drink somewhere, said Jakob, who seemed to be in a very good mood, but Alistair ran his fingers through his hair with increasing frequency as the meal went on, he looked pale, said he needed to go home straight away, gave them both a hug and was gone, while Jakob and Isabelle lost their way again and wandered hand in hand through the unfamiliar streets until they managed to hail a taxi.

Next morning Isabelle woke up feeling reassured and cheerful. Each day blotted out the last, she thought, and no sound came from next door. But there was one who would not let her forget: Polly appeared in the street whenever Isabelle went to the window or stepped out of the door. Once she jumped up on to the ground-floor window ledge, meowed until she had attracted Isabelle's attention, and then vanished again.

For a few days Isabelle worked almost nonstop, only going out of the house for shopping. She talked on the telephone to Peter, to the children's books editor, and to the young people who were starting up the audio-books publishing firm and who were thrilled with her design. She spoke to Andras, too; he had come back from Budapest in a bad mood, seeming to regard as a defeat what had actually been his own decision. Isabelle could tell from his voice that there were additional reasons for his ill-humor, but preferred not to ask about them, as though his answer might block off an escape route for herself. Andras was less reticent. –What's the matter with you? What's become of your nice, bright voice that was like a child's school-bag bobbing up and down? Is it possible you're changing?

She was fine, she insisted, and it was the truth, but all the same Andras was right. She *was* changing. She didn't know in what way, or what it signified. –You sound as if you've been

finding your life up to now really monotonous, Andras persisted. And Jakob, how's Jakob? he asked, but she couldn't think
what to say.

Jakob came home around nine, they had dinner, and he
went to bed early. He didn't ask why she had suddenly become
so domesticated. Perhaps he liked it. They embraced lovingly,
and that was all. And there was Polly. When Isabelle stood up
and went to sit in her workroom—it was already close to midnight—she heard a voice outside calling and calling, –Sara,
Sara, where are you? Then there was silence once more. Half
an hour later Polly jumped triumphantly up on to the window
ledge. Fiercely Isabelle pushed her off again.

The following day, when she had taken the tube back from
Camden Town, Jim was standing outside the Kentish Town
station exit as if he had been waiting for her. –Ah, there you
are, he said, grinning at her.

30

It's all going according to plan, he told himself, but that was rubbish: one thing after another was going wrong. He had actually received a letter, a proper letter in an envelope, addressed to him, which had been pushed through the letterbox together with a few bills and advertising leaflets and which happened to have landed on top of the pile. His name. Damian had written him a letter, after more than a year: how prudent, Jim thought scornfully, after he had deciphered the sender's name. Damian. Just his name, no address. The rest of the post was in a cardboard box in the kitchen, bills that were paid by direct debit from an account somewhere, bills that Jim had paid, and now this envelope with his name in big block capitals, just to make quite sure everybody can read it, Jim thought, furious, and left the letter untouched. But the following day he opened it after all, and fished the sheet of paper out of the envelope: that was Damian for you, able to force him to open the envelope and read those four lines, as if heaven knows what depended on it. Things were going really well for him, he wrote, and so he had stayed on a lot longer, months longer than he'd intended. But where? Jim wondered, turning the paper and the envelope over and over. Now he was coming back, though, *so I hope you can find somewhere else, mate. I'll be back in three weeks.*

In short, he was chucking him out. Jim tore the letter to shreds and gave the sofa a kick. His notice to quit. And he had no idea where he could go. Condescending, disgusting.

Because Damian had money, because he had parents with money, and he, Jim, had to be grateful for all the months he had lived here without paying a penny. He looked around; it was fairly tidy, just as Mae would have liked it, and one day, he'd thought, he would bring her here and say, this is your home. A nice little flat in a nice little street. A home. One day, he'd thought, he would find her. The "missing" posters of her had long ago been replaced by others, with other faces and other names, and only once had Jim seen a pair of crazy people standing in front of it, jabbering away to themselves.

He had gone to the pub on Holloway Road, but the brown-haired barmaid hadn't been there, and then he had picked up a girl, but before they turned into Lady Margaret Road he had pressed a banknote into her hand and sent her packing. He thought he'd go mad if he didn't sleep with a woman soon, but at the same time the idea of it revolted him. Dave had stayed with him for two nights, after a fight with his father, that had been the only bit of variety he'd had, though Dave had moaned on endlessly about how his sister had spent a whole night in the garden, how their father was going to throw him out for good because Dave had threatened to tell them at school that his sister didn't go to school, and who would be the one to suffer, –how I hate him, Dave had said and had started to cry, not like a child but like an adult. Silent, grown-up crying. Dave begged and begged Jim to take him with him, but Jim felt he could do without any extra hassle. He didn't want to send Dave to Albert. He had let Dave have the sofa, even though he himself preferred the sofa to sleeping in the bedroom, in the double bed. Once Dave brought the little girl along to Pang's Garden, and she ate her chips slowly, fixing on him a look of abject devotion because he bought her some chips, because he bought her a Coke. I must get away from here, he thought when he saw her, an ugly little thing with stubborn eyes. She watched with interest as a girl emerged from the trap door above the kitchen, all dressed up and happy, with a bow in her hair, and climbed precariously down the narrow stairs that were little more than a ladder. Hisham's boys came into Jim's mind, and he spat. Running around all dolled up and happy, while these two kids here, real English kids, looked scruffy and frightened, and gazed at him in awe as if he was God Almighty just because he stood them a Coke and some chips. It got on his nerves, the way the girl's eyes were positively glued to his face, and then she stuck out her hand and said, –Thanks, mister. Stubborn, she looked, trusting, guilty. Dave wanted to run errands for him, but he turned him down. The three of them walked back together, just like a family, Jim thought, that's what anybody would think, seeing the three of them side by side. He imagined himself living with Mae and two children and moving to the country, because this was no life here. And now Damian was coming back and throwing him out.

When the doorbell rang one lunchtime, Jim grabbed a knife and flung the door open. But it wasn't Damian, it was Hisham, and Jim, relieved, furious, lost his temper. –Where did you get my address from, you bloody bastard? He flew into a rage; Hisham walked past him into the room without saying a word, and Jim grabbed a plate and threw it at him, then hurled a chair with such force that Hisham barely managed to stay on his feet, and the chair broke. So much the better, let Damian come back and find the place trashed. In Jim's head there was something clear, bright, and Hisham stooped to gather up the broken pieces of crockery with a calm, vaguely troubled expression, like a nurse whose patient is pulling the tubes out of his arms, and Jim laughed and laughed. Hisham would even help to tidy up if Jim let him; this spurred him on and he kicked the television, which Hisham steadied just in time, ran into the kitchen and wrenched the cupboards open, everything that he had got used to, such a nice set of fitted units, specially chosen by Damian's mother, who right now was luxuriously

stretching out her fat arse on cushions somewhere in the
Channel Islands or in Switzerland, always with sunglasses on
her face because she was ashamed of her son, always willing to
pay up so long as she was left in peace, and Damian would
phone her, spin her some yarn about a burglary and phone the
police, and then Mummy would pay for the renovation, a new
life, perhaps? There was always a new life to be had, you just
had to make a new beginning, clear away the crap, start afresh,
undaunted, become a good person, lead a good life, like
Hisham, who looked ready to burst into tears any minute and
was probably already praying to Allah to save Jim, since that
bastard of a Christian God had other things to think about,
like his rival's human sacrifices hobbling on the stumps of their
legs around Baghdad or New York. That was all right.
Somewhere there was a home for the unfortunate and the persecuted, for the hand of the Lord watches over you. Wasn't
that what they said? A sweep of his hand sent the glasses flying
from the cupboard, and he trampled them to pieces with his
bare feet, because of the brightness and because he saw something in Hisham's face that he couldn't understand and that
scared him, and there it was, the thing he feared, something
outside himself that took possession of him, an angel who folded his wings around Jim's shoulders and closed his eyes so that
he shouldn't see what was happening to him. His garden, the
garden with the cherry tree in the middle and the wall all
around it, where Mae was waiting for him because she wanted
to live and because they were both entitled to their lives. She
smiled at him, contented, healthy, she opened her arms wide,
it was just that somebody always pushed in between him and
her, somebody who begrudged them life and happiness. She
would never have left him of her own accord, and it was right
that he should wait for her and not allow himself to be led
astray, not by Albert and not by Isabelle, who with her childish, reckless eyes was inviting him to kiss her, no doubt about

it, she was offering herself to him, he only had to say the word and she'd be wrapped around his neck. Mae loved him. There was something bright, it was only a hand's breadth away from him, but he must make a grab for it before it was too late, before Damian threw him out. He swung the frying pan triumphantly in his left hand, and spun around because Hisham was behind him, pale as that other angel who didn't protect him but betrayed him, the Angel of Death. But he would teach him not to interfere. Jim felt that Mae was close by, just a tiny step away, he tried to concentrate, just a tiny step and he'd be with her, and in his head something shattered as he drew back his arm to strike, there it was, just the way he'd experienced it with Mae, bright, but it shattered into tiny pieces, and he was going to kill Hisham. They looked at each other. Then Hisham lowered his eyes and turned away, as if he didn't want to be responsible or be a witness. He offered Jim the back of his head, holding that position, doing nothing to protect himself. He started to speak, too softly for Jim to hear what he said. –You bastard, said Jim. Now it was neither bright nor dark. Just the kitchen, the broken fragments, Jim's bleeding feet. –Bastard. It was quiet for a moment. As if the air were mixed with something, Jim thought, stuffed full of something that stopped you from breathing. –Better that way, said Hisham slowly. Look at that. He opened a drawer, then another, searching for something, not finding it. –For God's sake, he said to Jim, at least go and get some toilet paper.

He obeyed stupidly, not understanding what Hisham had in mind. Hisham bent down and carefully dabbed at his feet, then took hold of one of them. –It's no good like this, you'll have to sit down, the sofa will be best. His voice had lost all trace of expression. They went into the living room. Nothing had been destroyed, Jim thought; despite everything, all was well. He looked at his bleeding feet, which Hisham was carefully lifting up and resting on a cushion before starting to dab at them again. –What have you and Albert got going between you? asked Jim. –Nothing, said Hisham. Money, I needed money, and he knew that I've got a few addresses. He put the squeeze on me. Hisham looked up. –If you need money for your family, he began, then shrugged. –I haven't got a family, said Jim defiantly, and pulled his feet away. Where did you get my address?

Hisham tossed the bloodied toilet paper on to the table. –Do you think it's so hard to track you down, you or your girlfriend?

–I never asked for your help. I never asked you to play nursemaid.

–Shut up. Hisham stood up. If I'd known what I'd find, I certainly wouldn't have done it.

Jim let himself drop back against the sofa, folded his arms behind his head and tried to look unconcerned. He was afraid. There was no good news, not for him, and Hisham wouldn't be the bearer of it.

–Two of my wife's brothers disappeared, do you understand? I know what it's like when you're looking for someone and you don't even know if they're still alive.

–What's that got to do with me? Is that why you're poking your nose into my business? Jim's eyes strayed around the room. There was the chair on the floor, there was half of the plate. –What's all that about? he muttered. The past half-hour, from the time when he had opened the door to Hisham, was becoming blurred, disappearing like smoke in this air that was too thick, too full of something that he didn't understand. What is this, he thought, it's like a pain, why does Hisham want to hurt me? –Leave it, he said, you don't need to tell me anything.

–I've found her, said Hisham calmly. Mae. I've found Mae.

–Leave it, repeated Jim, but it was too late; he sat up straight, obedient as a child, placed his hands on his knees, felt the cuts throbbing, and the carpet would be covered in stains.

It's nothing, he thought. His mind was a blank. He thought of Isabelle standing in front of him, waiting for something. Perhaps Hisham could help him find a room, he was sure to have a car, he could pick him up from here and help him move, perhaps help him find a room outside London, in a suburb somewhere. Now, as if it were his own home and Jim were the visitor, Hisham went into the kitchen, opened the refrigerator and came back with two bottles of beer, like a brother, ready to help: he held out a beer, and Jim took it and gulped it down.

When he woke up it was just getting light. He was lying on the sofa with a blanket over him, his shoes were placed neatly side-by-side in front of it, and the room had been tidied up. On the table there was a glass of water, he didn't know what for. Next to the glass lay an envelope. He picked up the glass and smelt it, but it had no smell, apparently it really was just water. His feet hurt. Once again he smelt the clear liquid. He must have fallen asleep before Hisham left. He liked this early morning light, and he got up, gingerly slipped his trainers on, and, putting as little weight on his feet as possible, went over to the door that led into the garden. Not a garden, he thought, just a neglected patch of grass and some rubbish, two or three plastic bags that he had carelessly tossed out there himself. The grass was moist with dew or rain, he didn't know if it had rained during the night. As for Hisham, he wouldn't be seeing him again. A squirrel was busying itself in the branches of a tree that grew on the other side of the wall. Jim's mind was empty and clear, with nothing more in it than a few thin lines like the condensation trails of aircraft in a clear sky, lines that made no sense, just as Hisham made no sense, none of his actions or decisions did, not to Jim anyway. Neither hatred nor a thirst for vengeance, but rather, as Jim had been inclined to believe yesterday, a kind of brotherliness, as if Hisham were trying to draw him back and didn't understand that for Jim there was nothing to come back to, no wife and no nephews, no restaurant. But he shouldn't have trusted him. When it came down to it, Hisham was worse than Albert or Ben. Unpredictable. Cruel.

Jim went into the kitchen and opened the cupboards, looking for something to eat. He put the kettle on, fished a tea bag out of the packet, and waited. Then he got a brush and dustpan from underneath the sink and swept up the broken glass. The kettle whistled. It's like when you're feverish, he thought. You have thoughts, but they don't work properly, they go haywire. There on the coffee table lay the envelope. He'd brought him a beer and then held the envelope out to him. –I thought it was all Albert's doing, I thought he'd taken Mae out of circulation.

Jim jerked his hand suddenly and tea slopped over the rim of the cup. He hadn't touched the envelope. But Hisham wouldn't let up. –Your pathetic little lies. Take a look. I took some pictures of her so that you can pin her up over your bed.

He knew how you prepared yourself for physical pain, what you had to do to make it bearable, but this was different. For a moment he dared to hope. If it was different—could he have been mistaken? Hisham had pulled out a photo. –Do you recognize her? I haven't told her that I know where you are. But something's missing, thought Jim, there's always something missing. He had fallen asleep, hadn't he? Hisham had taken himself off because he'd fallen asleep, and had left the envelope lying on the table. –At first I thought I'd kill you. Hisham had talked on and on, as if his voice were in Jim's head, like lines or a sort of shading, something that got darker, denser. I've been asleep, thought Jim. It's nothing, he wanted to say. By now the sun was fully up; the squirrel had vanished. He went indoors and hesitantly picked up the envelope from the table. He would go away from here. The sun shone into the room, and he was afraid.

A shallow step, that was all, a shallow step close to where the rubbish containers stood, but he stumbled, fell flat on his face and lay there doubled up, with his chin cut open and his nose bleeding. Picking himself up with an effort, he crouched down behind the containers, which gave him complete cover, and wiped the blood from his face, but there was too much of it, too much blood. Then the light above the side door went out, and only narrow strips of light from the windows fell across the yard. There would be two of them, Pete the door-man had said, two young guys, and here they were, one of them with a small backpack over his shoulder, talking quite normally, confident of not being disturbed. The music got louder. A third of the profit, he'd promised Pete. As much cash as possible: clean out a few petty dealers and then take off, to Glasgow first of all, sell the rest and then see. He had only a few days, somebody would recognize him. –Aren't you scared? Pete had asked, grinning. They'll kill you, won't they?

Albert had stopped phoning him, perhaps he had Hisham to thank for that. Nor did he answer when Jim rang him. And no jobs, not a single one, as though Jim had ceased to exist. No calls from Ben either. Cautiously raising his head, he felt in his jacket for a tissue to wipe away the blood. It had been Pete's idea that he should wait in the yard outside the side entrance: he'd assured Jim that those two would do their dealing in the back lobby, and anyway in the club itself Jim would immediately attract attention. –Too old, mate, Pete told him, you might pretend to be an American tourist, but then you'd have to keep your mouth shut, so that wouldn't work. Once you open your mouth there's fuck all chance of anybody taking you for a Yank, however wasted they are. A third for Pete, if coming here again paid off. Broken Night, what a bloody stupid name for a club. Two bands and two DJs, give or take. Ecstasy, and always a few wanting hash or cocaine or heroin. –Every time, Pete had assured him, and asked with a grin: What about your cash, what did you blow that on? Cocaine? Or did you lose it on the way home?

He needed to find some water to wash the blood off. The chill-out room was at the back, and that was where the toilets would be too, right by the side entrance. He got to his feet, taking care not to stain his T-shirt, but the bleeding had stopped, and he headed towards the side entrance that the two dealers had disappeared into. One of them was actually in the lobby, no more than eighteen, and he eyed Jim irritably and said something in an angry whisper as Jim peered past him, looking for the door to the toilets. –Not much to be done for that one's mug, with or without water, Jim heard after he had finally found the door, and he gave a violent start, pushed the door shut behind him and went over to the wash basin. The mirror was spotted, rust had eaten away the metal, and the naked bulb on the wall was flickering. –Oh shit, he muttered, shit, and began to cry. But he saw at once that it was nothing, simply that the blood had got smeared into a broad streak from the right temple to the chin. Jim turned on the tap and stood there, not washing, staring at his reflection. It *had* been Mae in the photos, he'd known her at once. One shot had been taken from the right, in profile; she looked tired, tired in a different way from what he remembered, calm and at the same time sad, in an unreal, unfamiliar way—though he still knew her at once—rather, he'd thought, as if the picture had been computer-generated. She wasn't smiling, but standing there as though presenting her face to the police photographer, as if he'd said, now the second one, left profile, but after all that it still wasn't good enough and they'd had to do it on the computer, which wasn't a problem, no problem at all to alter a photograph on the computer. A photo proved nothing. And now turn around, he imagined the photographer saying, now the other side, and then he remembered that it was Hisham who had taken the photos, who had said, turn around, I want another shot, yes, like that, you needn't be ashamed, it's not your fault. But apparently she had been ashamed, and had hesitated to present her right side—that was it, wasn't it, the right and the left cheek, someone smites you on the right cheek and you offer them the other one? But this had been done with a knife. The cut must have damaged a muscle or a nerve, the corner of the mouth was pulled upwards as if by a cramp or a nervous tic, the scar ran all the way from the right eye to the chin, a quick, long cut, badly healed, lumpy. Then the photo showing her from the front.

Behind him the door burst open and a young lad rushed past him into one of the stalls and threw up. Jim bent forward and washed his face under the tap, heard the youth retching and went over to him. –Bloody hell, can't you just have a swallow of water and then get out of here? The lad straightened up, nodded nervously, came obediently out of the stall and drank thirstily. –Go on, get out, said Jim, taking him by the arm, –you're better off in the fresh air. He took him out through the side door, into the yard and then on to the street. –Now piss off, there's nothing in there worth staying for. He watched him as he staggered away, making an effort to look cool and turning to give a wave. Jim took up position by the side entrance. Judging by the length of time those two had been inside, they'd have sold most of their stuff when they came out. So there'd be rich pickings. The first one came out, waited a second, didn't see him, and trotted off. The blow took him so completely by surprise that he didn't cry out. Jim grabbed hold of him and dragged him behind the dustbins. With a knife in his hand, he rifled his pockets and found a few hundred pounds, some pills, five wraps of cocaine. Then the other one came out, glanced around quickly, and started running. Jim calmly watched him go and then looked once again at the guy lying at his feet. It was just his body, a limp object, he couldn't see the face, but then the youth groaned and moved, there was his voice, and

Jim knelt beside him, knife in hand, as he made a vain effort to say something, a name, Jim thought, but it was incomplete, mangled. A window was flung open and music slopped out like a liquid. Suddenly he felt sickened. Another few minutes and this one would come to, or the other one would be back. He hit him again.

In Pang's Garden he ordered a bag of chips and a spring roll, sat down on the wooden bench and started to eat. His nose was swollen, but the cut on his chin wasn't deep. He turned round and looked out into the street, so as to see Dave if he happened to pass by, but there were only a few giggling women pushing their way in, one with a snotty-nosed little girl who stared aghast at his face. He wouldn't have recognized Mae, not if he had seen her from the front. From a distance he might have—her body, her head, the way she moved, but not her face. She had told lies about him. All those months he had waited in Damian's flat, and she hadn't come. Hisham had come—Hisham who had beaten him up on Albert's orders and then taken him out for a meal—because he knew that Jim trusted him despite everything. He had discovered his address, he had found Mae. Dave knew the address, Isabelle possibly knew it. She was throwing herself at him. She and her husband had a whole house to themselves, and she was throwing herself at him. She'd sleep with him if he wanted. But he didn't want it, not that. As he stood up he bumped into the little girl, who clung wordlessly to her mother. She looked up at him, green snot in her nostrils, sniffed, and rubbed her nose with her little pink hand; he was sickened. Then he left. Although it was windy, the air was murky and stale, and he made a detour to see Isabelle. There were still some lights on. He wanted to ring the bell, but it was almost midnight. He could see Isabelle's husband on the first floor; she wasn't in sight. Her husband seemed to be tidying up, he came down to the ground floor holding a vase of flowers, walked over to the window and looked out, then was gone. Eventually, she herself appeared; perhaps she'd been sitting in the back room. She too came to the window, and she pushed the sash up and leaned her elbows on the windowsill. Hastily Jim ducked down behind a parked car. He could make out her face, smooth and luminous. But then Dave's sister's fat black and white cat strutted through the bars of the front gate, jumped up on to the windowsill as if it knew it was welcome, and meowed. But Isabelle took hold of it only to push it off again, using both her hands, with a gesture of fury and disgust. Jim grinned, delighting in the annoyance that the encounter brought them both, cat and woman alike. The cat's legs buckled, it spat and made a beeline for the car that he was hiding behind. It ran straight into the trap, almost colliding with his legs, and he grabbed it with both hands as Isabelle slammed the window shut and turned away as if she had finished with the cat once and for all. But here the cat was, in his hands, and he stood up, holding it tightly as it did its best to scratch him, walked to the corner of Ascham Street and hurled it with all his might over the wall there. But he had thrown short. Its head struck the top edge, and it dropped like a stone at the foot of the wall and lay where it had fallen, in the pool of light cast by a street lamp. Jim looked back at the house, but Isabelle was no longer there. If she had been watching him she would never admit it, thought Jim angrily. She would never admit that it filled her with satisfaction to see the cat lying there with a broken neck. He knelt down beside the animal and contemplated the plump body. No, the neck was all right, but the skull was smashed, blood was seeping out. Gently he touched the fur and rolled the cat on to its side to see if it was still alive. He shuddered. Cats had their pride, they possessed a soul, perhaps they really did have nine lives. No, it wasn't alive. Now he was sorry. In the house over there, no lights were showing anymore. But Isabelle was no better, thought Jim: filled with hatred, she had pushed the cat off the window ledge, and by tomorrow she'd have forgotten about it because she didn't care. But he would find her, tomorrow, he would remind her about it, tomorrow or the day after he would waylay her and speak to her. She was no better than he was.

31

Although the lawns were already turning brown, it was so pleasantly warm in the sunshine that they sat down by the pond and had some tea, –of course, said Bentham, the tea and the coffee here are very poor; he ate half of Jakob's muffin and looked contented. –This is laughable, of course, when one thinks of a proper afternoon tea. We used to go out rowing and then walk back home, where our house-keeper would already have laid the table and there would be cakes and jam, and toast of course. She urged us to eat fruit. She used to boast of her own good health, of never being ill. And it was true, she never had so much as a cold. But then a growth developed, and she became rather eccentric.

–A tumor? Jakob asked.

–No, not on the brain, but she began to behave strangely, even so. We tried to ignore it for as long as we could, until one day she started to slash the sofas and armchairs. Next morning she saw what she had done and wrote us a letter asking us not to try to find her. Graham was terribly upset, and so was I. She had scratched some marks on a cabinet, and we considered for a long time whether to have it restored.

He broke off another small piece of muffin and tossed it to a duck. –What a pity there are so few sparrows nowadays. Somebody told me that the Hebrew word for a sparrow is *dror*, meaning freedom. They appear to have emigrated. Since I learned their name, their Hebrew name, I mean, I am even fonder of them than before.

–And you've really never tried to find your housekeeper?

–No. We supported her by roundabout means, Graham found a way. We left the cabinet as it was. The past always finds objects to tell its story.

–Is it true that your name was Bensheim? Jakob asked.

–Yes, my parents anglicized it to Bentham. A few years ago I even went to Germany to have a look at the town of Bensheim. A pretty little place.

The breeze was strengthening a little. A boy carefully lowered his toy yacht into the water and the white sails dipped alarmingly, but the keel kept the boat from capsizing, and as his mother ran laughing towards him it was too late, the boat was already off on its voyage, righting itself and gathering speed. But the boy hadn't yet realized that it was sailing out of his reach; proudly he smiled at his mother, they stood hand in hand at the water's edge, and it was possible that it might reach the opposite bank and be brought ashore there. Jakob's eyes were irresistibly drawn to the mother, who reminded him of Miriam; she stood there straight and tall, and even if it ended in tears, thought Jakob, she would be able to comfort her son. To his deep satisfaction he sensed that Bentham was as taken by the scene as he was himself, and for a moment he was conscious of Bentham's hand on his arm.

–In springtime the countryside there is wonderful, so charming and inviting that I have imagined how it would be to spend every spring in the Bergstrasse region: no doubt each year one would be lost in wonder and marvel at it afresh. That is the best thing there is, marveling at beauty of whatever kind, even when it is ephemeral, even when it is has to be bought. I have given the idea serious consideration. There was a little house, a little villa, where I would have been welcome as a tenant.

–And your partner?

–He was all for it; for him it was less problematic, of course.

But then there was the accident. I had never imagined that I'd be the one to be left behind.

Bentham was silent for a while. –Being left behind appears to be my particular speciality. When you love somebody, you believe, with all the trustfulness born of that love, that you will meet death together.

–Apart from my mother, I've never lost anybody, said Jakob.

–That is quite enough, surely, at your age? Incidentally, it is not so much the pain that is destructive. Rather it is the blindness that it brings with it, the desire to keep your eyes shut, to see nothing that might distance you from the image of the loved one, and it takes a long time before you fully understand the nature of the past—that it is beyond your reach and cannot be changed, however desperately you strive to get close to it. And that you lose everything if you refuse to accept what is past and to see it from that remorseless distance, a distance that torments you chiefly because it is your own remoteness from things.

–And from people who are still living?

Bentham laughed. –You mean, surely that's more important? You are right. But I am one of those people who grew up with a geography that was missing, a home that existed as a photograph, an address, a name, but remained out of reach. I knew the turn of the banister in our Frankfurt house by heart, not from memory but from the photos, and the same with the chest of drawers on the first floor with the mirror hanging above it. For me that was always the embodiment of harmonious proportions, of a meaningful disposition. In England there was nothing of that kind for me. One has to learn that one can come back and find something new: that is the point of conducting a dialogue with the dead, with what one has lost.

Jakob looked around for the young woman and the child. They were standing on the opposite bank, the boy had found a stick and was leaning out as far as he could, while his mother held him tightly by the hand.

–I can't imagine living here permanently, said Jakob uneasily. Though I would like to. I like it here.

–Why would you want to stay here?

–It seems so absurd to let oneself be defined by where one was born.

Bentham laughed. –But it's not often that one gets to choose for oneself. There are some things one does get to choose, though. He stood up. –Come, let's walk a little now, I will at least spare you the conclusion to be drawn from my endless talking. Probably there isn't one, a conclusion, I mean. And besides, to be frank, much as I love this park—and just look, those two are still over there, waiting for their little boat to come in—a whisky would be just the thing right now. Such a very pleasant custom.

They walked southeastwards, crossing Devonshire Street, Bentham half a pace ahead, and Jakob remained silent until they reached the pub, where an elderly barman greeted Bentham with a brief nod and brought two whiskies to the table.

–Maude would disapprove, said Bentham. Not of this one whisky, but she would know that it will be followed by a second one. It's nice of you to bear me company so patiently. And I haven't even asked how you and your wife are.

–We're fine, said Jakob, then hesitated. He smiled. –I'm really fine. Bentham sat there contentedly, a little absently, his glass in his hand. I'm happy, Jakob wanted to say, but the statement was like a little wooden doll that you carefully stood up but that only stayed up for a moment before toppling over. Not bad, Jakob thought, you can keep it balanced, you only need to support it just a little, with one finger. –But it's confusing. I mean, the idea that one's life is really changing.

–You mean, changing without your knowing how, or what the changes are?

But Jakob felt that he was treading on thin ice here, and fell silent. To run a finger very gently over Bentham's hand or face, over the heavy lids and eyebrows, so as to be better able to remember his face afterwards—that was what he wanted to do. It was desire and yet not desire, not what he felt for Isabelle when he caressed her face, although now it seemed to him as if, at those times too, touching was only an aid to seeing. He drank and felt the effect of the alcohol, the way thoughts took on a different weight, so that, for all their clarity, they only surprised but did not hurt him. The thought that he was someone who neither took nor gave, his sympathy genuine but his involvement merely simulated. He would not reach out his hand to touch the mottled skin; he sensed that Bentham expected nothing of him, and he was saddened, but without rousing himself to do anything about it. His glass was empty, and although his mind was easy now, he knew that later he would be horrified.

–When people are only onlookers it does make them pleasant to be with. Bentham made a sign to the barman, who refilled their glasses. –Except for those who love them, Bentham added, drinking.

–What do you do when you stay away from the office for a few days? Jakob asked.

Bentham looked at him in surprise. Jakob felt himself blushing.

–And now you are blushing, how nice. Feel free to ask. I go to a small hotel, not always the same one, though usually it is. A small hotel that one would call dubious if it were not so extremely civilized and well run, with good rooms and good service. A certain number of young men frequent it to earn a little money. I have no objection to paying for amatory favors—that is a question of age, and the young men who have an entrée there are, shall we say, hand-picked, students for the most part, cultured, well bred. Not frightfully young, moreover, just young. You meet in the lobby, perhaps agree to dine or go to the opera together, and round off the evening in one way or another. A very practical arrangement. *You* are too young for it, or too old, depending on how one looks at it. Otherwise I should possibly recommend it to you.

–But I'm married, Jakob replied naïvely.

–One should be conscientious in these matters, you are quite right, but without being *too* strict about it. In any case, I often spend a few days there simply to escape the emptiness of my house. Those objects that tell a story of the past—one cannot always bear them.

Two men entered the pub and greeted Bentham, then remained standing at the bar.

–They're lawyers too, Bentham explained. He was rocking his head slowly from side to side as if to familiarize himself with its weight and, Jakob thought, to consider the nature of the statements that had been made and weigh up their significance for his companion. Jakob felt sad again because he recognized this as the first installment of a farewell. He was being put in his place, he felt it physically and knew that he had neither the necessary credentials, nor the strength to ignore the boundary. –It makes no difference what you call it, Bentham said, character, lack of ability, fate—there are always limitations. The question is what you try to do with them, what you make of them. It's still your life. Bentham smiled. When Graham thought I was being too melancholy, he would remind me that cheerfulness is an achievement of civilization. Once again he seemed effortlessly to know what was in Jakob's mind, and growled something that seemed to express forbearance. –Anyway, you shouldn't wrestle with me, I'm not the angel. His arms, squeezed into the arms of his jacket, and the short, mobile hands now lay quietly on the table between them, and Jakob nodded gratefully and at last raised his eyes and met Bentham's gaze. He felt the seconds slowly passing, as though there were a second-hand attached to his heart: each one a tiny movement of remembering, anticipated, preserved and at last free of all fear of misunderstanding between them. He was conscious of blushing again, but knew that this time Bentham would make no comment, and noticed too that he was beginning to tremble; he mustered all his strength, feeling as though he were being turned inside out like a glove. But where do we go from here, how shall I bear it, he thought, and how straightforward it was with Isabelle, where taking the conventional steps had been a substitute for a confession of love.

It was no more than five minutes' walk to the office, where Maude let him in and gave him the message from Isabelle and Alistair. He went quickly up to his room to collect his keys and a pullover and, feeling unequal to reaching the address he had been given under his own steam, he hailed a taxi. After being set down, he had gone only a few steps when he caught sight of Isabelle, and his fear of being unable to show warmth towards her proved groundless. She came bounding up to him and fell into his arms, and he was happy to hold her tight. Bengal's Secret, the restaurant where Alistair was waiting for them, was close by, and he noted gratefully that Alistair took charge, ordering and letting him eat without plying him with questions; he could see that Alistair himself was weary.

She hardly left the house, seemed to spend most of her time working, made no arrangements with Alistair, and showed little inclination to go out in the evenings at all: perhaps she was acting out of consideration for Jakob, for he went to bed early, even though he didn't fall asleep for a long time, sometimes hearing, from below, a door closing or a window being pushed up or down; he was glad of Isabelle's presence, glad to be lying there alone. Cowardice had prompted him, when Alistair was kneeling in front of Isabelle with his head between her thighs, to signal to him to leave; they had exchanged a goodbye kiss at the door, soothingly and tenderly Alistair had stroked Jakob's hair, and now Jakob wished he had not sent him away. Coming into his room one lunchtime, Alistair had sat down on the chest, taken a small mirror from his jacket pocket, and studied his face in it. Then he had gone over to Jakob, who was sitting at his desk, kissed his hair, and embraced him. –Neither of us, he said, is all that pretty anymore. He had mumbled this in an imitation of Bentham, stroked Jakob's temple, and left. Bentham stayed away from the office; as ever, Maude made no comment, and this time she seemed not to be worried about Bentham, but sometimes brought Jakob a piece of cake or fruit or a cup of tea in his room. During the day he was too busy to spend time brooding. An English investment company was interested in acquiring several apartment buildings in the north of the Prenzlauer Berg district of Berlin. The tracks belonging to the railway company that was for sale were in a sorry state. Miller's case was developing well, he had been to see Sahar and said she had foretold that he would lose something connected with water, obviously the lakeside property, and so he himself was now proposing a compensation settlement based on a sum that seemed to be acceptable to the other side but was substantial enough to pay for the renovation of the villa in Treptow. –Bentham doesn't see the sense of it, I know, said Miller. I'm too old to move to Berlin, I would do a lot of work on the house and end up selling it after all. That's the way it is when you have no children. –But Bentham doesn't have children either, Jakob had objected. –Of course not, but he has that young man here, your colleague, and more courage than I have, too. For a person who is alone in the world, the passage of time is ultimately a nonsense. Time means children growing up and having children of their own—or else the rather bald fact that there are days and hours and that you die.

Hans phoned the office twice, and they discussed going hiking together in the autumn; Jakob thought they wouldn't do it. –I miss you, said Hans. I'm starting to be very envious of you for being married.

Night after night Jakob lay stretched out in bed, his hands clasped behind his head, hoping that Isabelle was not coming up yet. The time passed far too quickly. He lay naked under the cover without moving, as though in this way he might induce his body to reveal to him what he should do. Towards morning he started out of his sleep bathed in sweat, relieved to know that Isabelle was beside him. She had recently taken to talking in her sleep, he couldn't make out what she was saying, but it seemed as though she often dreamed of a cat. If he was sure that she was fast asleep he would get up, go from room to room, stand at the window in the dining room or on the ground floor, in Isabelle's room, and gaze out at the street. He was pleased when he saw the white fox ransacking the dustbins on its way to Hampstead Heath, he liked the assurance of the animal's movements, the nonchalant way it crossed the street where it was so out of place. On one occasion the fox appeared to have made a kill: it dragged something that might have been a cat for some distance along the pavement, then left it lying there. Jakob opened the window to get a better view, but could not make anything out. He jumped when a man's voice began shouting on the other side of the wall—unmistakably angry, though he could not distinguish the words—and again when, shortly afterwards, something hit the wall with such force that it seemed about to come straight through. The first voice was joined by a second, apparently younger one, and perhaps by a woman's voice too. Unpleasant as Jakob found this, he could not tear himself away. Was it exceptional, he wondered, or did Isabelle hear the neighbors having rows like this every day and choose not to tell him about it? And if so, why was that? He was now wide awake and felt agreeably stimulated, much to his shame. Then a door slammed, and he went upstairs. Back in bed again, he worried that he had failed to secure the window properly, and started up at every sound. There were burglars, there was violence; when he got up, he was relieved to find everything intact.

The city was drowsy, one hot day followed another. Bentham returned; he was in excellent spirits and had found Jakob a new client, a London hotelier who wanted to purchase two large hotels on the island of Borkum. Quite a young man, Bentham said, he looked forward to being the first Jew to own one of the biggest hotels on an island once "honored" with the shameful designation "Free from Jews," and to laying on historical excursions for his no doubt predominantly ignorant and insensitive guests. Alistair was fired with enthusiasm at the idea of arranging a tour of inspection. –Where is this island, anyway? –Right up in the north, Jakob replied, but he had never been to Borkum and had to consult an atlas. –He's coming to see you tomorrow, Bentham told Jakob, his name is John Pilger. –Pilger? Jakob queried. –Why not? Bentham looked at them both in amusement, and Alistair tugged at Jakob's sleeve. –Let's go and discuss it over lunch. Anthony and Paul came up the stairs. –You're not invited, Alistair called out to them, but we're going to a North Sea island full of seals, we'll have two days eating nothing but crabs and whale meat. Anthony prodded Jakob in the ribs as he stood with his mouth slightly open, only half hearing the others' predictions of attempts at bribery or murder threats from the local council. He lowered his eyes so as not to stare at Bentham; he felt happy, and Alistair put an arm around his shoulders. –It'll be wonderful, said Alistair.

When he got home, Isabelle had prepared a pasta bake; the telephone rang, and she asked him to crack two eggs over the top of it, but he forgot that they needed beating first and laughed when, a quarter of an hour later, he saw what looked like a pair of fried eggs crowning the pasta and just starting to burn. Isabelle smiled too, but she was annoyed, and her voice

was cold and so implacable that he was taken aback. Just a little outburst, he thought, and yet it aroused in him feelings of
dislike and fear. After the meal they went out for a short walk,
and she took his hand and told him that Peter and Andras
would be moving the agency to its new premises next week.
–Do you want to go to Berlin? asked Jakob, but she shook her
head dismissively. When they got back, he put some money
into the bowl on the chest of drawers and was ashamed to see
the wilted bunch of roses that he had brought her a week ago.
It was easy to make up after a quarrel, but they weren't actually quarrelling, and where there was only silence there was no
making up. He would have liked to ask her why they were
drifting apart, though he wasn't sure if he only imagined that
they had been closer in Berlin. Perhaps it was just a different
kind of distance, perhaps she was preoccupied with something
she didn't talk about, and he thought of the noise from the
neighbors that he had heard one night. He said nothing but
hung around her, watching her as if to read in her face what
was to be done. He wanted to tell her about Miriam, if she
would only give him a sign, he wanted to make amends for
whatever he had left undone. Isabelle sat at her table, bent
over the plans of the future office in Potsdamer Strasse. –From
Wartburgstrasse it'll only be ten minutes by bike, she said. She
looked up and smiled. You could never read faces with the eye
alone, he thought, without expectations and doubts getting in
the way, you were never satisfied with appearances, always
wanting to probe to the very center, but maybe that was a mistake. He laughed. That tiny point, not even the size of a pin-
head, that was so bitterly fought for by whoever or whatever
aspired to be central. Isabelle gave him a quizzical look. –I was
thinking what a very strange notion a center is, when in fact the
absolute center is regarded as having no area at all.

–Were you thinking of yourself as the center, or me?
Isabelle asked.

–That's just it, said Jakob, neither you nor me, neither Berlin nor London.

–Hasn't that always been the way? said Isabelle coolly, and returned to her plans.

And yet, he thought as he lay in bed, without a center there could be no orbit. He listened for any sound from the ground floor, where Isabelle was still sitting, but there was a whole floor of the house between them, and although the doors were open there was nothing to be heard. As he was drifting off he imagined he heard a dull thud. But that's impossible, he told himself; then it stayed quiet, and he fell asleep.

32

They went to a café, but that wasn't the right thing, and they strolled towards the canal and along it as far as the aviary. Jim's hands were damp and he tried to kiss her: she felt like a teenager. When they reached the aviary he burst into tears, and it was so embarrassing and ridiculous that she looked around for help, as if Jakob might suddenly appear from nowhere to help her. But Jim, the tears still in his eyes, seized her by the shoulders and laughed at her; he drew her to him, and she obeyed. –Don't you like guys who show weakness? He thrust her away from him a little, but held her firmly by the arms and started to tell her something, a story, he said, a true story, about the flower girl and the prince who betrayed her, but she could scarcely follow it. He noticed and spoke even faster, she didn't know if he was talking cockney; he deliberately annoyed her, pulled her hair, then picked her up and carried her, legs kicking, to the canal and held her over the water as if he was going to drop her in. –Will you come home with me? he asked, asked again and again, laughed, gently set her down and kissed her tenderly on the temple. –You see, he said, suddenly serious, I've been waiting for you all my life. He took her hand and laid it on his heart, then pulled his T-shirt over his head and stood bare-chested before her. His smooth, strong torso was pale, and his veins showed up with unusual clarity in the bright summer sunlight, Jim saw it too. –I'm the winter, I'm death, he said, keeping perfectly still, you have to kiss me back to life. His nakedness startled her; there were people on the bridge over the canal leading from the zoo to the aviary, any minute now they'd start clapping, Isabelle thought as Jim went down on his knees before her. –Don't say you're embarrassed, he whispered to her. –Come on, kiss me right here, in front of them all. She leaned forward helplessly, it was hot, the wind very warm, she felt as though she had no weight of her own, yet her brain went on registering every move like an ever-watchful eye; she wanted to straighten up, he wouldn't let her. He didn't love her, he was lying. His lips glistened, he was smiling. –Kiss me, he repeated, I'll give you one more minute.

Two hours later they still weren't at his house, she was getting tired and no longer knew where they were, except that she could only tell from the position of the sun that they were walking eastwards; it was nearly six o'clock. She had had nothing to drink all afternoon, but didn't dare ask Jim for a break, and on he went, gripping her hand firmly in his, walking a little ahead of her, more or less pulling her along. When he finally stopped—she hoped she would recognize the street, but she didn't—she almost fell. Jim planted himself in front of her, his hands in his trouser pockets. –How do I know if I can trust you? he said suddenly. Then he turned and walked off; she stared after him, neither surprised nor angry, she was too tired, she just wanted to know where she was and how to get home. The houses looked like council housing from the seventies, then came smaller detached houses painted pink, yellow or light blue, and she walked on mechanically, hoping to reach a main road or a tube station; in one of the little houses, through an open window, she saw a woman standing in the kitchen, she need only have called out to her, while from another window a dog drew attention to her presence by its barking. But it wasn't far now, she saw, they had looped back towards Kentish Town, and when she came to the tube station, where Jim had intercepted her a few hours earlier, she stopped. The greengrocer who had his stall there was just packing up for the day. He called out a greeting to her, and it occurred to her that she ought to buy a few things, for Jakob, for having at home, for another dinner, a prospect as tedious as it was comforting, an empty evening with no television because neither of them had wanted to sit in front of the television while they were in London—as if they were visitors to whom time was precious. But their time was no more precious here than in Berlin. She bought potatoes, parsley, and chives; the stallholder had a scar below his right eye that reminded her of something, what it was she couldn't recall. She looked uneasily to right and left, in case Jim might be coming. The stallholder saw her looking and made some remark, while behind her people poured out of the tube station and thronged past her, and she didn't understand what he said, and didn't know what Jim had meant, why he didn't trust her and what she needed to prove to him. With a sudden bound the stallholder was beside her, shoving somebody else out of the way with a curse; she held a ten pound note in her hand, and, grinning insolently and brushing against her breast, he slowly counted out her change. Then he gave her an avocado, because she looked as pretty as a picture, he said, still grinning.

Standing outside the house, she approached the window, from which a faint light shone, but when she went to look through the panes she saw herself outside the house, her own face approaching the glass, her hands blocking out the daylight from right and left, and as she coldly studied her own reflection she knew that she was dreaming. Nobody answered her ring at the door, she felt cheap, she knew that she was running after him, without a shred of dignity, but her longing for him was so great that she stayed there outside the house until a voice from one of the upper floors made her jump, and then she was running, along one of those streets that curved so gen-

tly that you only noticed it afterwards, racing past the impos-
ing grey façades. Surely this is Regent Street, she thought, and
then she was in the Park; great areas of grass were fenced off,
because they had been freshly seeded, so she was told by an old
man who was holding a pigeon in his hand, but she could see
quite clearly that the grass was thick and tall. Through the
grass a cat was approaching, and Isabelle walked slowly away
as though she could deceive the cat, she knew that she would
wake up and find herself naked in a room that was brightly lit,
and she put her hands over her private parts. When she did
wake up she was sitting upright in bed, her vest wet with per-
spiration. Jakob had left quite some time ago. She could hear
noise coming from the street, and when she went to the front
window she saw a small piece of road-building machinery
trundling to and fro where the asphalt had been dug up some
days earlier, and there was a cement mixer standing nearby,
churning around. The sun was shining brightly into the room.
It was one of Jakob's vests that she was wearing, she drew it
over her head, it was like being touched, and then she showered and got dressed.

On the ground floor, coffee cup in hand, she once again
went to the window and pushed up the sash. Two men were
standing in front of the machine, a small digger, they were
laughing, their sun-tanned torsos were touching, they were
bending over the trench at their feet and laughing. One
jumped down into the trench, disappearing in it up to his
chest, then he stretched up and reached for his spade. The
other shouted something, gesticulated, held up his fists above
his head, one on top of the other, and turned them in opposite
directions, a brutal, vulgar movement, and the first man
slapped his thighs in delight, took a delight in slapping his
hands against his bare chest, and because they had switched
off the concrete mixer and interrupted its monotonous spinning Isabelle heard the slapping sound as clearly as if it had

been right by her ear. She gulped down her coffee, turned around and saw the office plans lying on her table, and on the chest of drawers the key, Hanna's key, that would no longer fit when she got back to Berlin. The books and papers were already being packed up, the shelves dismantled, –are you expecting me to empty your desk drawer, or what? Andras had asked, angry, disappointed that she wasn't even coming to Berlin for the move, –if only for a few days, you haven't even had a look at the new office! She had signed the lease faxed to her by Peter, committing herself, in line with her share of the business, to one third of the rent, one third of the caution money, one third of the expenses, –you could give me power of proxy, Andras had suggested, but Isabelle preferred to sign it herself. And finally there was Hans, who was taking care of the Wartburgstrasse apartment, had checked through the terms of the lease, and was keeping an eye on everything: –*der getreue Hans*, as Alistair said with his strong English accent—faithful Hans. In her drawer Andras had found the old photos, Alexa's photos. –I've put them in an envelope and packed them between some books. –Alexa's photos, did you say? –Who else do you think took them, Isabelle had replied petulantly. The keys. Photos. She wouldn't ask him to send the photos to her in London. She felt she was clutching at thin air. Jakob at the office. Her body still smelling of sweat, even though she had showered, night sweat, the sweat of fear. With sudden decision she picked up the bunch of keys and went out into the street. Now Jim was there, standing in front of the two workmen, who were looking up at him as though he was giving them his instructions. The shorter of the two saw Isabelle approaching, setting one foot before another, and Jim turned his head sideways to see what was going on behind his back, while Isabelle moved into the shadow of a plane tree and out again, as if her own movements were part of the play of light and shade on the asphalt, every gust of wind creating new patterns in place of the previous ones. By now Jim had turned to face her and stood with his legs apart, grinning as he said something to the two workmen that made them burst out laughing; as though in a scene that had already been filmed, she continued to advance and knew that she would obey him, would let herself be embraced and kissed on the lips. Her skirt was too short, the wind got under it and lifted it, and the men laughed again, the shorter one bending down, tilting his head to one side and peering up her skirt, and it was as if she could feel his hands on her; a furious rage rose up in her, and she took two quick paces towards him—he gaped at her in astonishment—and gave him a box on the ear. The noise shocked her. And there was Jim, stepping up to her like a flash and wrapping his arms round her from behind, while the other workman rolled about laughing and her victim stood there stupidly, not knowing whether to join in the laughter or make an issue of it. –Okay, now you get a kiss, announced Jim, holding her so tightly that she gave a loud moan; he had pushed his right leg between her thighs. The workman whose ear she had boxed came closer, grinning with satisfaction, but again she felt a surge of anger and kicked out as hard as she could in his direction, while pressing herself against Jim. –All right, the man made a gesture of resignation, she's your tart. Jim relaxed his grip and put his left hand on her breast, –but she'd better do as I tell her, and he squeezed her breast, kneaded it. Then he pushed her gently forwards until she was standing at the edge of the trench. The two workmen grabbed their spades and T-shirts, pulled a couple of bottles of beer out of a bag and took themselves off. Jim didn't let go of her but rubbed himself against her bottom, while she stared down to where three rats that had been clubbed to death lay in the shallow water, the rats the same dirty brown as the water itself, and beside them the cat, its intestines spilling out of its belly, stinking, but with its fur showing up brightly against the dark background. Jim moved forward to stand beside her, watching her face, then he picked up a long stick, pushed it under the cat's neck and lifted the animal a few inches out of the water; blood had trickled out of one eye and dried, the rats had started feeding on it, gnawing at the belly, but it was plain to see that the skull had been crushed. Somebody must have thrown it into the trench, into the shallow water. –They'll be covering it over with sand and filling it all in, said Jim, so if you want to say a prayer for the cat, now's the time. He idly poked at the pile of sand with the toe of his trainer. –Do you see its head? Well and truly smashed. It must have been lying around somewhere else for a few days, otherwise the rats would have got hold of it long before this. A gust of wind blew the stench into her face. With a high-pitched, aggressive screech, a seagull tumbled rather than flew down from a tree, made contact with the asphalt beside them, rose up again, repeated the maneuver once more, only faster, landing awkwardly this time, and Jim struck at it with the stick, but it dragged itself into the air again, climbing almost vertically. Isabelle retched. He took the keys out of her hand, the keys that were warm and damp like her palm, stuck his finger into the ring and jingled them in front of her face. –In a few days I'm off. She stood before him, pale, fighting down her nausea. –I'm leaving, do you understand? He turned and went up to her front door, found the right key and opened it. –Come on then, he called indifferently, stepping onto the threshold and waiting for her to follow. He seemed to know that Jakob wasn't there, and even if he were, she thought, it would be a defeat for Jakob, who never put up a fight, who had found himself a safe retreat. Jim let the door swing to, locked it behind them and pocketed the key. On the banister Jakob's vest hung like a white flag. Isabelle clung to the banister rail, using both hands. –Bastard, said Jim out of the blue. The telephone rang but he motioned to her to stand still, not to answer it. The answering machine came on and they both listened to

Isabelle's recorded message and the caller's breathing. It's Andras, she thought, straightening up. It was Andras. He said his name, then hesitated. –Sonja is pregnant, he said, I just wanted to let you know. Tears welled up in Isabelle's eyes. Jim eyed her curiously, then turned away and went upstairs before working his way down again from the top floor, from the bedroom, looking at each piece of furniture with his hands in his trouser pockets, as if to demonstrate that he wasn't touching anything, like a child on a visit to people it doesn't know, obediently trailing along behind its parents, bored and yet curious to see how other people live. He looked disgruntled, as though his plans had been thwarted. He pulled the key out of his pocket again and toyed with it.

She shut her eyes and leaned against the wall, expecting him to come to her, but nothing happened; a violet spot started circling in front of her eyes and disappeared again, and after that there were just vague shapes, no light now, although they must be the remnants of light, a private underworld of the retina, a realm of the dead for just a few minutes, three dead rats, one dead cat, still the furry taste in her mouth, and it was so quiet that she had to open her eyes so as to see Jim, whose breathing she couldn't hear, whose steps she couldn't hear.

–It's your fault, do you realize that? he said. The cat, that's your fault. He stood on the threshold of the double doors between the rooms and spoke without looking at her. –You pushed it off the window ledge, do you remember? Carefully, mockingly avoiding making any sound, he laid the key on the chest of drawers. –At night, and you thought no one could see you. He suddenly looked hard at her, spitefully, inquisitively, gauging her precisely as if trying to place and define her. –That's right, you push it off the ledge and shut the window. You don't need to understand anything, you don't need to understand that things have happened. That it hurts like a scar, that we don't forgive anything, ever, because that doesn't change anything, and because we can only turn away, or not. But everything is recorded, whether anybody knows about it or not. And I saw you.

–Jim? Isabelle's voice sounded squeaky. –It's so nice to look at your face, Jim went on, it always gives the impression that nothing has happened to you and nothing ever will happen to you. –Jim? She tried in vain to steady her voice.

–Oh, be quiet. He turned to go, then remembered that he had locked the door. As he looked at her again, his face twisted. –How pretty you are. You look like her. Except that your face shows nothing, it's all so smooth and perfect. –Who do I look like? Jim? Who is it that I look like? He made no answer. –Jim? I didn't do anything to the cat. It was an accident, it must have been an accident.

–Oh no, you didn't do anything to the cat. You haven't done anything at all, have you? You'd sleep with me right now if that was what I wanted. Why is that, actually? Because you fancy me? Or isn't your husband screwing you? You'd cheat on him and then say you hadn't done anything, wouldn't you? But I'm not interested. He picked up the key. –Give me a hundred pounds.

She stared at him. –Yes, he grinned, I can see there's money lying there. But I want you to give it to me. Personally, so to speak. Do you understand? As a little present.

The telephone rang, she was going to pick it up. Jim shook his head. –No, darling. You leave the telephone where it is and come over here and give me the money. Again they heard the recorded message, and then Alistair's voice. –Call me when you get home and we'll go out for a meal later. She went to the chest of drawers, trying to keep as much distance as possible between herself and Jim. They were twenty-pound notes: she picked them all up. –Count it out, Jim ordered. I'd like exactly a hundred.

She counted the money and handed it to him. He waited, then took it, –and a little kiss by way of a goodbye. His lips were cold. He raised his hand and took her by the chin, she flinched, but he stroked her cheek gently, lingered briefly on the mole, pressed it, and let her go. –I'll teach you, you'll see, I'll teach you how not to forget something. Then he went; he left the key in the lock.

33

Polly hadn't come back. –That little parasite, her father said indifferently, it's a good thing if she's gone. Sara pressed herself against the sofa, buried her face in the throw and whispered something to the tiger. –Stop licking everything! The blow struck her unexpectedly, but it didn't hurt, because the cushions gave a little. –Bloody hell, do you two have to wail all the time? When Dad said that, her mother would get up and go into the kitchen, sometimes she would leave the house, and then he would follow her. Run after her, yelling. Run after her, and neither of them would come back, not until the next day or the day after. Mum's first question would be whether Dave was back, and Sara would lie and say he'd been there and had said he was going to look for Polly and would be back, and Dad would give a scornful laugh and ask whether Polly hadn't been there too and gone off to look for Dave. –As far as I'm concerned they can both stay away, he would say, and Mum would go into the kitchen to have a cry, and Sara would hide away behind the sofa.

Now she was wetting the bed again every night, but nobody noticed because Dave wasn't back, and Mum just grumbled because of the smell, she would fling the window open and start grumbling. They'd have to chuck the mattress out. She said it accusingly, and Dad stared at her, stunned. –A new mattress? For the kid? Can't you get it into your head that she's retarded? She's not growing, he shouted, dragging Sara out from behind the sofa, –look at that. He grabbed her by the arm and held her tightly. –Do you call that growing? You know, I'm starting to wonder if she's mine at all. Look at her. Might do as bait in a mousetrap. New mattress! I tell you, this isn't how I thought my life would be. She pisses the bed, that's what it is. And where's that cat that you've stuffed so full of food? Died of a heart attack, I expect.

Sometimes he would stand quite still and just stare at the table, which was empty apart from an ashtray, tidy, clean, the brown wood wiped down, and you could see the grain, lines and curves running together or separating, with islands that were the knots. Sara wiped the table, giving each individual knot an extra rub with the towel, but he didn't see that, all he saw was the empty table. The table at which he and Mum and Dave and Sara had sat, with Polly rubbing round their legs, purring, begging. –You can go to hell, the lot of you! He was always saying that, and Sara wanted to ask Dave what he meant, but Dave wasn't there. –Do you remember when we moved in, two years ago? asked Mum in the kitchen. She was smoking, letting the ash fall on the floor. Everywhere there were tiny specks of dust, floating as if they had parachutes, princesses looking for their prince. –Like your dolls, only smaller, Dave had told her, –it's as if they were gently drifting down from an enormous blue sky, do you see? But Sara couldn't see them anymore. The ash fell on the floor, and she stared at the smoke rising from the cigarette. –Where's Polly? asked Mum.

The lady had put the cardigan round her shoulders and hadn't asked for it back, a blue woolen cardigan, softer than anything Sara had ever known. Hidden behind the sofa, behind the sofa and under the tiger throw where nobody would look. –Sara! called Mum. Hasn't Polly come back? Polly had come back two or three times after the lady had taken her into the next garden, but then not anymore. Dad shook his head and stared at the empty table. He and Mum and Dave and Sara, and the cat under the table. –Bloody hell, he shouted, banging his fist on the table. I suppose I don't even get anything to eat here now.

–Do you see, Dave had said to her, when he has that expression on his face you know he's going to start whistling, and then it's about five minutes before he hits the roof, do you see? He had taken Sara by the hand and pulled her into their bedroom. But now he wasn't here. She squeezed behind the sofa and felt for the cardigan. Perhaps she ought to take the cardigan back, so that Polly would come home again—take the cardigan back to the lady because it was hers, because you had to give one thing so as to get another in exchange. The way you made up for something, the way Dave had told her that she must make up for it when she had annoyed him. Only this thing with Polly was different, and she knew it. It was her fault. She was guilty. Because she'd hit Polly. Because she wasn't good and didn't grow. The cardigan hidden, squashed under the sofa, dirty. She sucked and chewed on it. Because the lady had seen her, seen her in the garden, with the horse, with her spear, her lance, just as she and Dave used to play at killing the tiger with the lance, –you have to aim straight for the eye, Dave had told her, then it's dead. –I was only trying to slay the dragon, she whispered. She must tell Dave, must tell the lady and take her cardigan back. –Now she's down behind the sofa again, Dad shouted. When are you going to start looking after her properly? It was you that wanted another kid, he bellowed, as if we didn't have enough on our plates already. He dragged her out from behind the sofa. –Clear off, d'you hear me? She ran into the bedroom. Dave would make Polly alive again. She was dead, that was why she didn't come home. Dave would make her alive. –Well, he's on his own now, she heard her father say, thinks he can sponge off us and then up and leave just when he's old enough to help out?

Come, little cat, Dave whispered to her. She buried her face in his pillow. Come! But then he saw Polly, turned away and walked off.

Next morning she turned over and listened. The bed was wet, and she pulled the blanket over the wet patch and wrapped herself in it. She was alone in the flat. From the street she heard the bell, the man with the hand cart was approaching the house and calling out, and she ran quickly to the window and saw him ringing his bell. But he wasn't calling out to her, the cart was empty, he didn't wave or look towards her, even though she had run back into the bedroom to fetch the doll, which she had stopped playing with, held the doll up to the window, keeping a firm grip on the torn legs, and waved the doll from side to side, so that at last he would look across and remember, so that he would know she was here, with her doll that he had spiked on the railings, so that he would know she was looking for Polly. But without a glance in her direction he stooped, took hold of the two handles of the cart and pulled, but could hardly move it, and now here was the bus that picked up the old people, the driver folded the step down and rang at the house opposite; it was a different man, and he quickly heaved the old lady from across the road into the bus and drove off again. The bell was already much further away now, its ringing was fainter.

That afternoon the children climbed into the garden, came up to the veranda door, pressed their noses to the glass and made faces. Sara ducked down behind a chair. They searched around in the grass, one of the boys put a bucket on his head like a hat, then walked about with it balanced on his head while the others formed a circle around him, clapping. Then they ran to the wall and climbed over into the next garden, where the lady lived who had taken Polly away.

Next day all the bread had been eaten and all the milk drunk. Sara fell asleep again, on the floor, and blinked, when she woke up, into the sun that was shining through the veranda door; there was the dust again, drifting through the sunbeams, floating noiselessly down and down, no longer dancing but drifting earthwards as if they were dead, the princesses were dead because the prince didn't come. She pulled the cardigan out from under the sofa, shook it out as well as she could, spread it on the floor with the arms outstretched, blue, bright, and gently stroked it. –The important things don't get lost, Dave said, they always turn up again, but he looked sad as he said it. She picked up the cardigan and set off, but it dragged along the floor, she had to hold her arm up higher.

Behind her the door clicked shut. Hesitantly she went out through the gate, stood on the pavement and looked at the next-door house, both arms wrapped round the cardigan. A man with a yellow rucksack walked by and gave her a smile. Round the corner the children were playing, Sara could hear them shouting and pressed herself against a car. For a moment she thought she saw Polly at the first-floor window, but it was just something white that didn't move, however hard she looked, and then it was only a flower, –what are you looking out for, a man asked in a kindly tone, and Sara clasped the cardigan tightly to her and said, –for my brother, I'm waiting for my brother, he's coming to fetch me.

Later she hid between the car and the tree trunk whenever anyone came by, and then night fell, there were lights on in all the other houses, only her house and the house belonging to the lady who had taken Polly remained in darkness. She hoped her parents would come home, just so that they would turn on the light, so that it wouldn't look as if none of the four of them would ever live there again. She stared at the windows. Auntie Martha had lived there and had died, and then she had moved in here with Mum and Dad and Dave and Polly, and Dave was gone. He had told her that grown-ups die, but not children, but he had also said that you found the important things again, that they turned up again, and now it was too late. Softly she spoke her own name, Sara, and then she softly called Polly. Polly and Sara. She crouched by the tree trunk, which had markings like a snake's. She was cold, but she mustn't put the cardigan on in case the lady came after all. She was afraid of falling asleep and missing her, and she murmured the names to herself in alternation, Sara, Polly. Perhaps Polly couldn't see her because she had gone away. She felt cold. She stood up and then began to call her. When hands grasped her shoulders from behind, she screamed.

He had been nice, he'd bought her and Dave a big bag of chips, Dave had said that Jim was a friend of his. –What are you doing here, he asked and told her not to be frightened and that he knew all about it. He knew that Dave hadn't come back and that Polly had disappeared, that the lady had taken Polly, he nodded and took the cardigan and said he would help her, he peered at the cardigan for a long time and sniffed at it, grinning, and then he held her firmly by the arm and pulled her down the street, away from the house, –but Polly, she said, Polly's in there. He pulled her further, across Ascham Street and further down the road, and she was frightened because she had lied to him. In the garden, she tried to explain to him that she had been in the garden, with a stick, but she couldn't say it, and he didn't notice anything, she wished so much that he would ask. –Little cat, Dave had said, I always know when you're not telling the truth. But Jim didn't notice anything, and perhaps he wasn't telling the truth himself. He held her tightly. He led her towards a house and down a few steps, and unlocked the door, –your brother's sure to come here, he sometimes comes here to sleep, he said, maybe he'll come later, and he pushed her forwards into a dark room and locked the door behind him.

34

Before she could ring the bell in Devonshire Street, Alistair opened the door, as though he had been waiting for her. –Everything just a figment of our little brain, he said, out of the blue. And our little life is rounded with a sleep. He joined her outside and leaned against the spiked iron railings, which had a bicycle locked to them on the inside. –Today Bentham asked me to go with him on his walk, though he generally takes Jakob these days. He was depressed, he often is, it's only with Jakob that he always shows his cheerful side, perhaps he wants to spare him, who knows? We went to Regent's Park, taking our usual route. There weren't all that many people around because of the chilly wind, because it was cloudy, or because the park looks awful, so parched. On the grass not far from the Inner Circle a woman was running in slow motion, and her hands were making strange but actually rather graceful movements, feeling the air in front of her before each step: it made our own actions seem far too hurried. It reminded me so much of the slow-motion images of the Twin Towers, do you remember? The people falling from the windows?

Isabelle drew her thin leather jacket closer around her and folded her arms. –Are you cold? asked Alistair. Jakob will be down in a second. What's the matter? He studied her, surprised, without a trace of mockery. Your face looks quite different. He bent and kissed her on the lips, holding her by the shoulders, and did not stop kissing her when Jakob appeared in the doorway. Then he abruptly detached himself from her and turned towards Jakob. –I didn't think you'd mind. The mockery returned to his eyes, and Isabelle went cold as she saw it: it was as though he knew all about her and Jim and was judging her. He threw her a glance and pushed her towards Jakob. Again she felt hands on her shoulders, other lips on her lips, but was left unmoved. She took a step back, eyed them both, passed a hand across her face. Alistair grinned and went to stand next to Jakob, leaning against him, and they drew closer together; Isabelle was the only one who jumped when a motorcycle came racing around the corner and accelerated still more, its engine screaming, followed by a police car with a policeman leaning out of the passenger window holding something, perhaps a gun. Alistair had put his arm round Jakob. A black limousine braked sharply, then pulled away again. As if at a command, both men turned to look at Isabelle, searchingly, expectantly. She for her part was looking at the building, hoping to see Bentham or Maude, someone to give her some sign, to explain what was going on, but the building seemed empty: even the library windows, which Mr. Krapohl usually kept open, were closed. Again a siren wailed, further away this time, to be joined by a second and a third. –Bloody hell, what's happening? Alistair stood up straight, letting his arm drop. The sirens wailed and wailed, –it must be somewhere near Great Portland Street, Alistair said. He got out his mobile and made a call. –Anthony, where are you, on the tube? Great Portland Street? He listened, –okay, that's fine, I just wondered what's going on, all these sirens. –What's up with you? asked Jakob, astonished. –No idea. Alistair returned the mobile to his pocket, grinning. –Do you hear that helicopter? Jakob and Isabelle looked up, there's nothing there, Isabelle thought, but then a helicopter appeared above the rooftops and hovered in the air, noisy, menacing. –Those are ambulances, said Alistair. Bentham told me that a friend of his who works at the Foreign Office has information that British soldiers are using torture in Iraq. And that they've shot people by mistake. *Unlawful killing*, they call it. An eight-year-old girl. –What does that mean, has information? asked Jakob. –There are reports, said Alistair, possibly even photographs, and Bentham got terribly worked up about it. Good Lord, I said to him, does anyone really imagine they *don't* use torture, the Americans, the British? But Bentham was appalled, he was really despondent about it. –He said nothing about it to me, muttered Jakob. Isabelle looked at him. –Jakob? she asked, but he did not hear her. The helicopter circled, gained height, flew off in a tight curve, heading south. –What are you talking about, anyway? she demanded. Something rattled: it was Krapohl pushing up the sash windows. Isabelle would have waved to him, but he wasn't looking down to where they were. She turned uneasily towards the street, which was now perfectly quiet, and the sirens had also fallen silent. –We *shall* be for it one of these days, said Alistair. After all, why should we of all people be left in peace? Isabelle looked at Jakob, who was slumped against the railings. Why does he never *do* anything? she thought, why doesn't he show some fight? She sensed that he was wrestling with something, and he didn't ask how she was, he seemed to have forgotten her. –Look at us just standing around like this, Alistair's voice sounded sarcastic.

–I want to go home, said Jakob quietly. He detached himself from the railings, hesitated for just a moment, then walked off without looking back. Isabelle and Alistair stood motionless. –What's the matter? Isabelle asked helplessly; she found herself struggling to hold back tears. –What ever is the matter?

–You should know, Alistair replied.

–But what was that about Bentham, what's it got to do with you people, the photographs and all that?

–What's it got to do with us? If British soldiers use torture in Iraq and shoot children? Alistair shrugged. –Nothing, probably. As long as we're all right, that's all that counts. He grinned at Isabelle, coldly, malevolently. –But that's not what this is about, said Isabelle.

–Possibly not, said Alistair. Come on, let's go somewhere for a drink. That'll give Jakob time to calm down. Or aren't you two actually quarreling?

Isabelle shook her head. –We're not quarreling. Jakob had already disappeared around the corner; she doubted if he would go home. He probably didn't know *what* to do with himself. –Why ever should we be quarreling? Alistair moved close to her and took her face in his hands. –How I wonder what you're thinking, what really goes on in that head of yours.

For two hours Jakob wandered around Camden in the hope of recognizing the street where Miriam lived, but could not find it. Eventually he took the tube back to the office. Mr. Krapohl was still in the library, shifting books from one shelf to another, everyone else had left and there was no trace of Alistair and Isabelle. Jakob considered calling Alistair on his mobile, then decided against it. Nothing has happened, he thought, but he felt uneasy. On his desk lay a note from Maude saying that Mr. Miller had called and would like him to call back. The second note lay under the first, it was from Bentham. *Let's go to Berlin. A short trip would do me good, and Schreiber is delighted at the idea. If this suits you, we fly tomorrow morning at eleven o'clock from Heathrow. If not, please give me a quick call at home. I have booked three seats, in case your wife would like to come with us.*

Jakob held the note in his hand, then folded it carefully. He could see Bentham as clearly before him as if he were in the same room. Then he put together the papers he would need for the trip.

Isabelle didn't come home until nearly midnight; she seemed a little tipsy and threw her arms round his neck without asking where he had been. When he told her that he was flying to Berlin with Bentham the next day, she seemed taken aback. She went to the kitchen and got herself a glass of red wine. –How long for? Jakob hesitated. –Only two or three days. Her face looked small. –Tomorrow morning? So soon? she asked.

She went to bed and fell asleep at once. He stroked the quilt where it covered her shoulder, she was breathing evenly, and he was ashamed not to have asked her if she would like to come. He had already packed two suits and some shirts.

In the morning she was still asleep when he got up, and he considered waking her. But then he just wrote a note to say that he would call her later, put some money on the chest of drawers in her workroom—there was only a single twenty-pound note in the bowl—and left the house. Like a thief in the night, he thought, but as he boarded the tube train he felt excited and happy. As soon as they landed at Tegel he would phone Isabelle.

35

I don't know, she said, and when Andras impatiently asked, –why don't you know how you are? she didn't answer. There was a hissing noise on the line, and it was difficult to imagine that it wasn't really and truly a line, a wire, something thin but solid that somehow linked them to each other. Andras turned and opened the window, although it was chilly outside, already autumnal, and leaned out a little, as if he needed, just once more, to increase the space between himself and Magda. He grasped the telephone firmly so as not to drop it, and since Isabelle said nothing it was her silence that he was holding in his hand, he thought, that he was holding out of the window and could take wherever he pleased. She said nothing. And after looking for a while at the television tower and the illuminated advertisements going on and off, pallid in the daylight, he turned away from the window, crossed to table at which Magda was sitting, took a piece of paper and a pen and wrote: *If you'll still have me, I'll move in with you*. Magda smiled, lightly touched his hand and went into the bedroom. –Isabelle, what's wrong? he asked again. She still said nothing, he could hear her breathing, shallow, rasping breaths, like an animal, he thought, pacing up and down in its cage, and it made him angry. –Andras, can you come over and see me? He felt the telephone growing damp in his hand. Three months ago—he felt a stab of anguish—if she'd asked him three months ago he'd have gone straight to the office in the middle of the night to book a flight. –Andras, said Isabelle, can you come?

–Has something happened? he asked, are things not okay with you? She caught her breath, for a moment there was complete silence. In the bedroom something rustled, probably Magda had lain down with a book, waiting for him to finish telephoning. From the attic he could hear footsteps, poor Herr Schmidt, Andras thought, what was to become of him when he himself moved out and the owners started doing up the building? He went back to the window, but instead of looking out he turned round and gazed at Aunt Sofi's and Uncle Janos's old sofa. Do you remember the red sofa, he almost said, but didn't. She knew anyway that he wouldn't come. Too late, he thought, except that that wasn't the right way to put it, because time and what happened in it were never quite the same thing, never a line which, even if it followed an irregular course, could always be retraced. Time connects nothing, he thought. Nor does it break anything up: it connects nothing, it breaks nothing up, however do we endure it? It was as though what connected him and Isabelle was as worn-out as the sofa, an object that was no longer needed, no matter how many memories were associated with it. –I don't think so, he said, then corrected himself. No, Isabelle, I won't come to London just now. She was silent, and then she laughed, laughed again with that familiar, beloved voice, that voice that was like a bobbing schoolbag, he thought, and he saw before him the girl in the red dress, running. –Are you doing much drawing? he asked, interrupting her laughter. –Are you painting again? she asked in return, and there was something unpleasantly acerbic in her tone. –I'm moving in with Magda, he said, maybe I'll take up painting again when I'm there.

–Is that why you won't come?

It cut him to the quick. –So, Sonja is really pregnant? Isabelle asked, and you've all moved to Potsdamer Strasse, and you're going to move in with Magda in Charlottenburg? Nothing will be the way it was, she said, then they both hung up.

Magda had fallen asleep over her book; he gently covered her up, wrote her a note and went out. There was very little traffic on Torstrasse, and he was thinking that he might phone Jakob, when suddenly a car appeared from nowhere, sounding its horn, and Andras leapt on to the pavement and tripped. He managed to put out his hands to break the fall, so that his face came to no harm, but his knee was cut open, the palms of his hands stung and the balls of both thumbs were grazed. More surprised than alarmed, he sat up and examined his knee through the tear in the material. He must have fallen on to a sharp stone or a piece of glass, blood was welling from a cut an inch and a half long, collecting and running down his shin under his trouser leg. He felt for a handkerchief in his jacket pocket, didn't find one, and remained sitting there while he waited for the blood to congeal. It didn't take long. When he cautiously stood up, tears came to his eyes, crossly he shook his head, but he was crying all the same, and had to laugh at himself. His heart thumped unevenly as he crossed back over the street and went hobbling up Choriner Strasse, laughing, blinded with tears.

Magda had just woken up. She looked at him wide-eyed with astonishment, carefully took his hands in hers and led him to the bathroom. –Haven't you got any antiseptic? she asked, and when he dumbly shook his head she gently bathed the wounds with lukewarm water. –Those trousers are only fit for throwing away, she pronounced as she knelt before him. –My poor love. He let himself be put to bed and tucked in.

As dusk began to fall he was aware of Magda getting up and creeping out, then he went back to sleep. When he woke he found croissants and fresh milk in the kitchen; on the clean plate lay a slip of paper with a drawing of a lorry and a question mark. He phoned Peter and asked whether there were any empty packing cases left. –Six, Peter said, what do you need them for?

–I'm moving in with Magda, today if possible. Andras was surprised to find himself listening anxiously to the silence that ensued. –Peter? Are you still there? Why don't you say something?

–You're moving in with Magda? Really? I can hardly believe it. That's splendid! I thought you were going to spend the rest of your days pining for Isabelle.

An hour later there was a ring at the door, and there was Peter with the empty boxes. –I've got to go straight down again, Sonja's waiting in the car. Peter hesitated, then with an embarrassed grin gave Andras a quick hug and disappeared.

Only the essentials, he thought, two boxes of clothes, two of books, two of papers, I'll deal with the rest later. When he had almost finished, he suddenly recalled what he had been dreaming, a dream similar to the one he had had a few months ago. She was standing in a bare room, naked under the neon lighting, older and smaller than he remembered her, an aging woman with a child's body. He couldn't see her face, she was hiding it in her hands.

He would write her an e-mail, he thought, suggesting she might like to come to Berlin for a few days. The new office was not completely sorted out yet, in Isabelle's room—she had a room of her own with a window looking out at the chestnut tree in the courtyard—the boxes and the computer were waiting to be unpacked, there was so much to do, and why shouldn't it be a sort of new beginning, *New concept—new life*, for her as well? There was a knock at the door, not a ring but a knock. For a moment it flashed through Andras's mind that it would be Isabelle standing outside the door, and his heart quickened with excitement. But it was Herr Schmidt. He had a little old-fashioned cardboard suitcase with him. –I thought you'd be moving out soon, he said grumpily, looking straight into Andras's startled face. –I'm sorry, Andras raised his hand helplessly. –Well, there it is, said Herr Schmidt, yesterday I found a suitcase, today I'm moving out. That's the way it goes. I spent the night at the railway station, even though I didn't need to. The snack bars are very good. Friendly. And then the suitcase, empty, next to the letterbox, you know, by the bridge. Not just a coincidence, I thought. So he's moving out, and I'll move out too. He picked up the suitcase, nodded and started down the stairs. –But can't we give you a lift somewhere? Andras called after him. And don't you want to take the hot plate with you? But Herr Schmidt shook his head, waved and went on carefully descending the stairs without looking back again.

36

He gave her a blanket and said she could sleep on the sofa, like her brother. It was half past nine in the evening, and he liked the way she lay there and perhaps really did fall asleep straight away. At half past ten he went out again, locking the door behind him, and walked up the street, and when he found the windows of number forty-nine dark he was angry, as if that ruined his plan. He had a plan. Tomorrow he would take a train to Glasgow, his things were packed, the bag waiting ready in the bedroom, he only needed to summon up the will. Pete, the doorman at the Broken Night club, had warned him that two ugly-looking types had been there, asking about him. Jim had happened to bump into him on the Iron Bridge, he still owed Pete the money, he hadn't actually intended to give him his share, and then Pete had been decent enough to warn him. He'd said with a grin that it was just a little good deed to give his karma a nudge in the right direction, and as far as Jim's karma was concerned, he could only advise him to get out of town, because if he was reborn right now it would most likely be as an earthworm or a sparrow. But there are hardly any sparrows left, Jim thought to himself as he went back down Lady Margaret Road, not even sparrows; he felt as if Isabelle had betrayed him. The kid was lying on the sofa asleep, and it seemed she wasn't just pretending, because when Jim held a lighter close to her thin hair she didn't flinch but went on breathing evenly as before. Sleeping. She even looked nice, it was nice to come home and find a sleeping child, only it wasn't his home, tomorrow he was off, and he drank a beer and went into the bedroom, though he usually slept in the living room so as to be able to hear the door and keep an eye on his things, but the sofa had the kid sleeping on it. He took off his jacket, threw it on the floor and stretched out on the bed. In the middle of the night he heard the kid whimpering, she had woken him up. Instead of going on sleeping she'd apparently got up; furiously Jim's hand clenched itself into a fist. There was a noise as though she had bumped into the table, probably the corner of the glass-topped table, bloody stupid, the table, the kid; maybe she was thirsty. But he was too tired and too lazy to get up, possibly it hadn't been a good idea to bring the kid here when Isabelle wasn't around, she might have gone away for all he knew. He listened and heard a faint whimpering. Then he went back to sleep.

In the morning something he was dreaming made him wake with a start; he was ducking away from something or other that was ugly. When he opened his eyes the girl was standing in front of him, looking just as she had when he'd found her yesterday, a pinched little face, not pretty, and then he noticed that she smelled. –Can't you have a wash? You stink. She retreated half a pace, and as he scrutinized her he noticed a dark patch on her grey trousers, some sort of jogging trousers tied with a cord at the waist. That was it, he thought, the mistake he always made, taking the wrong decisions, never the right one, not telling Ben to get lost, being too soft with Mae, and now saddling himself with this kid. She was standing there stiffly, any minute now she'd start crying, and she'd be sure to want something for breakfast, too, milk and cereal or bread and marmalade. He got up and was amused to see how the girl fled to the living room and sat down on the sofa, hands on her knees and head bowed, growing more rigid with every step he took towards her. If he touched her she'd snap in two like a china doll with a crack in it. But suddenly she jerked her head

up and looked directly at him, purposefully, uncompromising-
ly. He had to look away. He went into the bathroom,
undressed, shaved. Pursed his lips as he often did, as though
one day he'd be able to whistle, just like that, but only air and
spit came out. After finishing his shower he was still furious.
Wrapping a towel around his waist, he went into the living
room. She was sitting there, not moving. –Get up, he barked,
and she obeyed, grimly, unwillingly. –How about getting us
some breakfast, or do you think I'm here to wait on you? Sara
came out from behind the coffee table, but he blocked her
path. As he breathed in her smell he finally understood. –Shit,
have you wet yourself? Have you peed in your pants and on my
sofa? Jim grabbed her by the shoulder, scrawny as a bird, he
thought. He forced her to raise her head. But she didn't cry.
She stared blankly ahead of her, with almost superhuman concentration, but didn't cry. Just stood there. The last obstacle to
deal with before he took off for Glasgow, this kid and Isabelle,
before he could turn his back on this whole lousy city that
wrecked everything and left you with nothing. It was already
ten o'clock. Jim looked away. Suddenly there was something
bright in front of his eyes, dazzling him, he had to close them.
A harsh white light. –At least have a wash, he said, I haven't
got anything for you to put on. He went into the kitchen, heard
her footsteps, the bathroom door as she shut it behind her, the
sound of water. He put the kettle on and looked around for
biscuits and some bread, got out a tray and put two mugs on
it, grinned: Hisham would be pleased with him. He hunted
through opened packets left over from Damian's time. Wasn't
there any honey? No honey, but a jar of jam, dried out on top
but not moldy. Mae had made proper breakfasts, with bacon
and eggs, she had bought a toaster without asking him, to
make toast every morning. He carried the tray into the living
room, picked up the blanket and folded it, sniffing at it, and
ran his hand over the sofa, no longer warm from her body, and

dry. Unable to find the bathroom, she'd peed standing up so as to wet her pants but not the sofa. All that was missing was Isabelle, he thought. Isabelle frying eggs and asking if he'd like some bacon. He poured tea into the mugs and spooned jam on to a biscuit. His mobile rang. No number showed on the display, it was only his damned curiosity that made him answer it, yet another of his stupid wrong decisions, he was actually hoping it might be Hisham calling him. But there was nothing there, only breathing on the line, a woman, he thought, labored breathing and no reply when he asked who was there, who was on the line, damn it? –Who is that? he shouted, and then she hung up and he shouted: Mae? Is that you? Mae?

The girl had crept out of the bathroom like a mouse, quietly, slyly, had been eavesdropping on him, and now she went over to the table and started eating, cramming biscuits into her mouth; he looked away in disgust, pushed his mug of tea aside, got to his feet and picked up his bag, locked the door behind him and left the house. Let Damian find her, a greeting from his grateful friend Jim, half starved or even starved to death, because she wouldn't manage to open the windows, even if she climbed on a chair she wouldn't be able to reach the catch at the top, and nobody would hear her. A small parting gift. Jim held on tightly to the mobile in his trouser pocket, listening for it to ring again, fingering it, but it remained mute. He walked down Kentish Town Road, bought himself two scones at the baker's and started munching them. Off at last, he thought, first the station and then I'm on my way. He ran his fingers over the plastic and took the mobile out of his pocket. There was the bridge, the canal; Jim pressed the green receiver symbol and listened to the dialing tone, nothing, and without switching it off he tossed it into the water. A boy beside him grinned in bewilderment. –Hey, mister, why didn't you give it to me? Jim looked into the glazed eyes. –Spare us a pound, mister. Shaky hands reaching out, –or a ciggy? the boy begged again, and Jim put a hand into his pocket, feeling for a coin, but there was nothing, not a coin, not a banknote, nothing, all left behind in the jacket he'd been wearing yesterday. He rummaged through his bag; among the clothes there was a rustle of small cellophane bags, boxes of pills, –just don't try to be clever, Albert had pontificated, it won't work anyway, just keep the cash on you and the rest in a bag that you can dump, and that was exactly what he'd done, except that the jacket was lying in the bedroom: a small parting gift, he jeered at himself, that was the idea, wasn't it? The boy was still standing there, cowering, –clear off, Jim snarled at him, and he did as he was told while Jim straightened up, clutching the handle of his bag. A small group of tourists stopped beside him, chatting loudly; they were talking about him, he could tell from the looks they were giving him, not even surreptitiously, but quite coolly and openly. Two men were talking and two women listening, the prettier of them idly drawing invisible lines on the pavement with her shoe, holding her handbag firmly with both hands. Like a swimmer pushing off from a rock, Jim thrust himself away from the balustrade, here we go again, he thought, and was already walking briskly back up the road, not even a few coins for a bus, humming, past Pang's Garden, for the last time. He'd take a taxi to the station, he thought, order one from Peace Cabs: there were the men standing around, polite, with their quiet, pleasant voices, and they nodded to him in a kindly, polite fashion and handed him a card. For today? Around lunchtime today, that was fine, a good time, he need only phone this number ten minutes beforehand, where from? From Lady Margaret Road, and going to Liverpool Street Station? No problem, one of them gave him a reassuring nod, but the attention of the other two had been distracted, they were gazing across the road to where an old woman was dragging herself along behind her dog and a young woman was walking along, supple-kneed, languid, in a short skirt, not lifting her feet, scuffing along in open sandals with her soft, white feet: he cursed and dodged across the street, between the impatient, hunking cars, but she walked on without looking around, supple and sexy, her soles scraping on the paving stones—but slowly, as if she were trying to make it easy for him, offering herself again, shamelessly, even the Arabs noticed it, across the width of the road. He allowed himself to drop back, then caught up with her again. The skirt hugged her bottom, her thighs—inviting, repulsive. She didn't notice that he was close behind her, heard neither his breathing nor his footsteps, lost in her thoughts, self-absorbed, content, Jim thought, content with herself and with the carefree day that stretched out before her until the evening, when her husband would show up and at least get some dinner and a few friendly words in exchange for his hard-earned money. I suppose you don't sleep with him, do you, he had asked, so what does he get for his money? She walked with a bounce, supple-kneed, perhaps it was deliberate, perhaps she knew very well that a man was following along behind her, turned on by that little bum of hers, nicely rounded, sexy, and now they were already entering Leighton Road with him three yards behind her, his eyes taking in her honey-colored hair, her bum, her blouse with its light green and blue diamond pattern; he was following her or driving her along before him, to give her a surprise. I took off in far too much of a hurry before, he thought, with no money, no goodbye, but that can be put right. He reached forward, called her name and, before she could turn around, grabbed her by the arm, and there was her face. Surprised, childlike; she moved closer as if about to fall into his arms, filled with relief. He had to look away. She wasn't ashamed, held her face up to his, eyes open wide, lips slightly parted, innocent, and started to babble on about how her husband had gone on a trip without her, how she had asked a friend to come—all this with the expression of someone who had rights, who expected to be consoled—but he wouldn't, this friend wouldn't come, because of another woman, she pressed closer to him, he had to back away, but he held her arm, held her firmly at arm's length, and then started to pull her along. Bright, he thought, and he blinked, dazzled, his sunglasses were in his jacket too, he remembered what Damian had said about the brightness in which things were hidden, and felt the warmth of the arm beneath his fingers. He felt a longing for Mae that rent his heart.

37

After all the light outside it was dark in Jim's house, her eyes had difficulty adjusting to it, she breathed in the stuffy, slightly sour air, Jim stumbled and she bumped into him, felt his firm body. –He'll phone again, she said, I bet he'll phone again and ask if he can't come after all, and quite honestly I don't know if I still want him to, her voice like a bright, bobbing schoolbag, Andras had said, and she went galloping on, –you should have seen the photos that Alexa took of me, they were in my desk, where else should I have kept them? Nude shots, I think the worst of it is that they aren't pornographic, Alexa has probably got a whole collection, I ought to give them to my parents, can't you just imagine the two of them sitting in their shoe box, that's what I call their house, a shoe box, expensive, not Prada, but expensive, good quality, and their reaction if I send them those photos so they can see what I look like naked now that I'm grown up? She fell silent. He turned away and locked the door. –Jim? You know you said the other day that I look like somebody? He stood before her in the half-light, not quite as tall as Jakob and Alistair, but more compact, full of concentrated, angry energy. He had put his bag down. She stooped to pick it up, –leave that alone, he said sharply, –but I was just going to move it out of the way so that you don't trip over it. She studied his face, but was unable to interpret what she saw there, and it would be Jakob who would try to phone her, not Andras. He wanted to be rid of her, Jim wanted to be rid of her. –Jim? she said, what was it you wanted to show me? Nervously she fiddled with the top button of her blouse; he misinterpreted her movement, laughed out loud, and spread his legs slightly. To her right, where a sofa and a glass-topped table stood, something stirred beneath a blanket, a head emerged, a child's head, and two thin little arms came into view, reaching out, holding something dark-colored, and she didn't understand until Sara sat up, with her old blue cardigan, and Isabelle stole a quick look at Jim, who stood there watching and waiting. Sara crawled off the sofa and came closer, holding out the cardigan. –Your cardigan, she said, I've brought your cardigan so that you'll give me Polly back. Isabelle retreated a pace, –nonsense, she said, that's not my cardigan; she could smell the sour odor more distinctly and put out a hand as if to push the child away. The girl stopped, completely taken aback. –Polly? she said in a questioning tone. You took Polly with you, you left me the cardigan? She turned her head towards Jim, seeking his help. –Tell her where Polly is, he prompted Isabelle with a grin. He came closer. –Tell her what you did with her filthy cat. She could feel his warmth, the tense, hot body. But he was distracted, as though suddenly reminded of something he had forgotten: pushing past Isabelle, he reached for an envelope that was lying on top of the television, –that was it, he said, that's what you were talking about, wasn't it, the photos. Irresolutely he held the envelope in his hand; it's as if something is breaking up, thought Isabelle, breaking up into its component parts. Sara lowered the cardigan and looked imploringly at Jim. Slowly he put the envelope down again, and Sara picked it up and held it out to him again, as if this was something she could offer, since the cardigan didn't seem to work; then she held out the envelope to Isabelle, –leave that alone, Jim's voice cracked as he said it, and he grabbed the envelope and tore it up, so that small scraps fell on the floor, brightly colored, Isabelle saw, scraps of color photos, and among them bits of white paper, the remains of the envelope. The room was lighter now because the sun had dipped a little lower. –But you told me that the lady knows where Polly is. –Just shut up, will you? Your bloody cat's dead, got it? Dead, he repeated, because of her—he pointed to Isabelle—because she couldn't stand your cat, because she couldn't care less what happened to it. He turned to face Sara, his head tilted back, what a play-actor, Isabelle thought, but that wasn't so, it wasn't play-acting, not for Jim and Sara, who stood there confronting each other, and as it grew darker again, probably because a cloud had drifted across the sun, she smelled the stale smoke, the unwashed bedding, the dusty cushions that were never aired; on the glass-topped coffee table there was a glass. –Jim, she said, I want to go now. She turned and went towards the door. It was locked, and the key wasn't there. –Jim, let me out. I pushed the cat off the window ledge, that's all. No cat dies just because you push it off a ground-floor window ledge! Her voice sounded shrill, indignant, as if getting indignant would do any good. –Jakob was planning to ring, she said, but she knew that he wouldn't be worried. And even if he were, she thought. Jim watched with interest as she let go of the door and took half a step back into the room.—Jim? She managed to regain control of her voice. –You're lying, Jim said. His face twisted, he flung out an arm as if to grasp or to banish a thought, and as he did so his hand caught Sara, who was standing next to him, not hard, but he seemed glad to meet some resistance at last, anything that would move things forward. Isabelle stood a little straighter. –Sara, she said very deliberately, Sara, have you told Jim what you did to your cat? That you hit her with a stick, with a thick stick? Jim froze in astonishment. –What's that? But it was the meanness, the sheer meanness of her denunciation that made him take notice, that restarted what had been standing still like a broken clock mechanism, and even the cloud moved away from the sun so that it was brighter in the room and she could see his face and how it was changing, it was like watching a primitive film, a flip book. There it was, he was picking up a trail, with an offended, arrogant demeanor he was brushing aside whatever was irrelevant; she saw him taking deep breaths, he was still searching, searching for something, just as she was. –Maybe I should take you with me? he said to Isabelle, do you want to come along, you with your pretty, innocent face? He moved closer and stood behind her, his hands playfully encircling her neck and then sliding downwards under the material of the blue and green blouse, touching her more firmly, intensely. Sara uttered a whimpering sound. With a curse he detached himself from Isabelle, shot forward, two steps, raised his arm with his hand clenched into a fist, and was already drawing Isabelle to him again as Sara stood there swaying for another moment before she fell to the floor, bleeding. The small scream had come from Isabelle, but he clamped his hand over her mouth, relaxed it again, fingered her lips and forced them gently apart, –nothing's happened, he murmured in her ear, come on, he enticed her, caressing her until her lips opened and her tongue touched his finger. The child rolled on to her side, sat up and gave a single cough, and the blood ran freely down her chin and soaked into her T-shirt. The finger withdrew from Isabelle's mouth, Sara looked up at the two of them, ran her hand uncertainly over her chin and spat, spat again, Isabelle closed her eyes, racked with nausea, felt a light slap, heard his voice, his laughter, –you wanted her punished, didn't you? He leaned to the right. –Open your eyes! Pushed her forward, towards the girl, who was holding her hand out in front of her, a little blood-smeared tooth on it; she was not crying. There's nothing I can do, Isabelle thought over and over again, felt the warm body behind her and nestled against it, but he ruthlessly propelled her towards the girl, who looked steadfastly back at them, that tiny, huge distance. Jim murmured something, his hands gave

Isabelle a little push and abandoned her. She thrust herself back at him, as if he could comfort her, she wanted to close her eyes, to be enfolded in his arms, but he pushed her away. –You'd go begging for it anywhere, wouldn't you? Jim said. Do you know what you are? You're like a black hole, anything can be poured into you and it vanishes without a trace. Abruptly he seized her again and spun her around. –Nothing shows in your face, just occasionally a touch of fear. He scrutinized Isabelle, and his mouth twisted. –The girl stinks, haven't you noticed? With a hand on the back of her neck he forced her down. –She's peed herself. He let go of her and stepped back. –She's wet herself, he said calmly, take her things off. I want you to strip her naked. No, she thought, no, but she bent down, Sara recoiled and tried to evade her, and the tooth fell from her hand on to the floor. –Get on with it, Jim said dispassionately; he was looking around for something as if not quite knowing what to do, then he went into the kitchen and came back with a knife. Isabelle obeyed, watching her own hands with incredulity, hands that took hold of the girl's T-shirt and pulled it over her head, not roughly, not hesitantly, but precisely and deftly, as if she had rehearsed this scene a hundred times. Alexa ought to be here, thought Isabelle, with her camera, and starting to cry she laid the T-shirt to one side, drew the now limp body to her, fumbled with the knot and pulled trousers and knickers together down around the child's ankles, then lifted her up. Now Sara stood naked before her, wiping her nose with her hand, smearing the blood about, not crying; she stared at Isabelle, frightened and comforted, then she spat, carefully, spat out a second tooth, seeming not to understand what it was, and looked questioningly at Isabelle, who knelt before her, pale, breathless with fear and shame. Jim gave Sara a light kick with the toe of his shoe, once, twice, as if testing out an idea. Suddenly in the garden there was a hubbub of children's voices, a boy shouting out orders, the others answering with piercing cries. –Dave, said Sara, without looking at the door to the garden. Isabelle looked at her, the pinched, childish face, the drying blood. –Your stupid brother, said Jim absently, his right hand toying with the knife. –Let's all go away together and buy a little house, shall we? With a garden and a cherry tree in the middle. Then he advanced on the girl. –No, pleaded Isabelle, crying but not moving. –No? Jim echoed, grinning, but you won't help her, will you? You won't lift a finger for her. Hastily Isabelle undid the buttons of her blouse, pulled her skirt and panties off, getting them caught up in her sandals, and sat naked on the floor. –Not interested, Jim pronounced after coolly appraising her. Suddenly his left hand was in her hair. Gathering up as much of it as he could, he pulled it taut, held her down with a foot on her shoulder, brought the blade close to her scalp and made a swift movement. Indifferently he let the severed hair fall. –That's better, he said, as though he had at last found what he had been searching for. –Now for once your husband will be able to see that you've actually experienced something. He stood there, weary. Then he went into the bedroom and returned with a jacket over his arm, hesitated briefly, swept her clothes together with his hands and picked them up, went to the door, grabbed his bag and went out. He locked the door on the outside. Through the window she saw him climbing the steps, his legs, then just his feet, and the clothes falling on the ground. From outside came the sound of a bird; the children had gone.

38

Like an animal the girl crept behind the sofa when Isabelle stood up; feeling cold, Isabelle looked around and saw a blanket, but she was revolted by the thought of touching anything, walked aimlessly to and fro, then over to the window, and saw her clothes lying where Jim had dropped them. An elderly man, no doubt one of the other residents, opened the front gate, gave the pile a puzzled look, and nudged it to one side with his foot. Naked as she was, she didn't knock on the window, but once he had vanished into the house she reached up to the security bolt and tested whether the sash could be pushed up. Climbing out would be easy. She shut it again and half drew the curtain so that she could not be seen. Hearing a faint, regular sound coming from the direction of the sofa, Isabelle leaned over it to look at Sara, who was kneeling between the back of the sofa and the wall, with part of the blue cardigan in her mouth, sucking, chewing, her face swollen. Everything was so quiet. It seemed to Isabelle as if Sara was the only thing preventing her from leaving. Her next moves were clear and straightforward: she must look in the bedroom for something to put on or else wait until it was dark, hope that nobody would go off with her clothes, then run naked up the short flight of steps and fetch them. She must take the child to a doctor. She had to do these things, and then they'd be done: there was no point in putting them off. But it wasn't dark, and she stood there shivering and wishing she could get away from her own body, which she saw before her as it appeared in Alexa's photos, naked and alien.

Sara crawled out from behind the sofa, a corner of the cardigan clutched tightly in her hand. –Dave, she said without looking up. Isabelle smelled the urine before she saw the dark patch on the carpet. –Polly, said Sara, and began to cry, soundlessly, apparently unaware of the tears pouring from her eyes: Isabelle could hear them dropping on to the carpet where the pieces of the envelope and color photos lay scattered, together with clumps of her own hair.

In the bedroom, on the bed, she found a T-shirt and a pair of jeans, both dirty, the smell of Jim so intense that it made her retch, but she slipped into them, hurriedly, felt the hard material against her sex, and had to roll up the trouser legs and hold onto the waistband with her hand because there was no belt; she found a vest too, which she took into the bathroom for Sara, without switching the light on there, and now she needed to call out, to call Sara's name. From one of the upper floors a radio could be heard, much too loud, a voice soaring in jubilation, an aria, then the orchestra came in, somebody shouted something and the radio was turned down. A towel was hanging over the side of the bath, she held one corner of it under the warm water and attempted to call Sara, but achieved only a nervous little exhalation of breath. She put her hand over her eyes, pressed it against her forehead: it was as if something inside her had come apart, was breaking up, something whose pieces you would never collect up and stick back together, because you were too tired or too perplexed, and because you knew that a vital piece was missing, that the whole thing would never come together as you had hoped. Jakob, she thought, cautiously, as if he could hear what she was thinking and see her here. She wouldn't phone him. Nobody could tell anything by looking at her, Jim had said. In the semi-darkness she risked a glance in the mirror, and started back in horror. But if she combed her hair and tied it back, nobody would notice that a handful was missing. She picked up the damp towel and went into the living room. There lay Sara, with the cardigan in her mouth. –Sara, Isabelle whispered, kneeling in front of her. Gently she took the face in her hands; the eyes gazed at her blankly. Reaching for the towel with her right hand, she wiped over the blood that had dried to a crust, then stood up and went to the bathroom to rinse out the towel, and came back with it. Every wipe laid bare a small area of destruction, the split lip, the bloody gap where two teeth were missing, a broken nose, bruising and swelling. Gently she helped the child to her feet, Sara got up with difficulty but then trotted along behind her to the bathroom. She let Isabelle wash her face and hands with warm water and place another towel, a cold one, on the swelling. Then she followed Isabelle into the living room, to the window, and watched as Isabelle found her handbag and climbed out. –Polly, said Sara. Isabelle nodded, and lied. –Come on, perhaps she's back home again. She ran up the steps, dusk was beginning to fall. The clothes were gone, a corner of blue and green material was poking out of the dustbin, the rest now lay buried under a burst rubbish bag. Sara tried to climb up onto the windowsill, but slipped back, tried again, then gave up. Isabelle saw the swollen face and reached out a hand to help her. She had to lean into the room, the child clung to her hand but suddenly let go and looked at her distrustfully. But what am I supposed to do, thought Isabelle, tears coursing down her face, and she turned away. Then she set off.

Dave rang the bell, rang again, stretched up to the window and tapped on it, went back to the pavement and stood on tiptoe. There was the sofa, with the tiger on it. –Sara, he called, Sara, are you there? He stared distrustfully at the woman, who was using one hand to hold up trousers that were much too big for her. –Dave, she repeated, you're Dave, aren't you? He nodded, understanding only a part of what she was saying as she pointed down the road with her free hand, –she's at Jim's, she said, and repeated it again, at Jim's. She was trembling, Dave didn't know if he ought to do something, but then she turned away, and hesitantly he started off down the street to Jim's house. He sensed her eyes following him, looked back, and waved helplessly; she shook her head and seemed to be crying, and he started running. Nobody opened the door, but then he saw the open window and stooped down. –Sara, he called softly, Sara, are you here? On the sofa something stirred, and from under a blanket her face appeared, a pale patch. He swung himself up on to the window ledge and jumped inside. –Little cat, he whispered, what's happened?

Isabelle sat downstairs, still in Jim's clothes, it was getting dark, but she didn't switch on the light. At some point she stood up, went to fetch herself a glass of water from the kitchen and took it back downstairs, then forgot about it until later her gaze fell upon the round work table, where the glass was standing in a faint beam of light that slanted into her room from the street, through the leaves of the plane tree, wavering because a light breeze was making the leaves sway to and fro. It sounded as if it was raining, but she didn't get up to see. The telephone rang, and rang again, but stopped before the answering machine came on. The flashing display showed that there were five messages. At every car that slowed down outside the house, every sound from outside, she looked up, but then she might have fallen asleep, because suddenly there were voices next door, a commotion in which individual sounds only gradually became distinguishable, something banging against the wall several times in quick succession, a man's voice, followed by a silence that brought her to her feet, impossible to say how long it lasted and who might be gathering their strength for another onslaught, and she stood up and drank the glass of water all in one go, smelling the odor on the clothes, her hand mechanically holding the trousers up. Again the telephone rang, this time the answering machine switched itself on, and she heard Jakob's voice, –I've been trying to get hold of you all day, but although he sounded concerned, his voice was so bright and cheerful that she went towards the machine, –with Bentham, he said, we've really only been going for walks, and we're not meeting Schreiber until tomorrow, she listened for any sounds from behind the wall, and Jakob hesitated, –I'm sorry, I should have asked you if you wanted to come too, a thumping on the wall distracted her, it was like a signal, –don't be cross, said Jakob, she nodded her head mechanically, went over to the wall and pressed her ear to it, holding her breath. –Tomorrow or the day after, said Jakob's voice, before the connection broke off and another thud against the wall, sounding like a blow from a fist, made her jump. The trousers slipped down over her hips, she sobbed, caught her foot in one of the trouser legs and stumbled, but then she was by the telephone, dialing the three-digit number that was stuck on its black plastic casing, ready for emergencies; gripping the handset tightly, she repeated the address twice before hanging up while she was being asked her name, and once again she smelled the T-shirt's sweaty odor.

The police car had driven past the house as it made its way slowly down the road from the top end; it must have turned somewhere roughly level with the church, and now the blue flashing light circled several times around the room before it was switched off and the car doors slammed, almost drowned out by the furious bellowing, which broke off abruptly. She crouched down under the window, her body pressed up against the cold radiator, and only rose to her feet again when a second blue light approached and swept the room like a searchlight, and then she saw a paramedic carefully carrying

Sara to the ambulance, a second one following him, shaking his head and saying something, while the first went round to the passenger side and was handed a blanket which he gently wrapped around Sara before sitting her inside. Then the engine started up, and as it faded away Isabelle heard the woman's voice, sobbing, choking, she seemed to be at the front door, and then a man's voice was impatiently telling her to get in the car. Isabelle crouched down again and shortly afterwards heard four car doors being slammed, and when she stood up and looked out the street was empty.

39

J akob saw Bentham approach the entrance door, where he was welcomed by Maude and Alistair, and Alistair looked up briefly and waved to him before the taxi moved off, turned left and filtered into the traffic on Great Portland Street, then headed northwards along the side of Regent's Park. But nothing has happened, thought Jakob, Alistair says she's just in a state of shock. –If you can't get hold of your wife, send Alistair over there, Bentham had demanded, finally losing patience. –You do need to find out if something has happened, and then Alistair had found her at home, –but she wouldn't let me in, you really should come straight away, she had to call the police because of a fight going on next door. Jakob hadn't managed to grasp what had been going on, the girl, he had thought, it's sure to have been the girl, and Bentham had insisted on their flying back that same afternoon.

The taxi reached Kentish Town Road and turned slowly into Lady Margaret Road. In the morning light the Victorian façades stood out with such a sculptural, three-dimensional effect that Jakob felt he was seeing them for the first time, and the street looked thoroughly peaceful, windows gleaming brightly in the sunshine, the leaves of the plane trees showing the first signs of autumn: it was September. A man with a cart was obstructing the street, blocking the taxi's way, he was ringing a hand-bell, standing in the middle of the road outside the church, shouting something to the priest while still swinging his bell, and the priest was making vehement gestures.

Jakob held the flowers he had bought for Isabelle at the air-port carefully away from himself to prevent them dripping on his trousers. Isabelle was standing in the doorway as he got out and paid the fare, he glanced at the house next door and in at the window where the tiger throw was spread over the back of the sofa, but there was no sign of the cat that he had so often seen lying there, and he wondered where it was. Then Isabelle gave a tentative wave, let go of the door, and came towards him. But what's happened? Jakob wondered, why is she wearing those clothes? She reeked of sweat, he had to steel himself to embrace her. She didn't snuggle up to him, her eyes were closed, he looked at her face for a moment, and it wrung his heart. –It will be different from now on, he said softly. Her face was strange and sad, but there were all those years he had waited for her, waited to see her face again, and here it was, the smooth forehead and the mole on the left cheek, the clear, oval face, insecure, distressed. –It'll all come right again, he said, putting the flowers down on his suitcase and taking Isabelle in his arms. One must have pity, he remembered Bentham saying, but what had he meant, what had he been talking about? –It'll all come right again, he mur-mured and tried in vain to recall exactly what Bentham had said. Over her shoulder he looked along the street, where the houses were still standing, solid, sculptural, the ornate façades with their decorative columns and ledges that served no pur-pose; no one was coming this way from where he had seen the man with the cart and the priest, agitated and gesticulating, and none of the residents were to be seen, not even at a win-dow. The whole place was deserted, as if they had responded to a warning, Jakob thought, a warning to evacuate the street, and only he and Isabelle had known nothing of it. He turned his head towards the empty windows, towards the sofa with the ugly throw, but the smell was here, it came from those clothes, men's clothes, that Isabelle was wearing. –We must go inside, said Jakob. He stooped to catch the flowers that were about to slide off his suitcase. –Isabelle? he said, we can't just stand here. She opened her eyes and looked at him. –Yes, she answered, and slowly walked towards the door that had clicked shut.

ABOUT THE AUTHOR

Katharina Hacker's previous books, *Morpheus* and *The Lifeguard*, have earned her a reputation as one of the most discerning and elegant stylists in contemporary German literature. Born in 1967 in Frankfurt, she now lives in Berlin.